Shadows

Jackie McLean

TP

ThunderPoint Publishing Ltd.

Shadows

Simon Nolan

Thunderpoint Publishing Ltd

First Published in Great Britain in 2017 by
ThunderPoint Publishing Limited
Summit House
4-5 Mitchell Street
Edinburgh
Scotland EH6 7BD

Cover Image © Seita/Shutterstock.com
Cover Design © Huw Francis

ISBN: 978-1-910946-28-2 (Paperback)
ISBN: 978-1-910946-29-9 (eBook)

www.thunderpoint.scot

Acknowledgements

The characters and events in this book are fictional, the result of an overactive imagination. If, however, you have annoyed or upset me in the past and you happen to find characters that appear to resemble you, I am sure this is entirely, erm, coincidental...

A book doesn't emerge just out of one person's imagination and there are lots of people to thank for arriving at the finished article.

First of all, a special thanks to my friend Anne. It was in discussion with her that the storyline about the midwives came about. Yes, be careful who you talk to...

As before, my dear friend (she knows who she is) has provided invaluable insight into the nitty gritty and often mundanity of policing and being a detective (and yet she has stood by me when I have ignored all of that and made up a more exciting version of the job). The Fannuary joke that Alice tells in the story is a true one told to me by police friends, and I must say thank you for the steal!

Stuart Archibald of Theatrical Armoury Services was amazing, giving of his time and expertise to explain guns and shooting to me – and for not laughing too loudly at my dismal attempts at firing a couple of handguns. His wealth of knowledge is awesome.

For checking and advising on details of all things Turkish, my thanks go to Seref Isler.

The support of fellow crime writers and others in the crime fiction world has been immense, and has made a huge difference to my confidence as a writer. Special thanks go to Mark Leggatt for introducing me to the Noir at the Bar crew – in particular Dr Jacky Collins (Dr Noir) and Vic Watson, whose encouragement has been tremendous. Also to Wendy H Jones and Chris Longmuir (my fellow Dangerous Dames) and Tana Collins, Lesley Kelly and Amanda Fleet (Murder & Mayhem team mates), to Shirley Whiteside of Booked on Pulse 98.4FM, and to Kelly Lacey of lovebooksgroup blog. Group hug, group hug.

Not least, I'd like to thank the team at ThunderPoint Publishing Ltd for the journey. The hard work of taking a book to publication begins when the writer hands it over. Seonaid Francis is just the best editor.

Dedication

To Allison
my heart & soul

Monday

Chapter 1

Donna left her car at the foot of High Street, and made her way through the November squall along Old Shore Head. She paid no attention to the row of pretty cottages to her right or to the grey, tumultuous North Sea to her left, keeping her chin tucked into her jacket collar against the biting wind and the needling raindrops.

What a feckin' morning, she thought. And the lack of nicotine wasn't helping.

She'd gotten up earlier than she had to, in order to make this trip before work, her first day back at work in 18 months. But she had to do this. She couldn't face going back until she did *this*.

Her quick footsteps veered left around Market Gate and into the car park at Arbroath harbour. Surprisingly at this early hour, the car park was almost full. On the far side of the harbour, she could see as she squinted past the watery sun climbing out of the horizon, a creel boat was being unloaded. Fishermen and seagulls went head to head as the haul was manhandled into one of the harbour-side fish houses.

Donna's toes began to hurt with the cold as she continued on round to her left, leaving the creel boat at her back, and came to face the harbour wall. A seagull swooped past her face, very close, and its *yark!* made her flinch, her stomach tightening. As she approached the wall and came to a stop in front of it, her sudden anxiety remained with her.

She had to do this.

There it was now. The memorial plaque fixed on to the harbour wall, marking the spot where it had happened that day. Donna couldn't remember much about it as she trailed a finger across the names on the plaque, only knew that hers had very nearly been one of them – one of the five who had died right here, and the other six who'd lost their lives nearby during that awful week.

She shuddered, tried to shake away the terrible events that she did remember, and then caught the sound of a siren approaching from the distance just as her mobile rang.

Only minutes later, she pulled up on the lane that sat squashed between the amusement arcade and the sea front. Her eyes stung as she peered through the rain at the flapping yellow police tape that was tied across the pathway to the beach.

It hadn't taken long for news to travel, she thought, marvelling at how quickly a crowd had gathered there. She watched them huddle against the elements.

Her fingers twitched, seeking something to hold.

She grasped the car key, killing the engine. She eyed the packet of nicotine gum sitting on the dashboard, and then found herself reaching under the passenger seat to where her too-strict daily ration was stashed.

Just one, she told herself. God, she needed it. Today of all days.

She almost missed the end of the cigarette with the lighter, her jitters were so bad.

She took a long draw and exhaled slowly.

Aaaaahhhhhh.

With the squall calming and with a more composed eye, Donna studied the area around her, familiar in so many ways. The sea to her immediate right, the tide on its way out but still close enough to be spraying salt onto the road. A uniformed officer standing outside the amusement arcade's door. Large bins waiting to be collected; one lying on its side and trailing debris as if it had vomited plumes of sodden tissue paper the length of the walkway.

There was a silver estate parked up on the kerbside, and Donna now blocked entry to the narrow lane that ran on towards the harbour.

Up ahead, past the amusement block, stood the surrounds of the town's football park, and opposite that lay a stretch of grass that led onto the beach.

The grass marked the boundary set by the police tape, and from there the scene that awaited Donna on the sandy shore – the body deposited on the earth by a retreating tide – was being kept from public view.

She stepped from her car, shivered at the cool breeze that ruffled her jacket, and headed towards the cordon. The police officer at the door of the amusement block stepped forward, and instinctively Donna retrieved her warrant card.

"Just down there, Detective Inspector," said the officer,

indicating the way. Donna smiled an acknowledgement to him, and made her way down, ducking under the tape at the nearside so that she didn't have to go through the crowd of onlookers.

From the grass verge, looking out towards the scene on the beach, the first sight Donna caught of the body was the shoes. Gaudy purple high heels.

Moira cursed out loud as the heel caught on the uneven floor, and she almost fell headlong into the salsa club. But her expletives were drowned out by the giggling from her companions, and the force of the noise from the band inside.

Wide-eyed, Moira righted herself, and let her eyes dart left and right, taking it all in.

"Welcome back to the world," her friend shouted.

In her day, the dancing was the school disco. Had things changed that much during the years she'd frittered away in her hopeless marriage?

She raised her arms above her head, and followed her friends through the club, letting the purple shoes clatter as she went.

One shoe pointed straight up to the sky, while the other peeked from behind her waist, the leg attached to it lying at an impossible angle.

Donna stopped where another uniformed officer indicated to her, and she quickly pulled on a set of pale blue coveralls. As she tied the garments on, she could see Emma standing at various angles over and around the body, taking photographs. She watched as Emma carefully tread on the aluminium paving steps that were laid there to avoid further contamination of the scene. Then, following the route that the officer pointed out to her, Donna made her way carefully to where the woman in the purple shoes lay.

Getting closer, Donna's eye was drawn to the angry, swollen black welts around the dead woman's neck.

Moira twirled nervously at the pearls around her neck.

"No, he isn't," she said.

"He is," her friend insisted, shouting into her ear above the din from the salsa band. "He keeps looking at you. Go on, just smile, he looks well fit."

Moira glanced up, curious now to see this well fit man her friends were telling her about. Sure enough, leaning with one elbow on the bar, a slim and handsome forty-something flashed a smile at her. She ducked her head, ashamed to be caught looking.

"Did you see him?"

She took several long pulls from her cocktail straw, before letting a giggle loose.

"He looks nice," she admitted. "But it's been so long, I don't have a clue what you're meant to do."

"Just smile back," said her friend. "Let him buy you a drink. What's the worst that could happen?"

Emma did a double-take when she turned to see Donna.

"You're back," she beamed.

"Yeah, first day," said Donna, smiling at Emma. She glanced at Emma's tummy. "I didn't know you were…tell me you actually *are*, and that I haven't just put my foot in it."

Emma chuckled, and placed her hand on the bump. "Yes, I am. I'm stopping soon for maternity leave, so I'm glad we're getting a chance to work together before I go off."

Donna nodded to the body lying on the shingle. "Hope I haven't forgotten how to run a murder investigation."

"Ah," said Emma, raising a finger. "First mistake, detective. Don't assume it's been a murder."

Donna raised an eyebrow. "No?"

"Well, I know you'd think that, what with the strangulation marks," said Emma. "That's why I asked for a DI to take a look. But you never know. She could have fallen in, got her neck caught in a net. Or something. A corpse in the sea has a pretty tough time."

"That's what I love about you forensic types," said Donna. "Anything you can tell me about her?"

"Well, she doesn't seem to have been in the water long," said Emma, letting her camera fall to her side. "At least, not from what I can tell."

"Did she drown?"

Emma carefully walked a circle around the body. "I don't see any obvious signs. John will do a more thorough check when he gets here, but to be honest, there's no sure way of telling. The post mortem might not even be able to establish whether we're looking at death before or after immersion. We haven't perfected the science of drowning yet." She shrugged an apology.

"When you say *not long*," said Donna, "what's your best guess?

5

What sort of time-span?"

Emma moved her head from side to side, calculating. "We're likely talking days rather than weeks. Maybe even hours rather than days. A body in sea water…" She shrugged again.

Donna crouched down, close to the dead woman's face.

"Okay. Anything to identify her by?"

"Not yet," said Emma. "And I'm not aware of any missing person reports. But it could be too early for anyone to realise she's gone."

"Poor cow," said Donna. "Too old to be dressed like that. Picked up the wrong guy, maybe?"

Moira was captivated by his accent. She allowed her alcohol-induced haze to rationalise her decisions. It was a year and a half since she'd been with a guy. It was a reputable club, not some sleazy joint. Her friends were relaxed about him. He'd joined them at their table, and they'd all fallen in love with the handsome Latino. Oh, and what a dancer! Moira's purple shoes had tread on his poor toes countless times, and he hadn't complained once. So, when the taxi arrived and he held onto her hand a moment longer than necessary, she pulled him along with her.

He laid her down on her sofa, and caressed her fully-clothed body until she got into such a frenzy, she began to tug at his shirt.

"Stop being such a gentleman," she teased, aware that she was slurring her words.

He sat up, straddling her drunken form, and said, "Who else knows about Craigie Drive?"

"What?"

He slapped her face. Hard. She screamed.

"Who knows about the flat?"

Sobriety kicked in a fraction behind terror.

"Stop it," she cried.

"Tell me who else knows about the flat on Craigie Drive," he said.

"Look at those heels," said Emma. "And the outfit's for a night out. She could have been drunk and fell in the water."

"Or she could have been strangled and dumped in the water," said Donna. "I know what my money's on."

"And you do have that uncanny detective instinct thing," said Emma.

Donna looked across the water, and studied it for several minutes in silence. She looked at the clouds. They were moving quickly northwards and west.

"Is it plausible the tide could have moved her along the coastline to here from Dundee?" she asked.

Emma shrugged. "It would fit with my guess about her not being in the water long."

Donna crouched down again, her eye caught by some faint contrast on the skin. "See the mark on her arm there?"

Emma squinted her eyes as she looked in close and saw the barely discernible print. "Hmm, somebody had a strong grip on her. You calling it in as a murder investigation?"

"Damn right," said Donna, glancing up and down the coastline. "We need to estimate the scope of where she could have gone into the water, dead or alive. Whoever did this to her might not be far away."

"I'll get the coastguard," said Emma. "He'll be able to help with that." Her voice trailed off. She followed Donna's line of vision, knowing already that it was resting on the harbour up ahead. They could make out the tops of masts bobbing in the water, sheltering from the gusts, and from here they could see some of the harbour walls. They'd been repaired since the day Donna was thinking about. Emma shivered.

"We still haven't found him," said Donna. She remembered the sight of Evanton sprawled there on the ground that day while they cuffed him. How the hell had they let someone like him escape?

Emma let a silence fall between them. She folded her arms, stepped towards Donna, and said, almost in a whisper, "I know."

They stood gazing at the harbour until a sudden rain of hailstones brought Donna's attention back abruptly.

"To think," she said, wheeling around to face Emma. "I was heading out here for a sneaky fag, and now it's a feckin' murder scene."

"Welcome back, DI Davenport," said Emma, throwing her a wink.

Chapter 2

Taxis heading for the airport were the only vehicles on the road. Soon enough, they'd be joined by the long distance truckers making their way south from Aberdeen, then by commuters, and finally the school run.

Mirroring the widening flow of human activity, the first skein of pink footed geese swooped across the estuary from their nearby roosting fields to begin the daily noise-fest on the bay. The rest would follow soon, then the waders, the oystercatchers and the rock pipits would appear on the sands, and their numbers would swell with the growing clamour of the woodland birds here in the park.

The taxi headlights, the arrival of the geese, it marked the end of the night's hunt for the nocturnal beasts. Foxes slunk back to their dens. Owls ruffled their feathers, settling back into invisibility in the tree trunks. The white cat with the black eye patch and black ears strolled across the road, expertly zig-zagging past the taxis. Only one peep from a horn indicated that anyone had noticed him.

The cat picked up pace, paws flashing back and forth in perfect synchronisation. It stopped stock still for a moment in the centre of a large garden to the rear of Perth Road, glimpsing the tantalising movement of a tiny form in the hedge, before sprinting off, startled by the sudden barking of the dog in the house.

Up along Hyndford Street, along Glenagnes Street, and finally to the promise of warmth, food and sleep, when it reached Scott Street. By now a drizzle was on. There'd be no more sport for the cat until nightfall.

The flats were packed one next to the other and stacked four-high, but the road was broad and there was plenty of greenery. The cat made its way directly to one door, sat on the top step, and emitted a shrill meow.

"Ah, shurrup," came a grumpy response from within the flat next door. The cat ignored it and meowed again. Silently the door opened, and a spear of light stabbed the doorstep from inside.

"Chshush, chshush," Samira Chaudrakar gently ushered the cat

8

inside. "No mice this morning, good cat."

The cat rubbed the length of its body across her leg. Samira scowled. "You're all wet."

The cat sprang effortlessly into the hammock that was slung across the radiator, settled into the centre of it, and began the very deliberate process of cleaning every part of its body, methodically from one quarter to another. Its rhythm melted into the soft clinking of crockery as Samira stirred coffee into two cups.

Alerted to the sound of Samira emerging from the kitchen, the cat shot from the hammock, made Samira stumble and curse as it sped across her footstep, and ran ahead of her through the crack in the bedroom door. It pounced onto the bed and was immediately assailed by a torrent of insults and flailing human limbs.

"Get off, cat!" Natesh grunted.

Bad start to the morning. Then it got worse.

"Morning, fine young man," Samira beamed from his doorway. "Coffee for you."

"Mum," he groaned, "I told you not to."

As if it wasn't bad enough, being back here and having the cat pounce on his head at the first glint of sunlight. Since last Wednesday, when he'd had to have The Talk with Erin.

Not forever, just a break.

"Too eager," he'd told Donna when he'd sought her advice.

"Too eager, how?" Donna had asked.

"Having her suitcase ready by the second date," Natesh had said.

"Fair enough," Donna had agreed.

But he'd meant what he'd said to Erin. They could try again. He wanted to, but more slowly. He really wanted things to work out with her, he cared about her too much to botch it up.

He sighed and raised an eyelid. His mother beamed at him as she held forth the coffee mug. He shuffled onto one elbow and reached out for the mug.

"Thank you," he said, "but I'm very capable of getting my own coffee when I get up. You can stop treating me like a wee boy." He regretted the words as soon as they came out, sounding harsher than he'd intended. *Bloody cat.*

"Ach, but you're *my* wee boy," beamed Samira.

Natesh rolled his eyes. Then he smiled, a forced smile that said, *you can go away now.*

He wanted to check his phone in case he'd missed a text in the night from Erin, but Samira persisted by the door.

"What are your plans today?" she asked him.

"I'm on till six tonight, then heading out for a bite to eat with Donna," he said. "She's coming back here to watch the football."

"Ah, Donna," she said, with that tone in her voice, and twirled the end of her sari at him. "Now, why don't you two just get on and settle down together?"

"Mum, I've told you before . . ."

"Such a nice girl, I've always liked her."

"Not going to happen."

"But you've always been so close."

"She's my best friend," said Natesh. "And that's the way it stays. Anyway, she's with somebody, I told you."

"Ach, that won't last. You two are meant to be together."

Natesh rolled his eyes to the ceiling. "I'll see you this evening," he said as Samira turned to go.

Finally. Natesh immediately looked at his phone, and felt the ache of disappointment. No text from Erin. Facebook, then. Maybe she'd posted something. He flipped down the screen and suddenly caught sight of the chatter about a body washed up on Arbroath beach.

Crap, he thought. *What kind of friend am I?* It was Donna's first day back at work since the Evanton thing. He knew she'd almost decided not to go back at all, how torn she was about whether her heart would still be in the job. Whether she'd be up to it and if she was risking another bipolar flare-up. Now she'd be up to her neck in it in Arbroath, with no chance of a banter until God knew when. Still, he rang her number, just in case. But, as expected, the usual message played back.

He jumped when his radio came on suddenly, too loud. Damn, he hated that! He reached out his hand to hit the snooze button, just as the cat thought it would be funny to sink its claws into his knuckles. He roared in pain, knocked the coffee onto the carpet.

Great, he thought. *Just great.* He slumped back down onto his pillow, and scrolled through the online postings that were building all sorts of rumours and theories about the body, and almost decided to take a trip up there. But he hadn't picked up the car keys in eighteen months, and he couldn't do it today. He sighed, and sat back up. He'd give Donna another try. If she didn't answer, he'd play some *Planets Under Attack* until it was time to go to work. His car keys could sit where they'd been sitting since the accident. Even the draw of getting some juicy murder investigation gossip from Donna couldn't get him back behind the wheel.

With a wry smile on his lips, he watched his clock flip to 8.00, counted to three and heard the door close as his mother left the flat, right on cue.

Chapter 3

The white tarpaulin, hastily erected around the body, flapped and groaned against the wind coming off the shore. Inside it, Donna felt relieved to have some protection from the elements, and from the crowd of onlookers at the cordon. At least the dead woman was afforded some modesty now. The media had begun to turn up, and Donna wasn't confident that they'd be able to resist the pressure on them to try and scoop a photograph of the dead woman. And then all hell would have broken loose.

She shielded her eyes from the wind as she took a peek around the outside of the tarpaulin, her senses alerted to several vehicles pulling up close by.

"Morning, John," she called as she saw the pathologist making his way across the shingle towards her.

"Well, if it isn't Donna Davenport," John Ogilvie exclaimed. His thinning blond hair stood this way and that on top of his head as the wind ruffled it. "How are you, lass? When did you get back?"

Donna sighed. "This morning."

Ogilvie lowered his head to one side in a gesture of sympathy. "Well, take it easy, lass. You've got a whole team around you, eh? Don't try to tackle this on your own. Isn't that right, Emma?"

"Dead right, John," said Emma, wincing before the words finished coming out of her mouth.

Donna nodded her head and stood aside to let Ogilvie approach the body.

He crouched low over the dead woman. He examined her facial colouring, then ran a gloved finger lightly over the indent marks around her neck. He gently lifted one of her hands and teased at a finger nail. Then he pressed firmly but carefully on her chest.

When he was done with his cursory examination, he stood up, and circled around the body.

"First impressions?" asked Donna. She wasn't hoping for much. She knew – as Emma kept telling her – that bodies pulled from the water, especially sea water, were notoriously difficult to read.

"Well," said Ogilvie, screwing up his eyes in concentration.

"The colouration on her face isn't consistent with what I'd expect from the state of her hands if she'd been in the water long. The fingernails seem to suggest she's been in the water only a very short time."

"That's what I said," whispered Emma.

"Maybe not even as long as 24 hours, at a wild guess. In that timescale I'd expect to see foam still coming from the airways if she'd drowned, but there's none, eh? Not even when I press on the chest. That's not conclusive, of course, but it'd be unusual to find that in a recent drowning. We'll run a check for diatoms, but even if we don't find any, it's still not fool-proof."

"I said that, too," whispered Emma.

"All adds to a probability, though, right?" said Donna.

"Yes, if we're put to the test in court, we'll be able to say she was probably dead before she got in the water, given the lack of foam in the airways and *if* we don't find any diatoms. If it were me in the dock, though, I'd be wanting more proof, so don't jump the gun."

"I won't. But I'm hunting a killer, aren't I?"

"Most likely. Look at the neck and head. See the thumb marks?"

Donna and Emma leaned in to look again.

"Consistent with strangulation, obviously," said Ogilvie. "Clumsy, though. I've seen better jobs of strangling a victim. Your guy might be in a panic, probably been careless in other ways. Sea water's a bugger for getting rid of forensic evidence, though. I'd be surprised if we find anything under her fingernails, even if she put up a fight. But you never know, eh? Stranger things have happened. I'd wager your best shot at finding anything is to find out where she lived. If you can identify her, you'll most likely find plenty of material for us at her home. A guy this clumsy won't have thought to clear up after himself. That do you?"

"That's great, John, thanks," said Donna.

"Mind now, lass," said Ogilvie. "It could all change with the post mortem."

"I know," said Donna. "You can take her in now. I'm done here. You got everything you need, Emma?"

"Yes."

At her words, Ogilvie signalled to the waiting private ambulance, and the body on the beach began its next journey.

"See you at the morgue," said Donna. "I'll need to search her clothing."

"Right you are, lass."

Vidu watched from the cliff tops overlooking the beach. Police tape had prevented him from getting there by the normal route, and he'd skirted the town so that he could join the path from the neighbouring village on the other side. Crouching low behind a boulder, he watched the scene going on around the white tarpaulin shelter while constantly scanning for any sign that he'd been spotted there.

He dialled a number on his mobile, and waited for the connection.

He spoke rapidly, cringing at the ferocity of the reply.

"You *killed* her?"

Vidu mumbled an explanation. He'd only meant to find out if anyone else knew, and warn her off from talking.

"You killed her?"

"I didn't mean to," said Vidu, pleading in his voice. "It just got out of hand. I panicked. What do I do now? The police have found her."

"That's the second one. Fucking idiot. It's over. We need to pull out now. Get on the next flight, and bring Samira."

Sweat trickled from Vidu's forehead. "Samira, too?"

"She knows too much," said the voice on the other end. "I'm not going to risk her going to the police if she thinks we've gone. Has she told the boy anything?"

"No, she refuses."

There was a hesitation, then, "He doesn't know about me at all?"

"He still thinks you died when he was born," said Vidu. "Do you want me to tell him? Last chance."

Another pause, then, "No. I don't want him getting involved in your mess."

At the end of the call, he watched for several minutes more, until a tall woman in blue coveralls walked away from the tent on the beach. Then he scrambled along the cliff top path on all fours, keeping out of view, back towards the village.

Donna felt herself begin to shiver as her adrenaline ebbed, and she felt exposed again to the biting wind. She removed her latex gloves, but kept on the coveralls as she passed through the large group of people still standing at the police cordon. The waiting crowd thinned to let her pass unmolested.

A small group of press reporters remained waiting, and she stopped beside them. There was no point denying what she'd been dealing with. If she didn't give them information to report, then the grapevine would fill in the public imagination instead.

"We're investigating a possible murder," she told them. "We need to identify the victim, a woman in her thirties or forties. If any of you hear anything that can help identify her, any reports of a missing friend or relative, I need you to let me know." She dished out her card to the outstretched hands. "We'll be in touch later on today once we decide on a press conference."

A tall, lean man of around her own age stepped forward. She vaguely recognised him, but couldn't place him. "Adam Ridout," he said, handing over his business card to her. "I'm with the *Herald.*" He made a sound as though to say more, but stopped.

Donna glanced at the card, then back at Adam, and smiled. "Thank you," she said. "Hopefully we'll be able to talk to you more this afternoon."

There was a general murmur of thanks and farewells as the small group broke up, and Donna turned to go back to her car.

Chapter 4

Samira Chaudrakar tucked her bus travel card into her bag, and held onto her sari as the wind whipped at it, as she stepped onto the road to make her familiar walk to work. As usual, a group of smokers stood huddled in the doorway to the midwifery unit. She knew everyone there.

"Have you heard the news?" asked Craig, one of the new auxiliaries.

She registered surprise, midway through her gesture of waving away the cigarette smoke.

"Sadie's retiring. She finally got a package agreed."

"Not a very generous package," said Sadie, a woman who'd been working here almost as long as Samira had. "But these days, who expects much?"

"Ach, you'll be missed," said Samira. "You lucky thing!" She waved the cigarette smoke away from her again with a brusque gesture of her hand.

"Leaving do in two weeks' time," said Sadie. "Please tell me you'll be there? I don't want to be the only oldie amongst all these young things."

"Cheek of it," said Samira, laughing.

Making her way towards the reception desk, the chat was all about Sadie's imminent departure.

She dropped her handbag into the foot-well of her workstation, switched on her computer, and let it whir to life while she hung up her coat in the staff cloakroom. When she got back, two of the midwives were already standing there, discussing the final preparations for the antenatal class they'd be running that morning. They called out a jumbled greeting to Samira.

"No home visits today?" Samira asked them.

"Not today," said Vicky. "Moira's got the visits today."

"Are you going to Sadie's leaving do?" asked Rowen.

"Of course," said Samira. "I've worked with her for such a long time. It'll be strange with her gone."

"I know," said Rowen. "But we'll look after you."

"Talking of which," said Vicky, "the coffee machine's broken again. I'm nipping down to the canteen. What do you want?"

"Oh, a tea, please," said Samira. "Something to warm me up."

Vicky headed for the canteen, Rowen drifted off towards the antenatal room, and for a short time Samira was alone in reception. She straightened the photograph of Natesh that sat on her desk, and logged into her computer. Then like magic, midwives and other health personnel began to fill the unit and the phones began to ring. Maybe that was why Rowen and Vicky were always at work so early, thought Samira. It was the only chance of getting one minute of peace to do any preparation. For the rest of the day the team would be fitting in their work plans around one crisis followed by another.

It just wouldn't be the same without Sadie, she thought. Perhaps it was time to begin thinking about her own retirement? She shuddered, and began to twist the amber ring on her finger. What would happen to her then?

Her desk phone rang.

"Midwifery Unit," she answered, poised to write down the details of the call coming in. She listened carefully to the woman on the line.

"Let me just check for you," said Samira. "Can I take your phone number, please? I'll call you right back."

Samira stood up and walked through to the antenatal room, carrying with her the piece of paper she'd written on.

"Can I just check," she said, making Rowen look round from the information display she was arranging on a table. "You said Moira was doing the home visits today?"

"That's right, why? Is something wrong?"

"No," said Samira. "Just one of them phoning to say she hasn't turned up yet, but it's still early."

"I think she was putting her car in for a service today," said Rowen. "She's probably got on the wrong bus or something."

Samira nodded her head, and returned to phone to reassure the woman who had called. As she sat at her desk, she pulled the electronic diary onto her screen and checked Moira's schedule. She'd been due to do the first visit at nine. It was just ten past now. Some people were impatient, she thought.

Chapter 5

Donna pulled up at Bell Street. Eighteen months she'd been away, and she had butterflies flapping wildly in her tummy at the thought of going inside. The plan had been to come in this morning, and spend a couple of days re-orienting herself back into the job. Hadn't quite worked out that way, though, and she fretted about having jumped into it so quickly. How would she know if she was really up to running this murder case?

Her mobile rang, and it warmed her heart to see Natesh's name flash on her screen.

"You're psychic, aren't you?" she answered his call.

"Hey, so I'm right, then?" Natesh's cheery voice came over the line. It immediately helped her to relax.

"Go on, tell me."

"It's all over the place about the dead body on the beach," said Natesh. "You've been there, right?"

"All morning," said Donna. "Just the welcome back to work I needed. Anyway, aren't you supposed to be working this morning?"

"Man's gotta skive sometimes," he said. "The bosses have been glued to their screens, all talking about the body. Everyone's posting about it."

"Facebook, eh?" said Donna. "Didn't take long for that news to get out."

"Was it a murder?"

"You know I can't discuss it."

"Aw, come on!"

"I'll see you later, and maybe I'll be able to give you some gore to keep you going," she laughed, as she ended the call.

She got out of her car, and stood looking at the office complex that was Tayside Police headquarters. Inside this building were the corridors she'd walked, the doors she'd gone through, with a confidence that had always been unshakable, and never questioned.

Now she stood, apprehensive. She'd been out of it for so long. Maybe that was how it was supposed to be. After all, she'd already jumped to conclusions about the body on the beach. Was she really ready? And now she found herself glancing over her shoulder, a reflex of fear. The events that had led to her lengthy absence were never that far from her shattered mind.

She instinctively reached for her cigarette packet, only to realise it wasn't in her pocket any more. She was on rations. But she needed one now. She found herself caught between two giant anxieties. If she had another smoke now, she would run out before the end of the day. But if she didn't have one, there was a chance her nerve wouldn't hold strong enough to walk into Bell Street. Libby's face came into her mind, along with her voice saying, *I almost lost you once; over my dead body are you going to get lung cancer.*

She took a deep breath, locked her car, and forced her feet to carry her into the building, minus the nicotine.

She took the lift, and made her way to Ross's office. As she went, the smells and the sounds of the route, so embedded in her senses, brought back comforting familiarity, and she began to relax.

She knocked on Ross's door and stepped inside.

The tall, flame-haired Highlander was on the phone, but his face broke into a beam of sunshine when he saw Donna, and he mouthed *hi*, using his free hand to beckon her into a seat. Immediately, she clocked the sad effort at a moustache. Like a dead mouse hanging from the end of his nose.

The last of her first-day-back fears ebbed as she sat, returning Ross's smile.

"Donna," he said, when the call was ended. "It's great to see you back. How are you?"

"Oh, you know," said Donna. She couldn't take her eyes off the moustache.

Ross leaned towards her on his desk. His brows creased in concern. She saw his hand hesitate as if it was going to clasp hers. She wondered momentarily if she should scare the wits out of him by pouncing on it, and the thought made her smile.

"Really," he insisted. "I know it'll have been hard enough coming back after all this time. You could probably have done without the circus this morning. How did you get on with that?"

"Wait," said Donna, waving vaguely at his face. "What is that?"

Ross touched his moustache automatically, and grinned.

"That," he said, "is Movember. It'll be coming right back off on the first of December, believe me."

"Well, that's a relief," said Donna. "I thought you'd lost the plot."

The ice was cracked.

"Emma and John Ogilvie kept me right," she went on. "I suppose I'm a wee bit rusty, but it'll come back soon enough."

"Aye, it will," said Ross. "You're a detective in your marrow, Donna. Just lean on me when you need to. I don't suppose it's going to be easy, but then you never were one for doing things the easy way."

They both laughed, old friends, seasoned colleagues. Avoiding the elephant in the room.

"So, what did you find?" he asked.

Donna knew full well he was avoiding the discussion they should have been having.

"Woman in her thirties or forties, probably not long in the water, probably dead before she went in. Strangulation marks – clumsy ones – around the neck, and defensive marks on her arm." Donna preferred to avoid it, too.

"How do you want to take it forward?"

Donna steepled her hands as she thought about Ross's question. "I'd like Alice on the team for this one," she said. "Our first priority is to identify the woman and visit her home. According to John's gut, that's where we'll find the clues that we need to work out what happened to her and who did it."

"And what about your own workload?" asked Ross. "I want you taking it easy. You've been away a long time. And what happened here . . ."

"What happened here is dealt with," said Donna, hearing the unconvincing note in her own voice. "But, since you raised it, what's the latest on the hunt for Evanton?"

"One step at a time, Donna," said Ross. He looked at her with a steady gaze. "There's not much to report, anyway, but I will fill you in on every detail, don't worry." Then he smiled again. "God, it's good to have you back."

Ross looked past her shoulder as a knock came at his door. A uniformed officer entered the room. Donna stood up to leave, and Ross mouthed *see you later*.

Chapter 6

Samira got a shock when she saw the time. Twelve o'clock already. How had that happened? She quickly closed down the web site that offered tips on when it was time to retire, and reached for the next folder of case notes that needed to be recorded in the database.

It'll be so strange without Sadie here, she kept thinking. The morning's news of Sadie's decision kept making her fingers key in web searches on retirement instead of putting the information into the database. She looked around her desk. For the first time that she could remember, the pile of to-do folders was higher than the pile of those completed. Even Geri had noticed.

"Are you okay?" she'd asked Samira earlier, eyeing the pile. Samira had been mortified. Getting through the case notes like clockwork was what she prided herself on. Every woman's current details were available at the touch of a button to those who needed them. No need to waste time trying to track down information over the phone. Except today. What was wrong with her head? Had Sadie's news reached into the depths of her own desire to retire? She didn't think so. What else would she do? This was the only job she'd done since arriving in the UK all those years ago.

Suddenly Samira knew what it was that was crawling around at the back of her mind today and bothering her. Remembering the morning phone call about Moira being late, she quickly called up the electronic diary again. She clicked back, and only had to go back three days before she saw it. Moira had made a visit to Craigie Drive. Without thinking, she found herself deleting the entry.

Samira felt a cold sweat break out and her head swam. *Surely not again*, she thought.

She glanced left and right. Midwives were hurrying past her in both directions amidst the usual clamour of the unit that rang around in her skull. Nobody paying her any attention. Nobody asking about Moira.

She shook her head. The ringing. It was her phone.

"Midwifery Unit," she said automatically. She held the pen in her hand, aware that it was shaking, as she listened to the caller. She checked the time again. Anxiety rippled across her gut now. This was the woman with the twins. There was no way Moira would have missed this visit. With a frown, Samira replaced the receiver.

Chapter 7

One, two, three, four five, once I caught a fish alive.
  Six, seven, eight nine, ten, then I let her go again.

He chuckled as he sang the words softly. There she was: Donna Davenport. He was going to have to be more careful. While it was an unexpected bonus to see her out here, it wouldn't do to get caught out. With her return to work, he was going to have to learn her new routines.

He couldn't take his eyes off her. She was wearing that long, sleek leather jacket that he liked, and her mid-length blonde hair ruffled fashionably chaotic in the early winter breeze.

A remarkable amount of activity went on here. People leaving the building. Some arriving back from wherever. Mail delivery. Bin collections. Cars with screaming sirens racing from behind the complex every two minutes. It was a wonder he still managed to feel invisible while he sat watching her.

But who wouldn't feel invisible next to her? A shadow to her glow. Basking in her light.

Basking like a shark.

No, no, no, he wasn't a shark.

He would never harm her.

But you want to?

No!

He would only make her happy.

Lived to make her happy.

His heart rate quickened as she walked towards him.

Oh, my God!

But she walked on by, never glancing in his direction. Then she double-backed, walked the perimeter of the car park, and went back inside the building.

Well, he thought, now that she was safely inside, *no time like the present*, and he opened his car door and got out.

Focus, Donna told herself as she walked around the car park. Only an hour to go before her next smoke.

Ross would have her new team assembled for her by now. She

took one last look around, unable to shake the unnerving feeling that she was being watched.

Everything looked the way it always did. Except that burger van outside the gates, she noted. That was new. Takeshi's Japanese Takeaway.

Sushi burgers, she thought, *whatever next?* But it did seem to be popular. A line of uniformed officers and civilian personnel stood patiently waiting for their turn. She studied each one closely, but none were paying any mind to her.

She shook her head, trying to rid herself of the paranoia, and went back inside. There was a dead woman who needed her attention.

Donna slowed her pace as she neared the briefing room where she was about to meet her new team. The last time she'd been in there, she remembered, was when they were trying to track down the maniac who was storing a lethal cargo of the highly toxic chemical, MIC – the substance that was responsible for the world's worst industrial accident. She thought of Sergeant Ted Granger, due to retire before he was brutally gunned down in the line of duty on that case. And the young officer – what was his name? Dom Hilton, she recalled. New in the door. Now a name on a plaque on the wall at Arbroath harbour. She wiped away a tear, and cleared her throat.

"Donna!" The familiar gravelly voice made Donna stop before she pushed open the door to the room. She looked along the corridor and broke into a genuine and wide smile. Hurrying towards her with her arms held wide was Sergeant Alice Moone. *The General.*

"Oh boy, is it good to see you," said Donna from within the envelope of Alice's hug.

"When did you get back?" asked Alice, now holding Donna at arms' length and appraising her from top to toe.

"This morning," said Donna. "Just in time for the fun at the beach."

"Ouch."

"Yeah."

"So, how are you?" said Alice. "The last time I saw you . . ." She bit her lip and stopped talking abruptly.

"I'm okay," said Donna, looking at the familiar scars on Alice's face, that alarmed anyone meeting her for the first time, and had earned her her nickname. "Really. What about you?"

Alice shrugged. "I was off for six weeks after the carnage. I've had my moments, I think we all have, but it's so great to have you back. I've really missed you. Too much fresh air in here since you've been away."

"Ah, well, about that," said Donna. "You're not going to believe it, but I'm trying to give up."

"What?" Alice cackled loud and long.

"It's not that funny."

"You think?"

"I didn't say I *have* given up," said Donna, laughing along with Alice, and opening the door to the briefing room. "So, let's go find out who our victim is and what happened to her."

With Alice at her back, Donna walked into the room and saw three officers sitting round a table, a woman in an M & S suit and two uniformed men. Three pairs of eyes flicked towards Donna.

"This is DC Fran Woods," said Alice. "Joined us from Strathclyde about six months ago, you'll need your recovering lungs to keep up with her."

Fran leaped to her feet, dropping one of Takeshi's fast food wrappers onto the floor, and grasped Donna's outstretched hand. *Fuelled by burgers*, thought Donna, hoping desperately that it hadn't slipped from her lips.

"I've heard a lot about you, Ma'am," Fran gushed. "It's a pleasure to meet you, and I'm looking forward to working with you."

"It's Donna."

Fran blushed and looked at Alice.

"It's really okay," said Alice. "You can call her by her first name. You'll find other things to call her as you get to know her."

"You're so funny," said Donna.

Fran, along with the other two unknown officers, visibly relaxed.

"PC Stephen Morrison, and PC Thomas Akwasi," said Alice, indicating them as though they were a museum exhibit. "Just out of Tulliallan, so they're still fit and un-jaded." Their voices merged as they responded to their names and stood up to shake hands with Donna. Sinewy Morrison towered above the brick of muscle that was Akwasi.

"You another Movember victim?" Donna laughed, pointing at Morrison's effort of a moustache. He blushed, and turned to Akwasi for validation.

"Oh," said Donna, realising that his was for real.

There was an awkward moment, and just when Donna felt it was safe to move on, Alice spluttered a giggle.

"Ross asked me if I was doing Movember," said Alice, her voice rising to a yell in her hysteria, "but I told him, *Can't do Movember, I'm doing Fannuary!*" She doubled over, slapping her thighs as the room exploded into hoots of laughter and snorting.

Only Alice, thought Donna, relieved by the broken tension.

Then she caught Akwasi's eye as the room quietened again, saw the twitch at the upper corner of his lip. *What the hell is that about?* she wondered. Akwasi broke the eye contact and folded his arms, before turning away. Donna noted the negative body language. But first things first.

"Let's get to work," she said. "We have an unidentified woman in her thirties or forties, washed up on Arbroath beach, most likely still alive this time yesterday and most likely somewhere close to here in Dundee. Strangulation marks and defensive wounds, so we're looking for a killer. Any missing person reports in yet?"

"Not as of yet," said Morrison.

"Okay then," said Donna, "let's get ready to put out an appeal, in case we're none the wiser by the morning. Alice, can you arrange for a press conference early?" Alice tapped her hand to her head to indicate that she would.

"Fran, you come with me to the morgue -" Fran squirmed as Donna turned to the two PCs - " and you both stand by for the first hint of a missing person, and go and interview the informer." Morrison and Akwasi nodded in agreement.

"We need to find out who she is as soon as possible," Donna concluded, "while there's a chance her killer might still be in the area."

A uniformed officer knocked on the door and entered the room.

"Ma'am," he acknowledged Alice. "There's a punter in Interview Room 2, claims he murdered a woman. Says he'll only talk to DI Davenport."

Donna spun round to face the officer, but Alice remained calm.

"Wouldn't happen to be one Rory Thomson?" Alice said to the officer.

"Actually, aye," said the officer, sounding both impressed and confused. "How did you know that? We only just booked him in."

"Where there's a murder," said Alice, "there's Rory Thomson confessing to it. But how the hell did he find out about this one so quickly?"

"I'll go and ask him, shall I?" said Donna.

"Give him short shrift," said Alice. "This'll be the fourth murder the bastard's confessed to this year. I'm sick of him, attention-seeking nutter."

"Nutter, is he?" said Donna. "Oh well, takes one to know one. This'll be fun."

Chapter 8

Geri appeared at Samira's desk almost immediately, a look of concern etched on her face.

She smoothed at her dark blue tunic with quick hand movements. "The second one?"

Samira confirmed it, and showed her the details of the two callers.

"Did you check with the first one if she turned up?"

"Not yet," said Samira, already punching in the phone number. "I'll do that just now."

There was a pause, then her call was answered.

The woman on the line wasn't pleased. Moira hadn't shown up, nobody had been in touch with an explanation, and she'd waited in all morning. Samira was informed in no uncertain terms that people had better things to do than hang around all morning waiting for the midwife to turn up.

Geri tapped a number into her mobile phone while she stood there.

"Hetti?" she said. "Have you seen Moira today?"

A pause while she listened to the answer. Two paces to the left. Two paces to the right.

"Are you sure?"

Another pause, a longer one, during which time Geri began to chew at a fingernail.

"Okay, thanks, I will do," said Geri, and she ended the call. She turned to Samira. "Could you put out a call for the midwives in the building to meet here at once?"

Samira's heart began to beat faster. Geri was never one for being melodramatic. Something must be very wrong. Samira clung to a desperate hope that it wasn't what she thought it could be.

The clock on the wall seemed to boom out across the office while Samira and Geri waited for the midwives to arrive. When they did, most of their faces showed confusion, and there was a lot of chatter and commotion while they gathered.

"Does anyone know where Moira is?" Geri asked, as soon as everyone was there.

There was a murmur while they all looked around at each other.

"She was out with me, Binnie and Nadine last night," said Debbie, a short woman in scrubs. "We were at *Spice*, and she went home with a guy."

There was a mixture of responses, some relieved to hear a plausible explanation for Moira's lateness today, others finding the news a source of worry.

"Has she phoned any of you since she left?" asked Geri.

Three heads searched each other out, and all indicated no. Moira hadn't been in touch with any of them.

"She wasn't at home when I went to pick her up this morning," said Debbie. "And her phone just went straight onto answer machine. I just thought it was because she stayed with that guy."

"No," said Binnie from within the gathered midwives. "They definitely went back to her flat. I called the taxi for them."

"Wasn't she putting her car in for a service today?" asked Rowen.

"Tomorrow," said Binnie.

"Why, what's happened?"

"What's wrong?"

"Is she okay?"

Everyone began to speak at the same time.

"Look, I don't want to jump the gun," said Geri. "But Moira has missed her morning visits, and we've not been able to contact her."

An uneasy silence crept into the room.

"What should we do?"

The midwives subconsciously drew closer together, as Geri's words trailed off. A sense of foreboding rose like smoke, and embedded itself in their nerves. None of them had forgotten. It was nearly two years since the murder of Eleanor Wallace, one of their own.

Since the morning's news of a body found on Arbroath beach, her name had been mentioned more than once. No-one dared say out loud what they were all thinking now.

"There's probably some silly thing," said Geri, making a forced flippant gesture with her hands and trying to inject confidence into her voice, "like she forgot to mark in an annual leave day, or something."

But she got no response, no general murmur of assent. She felt the hairs on the back of her neck stand on end.

Chapter 9

Donna acknowledged the officer who opened the door to Interview Room 2 for her and followed her inside.

Sitting with his hands clasped in front of him at the room's table, sat a tidily-dressed man in his fifties. His face was clean shaven, well scrubbed, and his hair was clean and brylcreemed to within an inch of its life.

"Hello, Mr. Thomson," said Donna, as she pulled out a chair opposite him. Over her shoulder, she gave the date, time, and attendee details for the recorder. Thomson watched her with an intense, almost fascinated gaze.

"You wanted to speak to me?"

"I killed that woman on the beach," said Thomson. He spoke clearly, and he held his head high as he spoke. *Prissy*, thought Donna.

"That's an unusual thing to do," said Donna, "come into a police station and confess to a murder."

Thomson looked thrown for a moment, before recovering himself. "It's the right thing to do. I have a conscience, you know."

"Hmm," muttered Donna, having a chew on the end of a pen. "I understand you make a habit of confessing to murders, am I right?"

Before Thomson could say anything, she continued. "Why should I believe you this time?"

Thomson was clearly ready for this one. His face brightened. "Because it hasn't been in the papers yet," he said. It was his trump card. "If I didn't do it, then how else would I know about it?"

"It's been all over Facebook," Donna offered.

A cloud crossed Thomson's eyes.

"Look, I did it," he said, leaning forward. "I've confessed. You have to charge me, I know my rights." Donna tried to hide a smile.

"So, how did you kill her?" she asked, her voice flat, careful to keep exuding boredom.

"Well, if you're not interested," said Thomson, sitting back again and folding his arms. He looked up huffily into the corner of the grubby ceiling.

Donna looked Thomson over from head to toe. Everything about him spoke of care and precision. Everything in its place. All carefully planned. This was a man who didn't do panic and dash. Making these observations, John Ogilvie's words rang in her head. *I've seen better jobs of strangling a victim.*

"I'm looking for somebody a bit more cack-handed for this one," said Donna. "So, unless you want to be charged with wasting police time, you'd better make sure we don't see you in here again."

As she rose from her chair Thomson's voice grew urgent, his eyes widening with desperation.

"You'll regret this, you know," he said, also standing up, making to follow her before the uniformed officer caught his eye. "You didn't believe me when I told you I murdered Eleanor Wallace, and now I've gone on to kill again. You're the only one who can stop me."

Donna turned and levelled her gaze at him. He sat back down. He was panting now.

"Look, I'm in the middle of a murder investigation," she said. "A woman has died. Her loved ones have had their lives turned upside down. They'll never be the same again."

Thomson stared at her, eyes wide.

"If you have information that will help us catch her killer," Donna went on, "then, fine, you can talk to one of my officers. Otherwise, piss off and get out of my sight." As she left the room, she motioned to the uniformed officer to get rid of Thomson.

Donna made her way to the main entrance of the office complex, where a small group of people, uniformed and civvie, stood smoking and chatting. She wandered past them and out to the car park, then she stood for a moment shivering in the cold air.

Weird, she thought, going over the interview in her head. Thomson was no killer, she had no doubt, but there was something unnerving about him. She wasn't going to rule him out of this investigation just yet. She glanced at her watch, glad the working day was almost over, and more to the point that it was time for her four o'clock cigarette.

Chapter 10

It was good to be home. As first days back went, this one had been a challenge. Donna felt bad about going at the normal close of day, leaving Alice to co-ordinate the investigation on overtime, but Ross had insisted. And she hadn't argued back too hard.

She sank her shoulders under the water, savouring its warmth and the luxury of the bubbles. She wriggled her toes beneath the taps, and let the stress of her first day back ooze away. It seemed like a lifetime ago since she'd stood beside the harbour wall in Arbroath, re-living the terror of her last day at work eighteen months previously. But she'd taken the step. She'd come back, and what a come-back! She'd skirted over the details of the body on the beach, but was enjoying relaying the details of the day's other events to Libby, who was perched on the toilet seat, barely able to hold onto her mug of tea for laughing.

"You should have seen his face," Donna egged on the hilarity, the memory of Morrison's startled expression making her laugh aloud. "I bet he shaves it off tonight."

"How will you keep a straight face if he does?"

Their laughter echoed around the small bathroom, the recounting of Donna's first meeting with her new team a source of great amusement.

"I wish you didn't have to do this course," said Donna, suddenly growing serious.

Libby shrugged as she popped a handful of salted peanuts into her mouth. "At least it's just a one-off," she muffled through the nuts.

"Five days, though, that's rubbish."

"I know," Libby agreed. "But at least I won't have to be worrying about you eating properly while I'm away."

"No?"

"Danny's coming round with some frozen home-cooked."

"Result," said Donna, punching the air and sending a plume of bubbles rising. There were perks to having a chef for a brother-in-law.

"I thought you'd like that," Libby smiled.

Libby scooped up more peanuts, and Donna let her skin grow pink in the hot water.

She breathed in the delicate and pleasing scent of the bubble bath. Sandalwood, she noted from the bottle. Nice. These were the moments that kept her going during the difficult ones. In moments like this one, the nicotine craving was silent.

She realised her eyes had drifted closed only when they snapped open. Now Libby was sitting on the edge of the bath and looking concerned.

"Today's taken more out of you than you think," said Libby.

Donna yawned. "I'll be okay."

"You meeting up with Natesh later?"

"Yeh," said Donna, with a sheepish grin. "Not that I'm trying to wriggle out of visiting your folks."

Libby chuckled. "You and dad could probably do with some space from each other just now."

"It's not him," said Donna. "Your mum's been a bit bonkers lately. And that's coming from someone like me!"

Libby made a non-committal sound. "Well, I'll see how they are tonight. What's Natesh been up to these days?"

"Problems with Erin."

"Back at his mum's again, you mean?"

"Yup."

"Just as well he's got a sensitive friend like you, then," laughed Libby. "Mrs. Look-at-your-terrible-Movember-tache…"

Donna launched herself from the water, caught Libby around the waist and tugged her, shrieking and fully clothed, into the bath. Copious volumes of bath water lobbed onto the floor.

Chapter 11

After her bath, Donna had quickly dressed then driven into the city centre to meet Natesh.

They had time to spare before the game started. It was their thing, watching all of the televised Premier League games and betting against each other on the results. Since neither Libby nor Erin cared much for football, it gave them the chance to relax together in the way that old friends do, in a routine they both treasured, making sure they kept the contact during their busy schedules.

"Mmm, num num num," said Donna, savouring the vinegar licked from her fingers.

She and Natesh strolled along the waterfront, each carrying a fish supper and eating as they went. The front was decked out in twinkling Christmas decorations.

"The body might have been dumped right in here," said Natesh, pointing at the water that was calmly lapping the shore beside them.

"Good try," said Donna.

"Damn!"

They passed a couple taking a selfie on their phone; a cyclist whizzed past, all glaring Lycra and flashing lights.

"So, how will you cope without Libby for a whole week?"

"It'll be weird going home to an empty house," said Donna. "But she'll be back on Sunday, and the important thing is, she's asked Danny to stock up the fridge for me."

"Well, in that case," said Natesh, scrunching up his chip shop wrapper, "you got yourself a dinner partner for the week."

"Well, thank you, friend," said Donna. "But I'd prefer if Libby didn't have this sodding training course."

"You'd feel a lot better if you gave me a teeny weeny clue about the body."

Donna grinned. "Okay," she said, buoyed by his astonished expression. "But you'll have to catch me first!" And she broke into a sprint. Natesh plunged after her, yelling in glee.

At a bus shelter towards the end of the front, Donna stopped abruptly beside a pile of rags. Natesh slowed behind her, and his mouth fell open as a shaggy head emerged from the rags.

"Donna, hen," said the pile.

"Thought that was you," said Donna, crouching down level. "What are you still doing out here at this time? It's getting cold."

"Fell asleep, hen."

Natesh shifted his weight awkwardly from one foot to the other, not sure whether or how to join in. He froze when he suddenly found himself in the old man's glare. A gnarled finger shot out and pointed at him.

"Good God, is that that wee Paki lad you used to play with?"

"Marcus!" Donna scolded. "We don't talk to each other like that. Bit of respect, eh?"

"Ach, political pish," said the man.

"It is not," said Donna.

"Is that Tomato Man?" gasped Natesh, sudden recognition rocking him.

"*Tomato Man*?" said Marcus, indignant. "He can call me *that*, and I can't call him a…"

"This is Natesh," Donna hurried in. "And yes, he's my old friend. And yes," she lowered her voice aside to Natesh, "this is indeed Tomato Man."

"But how? What's he doing here?" Natesh was at a loss, and gaping again.

"Long story," said Donna. She turned back to Marcus. "You need to be getting home."

"Aye, hen, I'm just going," said Marcus. "You joined the police, didn't you?"

"That's right."

"You always were a bright one. Not like him." He stared at Natesh. "Trouble, you."

"Don't know what you mean," said Natesh, his voice more kindly this time.

Donna nudged him on, and they set along their way, with a wave from Marcus.

"Well?" asked Natesh, once they were out of earshot.

"Wife died, went to pieces, turned to drink," said Donna.

"That wasn't such a long story."

"Was for Marcus, poor bastard," said Donna. "But he still has the house, you know."

"Man, that's sad."

"Come on," said Donna. "Kick-off's in ten minutes."

They hurried across the road and into the housing scheme, winding their way purposely towards Scott Street. Fireworks were going off in all directions now.

Approaching the front door, Natesh fished a set of keys from his pocket. As he was about to place a key in the lock, the door flew open.

"There you are!" declared Samira. "Donna, how lovely to see you."

"You too, Mrs Chaudrakar," mumbled Donna, suddenly feeling twelve years old again.

"Come in, come in," Samira gushed. She fussed around Donna, brushing invisible debris from her shoulders as she was ushered into the flat.

Natesh rolled his eyes. Donna smirked.

"You two make yourselves comfortable," said Samira, marshalling them towards the sofa in front of the TV. "I'll be busy in the kitchen…"

"It's okay, mum," said Natesh. "We're just watching the football."

"Oh, but I'm sure you'd appreciate a bit of privacy."

"Honestly, it's fine," said Donna. "No privacy needed. Really."

An expression of disappointment emerged clear on Samira's face. Natesh shrugged at her, his eyes saying, *told you so.*

"What about this body, then?" he asked, turning to Donna.

Samira stopped in her tracks. "A body?" she asked, her voice hesitant.

"Yeah, work," Donna explained. "A body was washed up on Arbroath beach this morning. We're having trouble identifying her."

"What are you going to do?" asked Natesh.

"Well, if there's no progress by morning, we'll need to put out a media appeal for information. Until we know who she is, we've no way of knowing whether her killer is a risk to others. We need to assume the worst, so time is of the essence."

Samira shuddered and drew her shawl around herself more tightly. The way her hand flew to her mouth hadn't escaped

Donna's attention.

With the game underway, and Natesh installed as the centrepiece in a monument of crisps and beer bottles, Donna went into the kitchen. She appeared at Samira's back. She saw the older woman start at the realisation she was there.

"You've known me since I was a kid," said Donna gently.

Samira scrubbed furiously at a pot.

"You know you can trust me. If you know something, you can tell me."

Samira turned to half-face her. She twisted at the amber ring, then smiled. "Always working. Go, go! Watch the game and calm down your imagination."

Donna backed out of the kitchen. She'd seen enough fake smiles to know when someone was trying to cover the truth.

"All right," she nodded. *For now*, she thought.

Tuesday

Chapter 12

Fran stood back from the whiteboard, satisfied she'd tacked the photo of the dead woman onto the board straight. It was a solemn moment, with Morrison, Akwasi, Alice and Donna standing in a semi-circle behind her. They kept a moment's silence, looking at the picture.

Nothing in the picture was dignified. Nothing about the dead woman's skin or clothing to speak of a lost loved one. Nothing to show how she'd lived, how her voice had sounded, how she'd laughed or cried. Or screamed.

"Our Jane Doe," said Donna. "Until we know who she is and who did this to her, we're her next of kin. Everything about her matters to us."

"There's been no more information overnight to identify her," said Alice.

"Anything gleaned from interviewing the old boy?" asked Donna.

"Not really," said Akwasi. "We took his statement last night. He's walking his dog along the shore about six am…"

"That's early," Donna commented.

"I don't think an 87 year old guy is going to make that up to give himself an alibi for murder, do you?" Akwasi's voice threw sarcasm at Donna.

"Watch it," Alice warned him in a low voice. Morrison coughed into his collar. This morning he was clean-shaven. It was gone.

"Go on," said Donna, deciding she would have a word with Akwasi later, nip this in the bud.

Akwasi continued. "When the dog ran off to pee, and started barking, the poor bugger found a dead body on the beach. He called it in on his big-button phone."

"We interviewed a number of people who were in the area the night before," said Morrison. "But nobody noticed anything suspicious. Last known person on the beachfront was around 2am, and we've interviewed him. Nobody seen on CCTV walking by until the dog walker."

"Somebody needs to stop these dog walkers," Alice said.

"So, she could have washed up between two and six am," said Donna, smiling at Alice, "except the tide only started to go out, when, five?"

"Yes, high tide was just before five," said Morrison. "And the coastguard agrees that the body was most likely carried north-easterly."

"So we're looking down the coast, how far?" asked Donna.

"With the estimated time frame, he says he'd circle off the coastline to about St Andrews. Berwick if it's longer," said Morrison.

"Okay, have you got all that?" Donna asked Fran.

Fran nodded as she marked the details onto the whiteboard.

It wasn't much to go on.

"We'll go ahead with the press meeting," said Donna. "We need to identify her as soon as possible. Where are we at with that?"

"They're waiting for us in the press room, ready to roll in about ten minutes," said Alice. "We've got a sketch of her face ready to give to them. Gets her onto the evening news."

"Let's do it, then," said Donna. "And let's hope to God she's a local, so there's some chance of her being recognised."

"Yeah," said Alice, "and we can give her her real name."

"And find out her last movements," said Donna.

They all turned round at the sound of a rap on the door.

"DI Davenport?"

Donna walked towards the officer who'd popped his head into the room.

"I've been told to let you know we've had a report in of a missing person," he said.

Donna swung round to face her team. "Alice, hold that press conference another half hour, will you? Fran, come with me to see what we've got."

Fran almost fell over the chair next to the white board in her flustered rush to catch up as Donna swept from the room.

Chapter 13

Amin Chaudrakar sat in a rocking chair on the paved porch of his secluded villa, and watched the clouds gather across the Kaya Valley. A cool breeze made the surrounding pomegranate trees rustle. The villa was quiet these days, with most of the girls gone. Just chickens foraging around. The two murders in Dundee changed things. It was risky, but he decided to go ahead and send the final two girls. It was too late to back out of this one. Then he'd have to reconsider the whole operation. It had served him well over the years.

He continued to watch the clouds as he heard footsteps approach from the rear of the villa. He knew the sound of them. It was the American. The visitor stopped and stood next to Amin.

"Are the passports ready?" The American cupped his hand around his cigarette as he lit it, and closed his eyes as he inhaled.

Amin continued to gaze out beyond the shrubbery to the mountains.

"Firaz is on his way," he replied, without turning to face his visitor.

"And the blushing bride?"

Amin shrugged. "She'll be here, don't worry."

The American ducked back inside the house and dragged a stool, the antique rustic oak one, across the ceramic-tiled floor, making Amin wince in annoyance. Bringing it outside, he plonked the stool next to Amin's rocking chair and sat down. He offered a cigarette.

"Bad for your health," said Amin.

The American chuckled. "You would know, doc."

The rumble of a jeep engine droned into the morning air, and this time Amin looked over his shoulder, out towards the open gates of the compound that contained the villa. A large man with an assault rifle slung over his shoulder sat on a boulder by the gates, and raised a hand to reassure Amin that the approaching vehicle was friend, not foe.

"That'll be Firaz now," said Amin, and he rose from the rocking chair, stretching and yawning as he did. The jeep spluttered and clanged as it entered the compound, its horn sounding a thank you to the guard who let the ancient vehicle through. It came to a stop in a cloud of exhaust fumes, close to the rocking chair and sending the chickens squawking into the bushes.

The jeep had a single occupant, a young man with his long black hair tied back in a ponytail. He wore a khaki green t-shirt, revealing intricate tattoo work that covered every inch of both arms. He slung a leather satchel over his shoulder as he jumped from the jeep and grunted his greeting to Amin and the American.

"Let's see what you've got, Firaz," said the American, holding out his hand.

Firaz rummaged in the satchel, glancing at Amin, and produced a small booklet. He flipped through the pages, and held it out to the American with the chosen page open.

The American stared at the contents of the fake passport for a moment, then grinned.

"Bradley Feinmann," he said. "Back from another honeymoon, dirty bastard."

The three men guffawed.

"This is her," said Firaz, handing over a second passport. "Both of them have the entry stamps. Story is, you've been here on honeymoon for two weeks, and now you're off to Europe for the tour. Drop her off in Amsterdam."

"Check us out, jet-setters," said the American. He pocketed the two passports, glancing quickly at Amin, noting the absence of the usual instruction to return to the compound following the drop-off.

Firaz rattled his car keys. Amin reached into his jacket pocket and retrieved an envelope, which he tossed at the younger man. Firaz caught it and quickly scanned the contents. He didn't have to check. Amin was always good for the money. He nodded a farewell, and only minutes after arriving, he was gone.

Amin and the American strolled into the house. As they walked, the American studied the second passport again. "She looks a bit attitudey," he observed.

"They're the best ones," said Amin. "More convincing."

"Yeah," agreed the American. "Ain't that the case!"

Amin paused briefly to look at the photo that sat on top of the TV. A younger version of himself smiled widely at the camera, the woman at his side caught in a moment of frivolity, her eyes shining with laughter and her hand part way to covering the giggle that had escaped her mouth. He brushed his finger over her hand, smudging the glass that covered the photo, just where the amber ring that he'd given her gleamed.

"This is the last assignment I'll have for you," he told the American.

The American turned to him, surprised.

"There's been trouble," Amin explained. "Too risky."

"Fair enough," shrugged the American. "Guess my line of work doesn't come with guaranteed job security."

Amin chuckled, relieved.

"But I'm sure you'll want this final trip to go smoothly," said the American. "You wouldn't want me slipping up 'cause I'm scanning the vacancies ads, now would you? We can have a chat when I get back from Amsterdam."

The American wanted to be difficult, thought Amin. There was only one way to deal with difficult people.

Chapter 14

"You've gone awful quiet, Ma'am. I mean, Donna." Fran hesitated, unsure of the cue to be taken from the DI as they made their way back to the team room.

Donna was staring at the photograph of Moira Cowan that her worried colleagues had just handed in. She and Fran had agreed, out of earshot of the midwives, that the woman in the photo bore a striking resemblance to the one lying in the morgue. Then Donna had fallen silent, and had said nothing more while she and Fran walked.

As if coming out of a daydream, Donna looked at Fran. She handed over the photograph.

"Take this through, will you?" she said. "Get the details onto the evidence board."

"Ma'am."

And without any explanation, Donna turned around and marched towards the exit, leaving Fran to inform the team about a likely ID on the murdered woman.

Donna barely made it outside before lighting a cigarette. She watched gulls scrounging at the bins on the other side of the car park, and blew a stream of smoke into the cool air, as a barrage of thoughts assaulted her mind. Her heart, to her alarm, was beating wildly, like the gulls' flapping wings. She had to get it under control, and without resorting to popping more lithium pills. Was there a mania coming, or had she subconsciously stumbled onto something? She forced the thoughts apart and focused on them one at a time.

Moira Cowan.

Midwives.

Samira Chaudrakar's reaction last night. She knew something.

Samira had known, Donna now realised, that the body on the beach was Moira Cowan.

She inhaled and held her breath for a moment before releasing it, slowly, telling herself to slow down. To think. Slowly.

The racing thoughts began to calm and form an orderly queue. She wasn't losing it. Of course Samira must have been worried, she reasoned: her colleague was missing from work, and the news about the body on the beach had been all over the place. Samira had simply put two and two together, as anyone would have done.

Donna stubbed out her cigarette, and found herself automatically reaching for another one, but stopped herself. She turned and made her way back towards the team room, but couldn't shake a nagging whisper that there was something else.

"The description definitely fits the woman in the mortuary," Fran was saying when Donna entered the team room. She saw Fran steel herself, as she held up the photo of Moira Cowan that the worried midwives had brought to the station. Alice, Morrison and Akwasi stepped forward to look. Donna remembered the young DC's unease in the mortuary.

"Thank you, Fran," she smiled. Fran returned the smile, looking relieved.

"How do we run this with the press conference?" Alice asked Donna, taking the photo from Fran for a closer examination. "They're pissed off about the delay." She stepped forward and pinned the photo next to the one of Moira's lifeless face.

"We can't release any details of her identity until next of kin have been told and we have a positive ID," said Donna. "And pull the sketch - I don't want the appeal for information going out now."

"Are you serious?" asked Alice. "They'll form a lynch mob. I would if I was in their shoes."

"Would it do any harm to just go ahead as planned?" asked Fran.

"Donna's right," Alice sighed. "It looks as though we have her identity. It wouldn't be fair to pretend otherwise."

"And she's the right one to be making decisions about what to tell the press?" Akwasi whispered to Morrison, a whisper that was louder than it needed to be.

Donna held his stare for a moment. It wasn't worth it, she thought, and she turned to the white board, and pulled at her lower lip as the others debated press tactics behind her.

The dead woman - the murdered woman - had been a midwife. A midwife. That nagging whisper again.

"What is it?" asked Alice, suddenly at Donna's side.

Donna turned to look at her. "A midwife?"

45

Jumbled thoughts were trying to form at the back of her mind. She wasn't quite grasping a coherent one, but something was definitely there. Then she remembered Rory Thomson's words, the desperate attention-seeking words of a serial confessor, *You didn't believe me when I told you I murdered Eleanor Wallace, and now I've gone on to kill again. You're the only one who can stop me.*

"Eleanor Wallace," said Donna, a flash of inspiration lighting her eyes. Fran, Morrison and Akwasi turned to look at her.

Alice shuddered. "That was an awful case. Her murder left three children and her mother was really ill, wasn't she?"

"Wasn't she a midwife, too?" asked Donna. "I'm sure she was."

"Oh crap," said Morrison, "that's a coincidence."

"The hell it is," said Donna. "Alice, I need her file up."

Donna watched Alice's eyes narrow as she weighed up the information, taking in the implication of the DI's instruction, before hurrying from the room.

Donna turned to the remaining officers. "When Alice gets back, I want Eleanor Wallace's details up on the evidence board beside Moira Cowan's," she said. "Then I want you both," she motioned to Morrison and Akwasi, "to head over to the midwifery unit and interview her colleagues. Last known movements, family members, any oddities. You know the drill. No mention of Eleanor Wallace, though, understand?"

"Ma'am."

"Fran, I want you to get Moira's electronic diary sent through, and have a look for any similarities with Eleanor Wallace's file that strike you. Places we need to check out, that sort of thing."

Ha, no more nagging whispers now, she thought. She was on top of this. Her mind felt sharp, no uncontrolled racing.

"I'm on it," said Fran.

"It's time for the press conference," Donna continued. "God knows what I'm going to tell them, but I won't be long."

She left her three colleagues and made her way to Ross's office.

He was waiting for her, busy pretending that he hadn't been.

"Time flies," he said, smoothing down his suit. "What are we telling them?" They began walking down the steps to the floor below.

"The good news or the bad news?" said Donna. Ross frowned. "There's been a development."

"Well, they'll like that," said Ross. "Tell me they will."

"We had an illustration to give them, to help identify our woman," said Donna, "but we have a probable name now."

"Okay," said Ross slowly, "so, no picture. Why's that bad?"

"You remember Eleanor Wallace a couple of years back?" Now they were walking along a corridor whose office doors were mostly shut, creating a hum of muffled voices as they passed.

"Of course," said Ross. Donna saw his Adam's apple bob up and down, knew he was dreading what she might be about to come out with.

"You remember what she did for a living?"

"She was a nurse, wasn't she? Oh, a midwife," said Ross. "What's she got to do with your case?"

"We've just had a missing person report," said Donna. "With a photo. We're pretty sure it's our surfer - she's a local, Moira Cowan. And guess what she did for a living?"

Ross stopped in his tracks, his jaw tightened. "Please tell me not a midwife."

"Told you there was bad news," said Donna.

"And you think there's a connection?"

Donna shrugged. "It's too early to say. But there's no way I'm letting any of this get into the press today." A tea trolley came clanking towards them, pushed by a miserable older man dressed in a parody of waiter's garb. He didn't stop or make eye contact as he trundled by them.

"We need to tell them something."

"I know that," said Donna. It came out harshly, and Ross raised his eyebrows.

"Sorry," she continued. "I'm so fucking desperate for a cigarette." An overhead fluorescent light began to blink and buzz.

"Well, for God's sake have one before you go into that press room," said Ross. "And that's an order."

Donna had already reached into her pocket and lit one.

"We're going to promise them something big if they'll agree to hold the headlines a little bit longer," she said, slowly exhaling a plume of smoke.

Ross frowned. "They're not going to like being called in here to be told they can't print anything."

"They're not daft," said Donna. "They know it's a murder

investigation, early days, sensitive information, blah blah blah…"

"What exactly is that you're smoking?"

"Trust me," she smiled, as she stubbed out the cigarette into a bin as they passed it. They now stood in front of a set of double doors, from which a clamour of eager chatter, clinking of teaspoons and scraping of chairs tumbled.

Trust you? Ross looked even more nervous than he had done a moment ago as they swung open the doors to the press room and walked inside, shoulder by shoulder. It was impossible to look at her directly to gauge her mood. He trusted her with everything except relations with the press.

"Donna!" several voices cried in warm recognition. Ross felt a knot form in his gut.

Juanita

I remember lots of people, lots of noise and lots of dust. That was where we stopped, my mother, my grandmother, my aunts and me. They told me it was away from the fighting, but everywhere I looked, men were fighting. Not with guns, though. But they still fought all the time, and I often wondered why. Why did they run away from a war, only to bring it here with them?

Our tent was right on the perimeter of the massive camp. In a way, that was the best place to be, as at least we only had to guard the front of our tent. Behind us was the fence, huge, and we were told there were landmines on the other side, but I didn't believe that. You could see through the gaps, and every night we saw people, often in large groups, escape through the fence and get onto trucks that roared away across the plains towards Europe. Those were the ones who had the money to bribe the fence guards and to pay the traffickers.

We had no money. We'd escaped with nothing, and we had nobody left alive at home who could help us. We were stuck in the camp, with no way out. There was enough food in the rations we were given. But it wasn't any safer than the war we'd run from. With the fighting all the time, we had to take turns on look-out, my mother, my grandmother, my aunts and me, 24 hours a day.

My grandmother took unwell. One of my aunts had heard there was a doctor. There were doctors in the camp, but the risk involved in trying to get to them was too high. We knew that some of the Turkish doctors would come to the fence and offer free treatment from time to time, and so my aunt told one of them about my grandmother.

He was a kind man. The fence guards let him talk to us, and he listened while we explained about my grandmother's illness. He promised to return the next day with some medicines for her, and of course we thought we'd never see him again. But he did come back, and he gave us the medicine. There was a queue of people at the fence, all patiently waiting to see him, but he took the time to make sure we understood how to administer the medicines, and I remember him telling me to do my schoolwork, as that was my best chance of getting a proper chance in life. I took his advice. I'd have been 13 then, not long after we'd arrived at the camp, and he was the only kind man I ever saw there.

Chapter 15

Samira's heart jack-hammered so hard, she got a headache. She'd picked up her bag and coat, looking as casual as she could, but the police had arrived before she could slip away. She was sure her face was flushed. How was she going to make sure she didn't give anything away? Make sure the police didn't suspect she knew more than she was going to say?

The midwives gathered round her desk at reception, and she kept her eyes lowered, trying to steady her breath and hoping nobody noticed.

"Moira Cowan," said Geri.

The tall police officer was furiously scribbling down the details. Moira's name, address, age, anyone in the household, her routine, why they thought she was missing.

"I don't like this," Rowen whispered to Vicky. "They're not brushing this off. They know something." Geri caught her eye and shared the look of fear.

"Mrs Chaudrakar?" Samira jumped at the sound of her name, and returned her focus to the police officers.

"Are you okay?" asked Akwasi.

"Sorry," said Samira. "I, er, sorry, did you ask me a question?"

"We need the details of the phone calls you took," said Morrison, pencil poised over his notebook. "What time did you receive the first call?"

Samira felt a sweat flush across her neck and head. She screwed her eyes shut while she thought. "Ten past nine yesterday morning," she said. "I remember thinking it was a bit unreasonable to phone and complain when she was only ten minutes late." The noise of the pencil scratching on the notebook grated in her head as she provided details of the calls.

"And you say Moira was with you the night before?" Morrison's attention now shifted to Binnie, and Samira let out a quiet breath of relief.

Binnie stared at Morrison like a rabbit caught in headlights as she answered his questions. Meanwhile, Akwasi began to ferret around the paperwork lying on the desk. Samira's notepad with the details of the phone calls. Staff rotas and call routes for the day. She watched his hands closely, wondering if there was anything lying on her desk that could possibly give her away. She tried not to fidget with her amber ring, but the more she tried, the more irresistible it became.

She could feel her breathing quicken in her anxiety.

After what seemed like forever, the officers were finally finished with them.

"Thanks for your time," said Akwasi. "We really appreciate it, and we'll do everything we can to find out what has happened to Moira."

"Let us know as soon as you find anything out," said Geri, amidst the general hum of worry among the women.

"We will," said Akwasi, and the two officers left the midwifery unit.

In the burst of chatter that followed their departure, Samira quietly picked up her bag and coat, and slipped outside.

She'd never sneaked off during her lunch break before. Never left work early, even. She'd kept her head down all those times the others had boasted about their skiving. Not for her.

She glanced at her watch. Forty-five minutes before anyone would notice she hadn't come back.

She paused and let her eyes roam around the room. It was strange being home at this time of day during the week. All quiet. She swallowed back the tightness in her throat from the sudden grief. She knew this was the end. She was going to have to leave behind this place that she'd called home for more than thirty years. Thirty years! Her eyes widened almost in surprise at how all that time could have passed by so quickly. The memory of her bewildered, scared younger self arriving here for the first time played crystal clear in her mind. She recalled the silliest of details, like baby Natesh grabbing onto the teenage Vidu's ear as he fell asleep on their first night in their new home. Vidu had barely moved a muscle all that night, afraid of waking his nephew. And she recalled the heartbreak of watching Vidu go the next day with Amin's henchmen, to carry on the vile trade he'd begun back in Turkey. *Blood is thicker than water*, she remembered him smirk.

Samira shook her head to clear her thoughts. She had to pack.

Vidu was coming. She'd known since Eleanor Wallace had died that any more trouble would mean Amin would bring them back to Turkey. He'd made that clear at the time. If she didn't comply, well…she believed his threats about Natesh's safety.

Passport, where was her passport?

Natesh had a habit of sifting through old belongings and paperwork, an attempt she recognised to connect himself with something of his past. She'd seen his desperation, many times breaking her heart for him, his need to know where he'd come from. But it was best he didn't know. Sometimes Samira felt he'd seen through her story, but he never challenged her. Just kept searching old things for answers.

And now her passport wasn't where she'd left it. What had he done with it?

A bead of sweat formed on her forehead, and she heard herself panting.

She went into Natesh's room. Silent, dark with the curtains still drawn, the bed covers thrown back and several items of clothing strewn across the floor. She smiled and let a tear slip from her eyes. How was she going to let him go?

On his bedside table lay a book, face-down and open somewhere in the middle, and an array of paraphernalia, amongst which was a tiny figurine of a wrestling superstar. A remnant from his childhood. She picked it up, and placed it in her pocket.

She opened the drawer below, and a quick shuffle of her hand revealed her passport, carelessly tossed among the paperwork stashed away in there.

Letting out a breath of relief, she took the passport, and hurried from the room, failing to close the drawer.

Then she heard the knock on the door.

He was here.

Vidu slid into the flat as soon as the door was open, anxiously looking over his shoulder as if fearing he was being followed.

"You know we have to go now?" he said. "Right now."

"I got your message," Samira said, and indicated the suitcase to him.

She saw him hesitate. Squirm. She knew what he wanted to ask before he said it, but the words still tore her apart when she heard them.

"Are you going to tell Natesh?"

Samira fingered the wrestler figurine in her pocket. It was so unfair. Natesh deserved to know the truth. How could she just leave him with nothing but the torment of so many questions? But she knew the truth would destroy him, her untainted Natesh. He had a good life here, and she wasn't going to take that away from him. He was a grown man now, she told herself, trying to calm her fears for him. And he had good friends. Maybe he'd marry Donna. She never could understand why he scoffed so much at the idea; they were clearly very fond of each other.

Besides, there was now another reason why she wasn't going to tell him.

"You really think Amin wants to meet his son now, after all this time?" she asked.

"He does," said Vidu, reaching out to hold her by the shoulders. She flinched and he withdrew the gesture quickly. "And I want him to know me, too."

"Then you and Amin can both go to hell," said Samira. "Natesh is a good man, and if you make one move to contact him, it will be over my dead body."

She jabbed Vidu hard in the chest. He took a step backward, alarmed at her venom, but couldn't meet her eye.

"And before you get any ideas," Samira continued, "if anything happens to me, I've taken steps to reveal the whole story to the police." It sounded plausible, she hoped. She *could* have done.

"All right," said Vidu. "Point taken." He picked up her suitcase. "Let's go."

Chapter 16

Donna walked through the double doors into the press room. It must be a slow news day, she thought, surprised at the number of journalists in the room. Some of them turned around, and left their conversations hanging when they saw her.

Ross watched the effect she had on them, and allowed himself a wry smile. Having good media relations certainly helped with any investigation, but he was a little more nervous when it was Donna herself that they were interested in. Before she'd gone off sick, before all the Jonas Evanton stuff had kicked off, Donna had gotten herself into some deep shit over her wagging tongue in the company of journalists. *Rent-a-gob*, she'd referred to herself at one point, after conceding that she'd blabbed too much.

She and Ross were well aware that the reputation lingered, and any hint of an investigation led by Donna could mean the details they were really after – not just the official line – would flow freely. So they'd arrived en masse.

Ross had a bad feeling about this, but it was too late. Before he could have a word with her, she was caught up in a throng of *welcome back*s, hugs and *Donna dahling*s. But Donna kept walking steadily towards the liveried table with the microphones, politely returning the various greetings.

Donna and Ross sat down at the table. Their Press Officer, Martha, stood to the side of the room, holding a roving microphone, her lips moving silently as she made a quick head count.

There weren't enough chairs set out in the room, and only around half of the journalists there got a seat. The rest didn't seem to mind, and the buzz and clatter around the room gradually began to fade.

"Was this victim famous, or something?" Martha whispered to Ross. Ross glanced up at her and wiggled his eyebrows.

Martha, puzzled, stood in front of the table and introduced Donna and Ross. She invited Donna to open with her statement.

Donna pulled the microphone towards her mouth, and began. "Early yesterday morning, the body of a woman was found on Arbroath beach. My officers have been focusing on identifying the woman, and we do have a positive lead on this. Once we have verified it and informed the next of kin, then we can release the details to you."

The journalists murmured their agreement at this. Ross was well aware that if he'd been the one to say it, he'd have been bombarded with questions in protest.

"We are treating this as a murder inquiry," Donna went on, "although we have yet to establish the cause of death."

Martha invited questions from the journalists, and poised herself ready with the roving microphone. All of the hands in the room shot into the air at once.

"How does it feel to be back after such a long time, Donna?"

"How do you feel about Jonas Evanton's disappearance, Donna?"

"Do you have anything to say about Evanton's escape?"

"Do you think Jonas Evanton is still alive, Donna?"

Ross stood up. "If you could, please," he shouted. "We're here to share information about a woman who's been murdered."

"Is it true she was a midwife like Eleanor Wallace?" one voice rang out from within the throng.

"We can't confirm that," said Donna.

There was a rush of voices, and it was impossible to distinguish anything coherent. It was obvious that this was news to the majority of journalists in the room.

"Are you saying there's a serial killer on the loose?" The question came from a journalist that Donna knew well.

"Come on, Lindsey," Donna said to her. "You should know better than that." Lindsey blushed.

The atmosphere in the room was tipping subtly towards a more hostile incline. Martha decided it was time to wrap up.

"Ladies and gentlemen," she said, "Detective Inspector Davenport has told you all of the details we can release at the moment. We'll let you know as soon as more information comes to light."

Ross felt a twinge of anxiety ripple down his gut. The journalists had clearly come along to find out about Donna's return to the dead beat. Now the possibility of a serial killer had been sprung on them, and they'd been given scant details about either. He really didn't need a battle with the press on a case like this.

Chapter 17

Natesh groaned as he reached for the door. Locked.

He fished in his pocket for his key, then turned, startled, as something brushed against his leg.

"Harry Potter," he said, reaching down to pick up the cat. "What are you doing out here?"

He checked the time. Strange, he thought. His mother would normally be home by now. No, scrap that. She was always home by now, and Harry Potter was never outside this late in the day. Never.

Natesh was puzzled as he let himself in, and found the flat empty and quiet. In as long as he could remember, his mother had returned home from work at the same time each day, her routine unwavering. Except for the time he'd had chickenpox and she'd had to stay off work in case she carried the virus into the maternity unit, there had been no variation whatsoever in her coming and going. Ever.

He chewed his lip nervously as he went from room to room. But there was no sign of her.

Keep the head, man, he told himself. She'd said something about a retirement do at work. It must be today.

Trying not to fret, he went to the bathroom and ran himself a hot bath. He needed a soak after a long shift at the hardware store. He'd been unloading stock from lorries all day, and his muscles were screaming at him. A bath first, he decided, then he'd raid the fridge.

He cursed whatever it was that was keeping Donna's phone unavailable.

He took out a can of lager, grabbed a banana from the fruit bowl, and sat himself down in front of the TV, where he promptly fell asleep.

Harry Potter's whiskers brushing against his cheek awoke him abruptly. He checked the time. There was still no sign of his mother. No phone message, nothing. He was surprised that she hadn't called. Maybe they'd persuaded her to have a drink - the first in her life - and the thought of it made him chuckle.

Well, he thought, with the place to himself for the evening, perhaps now would be a good time to begin the slow reconciliation with Erin. At home, or dinner out, he wondered, weighing up the chances of it all going wrong again.

Suddenly he became aware of a noise, like water running.

Still groggy, it took him a moment to place the sound. *Oh crap!* He'd left the bath running.

He ran towards the bathroom, and his heart sank at the sight of the pool of water seeping from the bathroom door. Thank God they were on the ground floor.

He waded across the sodden floor, switched off the taps, and reached for a bundle of bath towels to begin the clear-up. His hands worked quickly, spurred on by the thought of phoning Erin as soon as it was done.

Chapter 18

Donna walked into the team room. The smell of fast food wafted from inside the door, and made her feel hungry. It was long gone tea-time. She glanced at Fran, who was picking at the remains of a bag of chips, the source of the aroma.

"Want some?" Fran offered.

Donna pulled a face, *no*, and stood in front of the white boards that now displayed the details of both Moira Cowan and Eleanor Wallace.

On the left, one of Emma's shots of the murdered Moira Cowan. It was a close-up of her purple face, and the bruising around her neck was plain to see. Even the faint thumb mark. Donna's memory filled in the details of the party dress and the purple high heels.

Below the photo, a list of bullet points outlining Moira's known details. Red marker ink circled *midwife* several times.

On the right, a photo of Eleanor Wallace, murdered around two years previously. She'd been shot, an almost unheard of method of killing in this part of the country.

Below the photo, a list of Eleanor's known details, and highlights from the post mortem report. The same red marker making circles around *midwife*.

Near the bottom of the board, the silhouette of a man's head, with a question mark scrawled on it. Arrows pointed to it from both Moira's and Eleanor's columns, with several question marks along them.

There was generally nothing clever about murder, Donna mused. The mundane conclusion usually turned out to be correct. No complex theory, no big conspiracy to unravel. Eleanor Wallace was having an affair with a man nobody knew. His DNA, matching no-one, indicated they'd been intimate probably only hours before her death. And Moira had gone home with a guy whose identity was sketchy. On both accounts, the man was foreign, Spanish, Latino. To Donna, it seemed reasonable to assume it was the same guy. Going after midwives, or hanging out in places where he was likely to come into contact with them.

But why did he have a gun? A possibility jumped into her head, one that had her doubting her own sanity again. There was one gang that was known to use guns. Abram Kozel's gang in Aberdeen.

She found her eyes sliding towards Fran's bag of chips, and her stomach gave her away. "Oh, go on, then," she said, holding out her hand. Fran tipped some chips into it.

She munched on the chips, and recalled the scandal surrounding the police cock-up over that one a couple of years ago: their ambush of the gang, following what proved to be a dodgy tip-off, had resulted in Kozel's supposed death, and along with it any hope of finding out where his shipments of arms and drugs were coming from. The newspapers had been full of it at the time, and the police had become a laughing stock. But the real story had emerged after Jonas Evanton had been jailed for his heinous crimes. Evanton had revealed his role in faking Kozel's death, offering information about the gangster's whereabouts in return for a move to a prison where he would be anonymous. The prison that he had then escaped from. Donna shuddered.

She walked to a nearby desk and quickly found a folder she wanted to check. Skim reading Eleanor Wallace's case files to confirm what she already suspected, she saw that DI Evanton had indeed been the senior investigating officer in the case.

Guns.

Kozel.

Evanton covering up: there was no record of a ballistics report on the bullet found in Eleanor Wallace's body. She made a quick call to Emma to follow it up.

She rubbed her eyes and scanned the room. Fran Woods, having wiped her greasy fingers, was flipping through another one of the folders containing details of the Eleanor Wallace case. Akwasi was talking to Alice, both of them engrossed in his notebook from his interviews with the midwives. Morrison was sitting on a desk in front of the white board. Despite his length, his legs swung freely back and forth, and now he was watching Donna intently.

"Sorry about your press conference," he said.

"It happens," said Donna, shuddering at the shouting match that it had turned into. "At least Moira's nearest and dearest aren't going to find out about her murder in the papers."

"Can we tell her colleagues anything yet?" he asked. "I've had several calls from them this afternoon. Sounds like they're worried about the body on the beach, and obviously Eleanor Wallace was one of theirs. They must be drawing conclusions."

"We need to get the next of kin first," said Donna. "Is there really nothing we have on that?"

Morrison shook his head. "Not according to her colleagues. They said both her parents are dead. She's divorced, no kids. They said there's a sister in New Zealand, though, but no details."

"Well, we'll find out in the house search," said Donna. She looked past him as a uniformed officer came into the room, brandishing the paperwork authorising the search. "Good timing," she said.

Chapter 19

Moira Cowan's flat was still and dark, with that air about it of having been unoccupied lately. Donna knocked loudly on the door again, and once again, there was no response. She peered in through the letter box, and only stale empty air came back at her. Alice was checking all of the windows from outside. No sign of anybody home.

At Donna's signal, Akwasi and Morrison kicked the door where the lock met the flimsy frame, and with an ear-shattering crack, the door flew open and clanged against the inside wall of the flat. Donna had seen curtains twitch in the surrounding flats when they'd arrived outside the building, and knew it wouldn't be long before visitors happened to turn up by coincidence at Moira's neighbours. She motioned Emma and Fran inside, and sent Morrison and Akwasi back downstairs to guard the building's external door like two cartoon bouncers.

"Hello?" Donna called into the flat, knowing that there would be no reply.

They found themselves in a square hallway, wooden floors, coats hanging on hooks to one side, a tall plant pot containing synthetic leaves, and in the far corner, a vacuum cleaner with its cord trailing across the floor. To the left, a door stood ajar.

"Hello?" called Donna again as she pushed the door fully open and peered inside. "Police. Anyone home?"

She scanned the large living room with its two sofas, large flat screen TV and its array of shelving and bookcases. Cushions had fallen off one of the sofas. Books had fallen from the bookcase nearest to it, and were lying as though tossed on the floor nearby. A broken wine glass tottered on the edge of the coffee table. Some spilt wine.

"We just want to be sure this is Moira's address," said Donna, finding herself compelled to whisper.

There was a door set into the wall to her left, and Donna carefully crossed the room, and with her gloved hand, she pushed this open. A tiny kitchen. Dishes waiting to be washed, a bin that needed to be emptied, but nothing odd. Donna returned to her colleagues in the hall. Fran was coming back through from one of two rooms at the other side of the flat.

"Bedroom in there looks tidy and unslept in," she said, pointing back at it with her thumb. "And the bathroom over there looks pretty normal to me, no signs of trouble."

"And this one's a general junk room," said Emma, who was emerging from the flat's only remaining room. "But it had this in it." She held up a passport, and showed it to Donna, open at Moira Cowan's details.

"Bingo," said Donna. "And chances are, this is where she was murdered. There's certainly signs of some sort of disturbance." She indicated the broken glass and fallen books. "But the place wasn't tarted up for visitors. So, if she came home with her Latino bloke the other night, she hadn't planned on it. My guess is she would've been drunk, and none too careful. So if he was here, there should be plenty of traces." She turned to Emma. "You can call your people in now, this is the right place."

Emma dialled a number straight away.

"Until forensics get here," said Donna, "let's find the sister's number. We need to tell somebody that Moira Cowan is dead."

At that moment, Alice came into the flat. "Any joy?"

"Joy," said Donna. "I'll need you to wait here with Emma. I'm off to talk to the Spice guy."

"Spice guy?"

"The owner of Spice," said Donna. "The place where Moira Cowan was last seen alive."

Chapter 20

Akwasi and Morrison strolled a little way past the front entrance to the block that contained Moira Cowan's flat. Then they turned, and strolled by it in the other direction. They'd been repeating this routine for the duration of the search, making sure curiosity didn't get the better of the neighbourhood worthies, who'd been trying to sidle closer to the building in the dark.

"I'm just saying," Akwasi continued their heated discussion, "that it's a man's job."

"You've got to be kidding," said Morrison. "CID needs brains. What does it matter if it's a man or a woman?"

Akwasi stuck out a petulant bottom lip. "You wouldn't understand."

"That's crap." Morrison couldn't believe what he was hearing. "What's not to understand?"

"You've no idea the stick I took off my family when I decided to join the police," said Akwasi.

"You sure about that?" said Morrison. He flinched, thinking for a split second that the flare in Akwasi's eye could lead to a violent outburst. But it didn't. Akwasi kept his voice low, conspiratorial.

"Look, young black guys get a hard time off the police," he told Morrison. "Harder than white guys, it's well known."

Morrison shrugged in a conciliatory agreement.

"So, joining the police doesn't make you popular, get it?"

"I suppose," said Morrison.

"So, just when I win them over, and they're proud of me," said Akwasi, his confidence picking back up, "my old man asks me, *So, who's your boss, son? What's he like?* and I've got to tell him it's a woman!"

"So?" Morrison said. "Your boss is a woman, it's none of your old man's business."

"You fucking don't get it," hissed Akwasi. "In my culture, men do men's jobs and women do women's jobs."

Morrison let out a harsh laugh. "In your culture?" He stared into Akwasi's face. "Mate, sexism isn't culture, it's just crap."

"It's not sexist," Akwasi insisted. "Men and women are

different. What's sexist about that? Each of us does what we're best at, that's fair."

"You'd better just stop this," said Morrison, stopping in mid stroll. "This isn't some backwater where you marry your cousin with six toes." This time, Akwasi's fist swung back, ready to throw, but he held it where it was. His eyes were wide with anger.

"Anyway," Morrison went on, "Davenport's got a good record. Clear-up rate second to none, apparently."

"Well, I've heard she's a nut job," said Akwasi, going for another angle.

"Aw, look, mate, I've heard enough," said Morrison, placing his palm in front of Akwasi's face. "If your poor wife wants to go along with your distorted view of the world, God help her. But don't bring it to work."

They abandoned their discussion suddenly, falling unnaturally silent as Donna emerged from the main door of the block.

"Don't mind me," she told them. "Forensics are on their way, this is Moira Cowan's place, all right. Keep tabs on who goes in and out."

And she hurried to her car.

Chapter 21

Ring o' ring o' roses, he hummed softly as he watched the house. Darkness had enveloped it hours ago, and he amused himself by sending clouds of his breath out of the car window. He kept the engine running every fifteen minutes on then fifteen off so as to keep warm without letting the engine idle for too long. She was late tonight, he thought, but the sound of an approaching car made him smile. *We all fall down.*

Donna pulled up across the driveway, too tired to pay enough attention to drive into it without hitting anything.

Typical, she thought. Staying on late to interview the Spice guy, and there was no CCTV. She recalled his slicked hair, black from a bottle, and his tight, satin-effect shirt. Open two buttons too many, with the obligatory gold medallion. She had a pretty good idea that a large bank deficit was the reason why the CCTV contract had been cancelled, owing to his fawning gratitude at her decision to leave off checking his insurance. The visit to Spice had given her nothing useful on the Moira Cowan case, but it never did any harm to know she could call in a favour from one of the city's less savoury characters.

Struggling to keep her eyes open, she rested her head on the steering wheel, as her mind tumbled around with thoughts of the anxious midwives, Evanton's role in the Eleanor Wallace case, and Moira Cowan's soulless home.

A burst of fireworks in the distance woke her with a start, and she quickly gathered her files and went into the house. She switched on the hallway light as she entered, and a sudden melancholy pitted her stomach as soon as she felt Libby's absence.

Only four more days, she told herself. And at least there would be decent food in the freezer, thanks to Danny. She dumped the files onto the kitchen table and opened the fridge expectantly. It felt like peeking into the living room on a pre-dawn Christmas morning as a kid, and she remembered that magical glow as she asked herself, *Has he been?* She experienced the same moment of anticipation, then she let out a whoop of delight. True to his word,

Danny had left a stack of cartons in the freezer for her, and she lifted out the one on top.

Without caring what was inside – it was going to be good, whatever it turned out to be – she popped it into the microwave, careful to follow Danny's handwritten instructions, before heading upstairs.

The house was dark and lifeless without Libby, and she switched on lights as she went. She began to think about the Eleanor Wallace case again. Around two years ago, the midwife had been shot dead. Guns were so rare in the area, only one source was known to the police: Abram Kozel. The Russian gangster and his mob of thugs had plagued the streets of Aberdeen, controlling the lucrative drugs and gun running trade. Violence flared up occasionally as rival gangs tried to cash in on the dealing, but Kozel always came out on top. There had always been suspicions that Kozel had police officers in his pocket, and that was eventually confirmed when they finally had Jonas Evanton in custody. A shiver ran up Donna's spine at the thought of him. They'd learned that DI Evanton had brokered himself a deal, turning a blind eye to Kozel's activities and keeping incriminating evidence out of the courtrooms on his behalf. Aside from the financial benefits to Evanton, Donna had to concede that the mutual agreement had probably saved lives: Kozel rarely had to enforce his authority by violent means. Still, if Evanton hadn't covered for them – and especially, if he hadn't allowed Kozel to fake his own death – then the police would perhaps have stood a chance of stopping the gang's activities. Then the cynic in Donna scoffed at the idea. Who was she kidding? Guys like Kozel never got stopped. Not by the police, anyway. They were no closer to catching the Russian now than they had been the day before Evanton notoriously became the first inmate to ever escape from Belmarsh high security prison, still on the loose 18 months later.

Shit, Donna muttered to herself, frustrated. Evanton knew the answers in this case. He'd been the SIO, in an ideal position to tamper with evidence. To Donna, this was proof enough that Kozel's gang had been involved in Eleanor Wallace's death. But why? And what had the gang been doing here in Dundee? If Moira Cowan's murder was linked, then it meant they were still here. But there had been no intel to suggest that. Unless…the hairs on the back of Donna's neck began to prickle…unless Evanton was still here too, helping to keep them under the radar.

She jumped at the crack of a firework nearby, and realised how tense she'd become. From downstairs she heard the microwave ping, and she smiled. *Eat some good food, kick up your feet and relax,* she told herself, forcing her breathing to slow down.

Passing the bedroom door, her eye caught on the red rose lying across the pillow.

Delighted, she scooped up the rose. Never mind that there was barely a scent from it. Supermarkets were good for removing all trace of nature from natural products. But it was the thought that counted. Libby knew this would lift her spirits.

Singing softly to herself, Donna took the rose back to the kitchen, and dialled Libby's number while she stirred the micromeal and set it for a final minute.

"Oh, it's good to hear your voice," said Libby. "It's been wall to wall droning all day here. I don't know how I'm going to manage another three days, and I'm missing you like crazy."

"Me too," said Donna.

Ping, went the microwave.

"One of Danny's meals on wheels?" said Libby. "It's late to be eating."

"Oh, I know," said Donna. "Been one of those days at the office. I only just saw your rose."

She felt the hesitation over the line. "Rose?"

"The one you left on my pillow," said Donna, already with a knot forming in her stomach. Libby was silent for a split second too long. "Ha, Danny must have left it there," she went on.

"What?"

No, that didn't sound right. Danny wouldn't have left a rose lying on the bed shared by his sister and her lover. That would have been weird.

So, where the hell had it come from?

"What's going on?" asked Libby.

"Er, nothing," said Donna. "Forget I said anything, I must have got mixed up, I'm really shattered."

The call ended awkwardly. Donna wasn't sure if Libby was

afraid or suspicious. God knows, Donna had given her plenty of reasons to be both.

The possibility of Evanton still being in Dundee suddenly came back to her. She looked at the rose, and winced as she caught her thumb on a thorn. She dropped the flower, and stuck her bleeding thumb into her mouth. The knot in her stomach grew, and she found herself unable to eat Danny's micro-meal after all.

Wednesday

Chapter 22

Natesh woke up needing to sneeze, and realised that a long strand of Erin's hair had fallen across his face. He lifted it off and leaned over her, listening closely. She was breathing so quietly, he just had to check. She murmured something incoherent and shifted slightly, as though she was aware he was watching her.

Natesh smiled and sighed. So much for taking things slowly. Who had he been trying to kid? Erin knew him like no-one else did, except for Donna. It was as if she'd looked right into his soul the first time they made eye contact, which was at his work while he was loading flat packs onto the shelves and she was there looking for a set of drawers. *Let me get your drawers down for you*, he'd said and had almost died of embarrassment as soon as the words had rushed out of his open mouth. She'd giggled. He cringed even now thinking about it, remembering how he'd desperately prayed to every deity he'd ever heard of to let him crawl into a very small space and never be seen again.

With Erin, he always felt good enough as he was. She made him feel like that. And in return he wanted to give her the world.

"Shurrup!" The voice from next door shattered his fluffy thoughts. He squinted at the time, then heard Harry Potter meowing on the doorstep. Natesh felt uneasy. Something wasn't right.

Careful not to disturb Erin, he got out of bed and listened intently. There were no sounds coming from inside the flat.

With his heart beginning to beat faster, he made his way quickly to the kitchen. All the lights were out. He heard the cat meow again, and again the neighbour's shouting. He hurried through the living room to the front door, and let the disgruntled animal inside. It regarded him with contempt before springing into the hammock on the radiator.

Natesh made his way back through the living room and stopped. Erin's jacket was slung in a messy heap over the settee exactly where she'd tossed it. Her shoes and his lay tumbled on the rug in the middle of the room. Natesh knew that his mother would never be able to resist tidying them away if she'd come through here last night. Suddenly he felt sick.

He ran into his mother's bedroom.

There was no sign of her.

She hadn't come home last night.

Natesh checked his phone. No messages.

Going back into the kitchen, he drew himself a glass of water and tried to clear his head, to think. Had he forgotten something? He fought to remain rational despite a nagging dread, as he watched his fingers key in Donna's number.

Donna's voicemail came on the line. She must be in work already, thought Natesh.

"Hi, it's me," he said after the beep. "I need to meet you. Lunch? I know you're busy, but... please...I need to see you. Give me a ring as soon as you get this." He thought about saying more, and after an awkward pause, he ended the call. Then a noise behind startled him, and he spun round.

"I hope you were phoning in a sickie," said Erin, standing naked in the doorway.

Natesh grinned and pulled her warm body into his.

"Coffee first," she murmured into his ear. Her voice made goose bumps travel across his neck.

"How about coffee *after*?"

"I can drink it really fast," she said, pulling away from him and turning towards the living room.

"I'll put in extra milk to cool it down," he called after her, flicking on the kettle and suddenly aware of the goofy grin he was wearing.

The kettle took forever to boil. Natesh paced back and forth, and heard the background chatter from the TV. He pictured Erin sprawled across the rug in front of it, and almost scalded his hand as he spilled water from the kettle in his haste to fill the coffee mugs and get through there beside her.

"Police are refusing to confirm yet," said the reporter on the TV as Natesh hurried into the room, "but local reports suggest the body found on Arbroath beach on Monday morning is believed to be that of Moira Cowan, a midwife from Dundee."

And then the world turned into slow motion.

He saw Erin turn her head towards him. Felt his muscles turn to water. Saw Erin's expression turn to alarm. Was sure she shouted something to him. Watched her hand go to her mouth. Then he realised he'd dropped both mugs, and the world returned to high speed again.

Chapter 23

Donna stood having a smoke in front of the Bell Street entrance. Worrying about the rose had kept her awake most of the night, and she needed a clear head this morning. The added jittering due to a lack of nicotine was not going to help. As if that wasn't bad enough, the news headline in the local paper was screaming,

DUNDEE SERIAL KILLER – WHAT ARE POLICE HIDING?

Silently cursing Lindsey Forsyth for the sensationalising speculation, her thoughts were disturbed by the sound of the main doors opening. She automatically stepped aside to let whoever was in a hurry get by, then stopped when she saw it was Fran.

"What's up?" she asked.

"Got some info for you," said Fran. Her hand clutched a piece of paper. "I was going through the list of house visits in Moira Cowan's schedule, as well as Eleanor Wallace's. There's an address, just the one, that both of them visited."

"Only one address in common?"

"Well, only one that doesn't check out," said Fran. "I've verified the others . . ."

"You've done that already?" Donna whistled. "Good work."

Fran blushed. "Thanks. Er, so, there's this one – Craigie Drive. It seems to be vacant, and I've been having trouble finding the owner's details. But I managed to trace it to this offshore property outfit, only there are no contact details."

"They must have bought it after 1980," said Donna. "The flats there are all Council."

Fran nodded.

"You phoned them already, didn't you?"

"Yes," said Fran. "The first sale of the flat, in 1983, was to a bloke called Edridge."

"Edridge?" Donna lost grip of her cigarette and it bounced silently onto the tarmac at her feet. "Damn it," she muttered.

"Yes," said Fran, squinting at the details on her piece of paper. "Marcus Edridge. Is something wrong?"

"I know him," said Donna, as the image of Natesh's *Tomato*

Man emerging from a pile of rags came to mind. Fran's face registered surprise.

"Do you?"

Donna nodded. "Retired doctor. Living on the streets."

Fran's mouth opened but words failed to come out.

"I take it Marcus Edridge sold the flat on to this property company?"

"He did," said Fran. She checked her piece of paper again. "Same year he bought it himself – 1983."

"Weird," said Donna.

"Even weirder," said Fran, "the midwifery records don't have anyone at that address on their system. It appeared once in each of Eleanor Wallace's and Moira Cowan's paper diaries, but not their electronic ones."

"Okay," said Donna, "go and get Morrison. I need you to pop over and get a Section 8, just in case. We need to search that flat, and I don't want any delays because we don't have the right bloody paperwork. I'll get Ross to email the request over to the magistrate."

Fran beamed, then turned and hurried back inside.

Donna turned to see a man she recognised arriving by her side from inside the building.

"Adam Ridout," he said, holding out his hand.

"The *Herald*," she said, remembering him from the morning on the beach. "At least you haven't printed that ridiculous stuff." She flashed Lindsey Forsyth's headline in front of him, then held out her cigarette pack after they shook hands. "Smoke?"

"Only if you don't rat me out," he said, smiling. He picked out a cigarette and lit it. He coughed as he inhaled. "It's been a while. Used to get through thirty of these a day. Now it's once in a blue moon."

"I'm trying to stop," said Donna. "It's murder, though."

Adam looked like he'd heard a punch line. "You know, I was two years behind you at school."

"Really?" said Donna. She stood back and appraised him. "Oh yeah, so you were. Oliver Ridout's wee brother?"

"That's the one," said Adam.

"How is Ollie?"

"On some tour of duty," said Adam. "He joined up straight after school, so I've hardly seen him since I was in second year or something."

"I heard you went on your travels, too?"

Adam looked at his feet and his cheeks reddened. "I did a bit of photography."

"Yeah, you did a bit!" Donna laughed. "Natesh told me about your award. Anyone would think it was him that had won it, he was that proud."

"Natesh is a good mate," Adam laughed, and he and Donna puffed companionably on their cigarettes in silence for a few minutes.

"So, I'm hearing rumours that Moira Cowan is the second midwife in two years to be found dead in the area," said Adam.

"Don't chance your luck," Donna smiled at him, "unlike Ms Forsyth – and don't think I won't be on her like a ton of bricks if her irresponsible reporting gets in the way of this investigation. But stick to the facts, and I'll keep you posted as we go."

"It's a fair cop."

"Well, good to see you," said Donna as she stubbed out her cigarette. "Duty calls, and all that."

Duty did indeed call, but so had Natesh. He'd sounded uncharacteristically stressed when he'd phoned, wanting to meet for lunch. Whatever was bothering him, it must be serious, Donna reckoned. It wasn't like him to call like that when she was in the middle of a murder investigation.

She said goodbye to Adam and made her way to her car.

Chapter 24

A blast of icy wind caught Donna off-guard as she rounded the corner towards Crichton's. So did the sight of Natesh standing in the doorway.

"What's happened to you?" She knew she'd failed to hide her expression of shock at his appearance. "You look like you've seen a ghost."

"I think something's happened to my mum," said Natesh.

"Okay," said Donna, softening her tone. She placed her hands on Natesh's shoulders and gently steered him into the pub. "Let's go and sit down, get some food, and we can have a talk."

Natesh nodded his head and allowed himself to be ushered to a table. He sat down opposite Donna, and a waiter materialised at the table to offer them menus and the run down of the day's specials.

"Fresh orange for me," said Donna, "and a double whisky for him." She knew Natesh wouldn't be driving. "We'll order food in a few minutes, thanks."

"Haven't seen you here in a while," the waiter began, then stopped talking when he sensed the atmosphere at the table. "I'll just be a moment with the drinks." He left Donna and Natesh alone.

"So, tell me," said Donna. "What's going on?"

"She didn't come home," said Natesh, his voice beginning to crack. Donna could see he was breathing rapidly.

"Has she phoned? Left a message?"

Natesh just scowled at her, and Donna shrugged an apology. She'd realised as soon as she'd opened her mouth that her questions were stupid. Suddenly, Natesh leaned across the table towards her.

"I heard on the news," he said, "about that woman being a midwife."

The people sitting at the tables on either side of them stopped their own conversations and several pairs of eyes swivelled in the direction of Natesh's raised voice.

"Shush," said Donna.

"Don't bullshit me, Donna," he pleaded, not caring that he was the focus of a growing audience. "Is it true? Was she a midwife? Because she's not the first one, is she?"

"For God's sake, Natesh," hissed Donna, "you know I can't talk about this here."

"Where, then?" Natesh stood up to go.

"Sit down," Donna ordered. The tone in her voice and the glare in her eye made Natesh obey at once. The waiter arrived with the drinks, sliding them onto the table before hurrying away again without making eye contact. "Drink that, and tell me what's happened."

Natesh grabbed the glass of whisky and took a large gulp. Then another. Then he coughed.

"You can go back to your meals now," Donna addressed the other diners. "Nothing to see here."

There was an awkward rumble of mutterings as the starers found themselves in Donna's sights.

"Right, so I got home yesterday," said Natesh, trying to focus his thoughts. "And she wasn't home. But she'd said something the other day about a leaving do, so I just thought she must be at that."

Odd of her not to keep telling you, though, thought Donna. She stopped the words from coming out of her mouth.

"She still wasn't home this morning," said Natesh. "She didn't come home."

"Have you phoned her office?" asked Donna.

"Ringing out or engaged," said Natesh. "And anyway, I felt better waiting to see you first. Just in case…"

"I'll give them a call," said Donna. She took a sip of her drink, then went to the door as she looked up Samira's work number.

The line rang and rang. Finally a voice, not Samira's, answered. "Midwifery unit."

"It's DI Donna Davenport. Who am I speaking to, please?"

A surprised pause, then, "The police? Oh God, something's happened, hasn't it? Oh God…"

"Try to calm down," said Donna. "Nothing's happened. I need to speak to Samira or Geri."

"This is Geri."

"You came and spoke to me yesterday, didn't you?" said Donna.

"Yes, to report Moira missing, but it wasn't us who told the news, we all saw it on the TV…"

"I'm not phoning about Moira," said Donna. "Is Samira at work today?"

Geri paused. "No. She hasn't come in yet. The union's running a thing on retirement, she's at that. I think it finishes at twelve, it's over in the Caird Hall. Bloody nightmare trying to get these phones without her."

"Thank you," said Donna, realising how tense she'd been when she experienced a sudden relief. She felt herself smile as she returned to Natesh.

"She's over at the Caird Hall," she told him. "At some event to do with retirement."

Natesh stared at her. "What? You mean to tell me I've been doing all this worrying, and she's just having a mid-life crisis? Man, I left Erin *naked* in my house!"

"Bottoms up," said Donna, and they clinked glasses.

Chapter 25

Donna pulled up outside the flat on Craigie Drive. With all the marked vehicles lining the street, and police officers posted at various points nearby, there was no disguising the fact that something major was going on. Four men in their thirties or forties stood nearby, swigging at bottles of something close to paint stripper, laughing loudly and pointing at the police activity. They were no strangers to trouble around here.

At least she didn't have to worry about Natesh, she thought, although something was definitely niggling at her about Samira. She'd have to deal with that later, though.

Police tape kept some sort of cordon around the immediate entrance to the block of flats, but onlookers were gathering, wondering if they knew who was involved, and kids were taking it in turns to try and run through the tape. iPhones and Galaxies swivelled in the air, filming the activity and making selfies in front of the scene. Donna watched two of the uniformed officers dart from one end of the cordon to the other, swatting the kids off like flies. Deciding quickly, she made a phone call.

"Adam," she told the delighted reporter, "you might want to take a trip over to Craigie Drive." It always helped to have a journalist's goodwill, she thought. And giving him the tip-off would send a message to Lindsey Forsyth – stick with the facts, or stay on the outside.

As she emerged from her car, she saw Emma crossing the road towards her, and Fran, Morrison and Akwasi coming out of one of the marked cars. They gathered in front of the graffiti covered entrance, and the officer at the door nodded them through.

Pulling on latex gloves as they went, the five trudged upstairs to where a door stood ajar behind a uniformed officer. Donna showed her warrant card, and took the first step inside. She tried the light switch with little expectation, and blinked in surprise when the hallway lit up. She glanced up at the old-fashioned glass shade that covered the bulb.

"I need some proper light in here, can't you open the curtains at least?"

"The curtains stay closed, doctor," said the man with the gun. "Not that anyone's likely to ask any questions around here, shithole. But we don't need an audience."

Dr Edridge followed the man further into the gloomy room, and placed his hand on the woman's forehead. He didn't need a thermometer to tell him she was burning with fever.

"We need the baby alive," said the man.

"For God's sake!" the doctor hissed, kneeling now at the woman's bedside. The man stood firm, making sure the doctor could see the gun.

Juanita shrank from the room. There was nothing more she could do now to comfort her friend.

Donna led her team into the flat, and the first room they came to was the kitchen. A gloomy affair, with a front missing from one of the drawers below the sink, and a cupboard door held closed by yellowing sellotape. Tea and coffee paraphernalia littered the nearside worktop, while two used mugs lay in the basin, a teaspoon sticking out from one of them. A withered plant sat on the windowsill, its soil dry.

Donna made her way to the fridge and opened it.

"There's stuff in here that's still in date," she said, scanning the contents and bringing out a block of cheddar cheese.

"Coffee, doctor?" An older woman appeared at the bedroom door. Juanita was peering over her shoulder.

The woman on the bed groaned and her eyes rolled. Blood appeared through the thin sheet that covered her lower half.

"We need to get her to a hospital," said Dr Edridge, ignoring the coffee offer.

"No hospital," said the man with the gun.

"She's dying."

"No hospital."

"The baby won't survive," said Dr Edridge. "They need specialist help."

"That's why you're here," growled the man with the gun. "Now, help her, deliver the baby safely, and you can go home. If the baby doesn't make it, neither do you."

"But there's nothing I can do this time! She needs to be in hospital." The doctor was on his feet now, pushing at the man's chest, his eyes blazing in anger.

"Cupboard full of clean towels," Donna reported.

"Shitload of disinfectant in here," called Morrison from the bathroom.

"Bins emptied."

"The phone line's live," said Fran, listening to a dial tone.

It was obvious that the flat had been vacated only recently. Had the occupants left it because of the murder investigation, Donna wondered? If Eleanor Wallace and Moira Cowan had been here, what had they witnessed? And why hadn't they told somebody about it? Had they been threatened?

"Let's just phone Samira," Vidu's co-henchman, Suleyman, said.

"What?" The man with the gun spun to face him. Dr Edridge stumbled and almost fell. "What the hell can she do to help?"

"This is our shout," said Vidu. "Samira can get one of the midwives to come here."

"Oh, and what then? You think said midwife will just keep her mouth shut?"

"We can't just do nothing," said Vidu. "And like I said, this is our shout. You leave this end of things to us."

"What, like you called in this useless doctor?" said the man, gesturing with the gun towards Dr Edridge.

"I'm telling you she needs to be in hospital!" Dr Edridge shouted.

The woman's moans were temporarily drowned out by the four men arguing.

"We'll give it one last chance," said Vidu, his forehead beaded with sweat. He turned to Juanita and the older woman who were now standing by the room door. "Get us some hot water, towels and disinfectant. The doctor will deliver the baby. Now."

The women vanished from the doorway.

Dr Edridge felt gently around the woman's abdomen. All he could tell was that something was dreadfully wrong, but with no access to hospital facilities or even a midwife's expertise, there was no way to tell what.

"I can't risk putting her or the baby through any more without knowing what's going on," he said. "I can get her into hospital without anyone asking any questions."

"No way."

"Then at least get me a midwife here," Edridge begged.

Vidu hesitated. When the women came into the room with the hot water and towels, it looked like such a futile gesture in the face of the howling and the bleeding on the bed. Finally he said, "All right. I'll phone her."

Chapter 26

Natesh put the phone down slowly, as if it was a fragile thing. A flutter of fear sprang up from his gut and gripped his chest. There had been no hiding it. The woman who'd phoned from the midwifery unit had sounded nervous. Worried.

Natesh had confirmed to her that, no, his mother was not home and, no, she hadn't come home from work the day before. They'd both pretended to sound casual about it and promised to contact each other when Samira's whereabouts were known. And it would be something really simple they'd both overlooked, right?

Natesh stood still, with his hand resting on the phone, wondering what he should do now.

He rang Donna's number, and sighed in frustration when her voicemail came on.

What would Donna tell him to do?

Have a look around, he heard her steady voice in his mind, *see if anything looks unusual, out of place or missing.*

Yes, he could do that. He would begin in Samira's bedroom.

He bounded upstairs and flipped on the room's light switch.

The room was tidy, the bed made, her dresser left neat and clean, her hairdryer hanging beside it on a peg, just like always.

Instinctively, Natesh walked across to the window and pulled the curtains closed against the darkness of the early winter evening. Guy Fawkes was tomorrow night, and the fireworks frenzy was starting for the night, with the first few crackers sending shards of colour across the black sky. Natesh ignored the noise and the spectacle of them, and studied the room. Nothing looked any different than before.

He stepped across to the old-style walnut double wardrobe, and opened its doors wide. It looked stuffed full of too many clothes, as it always had, except there was a gap on the top shelf. Natesh stared at it, puzzled. He was sure there hadn't been a space there before, but couldn't bring to mind what would normally have been up there. A bag?

Then he realised – Samira's suitcase. She'd never used it, as far as he could remember. She'd never gone anywhere. And now it was gone. Natesh felt his heart hammer against his ribs.

Bang! The firework right outside made him flinch, followed by another unexpected noise. Somebody was knocking at the door.

Leaving the wardrobe doors open and the bedroom light still on, Natesh turned and hurried down the stairs. Erin was working tonight. Perhaps it was Donna, he thought. She needed to know about the suitcase.

When he opened the door, however, his spirits sank as he saw it was Mr. Duffy, the miserable guy from next door. He looked less than happy to be standing there in the cold, and thrust a package at Natesh.

"This got delivered for you this afternoon," said Duffy. He immediately turned to go, muttering as he went, "Think I'm the bleeding Post Office, or something?"

Natesh brought the package inside and stared at it.

There was no post mark on the A5 manila envelope, simply his name scrawled across the front in black Sharpie ink.

He had thought his heart couldn't beat any faster, but now it did. He felt almost dizzy as he began to open the envelope and saw a glimpse of what was inside.

Chapter 27

"That was Ross on the phone," said Fran. "Er, I mean, DCI Ross. He's sending some extra uniforms round to secure the entrance."

Donna nodded in acknowledgement. This flat here in Craigie Drive, she was certain, held the key to finding the killer of Moira Cowan and Eleanor Wallace. They'd both come here during the course of their work, yet there was no formal record of why they should have done. And each of them had only visited here once, shortly before their deaths. It was in here. Donna silently thanked Ross for sending the extra resources. At least he was taking her seriously now.

"I'll get it," said the man with the gun. The knock at the door had coincided with a scream from the woman in the bed, and they'd almost missed it.

"No," said Vidu, "I will. She doesn't know you." He went to the door, and there stood a woman in her thirties, wearing dark blue scrubs. She had a pleasant smile, though full of concern. When she saw Vidu, she looked confused.

"What are you doing here?" she asked. "I was expecting Dr. Edridge…"

"My cousin is having a baby," the lie tripped off his tongue as though well rehearsed. "It's not going well, and the doctor needs help. Through there."

No sooner than she'd followed his gaze, there came a yell of agony from the room, and the dishevelled doctor hurried from it.

"Thank God you're here," said Edridge, taking hold of Eleanor Wallace's hand. "She's bleeding heavily, the bleeding started about forty minutes ago. I don't hear the baby's heartbeat any more." The doctor was out of breath as he spoke, and his shirt was sweat-soaked.

"Why isn't she in hospital?" Eleanor asked, while she quickly unpacked her case of equipment.

"I thought you said she wouldn't ask questions," said the man with the gun. Eleanor turned in surprise, noticing him for the first time.

"This isn't the woman I saw here the last time," said Eleanor. "What the hell is this, Vidu? What's going on?"

Vidu faltered. "Just help them," he said.

The woman on the bed gasped rapidly, then convulsed and was still.

"I want the full layout of the flat documented," Donna instructed.

Emma took photos while Morrison held tape markers where she indicated. Fran wrote details of everything she saw as she went. Like a swarm of locusts the team swept deeper into the flat, covering every square centimetre methodically as they went. Akwasi, following Emma's instructions, bagged samples as they went.

"Donna, you'll want to see this," said Emma.

Donna was at her side in an instant, and looking at the bullet lodged in a patch of decimated plasterwork. Emma's camera was whirring, and Morrison was placing yellow stickers around it as indicated by Emma.

"Why would nobody report a gunshot?" whistled Morrison. There were cynical chuckles around the room, and Morrison's face reddened.

"Emma, I want this bullet compared with the one that killed Eleanor Wallace," said Donna. "And both of them compared with anything we have on Kozel's guns."

"I'm on it," said Emma. "In fact, I retrieved the other bullet from the evidence room this morning, so I'll run them both together."

Donna knew in her heart that there would be a link; that this would prove to be the place where Eleanor Wallace was murdered. And that Evanton was in it up to his neck. "This is too good not to be where Eleanor Wallace was murdered," she said. "Get your team up here, this is a crime scene now."

"Right you are," said Emma. "I'll be back in a jiffy."

"What are we going to do?" Suleyman's voice was a shriek.

The man with the gun was pacing the room, frantic. The woman was dead. The doctor and the midwife had delivered the baby's lifeless body. How was he going to face Kozel now, after he'd persuaded the drugs baron to team up with Amin's men?

The doctor held his head in his hands, sobbing, while the midwife attempted to take the next steps. She took her phone from her bag.

"No you don't," warned the man, aiming the gun at her. She saw it for the first time.

"Are you crazy?" she gasped. "This woman and her baby have just died. Now, I don't know what's been going on here, and I'm prepared to keep it

that way, but they need to be taken to the morgue. They're dead, do you understand that?"

"Give me your phone."

"No."

She went to key in a number. A muted shot whipped from the silenced pistol. Eleanor Wallace dropped to the floor. A second shot, redundant, hit the wall that she'd been standing in front of, and sent a shower of plasterboard onto the floor. From outside the room door, Juanita screamed and her footsteps echoed along the hall as she turned and ran away.

"Eleanor!" cried Vidu, dropping to his knees beside the lifeless midwife.

"How do we clear up this mess?" asked the man with the gun. This time, there was fear in his voice. This was getting out of hand. A simple exchange had turned into a bloodbath that wasn't going to be easy to get out of.

"We need to bring in the surgeon," said Suleyman. "We've just lost Amin a ton of cash. He's not going to be happy."

"You're not serious?" said Edridge.

"Once the surgeon is done," Suleyman told him, "you can make the delivery and then you can do what you want. You won't hear from us again."

"Odd place to keep a freezer," Fran remarked, as they worked their way into the furthermost bedroom in the large flat. An electrical hum coming from it was the only sound in the room when they'd all stopped to look at it.

"Even odder that it's still switched on," said Donna.

"What about the baby?" asked Vidu. His face showed revulsion at the sight of the dead infant.

"Next door," said the man with the gun. "Until we hear otherwise." They all watched in silence as the doctor carefully wrapped the baby in a towel and took him from the room.

"Get those women to help us clean this place up," said the man with the gun. "We need to make sure there's no trace of what happened here."

Vidu scrubbed at his face and stood up, letting Eleanor Wallace's hand fall to the floor. He dragged his feet as he went to fetch Juanita and the older one. But a moment later, he hurried back into the room.

"They've gone," he panted.

"They won't get far," said the man with the gun. "Our guys are sitting outside." He walked towards the front door. "I'm going to make sure they don't talk. You make sure this place is clean."

"It's some size of a freezer," remarked Morrison. "Don't like the look of that."

The huge appliance stood against the far-side wall, filling the room with its low humming. Donna slowly stepped towards it, while Morrison recorded each step on Emma's camera.

All of the officers were now in the room or at its door, something about its odd presence alerting them.

Donna took in a deep breath and grasped the door handle, and pulled. White light and vaporous ice sprang out.

With a sense of relief, she announced, "It looks pretty empty. Just a whole load of polystyrene boxes. Freezer boxes."

Emma's camera whirred as Morrison photographed the inside of the huge freezer. Box after box, all lidless, was snapped, no contents in any of them. A series of deep drawers ran down one side of the freezer, but they were transparent, and even the officers who stood by the door could see that they were all empty. A collective sigh of relief seemed to fill the air.

"Creepy," remarked Fran.

One last drawer remained unchecked, below all the others, and this one wasn't transparent. Donna pulled the drawer fully open.

"Oh Jesus," said Fran as she registered with shock what she was looking at.

Juanita

Life in the camp got worse and worse.

The number of people escaping through the fence at night was huge, and we heard rumours that the governments in Europe were refusing to let them into their countries and that they were being kept in prisons in Greece and Germany.

At the same time, the number of people arriving in the camp from the war grew every day, and there were days when the food rations weren't enough to go around.

We'd been stuck there for about 18 months, but at least we were safe, my mother, my grandmother, my aunts and me.

We still lived in that same tent beside the fence, keeping our watch 24 hours a day.

After the day when the doctor had come, my grandmother had recovered quickly.

The doctor, Dr. Amin, had visited twice since then. He made the trip when he could, he told us, bringing what aid he could, from his surgery further north on Turkey's Mediterranean coast.

On one of his visits, he told me about the sea by his home, how it glistened blue like a sapphire.

How I longed to see it! The same Mediterranean Sea I had seen once as a young child, when we'd made what must only have been a two- or three-hour trip to the coast from our home in Kobani. The same sea, but now in a different world.

I took to watching Dr. Amin closely. One night, I saw a group of girls perhaps a little older than me, following him to a gap in the fence. They were giggling, excited. I saw the guard turn away while the girls got onto a truck, and they disappeared across the dark countryside.

I didn't see him again for several months after that.

Then, on the day of my fifteenth birthday, he was back.

We were so happy to see him.

While he worked on the other side of the fence, preparing his medications list, I asked him about those girls.

At first he told me I shouldn't be asking such questions, but I was persistent.

Eventually he told me that he knew the only way to get out of here was to pay the traffickers. It upset him that so many of us were unable to do that, and so he had started to help the poorest families. When the girls were old enough, he would bribe the guards to look the other way, and bring them to his town and pay for them to be trained to clean houses for rich people. That way, the girls could save the wages they earned, and buy their families out of the camps.

I begged him to let me go with him and find work cleaning the big houses.

Chapter 28

Morrison and Akwasi stepped forward to look inside the freezer drawer in the Craigie Drive flat, and immediately sprang back, as if burned. Fran's face was pale, and she looked as though she was about to throw up.

Approaching sirens heralded the extra officers that Ross had agreed to. Donna felt bile burning her gullet, and her head swam. Two days ago she'd crouched over the dead body of Moira Cowan on Arbroath beach. During her time in the Force, she'd seen her fair share of gruesome murder scenes. But the sight before her now, the lifeless body of a newborn baby lying in the open freezer drawer, its tiny form wrapped hopelessly in a towel, was truly shocking. The white towel glowed in sharp contrast with the infant's shock of black hair and doll-like dark eyelashes. Mercifully, the eyes were shut.

Donna placed herself in front of the terrible sight, blocking the others' view of it.

Midwives, she thought.

A dead baby.

Dr. Marcus Edridge.

Guns.

She felt momentarily dizzy, and the exchanges that took place between her officers during those first few moments sounded to her like they were being spoken underwater. Now, just as quickly, her head began to clear.

The body count in this case had now become three, and it certainly wasn't beyond the imagination to link them. This was sure to be the flat where Eleanor Wallace had been shot dead. Ballistics would confirm that. Donna wondered if Eleanor had known about the baby. What had been going on here in this flat, right under all of their noses? If Moira Cowan had come here, then it meant it could still have been going on as recently as last week.

She shook her head. Forced a slow breath from her abdomen, and turned to face the officers in the room.

Akwasi had moved to the far corner and was looking out of the window, although all that could be seen out there was the blackness of the November night. Donna saw him sway on his feet and look for something to hold onto.

My God, she thought. *This is probably his first serious case.* She put a stop to the jigsaw pieces flying through her mind, and focused on her team. They needed her direction. She could tell Akwasi wasn't going to hang on much longer.

"We need a medic in here right now," she said. Fran was already on her radio, making the request to the paramedics who were sitting outside on Craigie Drive.

Donna turned to Morrison. "I need you to stay here and make sure only those who need to be in here are." Then she called to Akwasi, "Thomas, come with me."

He turned to her, almost with a snarl on his lips. His face was ashen, his eyes watery. He cleared his throat and turned towards Morrison. Donna called to him again, this time her voice assertive. "With me, now."

She turned and strode to the door, just as Emma returned.

She saw Emma's expression turn from keen to puzzled as Donna placed an arm across the doorway to block her access.

"You don't want to be going in there," said Donna. "But get a couple of your guys. I'll be back in a minute, just going to make sure the place is properly cordoned off."

"What's the deal in there?" asked Emma, peering over Donna's shoulder.

"We've got another body," said Donna. "An infant."

Emma's hand went instinctively to her swollen abdomen. "Oh, my God," she whispered. "And this is all linked to the body on the beach?"

"That's my working theory," said Donna. "But let's see what the evidence says. See you in a minute."

Donna thumbed Akwasi into the hallway and walked with him out of the flat, while Emma instructed her own team. She nodded to the officer at the front door to the flat, and to the one who stood guard at the entrance to the block. She walked past the row of police vehicles that lined this part of Craigie Drive, past the clamour of activity that had now struck up around the vicinity of the block of flats, and on to the corner at the end of the street. There, she stopped under a lamp post and shielded her eyes against the needling drizzle of rain.

Akwasi stopped when she did, keeping a distance that only just prevented a whispered conversation. He began to rub at his arms, sending suspicious glances in Donna's direction.

Donna took a packet of cigarettes and a lighter from her pocket.

"Go and phone your wife," she told him. "Reassure yourself that your baby is fine, and be back here by the time I've finished this fag."

She lit it, while masking a smile at his look of surprise. Without having to be told twice, Akwasi whipped out his phone and pressed a button as he hurried on a few steps.

Donna turned and watched the activity back along Craigie Drive. The outer cordon was being widened as she watched, and more uniformed officers were arriving to assist with the door to door enquiries around the flat. It was only now that she noticed the cold, and she hugged her jacket closely around her body. She was just about to stub out her cigarette, when she heard Akwasi clear his throat behind her.

When she faced him, she saw his struggle to meet her eye as his gaze gravitated towards the ground.

"You think I don't get it?" she said softly. Akwasi shifted from foot to foot.

"Being shocked at what we just saw is okay," she went on. "Especially when it makes you think about your own baby."

Akwasi wiped his sleeve across his eyes, and finally looked at Donna. This time there was no hostility in his expression.

"Hell, if something like that doesn't upset you, then you're in the wrong job," Donna said.

"But I walked away," said Akwasi. His voice was barely audible. "Fran and Morrison just got on with it. I walked away, useless..."

Donna began to walk again, away from the direction of the flat, flicking her head for him to follow her.

"We've all got our weak spots," she said as they walked. "You just have to learn what they are, and work around that. My guess is Fran's going to go home tonight and demolish a mountain of burgers. That's probably how she copes."

Akwasi chuckled.

"But she won't feel good about herself," said Donna, and his face grew serious again. "Me, I've got bipolar disorder. It's a bit crap, and something like tonight can cause my mood to change. I've got to anticipate it, take action to prevent it, like go out running or something. That tends to work for me. You need to find your way of coping."

Akwasi was staring at her, his eyes wide. "I'm so sorry," he said, with his voice breaking.

"Well, let's not bullshit with each other," said Donna. "I know what you've been saying about me, and I know you're embarrassed I saw you upset. Am I right?"

"Ma'am…"

"Come on!" She shoved him hard, grinning. He stumbled.

"I'll have you for assault," he said, grinning back.

"Are we good, then?" she said.

"We're good."

"All right, then, let's get back to work." She started back towards the flat. "I'll need you to manage the cordon out here. This could be a long night, and the neighbours will get pissed off once they realise what it's like to live on a crime scene."

Back in the flat, Donna returned to the room with the freezer. It was a circuit of white-clad forensic examiners, watched by Fran and Morrison.

"Emma," Donna called, seeing her colleague hesitating in the hallway, "I'll need you to process those ballistics immediately. Don't leave your lab until you have something."

A confused expression flickered across Emma's face – surely Donna knew that wasn't how it worked? – before it twigged that Donna was giving her a legitimate reason, in front of the others, to leave the scene.

Now Donna was calling to Fran and Morrison while Emma hurried outside.

"Stephen, get the details of everyone who's been in here today."

"Ma'am." Morrison flicked open his notebook, looking relieved to have a task that didn't involve looking at the baby.

"And Fran, liaise with the medics. Stay with them."

Fran nodded. "Yes, Ma'am."

Donna strode from the room, and side-stepped the police barrier that was being erected around the front door. She hurried down the stairs past a clamour of personnel, and back out onto the street, before being joined by Adam Ridout. His face was flushed from the cold.

"What can you tell me, Donna?" he asked.

"It's a breakthrough in the murder case," she said. "Quick, give me a light. I've only got a minute."

Adam grabbed a cigarette from his own pack, and tossed it, along with a lighter, into Donna's open hand. She closed her eyes while she took a long draw. Exhaled. Then leaned towards Adam.

"We're expecting to confirm tomorrow that the murdered woman was Moira Cowan. She was a midwife." Her voice was a whisper. Adam's face remained flushed. "We've linked this address to her, as well as to Eleanor Wallace – the midwife who was murdered two years back. We've just recovered a bullet, and we're going to test it to see if it came from the same gun that shot and killed Eleanor."

Adam raised his eyebrows.

"I'm going to need anything you can get on what the neighbours have to say about activity in the flat. God knows, they won't tell *us* anything," said Donna. "And if your sources can give us anything connected to drugs, prostitutes, guns, you'll have the exclusive on what we've found. And it's big."

"I'm on it," said Adam. "I'll call you soon as I have something."

Donna stubbed out her cigarette, steeled herself, and marched back into the flat, hearing her name being called by more journalists who'd just spotted her.

Chapter 29

Donna stood, motionless, in front of the microwave while it warmed one of Danny's frozen meals. Her eyes stung with the effort of keeping them open. She remained standing staring at the microwave long after it had dinged. All she could see was that tiny lifeless form she'd uncovered in the Craigie Drive flat. Keeping Akwasi in one piece at the scene had been the only thing that had stopped her from dwelling on what they were actually dealing with, and now the images and the possibilities came tumbling into her head. Could the bullet in the wall have come from the same gun as the one that had killed Eleanor Wallace? Was Kozel's gang involved, and had Evanton covered it up? How was Marcus Edridge involved?

A sharp pain reminded her that she hadn't eaten since brunch with Natesh, and she made a note to go and see Samira. She recalled the older woman's reaction the other night when Natesh had mentioned the body. *She knows something,* Donna remembered thinking at the time. She'd brushed it off then, but now she wasn't so sure. She had to learn to trust her first instinct.

She reached into the microwave, promising herself that she'd phone Natesh right after she had a minute to return Libby's call. She took the meal through to the living room and sat down with it in front of the TV.

As soon as she'd eaten, she phoned Libby.

"Long day at work," she said in response to Libby's concern that she hadn't been in touch. And, "Yes, I'm fine," in response to the next set of questions.

She could tell Libby wasn't convinced, but did her best to sound simply tired. What she couldn't admit to Libby was her gnawing suspicion that something was going wrong in this case. The feeling that she was being watched. That rose on the bed last night. She shuddered, knowing she was going to have to deal with it head-on.

"Donna?"

"Sorry, head's spinning."

"Have you been taking your meds?"

"Oh, crap," said Donna, checking the time. "I missed one." Maybe that was why her imagination was trying to take off.

"I don't know," she heard Libby sigh. "I'm gone two days, and you're turning into a wreck."

Donna had to agree. Or was there something more to her niggling worries? Nobody at work would talk about Jonas Evanton. He'd murdered two of their own colleagues, not to mention the others he'd killed that day, and he'd been on the loose now for eighteen months, hiding in the shadows where they couldn't find him. How could a man stay missing for that length of time, when the whole police force was looking for him? Donna felt the hairs stand up on the back of her neck. Unless he wasn't hiding, she thought. What could be smarter than "hiding" in plain sight? He was here, she could sense him. And his hunger for revenge against her would be immense. There was no way he couldn't be here. But could he really have something to do with Eleanor Wallace, Moira Cowan, the baby? The fibres weren't meshing together, but they danced on the edges of Donna's mind, seeking a common thread. Or maybe she was overtired? Not ready to be back at work? She would know once Emma got back to her with the ballistics report on the two bullets.

"I'm on the next train home if you don't convince me you're okay," she heard Libby's voice over the phone. It shook her out of her thoughts.

"I'm just tired," she said. "But I have eaten one of Danny's hotpots. Yum yum."

She heard Libby chuckle.

After the call, she fetched her medication, then settled back down and dialled Natesh's number.

"Donna!" he exclaimed when he answered. He sounded out of breath.

"Erm, I haven't called at a bad moment, have I?"

"No." His voice squeaked.

Donna cringed. She was already on Erin's list of People We Don't Like. All she needed was to have disturbed them during a moment of passion.

"Wow, I didn't realise how late it was," she said. "Things are a bit nuts at work just now, but we'll catch up in a couple of days, yeah?"

"Sounds good," said Natesh.

Donna couldn't shake the unpleasant image of what she might have intruded on, so she put on her chirpy voice and ended the call.

At least Samira must be home, or he'd have said. She settled down in front of the TV and began flicking through the channels.

Natesh said goodbye to Donna, hoping he'd given nothing away. He was sitting on the floor in the centre of his living room. The contents of the package lay in front of him. A passport and what looked to be a bus ticket. A torn photograph. And a handwritten note. Natesh re-examined each item in turn.

The passport. It was an old one belonging to his mother. The photo in it was her younger self. It was her name, her date of birth. But the story about her fleeing with Natesh from the Sri Lankan civil war? This passport was Turkish. The stamps on it clearly showed Samira entering the UK with her child, Natesh, directly from Turkey. Not Sri Lanka.

And the bus ticket. Natesh turned it around and around in his fingers. Dated the same day as the day of departure on the passport, the journey was Fethiye to Ankara, one way. Natesh had checked online. Fethiye was at least a day's bus ride from Ankara. Samira had left with her baby, Natesh, leaving behind *what* in Fethiye? Or leaving behind *whom*? The man in the photo? Natesh stared at it.

He couldn't be sure that the baby in the bleached photo was him. But the woman was Samira, and the man standing next to her, grinning into the camera, bore a striking resemblance to himself. Natesh's heart had leaped in his chest when he'd seen it. Was that his father, who had supposedly died in Sri Lanka as part of the bogus story about Samira's flight from the armed violence? If it was, then there was something Natesh had to desperately find out about his own past, because he could see in the background of the photo a large building. And, while the letters were blurred, the sign on it said Fethiye.

On the back of the photo was written, *ölüm bizi ayırana kadar*. It hadn't taken Natesh long to find the translation online. *Till death do us part.* He felt a chill.

On finding the items earlier on, he'd run immediately to his room and searched his drawer for Samira's current passport. He knew he'd left it there not long ago, and now it was gone.

It was while he'd been staring at these items and wondering where Samira could have gone, that Donna had phoned. Lying to her, keeping anything from her, cut him to the core. And now, more than ever, he was desperate for her help. But he couldn't tell her about any of this. He had to work this out on his own, otherwise her life would be at risk. The hand-scrawled note he held in his shaking hand told him so.

Thursday

Chapter 30

He sat in the car across the street from her house. He'd arrived there about an hour ago, just as she'd come out the door, and had to think fast to avoid being noticed. He'd switched the car engine back on and looked down at his phone, so she'd think it was just one of her neighbours about to set off for work. And he'd pulled it off. Donna Davenport hadn't even glanced in his direction. He'd watched her in his rear view mirror, in her running gear, as she headed off down the street. An athlete. He was going to have to try and get in shape himself.

He hadn't been around when she'd been out for a jog before, so he wasn't sure how long she'd be. He checked his watch again. The car clock. The time on his phone. Definitely an hour now. She was going to be late for work. Where could she have gone?

He scanned the street. Most of the cars that had been there when he'd arrived were gone now. A dog barking in the bungalow at the end alerted him to the arrival of the postman. Pretending again to be preoccupied with his phone, he watched the postman's progress along the street. He watched intently as the red-topped youth sauntered past the car. No mail for her this morning. Perhaps he should send her a card? People liked getting surprises in the post. He mulled over the things he might say in his card.

But time was getting on, and she still hadn't returned.

What should he do? Get out and look for her? But if she suddenly came back, he'd be caught. There was no way she wouldn't recognise him. He couldn't risk it. Not yet. He wasn't ready yet. Where the fuck was she? What was she playing at? Bitch!

Donna eased off as she ran along East Dock Street. She'd made good time. She could take a shower in Bell Street and get changed there, be ready before Fran got in. Well, at least before the others did. She had a sneaking suspicion that Fran never left the office, ever. There were working time regulations in place to stop normal people being made to look like slackers compared to workaholics like DC Woods. Donna found herself smiling. They were a good lot, her new team, especially now that the ice between her and Akwasi was thawed. They were going to crack this case. Despite the lengthening odds, with it being three days now since Moira's body had emerged from the North Sea, Donna felt a flush of optimism. The strange link with Edridge to the Craigie Drive flat, the baby, the coincidence with Eleanor Wallace's murder, the case was looking more complex that it had done at first. With a complex case, three days wasn't so bad, and she was sure they'd get additional resources now that it was clear they weren't dealing with a run of the mill suicide or domestic.

But one thought kept returning to trouble her. The rose. Something had triggered it off in her mind again this morning, almost as soon as she'd left home, but she couldn't put her finger on it, and she just couldn't shake that feeling of being watched. For once, she knew she could trust the feeling. She didn't have to run through her usual checklist to test out whether a feeling of paranoia was justified or could be an early warning sign of a forthcoming bipolar flare-up. That rose had come from somewhere. She was going to have to be extra vigilant.

Showered and changed, Donna was making her way to the team room, when she heard Ross call her. She followed him into the nearest empty office, and they both perched side by side on the desk.

"That's the dental ID on Moira Cowan just in," Ross began. "Any more on the baby?"

"Two midwives murdered two years apart and a dead baby in a flat owned by a doctor," said Donna. "Ogilvie is due to get back to us with an initial report on the baby late today or tomorrow. I'm expecting a ballistics report from Emma today."

"We're going to have to go public on this, now," said Ross.

Donna put both hands in the air. "We do, but I'd hold the information about the baby for the time being. There's enough hysteria going on."

"Martha's called a press conference for…" he glanced at his watch, "…half past. We confirm Moira Cowan as the body on the beach, and we confirm her and Eleanor Wallace were both midwives, are you agreed?"

"As long as Moira's next of kin have been informed," said Donna. "I agree we need to release her name as part of this, but

I don't want some poor bugger finding out on the radio that their sister, aunt, whatever, had been murdered."

"Her name's been out unofficially for a couple of days," said Ross.

"I'd prefer to check," said Donna. She stood up, and walked quickly to the team room. Fran was there with Akwasi.

"Press conference at half past," Donna called to them as she entered the room. "Full disclosure, except for the baby. Thomas, any joy with the sister?"

Akwasi looked miserable. "I phoned her an hour ago, told her we had found her sister's body, murdered."

"Is she coming over?" asked Donna.

"No, she is not," said Akwasi. Donna's eyebrow rose in surprise. "Said she was going to check with her lawyer if she needed to do anything about selling the flat, but made all the excuses under the sun as to why she couldn't fly out to take care of the funeral."

"Unbelievable," said Donna.

"To be fair," said Akwasi, "she did sound pretty shocked. So, what now?" His voice was quiet.

"Her work colleagues," said Donna, realising that Akwasi had probably built himself up to his first time telling somebody that their loved one was dead. "Go round there now and tell them officially. Give them the option of coming to the morgue to view the body, but make sure you explain it's not necessary."

Akwasi stood up to go, and smiled weakly at Donna, glad of the direction. "On my way, boss."

Donna returned his smile, and added, "Tell them it's all going public this morning."

As she said it, she visualised the headlines. But there was no getting away from it. The man responsible for killing two women – two midwives – was still out there. And so was Jonas Evanton.

Her phone rang and she answered it before the second ring, her heart beating faster when she saw it was Emma.

"You were right," said Emma. "The bullet we found in the wall at Craigie Drive came from the same gun as the one that killed Eleanor Wallace. And it's a gun we know was used by Kozel's gang."

Donna felt goose bumps form on her arms. *Yes*, she thought, *you're out there, Evanton.*

Chapter 31

Ross was in a better mood after the press conference this time, Donna was relieved to note. She was also relieved to have been able to confirm all of the details of the investigation so far, without any information about the baby being leaked. She'd certainly learned a thing or two during her time off about behaving better around journalists.

"Nicely handled," he said as they left the press room. "I don't know how you do it, how you get them to eat out of the palm of your hand like that."

"It's my natural charm and good looks," said Donna. "And, of course, making them part of the hunt for this guy makes sense, especially when we're not getting anywhere fast."

"But turning the press conference around," said Ross, "*us* asking *them* the questions! That was genius."

"It was genuine," said Donna. "The press isn't some crazy beast to be tamed or tolerated. You treat them like that, what do you think they're going to do? Those reporters are human. Their job is every bit as legitimate as ours."

"And that's how you do it," said Ross. "Now, go get me some results."

When Donna walked into the team room, the waft of grill and carbs made her tummy rumble.

She saw Fran, Alice and Morrison huddled over something on the desk by the evidence boards.

"A sushi burger?" Alice prodded the object that sat among them on the desk. She sounded sceptical.

"It's fusion cuisine," said Fran. "That's what Takeshi called it."

"Ooh, so Takeshi said it, it must be true," Alice teased.

Fran's cheeks flushed red, and gave her away. Morrison snorted in laughter behind her back, and caught Donna's eye.

"Chief," he said.

Alice and Fran bounced away from the burger as if it had burst into flames.

"Don't mind me," said Donna, approaching it suspiciously.

"That's a sushi burger?"

"Tasty," said Fran. "Try a bite?"

"You try it first," said Donna. "If you're not throwing up by the end of the day, I'll get one."

"Can't guarantee that in this job," Morrison muttered.

"True," said Donna. "But at least we're going to be getting some more help – Ross is drafting in more boots for us."

"About time," said Alice.

"So let's recap on where things stand," said Donna, drawing their attention to the whiteboard. "John Ogilvie is dealing with the baby, and we'll have something from him, hopefully tomorrow morning. We're expecting the DNA results on the Latin lover, when?" She glanced at Fran for an answer.

Fran started. "Eh? What? Sorry…"

"The DNA link between Moira Cowan and Eleanor Wallace," said Donna. "When are the results due in?"

"Later today," said Fran, flustered to have been caught so distracted. She could tell by the look in Donna's eye that she hadn't managed to pull it off. It must be true what they said about Donna: she could see right through you.

"I'm expecting it to confirm that we're looking for one man," said Donna. "Tell me as soon as you get the call."

"Yes, boss."

"We know Moira was out with friends on Sunday night, so her time of death was during the early hours of Monday morning. The description of the man she took home is a bit vague, other than that he looked *Spanish, or something*," she used her fingers as quote marks, "and could be in his forties. He could be anywhere by now, I don't need to tell you. And we have the ballistics report from the bullet we found in Craigie Drive – it came from the same gun as the one that killed Eleanor Wallace, and it's been linked to Abram Kozel's gang. We need to find out why they would have been in that flat." She paused. "Have any of you noticed anyone hanging around here recently?"

"What?" said Alice. "Are you working on a theory?"

"Just wondered," said Donna.

"My arse," said Alice. "What makes you ask a thing like that?"

During the split second it took for Donna to weigh up what to tell Alice, the door slammed open and Akwasi ran in, clearly out of breath.

"Boss," he called as he hurried to the front of the room, "the midwives have reported another one missing." He was clutching a photo, and he waved it in front of Donna's face.

"Shit!" said Donna, as soon as she saw it. What the fuck was going on?

Chapter 32

Donna hurried to Ross's room while she rang Natesh's number. Not in service. Again. Not in service.

Ross looked up, startled when Donna barged in. His fingers stopped in mid air above his keyboard, and his eyes narrowed as she descended on his desk.

"This is going to sound crazy," she said.

"Even coming from you?" he tried, but she didn't smile.

"I know who's behind the murders."

"Really?" Ross sat back in his swivel chair. "You've had the breakthrough?"

"Just logic," said Donna. "Think about it. I read the Eleanor Wallace file. You know who the investigating officer was?"

Ross sighed. "Of course I do."

"She was killed just weeks after he was posted here…"

"Donna, don't go down this road."

"…shot with some Soviet semi-automatic…"

"But Moira Cowan wasn't shot."

"…the model that Abram Kozel and his gang use," said Donna, triumph in her voice. Ross looked wary.

"Are you sure about this?"

"Just had it confirmed," said Donna. She was beginning to shout. "Jonas Evanton's first case with us, you think that's a coincidence?"

"I think I want to see that file," said Ross.

"You can look at it all you want," said Donna. "It won't change the fact that we need to be open to the possibility that Evanton was involved in Eleanor Wallace's death, or at least in covering up the evidence."

"I can buy that he may have misled the investigation in order to protect Kozel," said Ross. "But aren't you stretching things to suggest he was involved in Moira Cowan's death, too? I mean, that doesn't make any sense."

"The hell it does," said Donna. "What's the one thing that'll be eating at him this past eighteen months?"

"You're thinking he's out for revenge against you?"

"I'm sure of it," said Donna. "Wouldn't you be, in his shoes?"

"You've got a point."

"So, the day I return to duty, there's another murder, obviously linked to Eleanor Wallace. He's trying to mess with my head."

"Do you seriously think he would have known when you'd be returning to work?" Ross tried to reason.

"He could, you know," she said. "Obviously he had inside help to get out of Belmarsh. He's the only person ever to have escaped from there, for God's sake, he could be getting help to find out anything he wants…" Her words began to race, and she could see that Ross was now looking at her with an expression of pity.

"Donna," said Ross. His voice was loud. Harsh. It made her stop and listen to him. "It can't be him. Think about it."

"I have been thinking about nothing else for the last three days," said Donna.

"I hate to be the one to say it," said Ross, "but are you really ready to be back?"

Donna slumped into the chair facing Ross, and lowered her head. She had to calm the rage that was building up inside her.

"What you went through was horrendous," said Ross.

"I know that," Donna spat out the words. "I got locked in the fucking nut house for twelve weeks as a result."

She regretted the words the instant they'd left her mouth. Hated the caricatured reference to the psychiatric ward where she'd experienced only calm, nurturing healing. Where the dedicated professionals had put her shattered self back together piece by broken piece following her ordeal at Evanton's hands.

After a moment of silence, Ross said gently, "These murders bear none of the hallmarks of Evanton's previous killings."

"But he obviously covered up evidence in the Eleanor Wallace case."

"You can't go about your work seeing him in every shadow," said Ross. "The search for him is still very much active, you know. And the search for whoever must have helped him. Maybe not on the same scale as last year, but believe me, Donna, if he was anywhere near here we would know."

"But…"

"He's not here, Donna, it's not Evanton. I do think, though, that you could have stumbled on a lead with regard to Kozel's gang. There's something that does make sense. I want you to pursue that line, but leave Evanton out of it."

She wanted to believe him. With every fibre in her being, she wanted Ross to be right. Evanton's ghost sat at her back wherever she went. He haunted these corridors in Bell Street. He lurked in every corner of this city's streets. But she knew that wasn't it. There was something else.

"Look," said Ross, "two women and a baby have been killed, possibly by the same person or persons…"

"A third woman is now missing," said Donna. "Missing person report just in."

Ross looked thoughtful. "Well, you're the best shot we have at getting them justice," he said. "Maybe bring this third woman home alive."

"There's something you need to know about the missing woman," said Donna.

A dark shadow crossed Ross's eyes.

"It's Samira Chaudrakar. My best friend's mother."

Ross sighed involuntarily.

"Do you still think there's no way it could be Evanton?" said Donna, as she stood to leave.

Chapter 33

Geri's face was ashen. Rowen held a tissue over her weeping eyes.

"I just thought it would look like she was sleeping, or something," said Geri, her tone flat. Her head shook from side to side as she spoke. "Did she…is she…?" Geri struggled with the words.

Donna looked up from her phone - still nothing from Natesh - and turned to face the two midwives. The spotless walls of the morgue's corridor pressed in close around them. Airless. Donna had to slow her breathing to stop all of the mis-fitting jigsaw pieces from crowding her head. She became aware, as if a cloud was clearing from her racing thoughts, that the two women needed her full attention.

"Sorry," she said, pocketing the mobile. "We can go talk in the lounge first, if that'd help?"

She watched Rowen and Geri glance at one another, each looking to the other for an answer.

"Come on," said Donna, "I reckon we could all do with a coffee."

"Thanks," said Geri. "I've never done this before. And, well…"

"I know," said Donna. She beckoned with a nod towards a room up ahead, and they trooped in.

The room looked like any other staff common area, and the two midwives huddled at the door, watching as Donna went straight to a cupboard that contained two shelves full of odd assorted mugs. She retrieved three, then plucked open an adjacent cupboard, from which she retrieved a jar of coffee.

"Tea or coffee?" she called over her shoulder.

"Coffee, please," Rowen and Geri replied together.

"Go, take a seat," said Donna, waving them towards a comfortable seating area. They went as directed and sat, hands clasped in front of their knees, listening to the kettle come to the boil.

As Donna stirred the coffee granules into the boiling water, soft footsteps arrived at the door. She looked up, and smiled.

"John," she said. "You must have superhuman hearing. How

did you hear the kettle all the way from your office?"

"Ah, rumour had it you were in the building, lass," said Ogilvie. "Thought I'd find you here." He stopped short in response to the flick of Donna's eyes.

"Two colleagues of Moira Cowan," she told him. "They've been paying their respects."

Ogilvie turned to Rowen and Geri, offering his hand.

"I'm so sorry," he told them. "This isn't a pleasant task. Are you okay?"

"This is Dr. Ogilvie," added Donna. "He's the pathologist."

Rowen and Geri introduced themselves. As they did so, Donna pushed the door closed and sat down, placing the coffee mugs in front of them.

"As I said, this is a murder investigation. I'm not going to patronise you by pretending we're not concerned about a possible link with Eleanor Wallace. Is there anything you can tell me about a flat in Craigie Drive? Number one-nine-two?"

Rowen and Geri stared back at Donna; she found no flicker of recognition at the mention of the address.

"We found something there yesterday," Donna said. "Something really terrible. You'll have noticed the extra police presence around today, and I'm afraid you're going to be hearing a lot about it soon, but for the meantime this is confidential. I don't want you to discuss with anyone what I'm about to tell you. Do you understand?"

She was aware of Ogilvie clearing his throat as he sat down beside her, and she steeled herself for what she was about to tell the two stricken midwives. Rowen and Geri affirmed that they understood Donna's instruction.

"We made a search of the flat yesterday afternoon," she began. "Forensics are ongoing, as we have reason to believe it may be linked to the murders. But we found the body of a newly born baby."

The midwives gasped.

"We don't know whether or how it fits with Moira and Eleanor's murders," Donna went on. Turning to Ogilvie, she said, "Will you be able to give us a time of death?"

Ogilvie sighed and looked at his hands. "Probably not," he said. "We'll be able to tell you how long after death the body was frozen, but there's no way to assess how long ago. The best I can give you on that, based on the level of frost on the body, is probably within the last five years."

"The baby's death could have been known to Eleanor, then, or to Moira. Maybe neither of them, or both, of course," said Donna. "But let's say one of them attends the birth, something goes wrong, and the baby dies. We know Moira disappeared after a night out, not during working hours. If she'd witnessed a baby dying, you'd know about it, wouldn't you?"

"Of course," said Geri. "It would be reported through the usual channels, and obviously Moira would have been upset about it."

"Okay," said Donna. "Bear with me, here. So, let's assume Moira wasn't present when the baby died. Could Eleanor have been there?"

The midwives looked at one another, but remained silent.

Ogilvie stood up and made an excuse to leave. *Not like him*, thought Donna. She caught his eye, and he looked away quickly. *He's hiding something.* As he left the room, Donna turned her attention back to the midwives.

"Eleanor was at work on the day she was murdered," she went on. "Could she have gone to Craigie Drive, and been murdered there, having witnessed the baby's death?" She seemed to be talking to herself, and nobody answered her question. "Did she say anything at all about being concerned about any of her visits? Any reason she didn't properly record her visit to Craigie Drive?"

The midwives shook their heads.

"Anyone in particular at work she may have confided in?" asked Donna.

"She was close friends with Christine Avery," said Geri. "She was part of our team, but she left shortly after Eleanor was killed."

Donna drew her notebook from her pocket. "Can you tell me how to get in touch with Christine?"

"Her details will be on the system," said Geri, "but she spoke to the police at the time. Don't you have them?"

"It would speed things up if you could pass them onto me," said Donna, preferring not to divulge that Evanton hadn't included any mention of Christine Avery in his so-called investigation.

"I can check," said Geri. "I'll ask Samira to look up the...oh!" Her hand covered her mouth and she began to cry again.

"What's happening about Samira?" Rowen asked Donna.

"We're treating her as a missing person, as part of this investigation," said Donna.

"Do you mean…?"

"That's all I can tell you," said Donna. "We've no idea of her whereabouts, but – no – we haven't found another body, if that's what you're asking. But we are worried about her safety."

Donna checked her watch, and gently ushered the midwives out of the morgue.

"It's really important we speak to Christine Avery," she told them. "If you could get me her details as quickly as possible."

As soon as they were back in the open air, she grabbed a cigarette from her pocket, lit it, and groaned in relief as she exhaled. Then she offered the pack to Rowen and Geri, and they both took one.

Chapter 34

Adam Ridout's fingers flew over the keyboard, getting his story ready while casting anxious glances at the clock. Copy deadline was looming, and Eric the editor was pacing the room, hovering around him. It was the biggest story to break in years, and it had to have broken so close to the deadline. And more, the details kept changing. First it was a possible suicide. Then maybe a murder. The speculation about a serial killer, and this morning's confirmation of a link, right enough, between the murders of the two midwives.

It was tricky getting the timing right on a story like this, but he felt the rush of excitement from having gained Donna's confidence. She didn't have to tip him off about the Craigie Drive flat the way she had. If he played his cards right, he could have the inside take on this before anyone else. He made a note to look up some of his less savoury contacts. He was sure that Donna would be as good as her word – yesterday she'd promised something big, if he could find anything connecting the flat to drugs, prostitutes or guns. His head spun at the thought of what he might be getting into. *It's big*, Donna had told him.

Adam could tell that Eric was trying to stay calm, trying not to shout, *Hurry up*!

When his phone rang, he cursed himself for answering automatically, instead of ignoring it. He saw Eric's eyebrows shoot to the ceiling and the older man's face grow purple, and he mouthed *Sorry*.

It was Natesh, and he sounded out of sorts. Adam listened to his request, surprised.

"Turkey?" he said.

"Yeah," said Natesh, not fooling him with the phoney calmness. "I need to get away for a bit. I found some family history stuff relating to Turkey, so I thought a trip out there would be, er, therapeutic. Do you think your photography mate would be able to help me find my way around for a bit?"

"I can ask him," said Adam, wanting to probe further, but aware of the hands on the clock. He reached into his desk, but couldn't find what he was looking for. "His name is Firaz. He was a great help to me when I was out there, and he earned quite a bit on the side from my photography, so yeah, I'm sure he'll help you, no problem."

"Thanks, man," said Natesh. "I'm getting a flight out of London on Saturday morning into Dalaman."

That's quick, thought Adam, sitting back in his chair. Several questions formed in his mind, and he was about to ask Natesh, when a sharp look from Eric had him sitting back upright. "Listen, mate, I'll call Firaz tonight, have him meet you at the airport, okay? He'll show you around, and tag along like a puppy to interpret for you. But I need to go just now, speak to you later."

Adam turned back to his report, his mind now distracted by his memories of Turkey, and puzzled by the call from Natesh.

Chapter 35

"I don't like it," said Firaz. He folded his tattooed arms across his chest. Defiant or nervous, Amin couldn't tell.

"You don't have to like it," said Amin. "It's what I'm paying you to do."

"And what happens when I get hauled in for questioning? I only just dropped off the American, don't you think they're going to notice that I'm back again?"

A rumble of thunder made Amin look up to the sky as the gathering dark clouds cast an unnatural gloom across the Kaya valley. The air was definitely cooling, at last. It had been a long summer, and such extremes of heat were exhausting. He stopped by a pomegranate tree, tapped on a number of the fruits before selecting one, and took a look around his compound.

Once a thriving hub of activity, with the girls chattering and working, the guards bellowing their mindless ruminations, and the constant pounding of target practice, Amin found the silence unsettling. The darkening sky only added to his unease. Vidu and Samira would be arriving later on today, following Vidu's bungling of the operation in Dundee. At least the departure of the American with the last of the girls had gone without a hitch, airport security none the wiser about their fake passports. Once the girl arrived at her destination in Amsterdam, he would receive payment enough to buy him some time to figure out his next move, and time to deal with the American when he turned back up to try and cause trouble. He'd always known the lucrative trade wouldn't last forever; he just hadn't foreseen Vidu's carelessness bringing it to an end yet.

Firaz had been a reliable worker. Discreet, always delivering the fake passports on time, and escorting the sham couples to the airport. In addition to the money, the young photo journalist had benefited from the security of Amin's bribes to authority figures who might otherwise have paid too much attention to his legitimate work. Amin could understand the young man's fears, but he couldn't trust anyone else to bring Vidu and Samira here from the airport.

"You're paranoid," said Amin. "Why would they notice you?"

"You didn't see the scene the woman made at the airport."

"Scene?"

"Yeah, she was a bit too enthusiastic. Practically jerking the American off while they were in the check-in queue. The guards didn't like it. And they saw me with them, they're not going to forget."

"Shit," muttered Amin. "We can do without the publicity." Coming to the attention of the Turkish authorities was never good, especially for someone of Kurdish stock, like Firaz. Amin was going to have to cut him loose after this last assignment.

Fat, warm raindrops began to pit the sandy ground. Amin and Firaz hurried inside the villa. It would likely be a heavy shower, but short. Enough to cause the dirt track leading away from the compound to run as a muddy stream for an hour or so.

They made their way through the villa until they came to a comfortable office. Amin sat in a rocking chair, while Firaz stood brooding by the door.

"You're right," said Amin. "You can't go back into the airport. Watch for her from outside the airport, have a taxi ready."

"I don't even know what she looks like."

On a shelf next to Amin was the photo of the smiling young woman with the amber ring. Amin picked up the photograph. "She looks like this. You've seen this plenty of times."

"You're losing it, old man," said Firaz. "She looked like that thirty years ago. Did you think about that?"

"Just get her."

"Well, I'm just saying, I don't like it."

Amin handed him a package. "Any trouble from the guards, there's plenty cash in there to make them forget they ever saw you."

Chapter 36

Adam Ridout hit the send button on his email. *There*, he *thought, deadline met!*

He stretched and stood up, and looked out of his office window. Blustery out there. The first stirrings of winter were sending grey clouds scudding across the sky. The open water further out to sea looked choppy, and the masts of the boats sitting in the harbour bobbed erratically.

His thoughts turned to Turkey. It would be getting blustery there, too, by this time of year. He just hoped Natesh's flight wouldn't run into the turbulence of the massive storm clouds that could linger over the area. Not for his first visit to the country, that would be unfortunate.

He opened a drawer and rifled through the debris inside. He was sure Firaz's number was in here. No point emailing him, it could be days before his old photography buddy accessed it. He needed the phone number. Natesh was in London already, getting his visa. He must be in a hurry, whatever he was up to.

Where the hell was that number? He and Firaz had kept in regular contact since he'd come back from Turkey, often sharing news of upcoming photography competitions and discussing techniques, ideas and the chances of winning. Acutely aware of the fine line his Kurdish friend was treading as a potentially dissident photo journalist, Adam was always careful to offer his support, and so he knew Firaz would be pleased to hear from him. If only he could find the number – ah! There it was!

"Hello?"

Firaz's voice sounded surprisingly clear, as if he was on the other side of the room.

"Firaz, man, how are you?"

"Adam? Hey, it's good to hear from you!"

They exchanged their usual pleasantries, and now that Adam had met the copy deadline, spent some time chatting about the next competition, before he remembered the real reason he was phoning.

"I've a friend arriving in Dalaman on Saturday," said Adam. "He's looking for a guide. Can you help him? Maybe meet him at the airport?" There was a pause on the line. "Firaz? You there?"

"Yeah, I'm here, uh, of course," said Firaz eventually. "Of course, I'll get him."

"Are you all right? Is something wrong?"

"No, man, everything's fine," said Firaz. "Just driving, you know? Surprised you can't feel the potholes over the line."

A picture of the jeep bouncing over dirt tracks made Adam smile. "Wish I was there," he said, meaning it. "I could do with a bit of sunshine."

"What's your mate's name, then?"

"Natesh," said Adam. "Natesh Chaudrakar. He's…"

"Chaudrakar?"

"Yeah…"

There was a bad sound over the phone. The screech of brakes? Tyres sliding across scree. The shriek of an angry hawk. Firaz swearing as he struggled to regain control of the steering wheel.

"Firaz? Are you okay? Are you there?"

Firaz pulled out of the compound and made his way through the Kaya valley forest until he found the route joining the main road to Fethiye and the airport. It was all right for Amin, he muttered to himself, it wasn't *him* taking all the risks. *He* just stayed there in his villa, while everyone else ran his errands in front of the authorities. Taking care to avoid sliding into a ditch, he was startled by his phone ringing.

"Firaz, man, how are you?" he heard. Well, if it wasn't Adam Ridout! But his joy at hearing from his friend turned sour when he heard the request to meet someone else from the airport. How would he explain away his frequent presence there lately? This was going to be tricky. But that wasn't all.

"Chaudrakar?" he spluttered. Surely not. What was going on here? Amin hadn't mentioned anything about this. He veered too close to a tree suddenly, and had to slam on the brakes and perform a skid on the hairpin track to avoid hitting it. His heart beat wildly. The screech of a hawk dive-bombing him from the tree made him break out in a sweat. He couldn't handle this any more.

Chapter 37

"Like hell I am!" Donna yelled at Ross. He turned his back on her, thinking his word was final.

"You're too close to this case now," he repeated.

"I am going to find this guy," said Donna. "You are not taking me off the case."

"For God's sake, Donna," said Ross, "this morning you were telling me you thought Evanton was the guy. Then you tell me you've a personal connection to the missing woman. The answer is no. I can't let you stay on this, the murders are now linked to the missing woman. I'm sorry, but...don't look at me like that."

Donna had her hands up, a peace gesture. Ross knew better than to believe it meant she had backed down.

"A compromise, then," said Donna. "Let me stay on the murders, and get Alice to lead on the missing person. I won't get involved. Emma will be here with our forensics, and I'll follow the leads that the evidence suggests. I'll forget about Evanton, I know that's not rational. You were right, there's probably a link with Kozel's gang."

She knew she'd won when she heard Ross sigh in exasperation.

"You're our best officer," he said. "That's the only reason I'm agreeing to this. Do not fuck it up." He dismissed her with a wave of his hand; she could barely contain the wry smile as she turned to go back to the briefing room.

As she walked, she listened again to Natesh's answer message. Where had he gotten to, she wondered. She knew he'd be frantic, searching, but if ever there was a time when they needed to be in touch, it was now.

When she reached the briefing room, Emma popped her head out the door.

"I thought I heard your size sevens," she smiled.

"What have you got?" asked Donna.

"Well," Emma said, pride in her voice, "we have a match. The DNA we found in Moira's flat comes from the same guy we know Eleanor Wallace last had sex with. It's one and the same Latin lover."

"Bingo," said Donna, meeting her high five.

"Unfortunately," said Emma, "we've no match with anything else on the database, so we've no way to identify our guy yet."

"We've got a sketch just about ready to go to the press," said Alice.

"Good," said Donna. "And we know there's a link to Kozel's gang, so we know we're not dealing with a small-time crook or a crime of passion. What would somebody like Moira Cowan or Eleanor Wallace be doing getting mixed up with those sorts of thugs? Could there be a link to prostitution, trafficking?"

Alice shook her head. "Kozel is into guns and drugs, never been linked to trafficking or prostitution."

"I want it checked out, anyway," said Donna.

She regarded each one of her team. Fran Woods, brimming with energy, she was relieved to note. Morrison, imposing and ready, Akwasi, compact and alert, and Alice, steady as a rock. They all looked back at Donna, waiting

She walked up to the whiteboard, taking in the growing list of details that were plotted below each photograph of the murdered women. The mystery Latin lover, indicated by arrows and question marks leading from each photo, was now joined by a drawn line, with a note confirming Emma's DNA match. Added to the growing array of information were Samira Chaudrakar's details, along with those of the Craigie Drive baby and Marcus Edridge. A note about the gun that killed Eleanor Wallace being of the same make used by Kozel's thugs was there.

"Some new information to add," said Donna, tracing her finger along the lines to the Latin lover. "Eleanor Wallace was close friends with one of her colleagues, a Christine Avery. Except Christine left shortly after the murder, and was never interviewed during the original investigation." *Scared off, or the notes removed from the file*, she thought, almost letting the words come out of her mouth.

She tapped her pen on the Craigie Drive address also linked to both photos. "Thomas, Stephen, get over to the midwifery unit later on and get whatever details they have on Christine Avery, and follow it up. We really could be doing with a breakthrough about now."

"Yes, boss," Akwasi and Morrison said together.

Donna turned to Emma. "I'll need the DNA run against Rory Thomson's set."

"The guy who confesses to everything? Surely you don't…"

"No, I don't," said Donna, "but when all this is over, I don't want any stone to have been left unturned. I am not going to be standing in front of the cameras with the *lessons must be learned* line."

"Fair enough," said Emma. "Consider it done."

Donna addressed the rest of the team. "So, we've had the dental record match to confirm Moira Cowan's identity. Fran's done some ace detective work, and we know the original owner of the flat – one Dr Marcus Edridge."

"Do we have him in for questioning?" asked Akwasi.

"That's complicated," said Donna.

"Complicated, how?"

"He's in pretty bad shape," she tapped her head. "We need to go through the hoops before we can talk to him."

She turned towards the whiteboard again. "Yesterday we found the baby in the flat. Ross had forensics taking up the floorboards all night."

A buzzer sounded, and Emma retrieved her phone from her pocket. "That's John Ogilvie," she said. "He's sent his initial report about the baby."

"That was quick," said Donna. "Never a good sign."

Emma quickly scrolled through the details she'd just received. "Oh, dear God," she whispered.

"Here, let me see," said Donna, reaching for the phone.

A brief silence hugged the room, breaths baited while Donna scanned the main points received from Ogilvie. In slow motion, she handed the phone back to Emma. No wonder Ogilvie had been acting strangely earlier when she'd been at the morgue with the midwives. This was the information he'd been hiding from her.

"I don't like the colour you've gone, chief," said Alice Moone.

"Change of plan," said Donna. "Here's how we do this. Alice, you're heading up the search for Samira Chaudrakar. Get round to her house, interview Natesh and all the neighbours, talk to the midwives, get CCTV as soon as you establish a timeline. Move heaven and earth, I want her found safe and well. Morrison, you go with her, and get Christine Avery's details while you're out."

Alice and Morrison sprang to life, and headed for the door.

Donna addressed Fran and Akwasi. "We're going to go and have a chat with Marcus Edridge."

"The doctor?" Akwasi failed to hide his surprise. "But I thought…"

"Forget what you thought," said Donna.

Alice and Morrison hesitated by the door, alerted to the tone in Donna's voice.

Donna took a pen to the whiteboard, and below the note about the baby found in the flat, she wrote *internal organs surgically removed.*

"Fuck," was the only word whispered around the room.

Chapter 38

Alice wasn't taking no for an answer this time. She knew the occupants were at home, she'd seen them stealing looks out of the window while she'd stood on Natesh's doorstep with Morrison, who stood slightly behind her, like a shamed schoolboy out with his mother. She banged harder on the door.

"Police," she called. "Open the door now, or we'll break it down." She smirked at Morrison, who returned a nod of admiration. This usually did the trick. And it did this time, too.

The door opened, and a wiry middle aged man stuck his head out. "What is it?"

Alice held open her warrant card. "I'm Sergeant Alice Moone, and this is my colleague PC Morrison," she said pleasantly.

The man gawped at her card and said nothing. He ignored Morrison.

"The woman who lives next door," said Alice. "Have you seen her about?"

The man shook his head. "Not today. Their cat usually sits on the step, meowing for about ten minutes every morning when she goes to work, but it wasn't there this morning. Woke me up, it did, not hearing it."

Alice saw Morrison's mouth twitch in a subtle grin while he busied himself with his notebook, jotting down the man's story.

"Next thing, the son comes round asking me to feed the damned thing," the man continued. "Saying he was going away for a bit. Well, that usually only means one thing, doesn't it?"

"He's not in trouble," said Alice, stifling his gossip. "When is the last time you saw Mrs Chaudrakar?"

The man stared at his slippers as he thought.

"What day is this?" he muttered. "Not yesterday." He used his fingers as though counting. "Day before, I think, about two. The son was on the doorstep, banging on the door, must have lost his keys. Then they left together about fifteen minutes later."

"Mrs Chaudrakar and her son both left the flat together on Tuesday afternoon?" said Alice.

"That's right," said the man. "Then he comes by this morning asking me to watch the cat."

"So, just to check what you're telling me," Alice pressed him, preventing him from closing his door. He shot her a look that would turn the sun blue. "You saw Mrs Chaudrakar leave her home on Tuesday, with her son? And you saw her son again this morning?"

"Yes, that's what I said," the man snapped. And this time he managed to slam the door shut.

Alice muttered something that Morrison didn't catch, then motioned for him to return to her car.

After a three-point turn, Alice pulled away from Scott Street, heading towards City Street. She seemed to be mulling over the information they'd just been told, then she turned to Morrison and said, "Did any of that strike you as odd?"

"The whole thing was odd," said Morrison. "Creepy old guy knows woman next door's every move."

"But what about the bit where our missing woman leaves the house with her son, the one who reported her missing?"

"Let's go speak to the son," said Morrison.

"He's a close friend of Donna's."

"You've got to be kidding?" said Morrison.

"I wish I was," said Alice.

Chapter 39

Donna stopped at a kiosk and ordered two coffees. She took the two cups and re-traced her steps until she stood in front of the mess wrapped in a pile of filthy rags that sat on the pavement. Fran and Akwasi stood at a distance, on her request, and watched, glancing at one another from time to time.

A movement from within the pile, then a pair of eyes on her.

"Donna!" a voice cried out. "How are you, hen?"

Donna smiled and sat beside the street beggar. "I'm all right, Marcus. You?"

"Ach, you know," he said. His eyes focused on the coffee, and Donna extended one to him. She recoiled at the gnarled, ingrained hand, and looked away in case he noticed. She saw Fran and Akwasi hesitate, as though wondering whether to intervene. She indicated, *no*, with the slightest tilt of her head.

"How's your mum?" asked Marcus.

Donna shrugged, and turned her attention fully on Marcus. Not for the first time, she wondered how it was that he could have gone from the slightly eccentric gent next door to this.

She lit a cigarette.

"Smoking's bad for you, hen."

"So is living on the street," said Donna.

"Well, you've got a point." The old man gazed up at the sky, seemingly deep in thought. "You're at university now, aren't you?"

"Yeah," said Donna gently.

She blew smoke lazily up towards the clouds. He slurped his coffee.

"How's your mum?" Marcus asked again.

"She's fine," said Donna, trying to keep the hint of impatience from her voice.

"I've got some tomatoes for her," said Marcus. "Have them for her tea, eh?"

Donna thought back to the times Marcus would arrive at the door with tomatoes from his garden. It had been his pride and joy, and Donna and Natesh had enjoyed many a summer's day hiding out among the various nooks and crannies in the wondrous jungle.

"You're at university now, aren't you?"

Donna glanced up again at Fran and Akwasi, before taking a photo from her jacket and showing it to Marcus. "Have you seen him around here lately?" she asked.

Marcus studied the photo. "No, that's not him," he said.

"Not who?"

"You've got a shadow."

A shiver ran down Donna's spine. "What do you mean?"

"How's your mum, hen?"

"Who's my shadow?"

Marcus turned towards her and seemed to notice her for the first time. "Donna! It's good to see you. How are you, hen?"

"I'm good, Marcus," she said. "Are you staying at the hostel?"

"Horrible place, that," said Marcus. "Good job it's getting demolished."

"Where will you go?"

"Nothing wrong with right here, hen," said Marcus. "Just wish the flemmin' social worker would leave me be. Wants me to go into some kind of sheltered housing, but what's the good in that? It won't have a garden, will it?"

"What about Craigie Drive?" said Donna.

Marcus froze. His hand began to shake, and some of the coffee spilled onto his blanket. He seemed to be breathing rapidly, then he suddenly returned to his previous demeanour.

"Donna, isn't it?" he said, smiling, a smile that didn't fool her. "You joined the police, didn't you?"

"That's right," said Donna. She put the photo of Jonas Evanton in front of him again. "Have you seen him around?"

Marcus screwed up his eyes as he studied the photo. Eventually he shook his head slowly. "Not for a long time, not since all that stuff in the papers."

"Well, that's good," said Donna. "About this shadow you mentioned?"

"Tell your mum I've got some tomatoes, hen," said Marcus.

Donna bit her lip, partly in frustration and partly in sorrow.

"I need to go now," she said softly, as she stood up and looked down the street at the shoppers going about their everyday business. She nodded to Fran and Akwasi, and they left Marcus sitting on the street, slurping his coffee.

Chapter 40

The driver remained silent during the journey. His tattooed arms held firm to the ancient jeep's steering wheel, as rocks and potholes competed for the vehicle's destruction. The motor roared in protest, and was frequently interrupted by clanging and wailing from the jeep's tortured engine. The lack of conversation was pragmatic. Any spoken words would have been swallowed up in the clamour, and lost to the heavy, humid air.

Samira sat in the passenger seat, her attention drawn alternatively between the inked serpents that entwined the driver's arms and the countryside that rumbled past along the roadside. How could a place have changed so much, yet not changed at all, Samira wondered. The warmth seeping into her bones and the smells of the countryside took her back to those early days.

The huddle of tired but excitable medical students trooped off the army truck, driven not by military but by a chain of friends of friends who'd brought them out of the danger zone to begin a new life here.

Among them, newly-weds Amin and Samira Chaudrakar, along with Amin's young brother, Vidu.

The bride Samira twisted the amber ring on her finger, wondering not so much about what lay ahead for them here in Turkey, as about what was to become of their revolution-ravaged home.

"Come on, Vidu," she encouraged the boy, taking his hand.

She knew the driver was avoiding the tourist route. The roads out of Dalaman were good. This one could barely be described as a road. She knew its every turn. Yet she was confused. She knew this area well enough to know that they weren't headed towards Fethiye, after all. In all of the years since she'd left, it had never occurred to her that Amin might have moved to a different base. Why would he have? He was able to bribe the local police officers so that he was left well alone. She tried to work out where she was being taken while the memories flooded in.

"It's so peaceful!" Samira admired the spacious villa that was surrounded on

three sides by forestry and whose open side looked out onto the vibrant, shimmering Fethiye marina.

Vidu's football thudded endlessly against the villa's concrete walls.

The hoarse screech of a hawk overhead pierced the air.

The rumbling and tooting horns from the main road provided more than background noise here.

"Peaceful?" Amin laughed.

"No gunfire," she said, and he stopped laughing.

The weeks were turning into months, and they'd received little news from relatives back home in Iran. Correspondence with the few family members they still had there was patchy, and the news was never good. There was little prospect of their returning.

A knock on the villa door disturbed her thoughts. She caught Amin turning to avoid her look of disapproval, before he went to open it.

She and Amin had worked hard at their studies in the local medical facility, treating mainly agricultural injuries. But lately Amin had begun to spend more time at the so-called foreign hospital nearby. It hadn't worried Samira at first, but now his colleagues from the hospital were turning up at the villa, holding strange, hushed discussions that unnerved her. She tried to ignore the small voice at the back of her mind that fretted over the snippets that she overheard. There was enough to be worried about.

By now, her bump was obvious. Vidu was speaking more Turkish than his native Farsi. Samira wasn't sure when it had begun to happen, when they'd drifted from the other medical students they'd arrived here with.

Then one day, Amin sat her down on the rocking chair on the villa's porch.

"We don't have to go back. We can make a life here in Turkey for the four of us."

Shocking as it was, it nevertheless sounded appealing. Samira had been worrying about the future that lay ahead for their baby, due in only twelve weeks' time. The atrocities she was hearing about at home seemed to be escalating, and everyone they knew was trying to flee. Surely they'd be crazy to head straight back into it?

"But how?" she asked. "How can we remain here legally? How would we support ourselves?"

"Do you trust me, Samira?"

Yes, she trusted him, of course she did. He was the love of her life. She was captivated by him, with his easy charm and his handsome features – a beautiful man, she often thought. And she was carrying his child. She had to trust him.

"We can stay here in the villa," he told her. "I've been offered some work at the foreign hospital."

It didn't really surprise her that he could work there under the radar. The hospital, that ordinary Turks weren't allowed to attend, took wealthy overseas clients who paid large amounts of untraceable cash for prompt treatment and the utmost discretion. It sat uneasily with Samira, but what was the choice? She had to think of the baby and Vidu.

Fethiye. She was sure it was the same road sign she'd passed so many times all those years ago. The last time she'd seen it, she and Vidu had been fleeing for their lives, with Natesh carefully wrapped against the fear and anguish.

By the time little Natesh was taking his tentative first steps, Vidu was growing up fast. His voice was deepening between the squeaks, and he was shooting up in height, taller now than his brother the doctor. He was a wiry, gangly teenager, no longer the scared boy who'd clung to Samira's hand, the language of his birth home long forgotten.

When she discovered that he'd begun to attend the foreign hospital with Amin, she knew she couldn't leave him behind. She couldn't risk leaving him to become part of the vile trade that Amin now aided. She knew that Amin's work would be found out one day, probably by another gang rather than by the police. The authorities would be no use to her, an illegal in Turkey, even if Amin wasn't providing backhanders to keep them out of his business.

"It's mutually beneficial," Amin tried to reason, the night she discovered the true nature of his work at the hospital. "They get hard cash. They're practically lining up to sell a kidney."

Always sounding so reasonable. Samira felt sick, suddenly seeing for the first time the opulence of all the material comforts here in the villa. Comforts that were well beyond the means of the Turks who lived in the surrounding areas. Indeed, well beyond the means of other doctors she knew. She'd benefited from the foreign hospital, a luxury she hadn't questioned when her baby was born there.

It made sense now, why – in the two years they'd lived here, openly extravagant – there hadn't been a single visit from the police.

With the baby, Natesh, now taking his first steps, the time had arrived.

She retrieved her stash of savings, carefully hidden and amassed over the months, along with the fake passports she'd acquired, and fled with Natesh and Vidu.

As the plane ascended over Ankara, she'd gripped Vidu's hand. Where she was taking him and baby Natesh was to an uncertain future, but away from the danger inherent in Amin's activities. They'd be free, she would make sure of that.

Then Vidu turned to her, and told her something that marked the beginning of the real nightmare — that he was, after all, bringing Amin's work with him.

Blood is thicker than water, she recalled his words that day again, as she turned the tiny wrestling figurine around in her pocket.

They veered away from the direction of Fethiye, into the Kaya Valley. He was here, then. She knew the route. She braced herself for the sharp left that would take them off the road to Kayaköy and through the forest on towards the villa. Almost on the count of three, the jeep veered left.

Friday

Chapter 41

Donna stretched and yawned, and while her guard was down, inadvertently let in a goal. Danny threw down the controller and copied her yawn.

"Call it a night?" said Donna. Her brother-in-law agreed. They'd been playing FIFA Manager, concentrating intently for hours, and now it was two in the morning.

They went around the downstairs rooms, switching off all the lights.

"I really appreciate this, you know," said Donna, as she trudged upstairs, dog-tired.

"No sweat," said Danny at her heels. "And I won't even say a word to Libby. She'll think you kept the place tidy all by yourself."

Donna was genuinely grateful. Libby was due back some time tomorrow, but with the murder investigation growing arms and legs the way it had, there was no chance she'd be able to spend time tidying up, although she did marvel at the mess she'd managed to create during Libby's few days away.

"I'll try and not wake you in the morning," said Donna.

Danny laughed. "It'd take a bomb to wake me. Don't know how you're going to manage getting up, though. You're exhausted."

Donna shrugged. "Somebody's got to do it."

She ruffled his hair as he pushed open the door to the spare room, thinking how glad she was to have him stay over. And not just because of his help with the house. It was just like old times. With a start, she realised that she was feeling content, something she hadn't felt since finding the rose. Having Danny around had helped keep her mind off it, except now she was thinking about it again.

Lying down in bed, she tried to force her mind onto some of the chat she'd enjoyed with Danny, but as she drifted off into a fitful sleep, the image of the rose stayed with her. It grew thorns. Sharp and gnarled, wrapping themselves around her arms, her neck, piercing her skin and glistening with her blood. The petals of the rose formed a grotesque grin, bleeding lips taunting her, and glaring eyes. Eyes she knew and abhorred. She struggled to move out of their gaze, away from the sneer, but she couldn't move, caught fast by the creeping thorns. The more she tried to kick and struggle, the sharper the thorns tore through her flesh.

"Donna!"

Donna sprang up, startled by Libby's voice. Momentarily disoriented, she stared blankly at Libby, then jumped to her feet and clasped her close. She realised her heart was racing and that she was fighting panic.

"He's been in here," she said. "Evanton left that rose, it must have been him."

"What?"

As Donna's conscious mind regained clarity, she was relieved to find that Libby hadn't caught her rambling words.

"I'm sorry," she said, slowing her breathing and using all her energy to still her careering mind. "Bad dream. Anyway, am I late for work?"

"I got a seat on the earlier flight," said Libby, "so...Surprise! I'm home!"

A noise like a cow mooing with a sore throat erupted from the spare room. Libby jumped.

"Oh, Danny stayed the night," said Donna.

"I thought as much," Libby grinned. "You left FIFA running, and all the downstairs lights are blazing."

"What?"

"The downstairs lights...Donna, are you okay? You've gone awfully pale."

Donna's breath caught in her throat as she felt her skin grow clammy and her head go dizzy. She clearly remembered switching everything off downstairs. And she was pretty sure Danny wouldn't have woken, gone down there, and switched it all back on.

"Look, I'll be honest," Libby said, sitting down on the edge of the bed. "You didn't sound so good when I was speaking to you on the phone. I thought maybe going back to work, straight into a murder investigation, maybe I shouldn't have gone away on that course. I re-arranged my flight to get back as soon as I could."

Donna's heart was racing. The rose. Now the lights. What was she going to tell Libby? *Oh, while you were away, Jonas Evanton's been dropping by*. Was there really no other explanation? She was aware of Libby staring at her while she sat trying to think of what she should say.

But there was no option.

Donna took a deep breath. "There's something I need to talk to you about."

Libby's face grew pale.

"I think he's back," said Donna. She watched, her heart aching, as she saw the range of emotions crumple Libby's face.

"You mean Jonas Evanton, don't you?"

Donna nodded, *yes*.

"What makes you think that?" There was denial in Libby's voice. "I mean, there's been a huge manhunt going on now since he escaped. There's no way he'd risk coming back here. Is there?"

"He doesn't like unfinished business," said Donna. "And I think he'll be so consumed by the need for revenge that he's not going to be acting rationally."

A moment of silence hung between them. Libby's brows formed a tight knot on her forehead. "What are you basing this on?" she asked, finally.

"We're looking for the same killer in the Eleanor Wallace and Moira Cowan cases," said Donna. "Evanton was the SIO in the Eleanor Wallace case, and I've found out he tampered with the evidence."

"But that doesn't necessarily mean..."

"That's what Ross said."

"You've told Ross about this?" Libby's voice rose an octave and her eyes widened.

"It's more than that," said Donna. "I can't really explain, but I've got this feeling. I can *feel* him. He's here."

Libby let out a sigh, and let her gaze slip to the floor. Donna knew what she was thinking.

"It's not my imagination," she said. "On Tuesday night, there was a rose lying on our pillow – the one I thought you had left. But you hadn't. And last night, Danny and I switched off all the lights. I made sure of it."

She felt the jolt. And knew that Libby believed her.

Chapter 42

Donna's head began to buzz as she drove through Dundee. The rush hour traffic had been and gone, and the sun was midway in its travels up the eastern sky. A pleasant winter's day promised, dry at least, but clouds gathered in Donna's thoughts as she remembered the shocked expression on Libby's face after she'd told her about the rose and the lights and her conviction that Evanton was behind the disturbing acts. She was investigating a murder that had Evanton written all over it, hiding evidence that linked Eleanor Wallace's shooting to Abram Kozel. She just hoped he hadn't managed to get to Christine Avery, potentially the only person who might have known what Eleanor Wallace had been doing at Craigie Drive.

The local radio station was, understandably, giving the story a high profile, and every newsagent she passed displayed the developing situation for all to see, now that she'd confirmed to the press that there was a link between the two murders and that Evanton had tampered with evidence in the Eleanor Wallace case. If Evanton hadn't scared Christine Avery off, there was a chance that all this publicity would have.

She had to brake suddenly to avoid running into the car in front of her, and took a deep breath to focus her attention. She ignored the other driver's obscene hand gesture, but she couldn't stop her eyes darting here and there, looking for a glimpse of him in the shadows.

You're clever, Evanton, she muttered to herself, *but not that clever. God help you when I find you – and I will.*

She pulled up in her parking space at Bell Street, and decided to take a walk round by the front entrance, have a look at anyone who might be sitting in the visitor car park. As she walked around the barrier that separated the two areas, her heart sank. A group of around a dozen journalists were jostling for space at the front doors. She caught Adam Ridout's eye, and he darted from among his colleagues to join her.

"This has nothing to do with me, honestly," he said, slightly out of breath.

Donna motioned for him to walk with her as she lit a cigarette and offered another to him.

"The jungle drums are saying Moira Cowan's ex husband has been picked up for questioning," he went on. "Is that right? Is he a suspect?"

"Are you serious?" said Donna. "I didn't know that. Off the record."

"The sources are pretty reliable," said Adam.

"Shit," said Donna. She stubbed out her cigarette, and turned back towards the station. She marched ahead of Adam, and whispered back to him, "Thanks for the heads-up. And I haven't forgotten I promised you a trade. I'll give you a call later on." She winked at him, then kept her head down as she passed the rest of the journalists, ignoring their questions as she went inside.

When she strode into the team room, several uniformed officers sprang back to let her pass. She aimed straight for the far end of the room, where Akwasi was standing in front of the white board. Fran was sitting at a desk next to it, flipping through some paperwork, and looked up with a start that alerted Akwasi. He swung round, and his eyes opened wide at the expression on Donna's face.

Alice and Morrison were huddled in discussion in the corner of the room, but abruptly stopped talking when they saw Donna.

"Moira Cowan's ex husband is in?" Donna demanded, throwing her bag and jacket down on Fran's desk. Fran jumped. "Well? Is he?"

"He's just been brought in," said Alice, moving to place herself between Donna and the other officers.

"And I had to fucking find out from the press?" said Donna.

"Calm your pants," said Alice. There was a stifled snigger behind them. "It wasn't us who picked him up. It was Aiden Moore doing the rounds in Arbroath. He found Cowan trying to stuff a bag of cocaine into a drainpipe, and he thought you'd be interested in having a shot at him."

"Really?"

"He tried to phone you," said Alice. "But he's through there with Cowan just now."

"Well, why didn't you bloody say?" Donna muttered, patting down her pockets and taking out her phone. Sure enough, there was a string of missed calls. She flipped the silent mode off. A small smile crept to the corner of her mouth. She would always be pleased to see Aiden Moore.

"Might want to let Cowan stew a while," said Akwasi. "Apparently he's not a happy bunny."

"Besides," Alice chipped in, "you've got another visitor. You asked for Rory Thomson?"

Donna tutted. What was it that was niggling her about Thomson? He wasn't the killer, she was convinced of that. But there was something about him. Something that was tangled up in all of this. Surely he couldn't be working with Evanton?

"Tell Aiden I'll be with him as soon as I've dealt with Rory Thomson," she told Alice, as she scooped up his file that was lying on Fran's desk.

As she walked to the interview room, she mulled over the possibility. Evanton could certainly oil an ego like Thomson's to carry out some of his dirty work. And it certainly fit with the way he would work. Manipulating. Hiding.

She strode into the room, and banged the door shut behind her. She locked eyes with Thomson, and saw the expression on his face change to confusion and then to alarm. By the time she reached the table, he was beginning to edge backwards from it in his chair.

"Where is he?" she demanded.

"What? Who?" Thomson whined.

"Don't piss with me, Thomson," said Donna. "What has he promised you? Or has he threatened you? That's more his style."

"Ma'am," cut in the uniformed officer in the room. He wore a worried frown. "We need to record the details…"

"Sod the recorder," said Donna. "For once, he's not going to confess to anything. Are you?"

Thomson looked at the uniformed officer in alarm. The officer hesitated, then returned to his seat in the corner of the room.

"Where is he?" she demanded again.

Thomson gulped, and a sweat formed across his forehead. "I don't know who you're talking about."

Donna slammed the file down on the table. Thomson stood up and took a step backwards. The uniformed officer craned his neck to see the file.

"I really don't," Thomson garbled. "Who are you talking about?"

For each step that Donna took into his personal space, Thomson took a step away, until they looked as though they were practising some strange ballroom dance around the small space.

"Make no mistake, Thomson," she said, her voice a hiss in his face, "you'll regret crossing me far more than you'll ever regret grassing him up."

Thomson's eyes were wide, and Donna saw his expression change again. Almost imperceptible, but looking at her as if he didn't recognise her. She felt momentarily unnerved by it, but couldn't explain the sensation. She had to get out of here, clear her head and think rationally.

She turned to the uniformed officer. "He's here to volunteer a set of DNA samples. The doctor should be here any time." And over her shoulder to Thomson, "Don't even think about refusing permission for the blood sample."

Thomson glared back at her, indignation in his eyes as he wiped the sweat from his forehead by dabbing at it with a white cotton handkerchief.

When Donna left the room, she saw the doctor heading towards her.

"You're quick off the mark," she said.

"Your lot's been keeping me busy in here this morning," said the doctor. He nodded towards the interview room. "Bloods, I believe?"

"Make it hurt," said Donna, and she went on her way.

Back in the team room, she pulled a chair to Fran's desk and leaned in, conspiratorial.

Fran's eyebrows piqued.

"I want you to follow Rory Thomson."

"Seriously?"

"He knows where Evanton is," said Donna, choosing to ignore Fran's expression of doubt. "Follow him, and when you see him make contact with anyone who could possibly be Evanton, get back to me straight away. Do not approach either of them, is that clear?"

"Yes."

"Once you give me a location," Donna went on, "I'll get a full team out."

"Where is Thomson now?" asked Fran.

"Interview Room 3," said Donna. "He'll be with the doc for about another twenty minutes. Be discreet."

Fran silently gathered her belongings and slunk from the room.

Donna looked around the room. Most of the officers were on the phones.

Alice and Morrison were gone.

"Hold the fort here," she told Akwasi. "I'm going to talk to DCI Ross."

Chapter 43

Ross was on his phone when Donna went into his office. He gave her a quick wave, and she sat down opposite him. Talking things over with him would help, but she decided not to say anything about telling Fran to tail Rory Thomson. Best to keep that one quiet. Just for now.

"So," said Ross once he was off the phone. "I hear we've got Moira Cowan's ex husband in?"

"Well, I'm glad somebody told *you*."

Ross raised his eyebrows. "How are you playing it? Do you think he's going to know who the Latino is?"

"Not likely," said Donna. "Moira only met the mystery guy for the first time on Sunday night, according to the midwives. Nothing from the nightclub, by the way, their CCTV is gubbed. But we've a lead on somebody who might know. Eleanor Wallace was friendly with a Christine Avery, who left the midwifery unit shortly after Eleanor was murdered." She saw Ross jot the name down on a pad of paper. "We know Eleanor was seeing this guy on the quiet, and chances are she would have confided in her friend Christine."

"But she left the midwifery unit? To go where?"

"Working on it."

"Okay," said Ross, "so, what else?"

"The bullet we found in Craigie Drive is confirmed as being linked to Kozel. I'm having links to prostitution, trafficking, that sort of thing, checked out."

"With Kozel's gang?" said Ross. "Doesn't sound like his thing, but you're right. It definitely looks like he's in the middle of all this."

There was a second of silence between them.

"Is there anything yet on Samira Chaudrakar?" Donna asked. "I'm asking for my own benefit, not to step on Alice's toes. I need to know."

"I understand," said Ross. He coughed awkwardly. "Have you spoken to Alice about her door to door yesterday?"

"No," said Donna, alerted to Ross's discomfort.

Ross stood up. "Do you want a coffee?"

"Am I going to need one?"

"Probably."

She sat fidgeting while Ross fetched a couple of coffees from his Tassimo. He placed the cups down carefully on his desk, and eased himself back into his seat.

Donna looked uneasy. "What happened?"

"Alice interviewed the neighbours," said Ross, "and they saw Mrs Chaudrakar leaving her address. Carrying a suitcase. With a man. Shortly after she disappeared from work."

"A suitcase? But that doesn't..." Donna scratched at her head. "Is there a description of the man?"

"There's more than that," said Ross. He slid a grainy still from CCTV footage across the desk for her to see. Donna looked in close, then bounced back in her chair, letting out a gasp of surprise.

"That's Natesh," she said. She looked up at Ross. "What has this got to do with Samira disappearing? My God, Angus, you're not trying to tell me..."

"This is from footage looking onto the ATM on City Street, just off Scott Street," said Ross. He spoke over Donna's protests. "We've got Samira making a cash withdrawal around ten minutes after the neighbour said he saw her leaving with the suitcase. And the man. The neighbour also identified him as Natesh."

Donna picked up the picture and stared at it.

"I'm sorry," said Ross, "but it does look as though she left with Natesh. Is there anywhere you can tell me they might have gone?"

"No, Angus, this isn't right," said Donna. "Natesh was worried sick about his mother disappearing. It was him that reported her missing."

"Look, I know he's your friend..."

"He's been my best friend most of my life." Donna's voice was rising. "I know him. There's no way he has anything to do with this. No way."

"Like I said yesterday," said Ross, "you're too close to this case. Let Alice handle it. But we've a call out for Natesh, to bring him in. So, any contact you have with him, I need to know."

Donna's face was pale now. She slumped back in her chair, miserable.

"I'm sorry," said Ross. "I know this can't be easy for you to take in."

"There's nothing to take in," said Donna. "Whatever you think is going on here," she tapped the CCTV picture, "Natesh is innocent. He has nothing to do with any of this. And you can stop looking at me with the pity. I'm going to show you."

"Leave this one to Alice," said Ross. "That's an order. And it's not often I feel brave enough to give you an order. Now, go and deal with Peter Cowan."

Ross dismissed her from the room, and scooped up a set of papers from his desk as she left.

Donna made her way along to the interview room containing Moira Cowan's ex husband. She had almost reached the room, when she realised she was in no fit state to interview anyone. She had to get her head together. A smoke. She needed a smoke.

Quickly turning towards the nearest fire exit, she tried Natesh's number, and although she fully expected to hear the voicemail message, she still cursed at it when she heard it.

Her thoughts alternated between outright denial that it could have been Natesh in the CCTV picture, to a sick dread that there was something going on with him that she couldn't explain.

He'd clearly been very agitated on Wednesday, when she'd met him for brunch, thinking something had happened to Samira. That hadn't been faked, even if Natesh was capable of fooling her. There was no way he knew Samira had left. But then, when she'd spoken to him on the phone that night, she'd felt discomfited, thinking at the time that she'd disturbed him and Erin. But had Erin really been there at the time? Before she realised what she was doing, she was looking up Erin's number.

"Hello?" Erin's voice sounded neutral. She certainly didn't sound worried about anything.

"Is Natesh with you?" asked Donna. There was no point in the pleasantries.

"No, he only heard about the funeral at the last minute," she said. "I couldn't get time off to go with him."

"Funeral?" asked Donna. "What funeral?"

"A relative of his down south," said Erin, her voice betraying her surprise at Donna not knowing. "Didn't you know?"

"When did he leave?"

"Wednesday night," said Erin.

Donna thought quickly. "Sorry," she said, "it's been a long week." The call ended awkwardly. There was no funeral for a relative down south, Donna knew. Why had Natesh told Erin that there was? What was going on, then, on Wednesday night when Donna had phoned him? Her chest was tight.

She lit a cigarette, feeling instantly calmer. She made a note to send a couple of officers round to talk to Erin in more detail, for the record. She stood watching the journalists milling around the entrance to the building, from her vantage point at the fire exit, but didn't see Adam there any more. By the time she'd finished the cigarette, she felt sure in her own mind that she would get to the bottom of what had happened to Natesh, that it was going to be okay. She turned her thoughts to Peter Cowan, and made her way back inside.

She knocked on the interview room door and walked in.

She barely glanced at the dishevelled creature that sat in the room. Instead, the uniformed officer who stood beside him caught her eye.

"Hello, Aiden," she grinned.

Aiden beamed back at her. "Donna."

"I'm glad you're here," she told him. "And thanks for bringing this one in. Come on, sit with me."

They sat down at the table, facing Peter Cowan.

He looked up, making brief eye contact with each of them.

Donna watched his shaking hands as he tried to hold them clasped on the table in front of himself. She saw the beads of sweat across his forehead, and the damp patches around his grubby t-shirt. This was a scared man.

Donna reached round to switch on the tape recorder, introduced the session, and turned again towards Peter Cowan.

"Where were you on Sunday night?"

Cowan screwed up his eyes. "I don't know."

"End of the week," said Donna. "What do you normally do on a Sunday?"

Cowan shifted in his seat. "I don't know. Fuck sake, I can't remember."

The sweating was more than fear, Donna saw. Cowan needed a fix.

"Heroin?" she asked.

Cowan drew his palm across his brow. "Please, I need it now," he whined. "Methadone, anything, know?"

"When's the last time you saw Moira?"

"What?" Cowan's head snapped up, and Donna saw the confusion etched in his expression. "She doesn't use."

"Did you see her on Sunday night?" Donna asked, already sensing she knew the answer.

"I've not seen Moira for months," said Cowan. "Bitch threw me out, didn't she? Won't let me near the house, even though half the stuff…"

"Did you kill your ex-wife?"

Cowan sneered. "I will if she won't fucking let me have my stuff back." Then he stopped and looked at Donna, utter astonishment taking over his face. "What are you saying?" he demanded.

"Moira was found dead on Monday morning," said Donna. Her voice was softer now.

Cowan's mouth formed a grotesque band across his face, and tears welled in his eyes. "Moira's dead?" His voice cracked. A sob shook his shoulders, and he clutched at his chest. He stood up. Donna felt Aiden tense himself beside her. "No!" It was almost a wail. "Don't say that," he whined. "Don't fucking say stuff like that!"

"I'm sorry," said Donna. "I thought you knew."

Cowan sank back into his seat. The tremor in his hands was more marked now, and his clammy skin had grown a shade paler.

"Moira's dead?"

Donna could see it wasn't an act. The information had come as a shock to Cowan.

"Was Moira involved with anyone lately, that you know of?" she asked. Cowan looked at her, but he was staring at something inside his own shattered mind. He shook his head.

Donna placed the CCTV picture on the table in front of Cowan. Aiden crooked his neck to take a look. "Have you seen this man before?"

Cowan's face blanched, and his eyes quickly flashed from the photograph to meet Donna's gaze.

"Bitch!" he shouted, getting to his feet again. "You're fucking trying to get me to grass him up, I fucking knew it. What kind of fucking twisted thing is that to say about Moira?"

"Calm down, Mr Cowan," said Donna, also standing up. She was a head taller than him. Still, he squared up to her, clearly angry, a man who thought he was being conned. Aiden stood up to assist Donna, but she waved him back, continuing to stare down Cowan.

"I don't care about your habit or your dealers, Peter," she said calmly. "But somebody killed Moira, and we think he's got someone else now. We need to find him before there's another victim." She held up the picture again. Cowan recoiled from it, and sat heavily onto his chair. Donna matched his actions and took her seat.

"Did he kill her? Was it him?" His voice came in gasps now.

"Who is he?"

"Never seen him," Cowan whispered, a fraction before Donna had finished asking.

"Come on, Peter." She wanted to grasp him by the shoulders and shake him. But she wasn't sure she could handle him identifying Natesh.

She got up and left the room, leaving Peter Cowan slumped with his head on the table.

Aiden hurried out behind her.

"Who's the guy in the picture?" he asked.

Donna paused to think. "Somebody that Peter Cowan's scared of, that's for sure," she said. She looked at it again. It certainly resembled Natesh, but that could be because he was the closest match to the man in the picture that they already knew. The guy in the picture might be anyone who looked like Natesh. It just wasn't clear enough. It could equally, Donna thought, be one of Kozel's men. That would explain Peter Cowan's fear, since he would almost certainly be getting his drugs from the Russian's gang.

Donna's phone rang, and Aiden watched her intently as she acknowledged the information she was being given.

"Thanks, Thomas," she said into the phone. "Come down to Interview Room 2 with one of the DIs. I need you to turn the screws on Peter Cowan. He knows the identity of someone we could be interested in."

She turned to Aiden. "Can I give you a lift back to Arbroath?" she asked. "I'm off to interview Christine Avery. We've traced her to your patch."

Chapter 44

"Thanks for this," said Donna as she got out of her car. They'd run into the afternoon school traffic but arrived at the small housing scheme next to Arbroath Academy in good time. Curtains twitched at windows, and kids lingered at the corner of the street, surreptitiously watching the tall DI and the uniformed Aiden Moore as they emerged into the cul de sac.

"Glad to be involved," said Aiden. "I've been looking forward to the chance of working with you."

They made their way to number four, and Donna rapped on the door.

A light came on in the hallway of the house, and a woman in her thirties opened the door. She looked surprised as Donna introduced herself and Aiden, then a little alarmed.

"Do you mind if we come in and have a word with you?" asked Donna, after confirming that this was Christine Avery.

"Is it Billy?" Christine asked immediately. "Has something happened?"

"No," said Donna. "We think you might be able to help us with some information, that's all. Nothing to be worried about."

Christine looked relieved, and then she showed Donna and Aiden into a spacious kitchen.

"Can I make you a tea or coffee?"

"No thanks," said Aiden.

"That would be lovely," said Donna at the same time. They looked at each other. "Second thoughts," Donna went on, "we'll not be staying that long. Just a couple of questions to ask."

Christine sat down beside them at the kitchen table, and Donna recognised a look in her eyes that suggested she already suspected they were here to ask about Eleanor Wallace.

"We're investigating a murder that we believe to be linked with Eleanor Wallace's murder," said Donna.

Christine's hand went to her throat, but she didn't say anything.

"Am I correct in thinking you were a friend of Eleanor's?" asked Donna.

"Yes," Christine nodded her head. "Yes, I was."

"We're trying to find out about the man Eleanor was seeing before she died," said Donna.

"I…I don't know anything about that." She licked her lips rapidly.

Donna and Aiden exchanged a glance.

Donna leaned across the table towards Christine.

"Did he threaten you?" she asked. "Make you leave your job and hide away here like a hermit?"

Christine made brief eye contact with Donna, then looked at her feet again and said nothing. Her shoulders were tense.

"He's killed again," Donna said quietly. "And now a third woman has gone missing. Any information you have could really help us bring her home safely."

"A woman is missing?" Christine asked.

Donna and Aiden remained quiet.

Christine began to fidget. Then she gave into the compulsion to end the growing silence. "She'd only been seeing him a few weeks, when…when she thought something wasn't right."

"What made her think that?" asked Donna.

Christine looked nervously around the kitchen, and her attention lingered on the window, as if she was afraid they were being watched. She shook her head vigorously. "I can't say…I don't know."

She reached for a packet of cigarettes, and looked surprised when Donna accepted one when she offered it.

"Look, nobody has to know the information came from you," said Donna.

Christine chuckled, her cynicism obvious. "The whole street's just seen two cops come into my house," she said.

"Who's Billy?" asked Donna.

"What?" Christine stiffened.

"When we came to the door, you asked straight away if we were here about Billy."

"He's my boyfriend," said Christine. "He's been in trouble a couple of times. Nothing serious. Why?"

Donna shrugged as she exhaled some smoke. "It'd be a good excuse to tell people why we were here. Any information you can give us about Eleanor's guy won't be attributed to you. Anyone asks, we'll say we came here looking for Billy. And, I suppose, one good turn deserves another, don't you think, Aiden?"

Aiden, though caught off guard, kept his composure. "I'm sure we can think of something."

This time Christine held eye contact with Donna. Slowly, the muscles in her shoulders began to relax.

"She never told me his name," she said. She stubbed out her cigarette into a glass ashtray sitting on the table. "He was married. But she got scared of him. Out of the blue one day, he said his sister was pregnant, and asked Eleanor to go and see her." Christine was on a roll now, and couldn't stop talking. Aiden was scribbling furiously into his notebook.

"I remember Eleanor telling me she thought it was weird."

"Did the supposed sister live in Craigie Drive?" asked Donna.

Christine's eyes widened. "How did you know that?"

"I'm a hot shot detective," said Donna. "Why did Eleanor think it was weird?"

"Well, the guy was pretty well off, according to Eleanor," said Christine. "But his sister lived in this shitty little place. When Eleanor went to visit, there were two men in the flat and another two women. None of the women spoke at all while she was there. Eleanor thought they were foreign, but the men were local, or hereabouts. She was surprised the pregnant woman wasn't already linked in with a midwife, especially as she was really young and this was her first baby. She told me the whole thing felt like a sham, maybe prostitutes being brought into the flat to see through their pregnancy."

"Did she or you have any experience with that kind of thing?" asked Donna.

Christine shook her head. "We'd heard of it happening in other places – Glasgow, Edinburgh – but never expected to come across it here."

"I take it she confronted her lover about it?" asked Donna.

"She did," said Christine. A pained, faraway cloud shaped her expression. "That's when he got nasty, told her just to see to his *sister* and not to tell anyone about it."

"She agreed to that?"

"She was scared," said Christine. "After that, she didn't say very much, but it was obvious he'd threatened her."

"Did she tell you anything about the other people in the flat?"

asked Donna. "Any names? Anything at all that we could follow up? We really need to find this guy."

Christine thought for several minutes, lighting another cigarette as she did. Donna could tell she was trying hard to remember any detail that she could. Finally, Christine tapped a finger on the table.

"She did mention one name," she said. "Juanita. I'm sure it was Juanita. As far as I can remember – and it's all pretty hazy, so don't quote me on it – but I'm sure Eleanor said she thought this Juanita worked the streets in Aberdeen. It kind of rings a bell with me now, because they tend to be Russian or Eastern European, don't they?"

Donna made a note of the information in her own notebook. She had to agree. There weren't many Juanitas working Aberdeen, not amongst all the Natashas. She'd send a couple of uniforms up to liaise with the cops there. If any such woman existed, she could be the one to lift the lid on what had been going on at Craigie Drive, as long as she wasn't scared shitless.

Juanita

One day, soon after I'd begged Dr. Amin to let me go with him to learn how to clean the big houses, he came back to the fence. There had been some rain, and the camp had turned into a mud bath. We were shivering from the cold, and I found my mother weeping in the tent, unable to cope with the thought of another winter there.

As soon as I saw Dr. Amin, my heart leaped, and I forgot all about the mud and the cold.

I told one of my aunts. To my surprise, she was overcome with joy at the prospect of my getting out. She told me, if I had the chance, I had to take it. I promised her that I would work hard and save up the money to bring them out. We fantasised about having our very own smallholding in Dr. Amin's town, beside the azure sea.

I was one of eight girls that were to leave with him that night. As I'd seen before, when it was time to go, the fence guard looked the other way, and we clambered onto the jeep.

The journey across country was uncomfortable, and after a while, surprisingly boring – endless flat plains. One the first night, the driver stopped for a few hours' rest in the jeep by the side of the road, but none of us got much sleep. It was daylight the next day by the time we reached Dr. Amin's town. Fethiye, I later learned.

I was surprised, but delighted, to find that not only were we to stay in his town, but actually in his home. It was a villa with a paddock, a large yard, and surrounded by high walls. He told us we were free to come and go, in and out of the compound, around the town. Free!

We lived there for around a year. We were happy, confident, well-fed. You have no idea how wonderful that was for us.

Dr. Amin did give us some rules. He was keen for us to receive an education, and he arranged for us to learn English. He was very strict about making sure we attended the English lessons. But the rules made us happy, too, because we knew he was looking after us.

Now that I think of it, it was clever of him. After all, the police wouldn't be looking for happy young women who came and went as they pleased, would they? I suppose they would be looking for women who appeared to be abused or terrified. Yes, very clever.

A year passed quickly in the compound. We were kept busy with English lessons, and learning how to shop, to cook, to clean, and to mend clothes. The eight of us who'd arrived together tended to go to the markets in Fethiye together, although we were never told that we couldn't go out on our own.

There were two American men and a Russian who came to the compound from time to time. We learned that these were the men who would accompany us to Europe.

Dr. Amin explained that the Europeans didn't like refugees from the camps, and that Turkish security were keen to stop us from travelling, so as not to upset their European neighbours. So there was a plan. We were to be given passports, with new names. European names, Dr. Amin said, were best. There'd be fewer problems. I chose the name Juanita.

We were to travel with one of the men, pretending we were newly-weds.

To us, it sounded exciting and daring, and never once did any of us think to question Dr. Amin. After all, he'd rescued us and looked after us all this time. We'd have done anything for him.

Chapter 45

Fran had put some thought into this. She'd changed into her gym gear, and stood at the front desk, bag slung over her shoulder, looking bored. Rory Thomson was not going to suspect she was a cop. She'd already warned the officer at the desk to ignore her as she was undercover. The officer occasionally glanced up at her and guffawed, but played along, and soon forgot about her for real when an indignant Rory Thomson arrived to complain loudly about the appalling way he'd been treated *in there*. All the while, Fran made a show of blethering on her phone, being somebody who was not in the least bit interested in following Thomson. Even though her heart was hammering her entire rib cage and her cheeks were flushing crimson.

Thomson, having made his scene, straightened his jacket and left the building. The officer on the desk smirked and raised an eyebrow at Fran as she sauntered into the car park, some way behind but within sight.

Watching Thomson retrieve his car keys from his pocket, Fran felt a twinge of panic. She'd left hers on her desk. She knew he'd be gone by the time she got her own car from the back of the building, and was pondering her options when, to her relief, Thomson put the keys back in his pocket and marched off towards the pedestrian exit. This was her lucky day. It looked like Thomson was so pissed off that he was going for a drink. Or maybe Donna was right. Maybe he was going to meet Jonas Evanton. Fran felt the adrenaline rush as she held back the urge to sprint after him. She had to be clever about this. He couldn't suspect he was being followed. As she watched him over the top of her phone, and inched her way across the car park so as to keep Thomson in view, she could picture the commendation she would receive for being the one to find Evanton, the cop-killing traitor they'd all been hunting for so long. *Oh yeah*, she thought, she'd make DI in no time.

She watched Thomson as he strode out of the gates and past the burger van. Wherever he was going, he was in a hurry. *Like he might be going to meet someone*, she thought.

She made her way to the edge of the burger van, keeping well back from Thomson, but never letting him out of her sight. Then she heard Takeshi's voice ringing out from the van.

"Well, if it isn't my favourite detective!" he called.

"Shush" she tried to quieten him, terrified he would make Thomson turn around and spot her. But Takeshi went on, undeterred.

"What is it you say here, I didn't recognise you without your clothes!"

Despite herself, Fran giggled. She enjoyed the moment imagining Takeshi's dark eyes roaming over her unclothed body.

He leaned across the burger counter and grinned at her.

"You know," he said in that voice that made her tummy flip, "I wonder what you would wear out to dinner?"

"Are you asking?"

"Is that a yes?" He beamed at her.

They stood grinning hopelessly at one another, then Fran suddenly looked up. Thomson was gone. Her heart raced, now with dread. In every direction she frantically looked, Thomson was still gone. Shit!

"Sorry, Takeshi," she said quickly, "I need to go." And she sprinted off down Marketgait in the direction she'd seen Thomson going only a moment ago. But he was nowhere in sight. Vanished. He could have gone along Douglas Street, or up by the roundabout. Hell, he could be sitting in any one of the cafes that she'd just run past. Or maybe his car had been parked out here and he was long gone. Damn! What was she going to tell Donna now?

Chapter 46

Donna arrived at Scott Street, after dispatching two officers up to Aberdeen to look for Juanita, the woman mentioned by Christine Avery as a potential witness to the events that had taken place in Craigie Drive.

"How do you want to play this one, Chief?" asked Alice.

Eyes were peering at them from windows all around Natesh's front door, the front door Donna had gone through countless times for as far back as she could remember. The doorsteps she'd skinned her childhood knees on, sat beside the boy Natesh as they'd chalked pictures and studied ants. Been shooed off to play by an irate Mrs Chaudrakar.

The memories flooded her thoughts all of a sudden in that moment, while her team stood ready for action at her word.

"Do one room at a time," said Donna. "Morrison, do the measurements with Emma. Fingerprints, samples, photos, the works. Akwasi, secure the front door after we go in. The back garden's covered." If there was anyone in the flat, they weren't getting out unobserved.

One of the officers prepared his stance, ready to force the door open.

"No need," said Donna, stepping forward. She handed the perplexed officer a key, and gestured for him to unlock the door.

It seemed like an anti-climax, opening the door with a key, and as soon as it swung open, it became clear to all of the team assembled that the flat was empty. Abandoned.

The first thing that Donna became aware of was an assault on her nostrils from Harry Potter's malodorous litter tray. She knew it lay in the kitchen, at the far end of the flat, and never once in all the years she'd come here had she known the litter tray to smell at all. Mrs Chaudrakar always kept it spotless. Which meant it couldn't have been Natesh she'd left here with – Samira would never have left the litter tray like that unless she believed he would still be home to see to it. But who would believe that? She was going to have to trust Alice to come up with the evidence.

"No-one's been here for at least a day," she said. No-one

questioned her.

They moved further into the flat.

"The living room," said Donna, pulling on gloves. She stopped abruptly by the door, seeing the torn envelope addressed to Natesh. She went to pick it up, then felt an odd lurch in her stomach, suddenly feeling like she was going to be sick. She had to leave this to Alice.

"Over here," she managed to say. "This is definitely unusual. Check it out." She took a deep breath before continuing, and noted that the rest of the living room looked normal. "We need a thorough search of the chest of drawers there, the cupboard, under the rug, everything. We need to know who's been here, other than the Chaudrakars, Erin and me. And anything that can shed light on where they've gone, or why they might have left." She clapped her hands twice. "Get to it."

A hum of low level murmury began to fill the room as the team worked across it inch by inch, moving methodically from one end to the other. Donna left them to lifting, looking, removing, bagging, recording and commenting, as she paced the room's perimeter, scanning every surface for any clue at all. She was surprised by the amount of material being removed from the familiar surrounds.

"I need to go and speak to Fran," she told Alice. She knew, as Alice did, that her conflict of interest was making the officers on the search uneasy. Alice nodded her approval, and Donna told the officer at the door that she was leaving the scene. He quickly updated his list and waved her through the door.

On her drive back to Bell Street, she felt the anchor of her life-long friendship with Natesh suddenly shift. How was he involved in all of this? What had she failed to notice? But the anchor held firm after all, and she found herself fearing for his safety. Whatever he'd become involved in, she knew in her heart it wasn't of his doing.

When she got to the team room at Bell Street, Fran was sitting quietly at her desk, her face red.

"Er, let me go and get you a coffee," Fran said as soon as she saw Donna. Donna had no time to reply as Fran zipped out of the room.

Donna's heart sank, guessing that the reason for Fran's

demeanour and her lack of update during the day meant she must have lost Thomson. How, she had to hear. Her mobile rang.

"You should know," Alice said to her when she answered it. "We found some baby clothes in Mrs Chaudrakar's room. Could be Natesh's from when he was a baby, but they look fairly new. And they were hidden under floorboards."

Donna's heart sank again. "Good work," she managed. "Report directly to Ross on this one, but keep me in the loop, yeah?"

"Understood," said Alice. "Best to keep yourself right."

"He's innocent," Donna whispered to her. She could almost feel Alice's pity bleed across the static.

Saturday

Chapter 47

Donna stared at the picture of Natesh, and handed it back to Ross.

"Do it," she said. "But I can guarantee you, he's not the guy. Something's happened to him."

"I understand," said Ross.

"I really don't think you do," said Donna. "I've known Natesh almost all our lives. He isn't the guy. We need to be worrying about him, not treating him like a suspect."

"I get that," said Ross. "You know I've always liked Natesh. But you have to admit, it's not looking good for him, is it?"

Donna hunched her shoulders.

"What about his mother?" Ross was on the ball this morning.

Donna thought back to that evening in the kitchen with Samira. She'd been hiding something. Had Donna avoided following it up because she was too close to the family?

"I'm not so sure," she conceded. "I got the feeling the other night that she knew something about what was going on."

She thought back again to Monday night. The night when all this investigation was about was a routine ID of a Jane Doe. How had it turned into this nightmare? Linked to another murder. A dead baby. Kozel's gang. Evanton.

"Something she could have dragged her son into?" asked Ross.

"No," Donna's thoughts returned to the present. "Natesh would've told me."

"But he didn't tell you he was leaving?"

Donna chewed her nail. She knew there was a piece of this puzzle that couldn't be deduced. How were they going to find it?

"For the record, Donna," said Ross, "I need to know some things about Natesh's background."

Donna nodded.

"How long has he lived at that address?"

"As far as I'm aware," said Donna, "since shortly after birth. But you'll have to check that. Certainly since 1986, the year before we both started school."

"Anyone else ever lived there with them?"

"No," said Donna. "Just Natesh and his mother. She fled the

civil war in Sri Lanka when Natesh was a baby. His father was killed there. I never knew of any other relatives. Mrs Chaudrakar certainly never made mention of anyone she kept in touch with."

Ross was jotting down the details as Donna spoke.

"What about relationships?" he asked. "Did she have anyone?"

"No," said Donna. "She always kept herself very much to herself. Come to think of it, she was always a bit of a hermit. She went to work, then home every night. Never an exception."

Something was stirring at the back of Donna's mind. She saw it in Ross's eyes, too, when she looked into them.

"Samira Chaudrakar flees the civil war in Sri Lanka following her husband's death," he said. "She's homed in Scott Street, employed in the midwifery unit, and doesn't move from either during 30 years. Doesn't have any contact with her previous life. Doesn't socialise. Have I got that right?"

"About sums it up," said Donna.

Ross leaned forward and rested his chin on steepled fingers. Donna could see in his eyes that he was trying hard to find a plausible story for Samira and Natesh, a reason to be on their side.

"Have you ever verified that she actually did travel from Sri Lanka?" he asked. Donna's heart began to beat faster as she shook her head, *no*. He was onto something. "Any trips back there?"

"Never," said Donna. "Natesh doesn't even have a passport."

"Are you sure about that?" asked Ross.

"Certain," said Donna. "In fact, I was going on about it to him just the other day. No passport."

"Bear with me for a moment," said Ross. "What if the Sri Lanka story was a cover? What if Samira is in hiding here?"

"Witness protection?"

"Let's suppose that's the case," said Ross. "Is it possible that Kozel found out, and has her over a barrel?"

Donna mulled it over. It was certainly possible. "So, Samira either really did flee the civil war in Sri Lanka," she thought out loud, "or she's on a witness protections scheme and that was her cover, until Kozel found out?"

"I'm willing to consider it as a line of enquiry," said Ross. "Look into it, see if it fits. Until then, we can't risk releasing Natesh's picture, just in case."

Donna tried to block out the racing thoughts screaming around inside her head. Witness protection? It might explain some of what was going on, and she was grateful to Ross for the lifeline. But the thoughts of witness protection brought Evanton to the forefront of her conscious mind. He had to be wrapped up in this, somehow. Witness protection or not, Natesh was in danger, she knew it.

"It still doesn't explain why Natesh has disappeared, though," Ross's words swam into her head, and commanded her attention again. "If, as you say, he doesn't have a passport, then he must still be in the country. We'd better check with the Passport Agency anyway." He looked at her for a moment, and flicked his head towards the door. "The sooner the better."

Donna took her opportunity. She had places to go. And the less that Ross knew about what she was planning to do next, the better.

Chapter 48

Donna left her car parked by Arbroath sea front and walked along the sandy path towards the town's High Street. She lit a cigarette as she walked, and enjoyed the feeling of the cool breeze from the sea in her hair. Images, words and arrows tumbled around in her mind, desperately seeking some way to connect, some pattern or formation that would yield any kind of sense.

Moira Cowan, she thought, as she passed behind the football ground and looked over to where the police tape had protected the body washed up on the shore five days ago. What did you know about the baby in Craigie Drive? What story could you have told? Who was it you could have incriminated? Did Peter Cowan inadvertently get you involved? How the hell does he know Natesh, or Natesh's double? Cowan had still refused to tell the police who he thought it was in the CCTV photo.

She stamped out her cigarette, and tapped Natesh's number into her mobile. She knew it was futile, and sure enough, she got the *not available* message.

"Where are you?" she said aloud, anger in her voice. *Why did you just vanish? How does a witness protection scenario play into all of this?* What had Samira been hiding on Monday night? Could she have known what had really happened to Moira and Eleanor?

And Marcus Edridge, her old neighbour. What was his connection to Craigie Drive? Was there a medical connection with the midwives? *My God*, thought Donna, *did he have something to do with removing the baby's organs?*

Rory Thomson, for God's sake. How was he involved?

The only real hope right now of joining all the dots and making sense of who fitted where in this nightmare jigsaw puzzle was to find Juanita, the woman that Christine Avery had mentioned. If any such woman existed, then in all likelihood she was a witness to what had gone on in that flat. Donna knew she'd been lucky to get the resources to send the two uniforms back up to Aberdeen again today to try and find her. She wasn't sure she'd get a third day if they drew another blank.

Christine Avery had been afraid to talk at first. But not terrified.

Donna lit another cigarette as she came to the harbour. She stopped, once again, at the memorial plaque. If Christine Avery wasn't terrified, then at least it meant Jonas Evanton hadn't gotten to her.

Jonas Evanton. She made herself say the name out loud while she stood facing the memorial plaque. She'd heard about his murdering rampage that day, the day he'd slung her bloodied body into his truck and driven it here with his intention of causing massive destruction. The memory was hazy, but she recalled the physical pain of regaining consciousness on the floor of the truck. Of seeing Aiden Moore as he hid out of Evanton's sight, quietly reassuring her that she'd be okay. She remembered the agony of reaching outside the truck door and grasping at Evanton's foot as he attempted to descend from the truck's rooftop and make his escape. How her simple action, taking him by surprise, had led to his falling and his immediate capture. The venom in his eyes while they led him away in handcuffs had promised revenge one day. Revenge that Donna had no doubt he would exact.

Was that really what could be going on now? Or was Ross right about that? Did Evanton's role in all of this end with his meddling in the Eleanor Wallace case to cover up for Abram Kozel? But the rose. The house lights. Donna shuddered as she walked on from the harbour towards the foot of High Street.

He was here, she could feel it in her bones. But how? How was he doing it? At least they were having extra security fitted around the house today.

She blinked when her phone rang.

"Emma?" she answered. "You've got something?"

"Just to rule out Rory Thomson," said Emma. "His DNA doesn't match anything."

Damn! thought Donna. But her instinct was stronger than DNA results. She knew in her marrow that Thomson was part of this, and he was going to be the one to give away Evanton's whereabouts, despite Fran's blunder.

She turned right onto the foot of High Street, and made her way up to *The Bampot*.

Fran still felt the flush of shame on her cheeks. She'd lost Thomson, and the memory of her undignified rush around the vicinity made her squirm.

She was going to have to pull something special out of the bag to impress DI Davenport and salvage her dreams of promotion. As far as she was aware, Donna hadn't talked to the others about her belief that Jonas Evanton was back. Tracking him down herself would give her just the ticket.

With her hands trembling, Fran noted the address, and quickly returned the file. She slipped, unnoticed, from the complex and left Bell Street by a side exit.

In her car now, she read the details from her notebook, and set her SatNav to the address she'd found.

Danny smiled widely and grasped Donna in an embrace as soon as she stepped into *The Bampot*.

"Any update?" he asked.

"We're having the security stuff put in today," said Donna, "and Emma's team are doing a sweep of the place for fingerprints and the like."

Danny whistled. "Does that not freak you out?"

"It's freaking Libby out," said Donna. "But part of her thinks it's me being bonkers, so she'll cope."

"Are you being bonkers?"

"Somebody's been in the house," said Donna. "I'm investigating a high profile murder case. Can't take any chances."

She saw Danny frown, and was glad she hadn't told him that she believed the *somebody* to be Jonas Evanton.

"Anyway," she went on, lightening her voice, "I have a secret rendezvous to be getting on with."

"Over there," Danny grinned, thumbing towards Adam Ridout, who was sitting at a table in the far corner of the restaurant, studying his phone and attempting to look as though he wasn't watching Donna and her brother-in-law.

"I'll pop round later on this evening," said Danny, as Donna made her way to Adam's table.

Adam waved a greeting as she approached. They chatted about mundane things while they decided what to have from the menu. This was the second time in a week that Donna had actually had the privilege of sitting down to a meal during her working hours. Normally she had to make do with grabbing fast food on the go.

She was aware of the family seated nearby, and she leaned towards Adam, speaking quietly, so as to avoid being overheard.

"Okay, so we've already released information that Eleanor Wallace was killed in the flat on Craigie Drive," she said. Adam nodded his head. "And our confirmation that the man linked to her death is the same man we want in connection with Moira Cowan's murder. But we made a crucial discovery at the flat on Thursday evening, and this is what we haven't released yet. We found the body of a newborn baby."

Adam began to respond, but Donna held up a hand to quieten him while she continued. "The initial forensic report confirms the baby's internal organs had been surgically removed."

"My God!"

Donna went on, "The flat was once owned by Dr. Marcus Edridge, a retired Dundee GP, and we're looking into the possibility of his involvement. And we've heard from the midwives that the flat may have been used by prostitutes who got pregnant. Prostitutes having babies, a doctor, midwives, organ removal…God, this is turning into one hell of a case."

Adam reached for his notebook, eager to give Donna some information in return for her candour, but she placed a hand on top of it, stopping him from opening it.

"There's something else more important," she said. "To me."

Adam's pained expression gave away his desperation to know what she was talking about, while their food was served. Once the waitress left them, they huddled back together. To any onlooker, they would appear to be a couple romantically absorbed in one another, not a detective and a journalist swapping secrets in a murder investigation.

"Natesh is in trouble," said Donna.

She knew she'd made the right call when she saw the brief flicker of excitement on Adam's face. He knew something about Natesh, all right.

"Let me spell this out," she continued. "Natesh is my best friend. I know he's innocent of any wrongdoing, but there's a stack of evidence painting a very bad picture."

"In what way?" asked Adam.

"Well, you know Moira Cowan and Eleanor Wallace were both midwives," said Donna. "The other thing we haven't released to the press yet is that Natesh's mother, who works at the midwifery unit, has been reported as missing."

"You have got to be kidding me?" Adam found it hard to disguise his surprise.

Donna shook her head. "I wish I was. We're concerned for her safety."

"Is this on the record?"

"Yes, you can print what's happening, but please don't mention Natesh or Samira by name."

"Got it," said Adam. "How is Natesh in trouble?"

"He's been identified by a witness and on CCTV as having left home with Samira around the time he reported her to be missing."

"But that doesn't make sense."

"You've got that right," said Donna. "Every time we get somewhere with this investigation, it opens a new can of worms. A warrant is out for Natesh's arrest, but I think something's happened to him. Have you heard from him recently?"

Adam was clearly shocked. "Look, Donna, all I know is Natesh phoned me the other day – Thursday, I think – asking me about travel to Turkey."

"Turkey?" Now it was Donna's turn to be astonished.

"Yeah, he gave me some cock and bull story about a trip to do with family history research, and he sounded kind of weird. Not like himself at all, you know?"

"How so?"

Adam screwed up his eyes, thinking back. "I can't believe I didn't press him on it," he said. "I was up to my eyeballs at the time, but I could tell something wasn't right. He was agitated."

"How can Natesh go to Turkey?" said Donna. "He doesn't even have a passport. What exactly did he say to you?"

Adam sat back in his seat, and his gaze fell on the wall behind Donna's shoulder, as he thought back to Natesh's strange phone call.

Here it is, thought Fran, as she rounded the corner onto Kirk Street. She looked up to the windows above the commercial units, then scanned the charming town square to find the doorway that sat between the bank and a pub. Without pausing, she hurried to the door. She pressed the buzzer for the flat, but got no response. She waited a moment before pressing it again. Making sure there was nobody home. Then she pressed the buzzer to the top floor flat.

A muffled voice answered.

"Sorry," Fran spoke into the intercom. "I've forgotten my keys. Could you…"

Before she could finish, she heard a sound of annoyance, then the secure lock was released and she was able to let herself into the building. At least the annoyed neighbour wasn't going to know the police were here snooping.

The heavy door closed silently behind her on well-oiled hinges, but clanged loudly when it locked. The first thing Fran noticed was the pair of fresh curtains hanging on the first-floor window. On the landing stood a table, with a vase of fresh-cut tulips, giving the close the impression of being carefully tended and cared for. The paintwork was precise, the stairs spotless, and the air was pleasantly fragranced.

Who knew? thought Fran, who was more used to dodging used needles in urine-reeked stairwells.

She made her way slowly to the second floor, where her target lived.

She knocked on his door.

No answer.

She peered through the letterbox.

Only silence, no movement inside.

Fran wiped her forehead, and glanced back down the stairs. There was nobody about. Keenly aware that she had no warrant, Fran slipped on her latex gloves and took her bank card out of her pocket. She slid the card into the space between the Yale lock and the door frame, pushed it as far into the crack as it would go, and gently levered the lock back from the latch. If she was the one to find Evanton, she reasoned, then her methods would be overlooked. She knew for a fact that Donna was one who often managed to get around the rules. If there was nothing to find, then nobody had to know she'd been here.

Inside, the flat was pleasantly warm, and well lit by sunshine streaming in through well-positioned windows. She trod carefully along the plush hall carpet, and looked quickly inside two rooms as she passed them. On the first impression, this was a flat that had had a lot of money spent on it. All the finishings were to a high spec. The bathroom was modern, the wall coverings right out of a Home Styles magazine. The kitchen, Fran noted as she walked by, looked clean and fitted with all mod cons. She came to the end of the hallway, and stood in front of a closed door. Her heart beating rapidly, she grasped the door handle and let herself into the living room.

Again, it was tastefully decorated. Plush furniture. An expensive TV mounted on the wall. A spectacular marine tank in the corner, displaying corals and colourful fish, meticulously sea-scaped.

But as soon as Fran turned her head and saw the wall adjacent to the door, she stopped in her tracks. With her eyes widening in alarm, she slowly approached the wall and studied the detail.

Oh, my God!, she whispered, as she drew her phone from her pocket. She needed to photograph this.

Then her stomach lurched as she heard a boom from outside, and she knew the flat's occupant had come home. As if that wasn't bad enough, it sounded as though he wasn't alone.

Chapter 49

Donna sat facing Adam while he finished the last of his coffee. He'd told her that Craigie Drive's more shady characters said the flat had something of a revolving door, with lots of residents coming and going, none of whom were known in the area. It fit with the prostitutes theory. And, crucially, that a source of a source was able to confirm the presence of one of Kozel's thugs in the street several times during the past couple of years. At least some of the pieces were coming together, Donna thought, as her mobile rang. It was Alice's number.

"I have to take this," she said, heading for the door. "Back in a minute."

As soon as she stepped outside *The Bampot*, she wished she'd flung on a jacket. The rain soaked through her shirt immediately, and she shivered.

"Update for you, chief," said Alice as soon as Donna answered. "We've got Natesh in London two days ago getting his passport…"

"…and a visa for Turkey?" Donna cut in.

"Ooh, not just a pretty face," said Alice. "The Passport Agency told *me*; how did *you* find out?"

"I'm a detective," said Donna. "But don't worry: you've got nice shiny buttons."

"The shiny buttons trump your detective thing," said Alice. "Where are you?"

"I'm in Arbroath," said Donna. She didn't want to admit to her meeting with a journalist, not even to Alice. "I'm going to see if Aiden Moore has any more for me after our chat with Christine Avery. Where are you lot?"

"Morrison and Akwasi are downstairs talking to the midwives," said Alice. "I don't know where Fran's got to – she left a cryptic note saying she was off to check out a promising lead."

Donna paced back and forth across the entrance to *The Bampot*. "Listen, Alice, Ross and I were going over the Chaudrakars' background."

"He said."

"Do you buy the witness protection theory?" asked Donna.

"It's plausible," said Alice, not sounding that convinced. "Using the Sri Lanka thing as a cover story. What are your thoughts?"

"Same as you," said Donna. "But you know what I'm thinking?"

"Not unless you tell me."

"They've both vanished," said Donna, "and we know Natesh has gone to Turkey."

"Right," Alice drew out the vowel, wondering where Donna was going with this.

"Either Natesh is being set up, or he's in danger," said Donna. "I'm going to have to go and find him."

"I understand," said Alice. "You're going out to Turkey?"

Donna paused before speaking again. "I don't think I should go alone. We don't know what we're dealing with, and I reckon a woman travelling alone to Turkey might get her share of unwanted attention."

Alice remained silent.

"So, have you got suntan lotion and mozzie spray?" said Donna.

Alice whooped. "Do I get to try the raki?"

"Just don't put it on expenses," said Donna. "Go and talk to Ross – we're going to need some help from the police over there. I'll see you after I've spoken to Aiden."

Donna ended the call, sure she could feel Alice dancing around the team room. Shaking the raindrops from her hair, she went back inside *The Bampot* to say goodbye to Adam and settle up the bill. Then she'd pop over to the station to see Aiden, she thought. Then at least she wouldn't have lied to Alice.

Fran scarpered across the living room and dived behind the sofa, just as the front door opened. Bracing herself, she drew her phone from her pocket. She needed to photograph the wall. She aimed quickly and took a burst of photos, then ducked back down.

She sent one of the photos in a hurried text to Donna, giving the post code of her location. Chances were she'd need assistance pretty soon, and she hoped Donna would make sure she wouldn't face disciplinary over skipping the correct procedures.

The living room door opened, and she heard his voice more clearly now. But something wasn't right.

She angled her head so she could peek around the side of the sofa, and suddenly she found herself staring into a pair of eyes that made her skin freeze in terror.

She dropped her phone, and tried to scream, but the sound stuck in her throat.

Chapter 50

"Speak of the devil," said the officer on duty as Donna walked into Arbroath police station.

He said it while he held his phone to his ear, and beckoned Donna to the check-in desk.

"Always a good sign," said Donna. "What's up?"

"Aiden Moore's got a woman in asking to speak to somebody about a missing person," said the officer. "He thinks it's to do with the body on the beach case. Just asked me to ring Bell Street to see if you want to talk to her."

"Point me in the right direction," said Donna. She felt a race of excitement run a circuit around her body. If another one of the midwives had gone missing, they'd have phoned her directly – she'd told Geri and Rowan to do so if they thought of any piece of information that might help. No, her instinct told her *this* missing person report was about to plug one of the missing jigsaw pieces she needed.

The officer pressed a string of keys on the door lock from his side of the desk, and let Donna through.

She was aware of a hush falling over the busy office she came into, and although it only lasted a second, she knew all eyes were on her as the officers there attempted to return to their conversations. She understood their reaction. She would, after all, be forever associated with the most appalling set of murders they would ever encounter in their careers.

At that moment, Aiden emerged from a side office.

"It's true, then," he smiled as he held the door open for her. "You really are psychic."

"Good observation," said Donna. "You'll make a fine sergeant."

Aiden's face reddened, and his mouth opened slightly in surprise. "How did you know?"

"Psychic hunch," Donna shrugged. "That, and the study folder sitting on your desk over there."

They both turned and looked at the nearby desk, on which sat a photo of Aiden with his girlfriend and their baby, along with the tell-tale Police Leadership Programme folder.

"I tried working on it at home," he said, "but the minute I sit down, the baby senses it."

"Well, you won't have to worry about getting your competencies signed off," said Donna. "I'll do it."

"Cheers!" He looked delighted. Having a DI vouch for him would give his career chances a boost.

"But first," said Donna, "what's this about another missing person?"

"She came in about half an hour ago," said Aiden, leading Donna through the second office. A woman in her thirties sat hunched and pale, clutching a plastic cup of steaming tea. Dark circles sunk her bloodshot eyes into her skull. What looked to be normally well-tended hair, cut into a current style, today sat nest-like on the woman's head. The make-up had been applied sometime before today.

"This is Mrs Chalvez," said Aiden.

Donna sat down opposite her.

"My husband is missing," said the woman immediately. "He's been gone for a week, it's so unlike him. I phoned the police on Tuesday, but I was told to wait for a week…"

Donna glanced up at Aiden. His cheeks flushed and he stared at his boots.

Mrs Chalvez continued. "He missed our youngest son's birthday yesterday, so I know something has happened. I checked with all the hospitals, and nobody has any record of him."

"Okay, Mrs Chalvez," said Donna, her mind jumping ahead, wondering if he could be their mystery Latino. "Let me take some details, and I'll do what I can to help. What's his name?"

"Vidu Chalvez," said the woman. "I know something terrible has happened, he would never go off like this."

"Don't worry," said Donna. "There's usually a perfectly reasonable explanation for these things." *Like, he just murdered a woman.* She glanced at the woman to make sure she hadn't said it out loud. "Do you have a recent photograph?"

The woman searched in her bag, and pulled out a colour photo, which she handed to Donna.

Donna stared, open mouthed at the face beaming out of the picture.

"What is it?" There was panic in the woman's eyes. "You know

173

something, don't you? Please, tell me what's happened to him."

Donna glanced at the woman, then back at the photo. She forced a smile.

"Don't worry, Mrs Chalvez," she said again. "I'm sure we'll find him. It would really help if you would let us come and have a look around your home. Perhaps allow us to take away some items to test for your husband's DNA. A toothbrush, maybe?"

"His DNA?" spluttered Mrs Chalvez. "Oh my God, is he dead?"

"Don't worry," said Donna. "I'm sure he's absolutely fine. Like I said, this is routine work to help us investigate. Trust me, we'll do everything we can to find your husband." *Like you wouldn't believe.*

She stood up. "Aiden, a minute, please."

Donna and Aiden walked out of the room, Donna holding the photograph after reassuring Mrs Chalvez they'd be back in a moment.

"Can you get this photo scanned and emailed over to Angus Ross, along with the Chalvez details?" she asked.

"Of course," said Aiden, taking the photo from her. "You recognise the guy?"

"Yes and no," said Donna. She brought her phone from her pocket. "I'll give Ross a quick ring…What's this?" She saw a text from Fran, opened it, and saw the photo that Fran had taken, along with a post code. No message.

"Forget that," said Donna, her words rapid. "Get me the address for this post code, and call out all units. We've an officer in trouble."

She took off at a sprint through the main office. Aiden followed close behind, yelling into his radio for the address belonging to the post code.

The officers at the desks listened to Aiden's words, and with barely a hesitation, they all jumped up to run after him and Donna.

Donna sprinted through the retail car park that sat next to the police station. It was the quickest way to get to Kirk Street, the address verified quickly by Aiden. She held her warrant card out, ready to shout, "Police!" if need be to clear her path of dawdling shoppers. But the pedestrians parted of their own volition to watch the spectacle of the tall detective leading a race in which she was pursued by five uniformed police officers.

Donna could hear and feel Aiden running at her back as she raced through the car park and on to Applegate, with its freshly painted fishermen's cottages now hosting numerous local businesses, then turned right onto High Street. In a matter of minutes from leaving the station she was bearing left onto Kirk Street, and as she drew to a halt outside the address that Fran had texted, she could hear police sirens approaching from the longer route that the patrol cars had to take.

Heaving for breath, Aiden and the other four officers who'd run with Donna looked to her for instruction.

"Jade and Gareth have tasers," said Aiden, indicating the two.

Donna nodded to them. "Get ready."

The two officers withdrew their weapons and held them, ready to use.

"We've no idea what we're going into," said Donna, "but there's an officer in trouble. I'm going in now, but I'm not asking you to come with me before reinforcements arrive."

She pressed the top floor buzzer.

"For God's sake!" came the reply over the intercom.

"Police," said Donna, and pushed her way through the heavy door as soon as the lock released.

Aiden glanced at his colleagues, then followed her inside, the other four on his heels.

They took the stairs quickly and in silence, only exchanging glances of surprise at the tidy and well-kept interior, and stopped when Donna pointed to one of the doors. Jade and Gareth took up positions on either side of her, their tasers ready. Aiden and the remaining officers stood behind Donna.

Donna took a moment to consider her options for entering the flat. The door looked too solid to attempt to break it open. She didn't have time to wait for a battering ram to arrive.

She was about to hammer on the door and yell an order through the letterbox, when she heard footsteps shuffle towards her from inside, and the door began to creak open.

Donna resisted the urge to take a step backward when she saw the bloodied figure that appeared in front of her.

Chapter 51

Natesh stood in line as the passengers shuffled towards passport control. He suddenly felt vulnerable, unable to read the Turkish notices and unfamiliar with the guards' uniforms. He watched each person as they approached the security guard, saw how they handed over their passports open at the photo page, with the visas tucked inside. He held his own passport and visa at the ready.

He noticed how the security guard barely glanced up as the passengers went through. Made no comment. No flicker of facial expression. Still, his nerves heightened as it came closer to his turn.

Now in front of the guard, Natesh placed his documents in the booth. He held his breath as the guard looked up and made eye contact. Then the uniformed man took a sticker from a drawer, placed it on Natesh's visa, and returned the paperwork. Natesh only realised he was rooted to the spot when he saw the guard reach for the next person's passport, while waving him on with an impatient flick of his hand. Natesh felt the corner of his mouth twitch in relief and he scarpered after the other passengers towards baggage reclaim.

For a four-hour flight, he reflected, he'd been travelling for around nine hours, and he felt suddenly tired and vulnerable, worried that he had made a mistake coming here. Wondering if he should he have told Donna, after all.

Then the contents of the package burned in his mind's eye: the photograph of him and Donna the night they'd walked along the Dundee waterfront with their fish and chips, taken unawares; the note making it clear that Donna would be harmed if he told her anything. Whoever had left him the package must have been following them that night. Must know the people who mattered most to him. *And these people had his mother.*

The airport exit was where Adam had told Natesh that he'd meet Firaz.

Not sure what to do, he followed the other passengers until he spotted a line of people holding up signs To his relief, he saw a card bearing his own name.

The man holding it up was wearing sunglasses, a vest and jeans, and he was looking bored, chewing gum. The stance made Natesh think about Donna, and he felt a pang in his heart, knowing she'd be upset and angry about his disappearance.

"Hey, man, you must be Firaz?"

Firaz looked Natesh up and down, clearly unimpressed, then clapped him on the shoulder by way of greeting, and almost smiled.

"You made it here in one piece?" Firaz said.

"Yeah," said Natesh. "It's a tiring journey, though."

"First time in Turkey?"

"First time anywhere."

Firaz whistled, and stared at him, as if wondering whether to believe him. "So, let's go," he said finally. "I have you a hotel nearby. Get some sleep, and we can talk tomorrow about what you want to see."

"Thank you," said Natesh. The prospect of a bed, a pillow, was a welcome one, even though he doubted that he'd be able sleep. Or maybe he was already asleep, he thought, trapped in some terrible nightmare. His head ached, and he realised he'd drunk only one small bottle of water since beginning his journey

He followed Firaz out of the airport building and across a large parking area. Late at night in November, and there was still warmth in the air. Natesh felt wretched. This place was as alien to him as the dreadful pit his life had fallen into.

Firaz walked in between buses whose engines burred, calling out words that Natesh could only guess at to the drivers, and headed into a melee of taxis. Firaz stopped in front of a battered old jeep and thumped the hood.

"Here is my vehicle," he said. "In you get, but don't put your feet there." He pointed to a square of cardboard sticking out from under the front seat.

"Why not?"

Firaz lifted a corner of the cardboard, and Natesh looked down, only to find himself staring at the road surface beneath the car.

"Welcome to Turkey," Firaz laughed, a bitter note.

The vehicle shuddered into gear and groaned as it rolled forward and joined the Dalaman traffic.

They were in the jeep for only twenty minutes, but Natesh felt his knuckles glow white as his rib cage jarred on every turn of the wheel. They came off the main highway and onto a gravel track, passing a row of crumbling flats, where the jeep screeched to a halt. To Natesh's alarm, Firaz got out, and waved him to follow.

Natesh threw a worried look at Firaz. "Has the jeep broken down?"

"No," said Firaz, "this is your hotel."

Natesh looked up and down the street. He didn't see anything that looked like a hotel. To his dismay, Firaz was pointing at a door that was squeaking loudly as it swung on its hinges. It belonged to a narrow building with a glassless window high up, its walls peeling pink paint. A dog casually walked out of the door, sat down by the roadside and began to scratch itself.

"You want an authentic experience, right?" said Firaz.

Natesh glanced at him. What on earth had Adam told this guy?

Half an hour later, Natesh was lying on top of his hotel bed and wondering what his next step should be.

Chapter 52

Rory Thomson stood facing Donna, the door to his flat now fully open. His breathing was rapid. Sweat beaded his forehead, and his hair was a mess. The front of his shirt was soaked red with blood. In his right hand he held a golf club, the club face congealed with what Donna thought looked like blood and hair.

"What have you done with her?" Donna hissed in his face, barging her way into the hallway.

Thomson pivoted on the spot to keep his eyes fixed on her. "In there…in there," he stammered, pointing with the golf club towards the living room. His voice was cracked. He put up no resistance when the uniformed officers bundled him against the wall, and dropped the golf club to the floor when they told him to.

Donna hurried to the door at the far end of the hall, as pointed to by Thomson, and pushed it open. To her immediate right, her eye caught the wall that was covered in photographs and news clippings. Of her. She faltered at the sight. Then a groan from the opposite side of the room made her spin round.

Fran lay on the floor beside a dining table. Around her were the smashed remnants of a chair, and next to her lay the body of a large dog. Fran was trying to sit up, and a long gash glared angrily across her forehead.

Donna and Aiden hurried to their injured colleague, Donna radioing for an ambulance. She could hear boots running up the stairs towards them, their reinforcements. Donna knelt by Fran and cradled her head.

"What happened?" she whispered.

"The dog," Fran whispered back. "Dog tried to attack me. Thomson fought it off."

"Thomson helped you?" Donna asked, surprised. She looked closely at the dog. It lay motionless, not breathing, its head a bloodied pulp.

Donna listened to the racket back at the front door, as more police colleagues spilled into the flat. "Tell them to wait outside," she said to Aiden. "And get Thomson. I need to know what happened in here."

Aiden hurried from the room and returned moments later, leading Thomson, flanked by two officers, towards Donna.

Donna glared at Thomson. Then her expression turned to one of puzzlement. The man was clearly distressed. His breathing was still rapid, and he seemed close to tears. He plucked endlessly at his bloodied shirt, and his eyes stared in horror at the dog.

"I didn't know she was in here," said Thomson, indicating Fran. "I came home, and the dog...I'm looking after my brother's dog...it just went berserk and ran at the window there." He pointed to the window behind Fran. "I didn't know what was happening, it was a moment before I realised somebody...she...was hiding there."

Donna glanced at Fran. Fran avoided her eye.

Thomson's voice quavered as he continued. "She was screaming...the dog was...I had to stop it attacking her, and I...I hit it with the golf club." He began to sob, and sank down into a chair.

The ambulance siren filled the air beyond the window, and stopped abruptly. Commotion at the doorway ushered in the paramedics.

"You're going to be fine," said Donna to Fran, as the paramedics moved in to take her place.

Two more paramedics hurried into the room. Donna pointed them to Thomson. "I want him kept under guard at all times," she told them. They nodded their understanding, and two police officers joined them next to the distressed man.

Donna focused on the wall that was covered in photographs of herself. A shiver ran down her spine as she took it in.

"I'm okay, really," she heard Fran protest. The paramedics were strapping her into a transport chair.

"Just get you checked over," one of the paramedics was telling her. "That's a nasty cut to your head."

As they wheeled her past Donna, Fran said to her, "Can you try and get a message to Takeshi for me? Tell him I've been taken in?"

Donna nodded and tried to smile. "I'll ring the office, find out if he's still at his burger van."

She felt a twang of annoyance, wondering if this new relationship had clouded Fran's judgement a step too far today.

Chapter 53

Morrison and Akwasi arrived at Ninewells and sat themselves down at Fran's bedside. Donna excused herself, to make her way back to Bell Street. She had plenty to discuss with Ross. The photograph brought in by Mrs Chalvez. The photographs on Rory Thomson's wall. *This* mess.

She stopped outside the hospital room, hearing Fran re-live her adventures, as Morrison and Akwasi sat rapt in front of her. Admiration shone from their faces. They weren't ribbing her now.

"And you should have seen it," Fran was saying. "This whole wall, covered in photos and news clippings. Look." She was showing them the photos she'd taken on her phone.

"But I totally crapped myself when I heard him coming up the stairs," she was going on. "Talking away to someone, too, I thought there's no way I'm going to be able to handle two men on my own."

"Oh, I don't know," said Akwasi, with a bawdy laugh. "What did you do?"

"I hid behind the sofa."

The three officers burst into peals of laughter.

"And then, he comes into the room, having a full blown conversation with this huge dog! I'm not kidding you, I thought I was going to piss myself when it spotted me…"

Donna found Alice and Ross pouring over an open file. They were the only ones left in the office, two steaming mugs of coffee at their hands. They looked up at Donna's approach, and she saw then that it was Natesh's file they'd been discussing.

"I think this is something I can help you with, lady and gentleman," said Donna, waving the photograph of Vidu Chalvez in front of them.

She saw the pity in Alice's eyes, and the annoyance in Ross's, but she grinned in response and placed the photograph on the desk in front of them, slapping her hand down triumphantly as she did. Then she stood back, hands on her hips, and watched for them to respond.

"Who is this?" asked Alice, picking up the photo. She screwed up her eyes as she looked at it. "It's a dead ringer for our man Natesh."

"Isn't it just?" said Donna. "Add on a few years."

"Let me see that," said Ross, taking the photo from Alice. "Well, I'll be!" He sat back in his chair, staring at Chalvez. "Where did you get this? Who is it?"

"This, my dears," said Donna, "is one Vidu Chalvez. Reported missing this afternoon by his distraught wife. He's been gone six days. I think this changes things somewhat for Natesh, doesn't it?"

"It does," said Alice. "But why the hell has he gone to Turkey?" Donna frowned. She had no answer to that.

"And what's this we got through about Rory Thomson?" said Ross.

"Looks like that explains why I kept feeling so unnerved," said Donna, trying to sound flippant. "I had a stalker all this time!"

"You're letting go of your other theory, then?" said Ross.

Donna noticed that Alice didn't ask what he meant. "You told Alice?" she said.

"He needed advice from somebody who knows just how crazy you can be," said Alice, chuckling. "You really thought Evanton was involved in all of this?"

"Evanton *was* involved in all of this," said Donna. "At least in the Eleanor Wallace case, hiding evidence."

Alice pushed her chair back, and gazed at Donna. "You thought Evanton was watching you, when it was Thomson all along."

Donna nodded, but didn't say anything.

Alice went on. "But you're still not convinced, are you? You still think Evanton's back here?"

"I can feel it," Donna burst out. "I don't know how to explain it, but I can just feel it! He's here."

"Oh, for God's sake," Ross muttered.

"Wait," said Alice, placing a light hand on Ross's arm. "Why don't we run it as an alternative line of enquiry? Let's face it, we're not getting anywhere fast with the one we're currently going with, are we? And, well, Donna quite often has that uncanny sixth sense about things."

Ross stared at Alice. "You're not being serious."

Alice shrugged. "Why not?"

"I don't believe I'm hearing this," said Ross. "The pair of you are barking."

"You'll be glad to be sending us off to Turkey, then," said Donna, winking at Alice.

Ross sighed, the heavy groan of defeat. Eyeing the doorway, he said, "Well, I suppose this is the time to discuss it, since nobody's here. This operation of yours needs to be kept to a tight circle. We don't know what kind of risk might be involved. If it's a witness protection gone wrong, the last thing we want is you two getting landed in the middle of it."

"What could possibly go wrong?" Donna and Alice both said at the same time.

Chapter 54

Arriving home, Donna paused, with her hand on the front door. She looked at the new security box that now sat above it, its blue light blinking. There wouldn't be any more visits from Rory Thomson, she thought, but she still felt better for having the extra security fitted.

Her stomach began to churn as she entered the house. A tantalising waft of home cooking met her in the hallway, the promise of a much needed night in with Libby. But she was going to have to explain to Libby what had happened, and what was going to happen next. She wondered, not for the first time, if being a cop was really worth the crap it brought into a relationship.

She mustered up her mojo, and sang out, "Hey, honey, I'm home!"

Libby appeared from the kitchen doorway, wearing a dish cloth slung casually over her shoulder. And nothing else.

"Thought I'd help you unwind after a stressful day at the office," she said, her voice silky and husky.

The Talk could wait, Donna decided quickly.

They lay back on the settee, legs entwined, catching their breaths. Donna had thrown herself into their lovemaking, pushing all notion of the ever expanding murder enquiry far from her mind. But now the details crept back, like guilty secrets. She glanced at Libby, and Libby recognised the look. She sat up, drawing her arms around her knees. Donna sat up, too.

"There have been a couple of major developments," she said, not quite able to decide which part to begin with.

"Is there a good-news-or-bad-news option?" asked Libby.

"Kind of." A cigarette would really help right now, Donna thought. "One of our leads, Rory Thomson, is in custody."

"One of your leads? You've solved the case?"

"Turns out he wasn't involved in the murders at all," said Donna.

"But you've arrested him?"

"He was stalking me."

Libby got to her feet, uttering a cry of alarm.

"It's okay," said Donna. "We're safe. He's under lock and key. And, hey, at least it wasn't Evanton."

"Not funny," said Libby, looking fit to faint. "I suppose I didn't really believe somebody had been in here, that there had to be some other explanation." She waved her hand in the air in a vague gesture.

"What, like I imagined the whole thing?" said Donna. "For God's sake, there was a rose on our bed. I didn't imagine that."

Libby look frantically around the room, and began to wring her hands as though attempting to cleanse them of some filthy intrusion.

"As I said," Donna cut in, talking slowly and calmly, "we're safe. He was a harmless saddo with an obsession, and he's in a secure unit now."

"This job of yours is putting years on me. But, like you said, at least it wasn't Evanton."

Donna decided this wasn't the moment to admit her conviction that he was still involved in all of this, somehow.

"But there's something else, isn't there?" Libby went on, eyeing Donna keenly.

Donna's stomach lurched. She pictured a time when this sort of stuff wasn't part of her every waking – and dreaming – moment. But reality had to be dealt with.

"It's about Natesh."

"Is he okay? Have you found him?" Libby sat back down next to Donna.

"We know where he's gone," said Donna. "He flew out to Turkey, but we don't know why, and I think he's in danger."

"Do you have contacts over there who can help?" asked Libby. Donna hesitated. "Wait," said Libby. "I know what's coming next. You're going after him, aren't you?"

"I have to," said Donna. She saw Libby bite her lip. "It's all very hush hush, but one theory we have is that Natesh and his mum are on a witness protection scheme."

"What?"

"It's just a working theory," said Donna. "It's possible Samira made up the Sri Lankan story as a cover. But we don't know. Just that she's missing, and something – or someone – has led Natesh to go looking for her in Turkey."

"But what about your own safety?" asked Libby.

"There's two of us," Donna shrugged, trying to sound confident. "Alice Moone is going, too." She hoped she'd said it quickly enough to be able to pass over it. But she hadn't.

"Alice Moone?" said Libby. "The bullet and blade magnet?"

Donna hesitated. It was true, Alice did have a reputation for getting into the thick of it, as her scarred features testified.

Libby rolled her eyes.

Sunday

Chapter 55

The battered black jeep crunched the stony track that led through the pomegranate and fig trees to the gates of the compound. When Firaz turned off the engine, the air filled instead with the sound of bird calls, the dawn chorus mingling with the haunting call of the muezzin as it drifted across valley. Firaz ignored them, and turned his attentions to the gates. Inside, a large man stood up, roused from his slumber by the noise of the jeep. An assault rifle was slung over his shoulder. The man yawned and rubbed his eyes, then seeing that it was Firaz, opened the gate and nodded him in.

"Early," grunted the man.

"Errands to run," said Firaz.

The guard looked sceptical, and slumped back onto his boulder. He muttered something disagreeable, and lit a cigarette. "What's going on?"

Firaz sat beside the guard and took his offer of a smoke. They took several puffs, watching the sunlight spill over the top of the compound's walls, while Firaz considered his response. The guard was a tight-lipped man, but he knew all the comings and goings around the compound.

"Amin's wife and brother," Firaz finally said. "They seem to be settling in okay? You seen them about much?" They'd been here a few days now.

The guard grunted, whether *yes* or *no* was unclear.

"I think the old man has a son, too, did you know that?" said Firaz.

The guard appeared to contemplate the information, and squinted his eyes in Firaz's direction while he took a final draw from his cigarette.

"Nah," he committed to responding, as he stamped out the smouldering tip under his mud-caked boot.

"Lives in the UK," Firaz went on. "Turned up at Dalaman Airport last night."

The guard's eyebrows rose in surprise. But not by much.

"You didn't know, eh?" said Firaz.

The guard shifted on his boulder. It was his business to know everything that went on around this place. But things were getting a bit strange lately. The operation had wound down considerably, and now the old man's wife and brother were here.

"What do you know?" he asked Firaz. The words were grudging, coming from an admission of failure on his part.

"Not much," said Firaz. "Has Amin said anything about why the wife and brother are here?"

The guard set his rifle down on the dusty ground, and stretched out his arms, entwining his fingers and cracking the knuckles.

"Not to me," he said. "You're the one he sent to collect them."

"Yeah, he did," said Firaz. "But he didn't ask me to collect his son."

He saw something close to discomfort register on the guard's face. The big guy was rubbing his hands together, processing this new information.

"A mutual friend asked me to show him around," Firaz went on. "I don't think the old man knows he's here."

"Then why would he be here? And how do you know it's his son, anyway?"

It was the most Firaz had ever heard the guard speak real words.

"A guess," said Firaz. "His name's Chaudrakar. Looks of an age to be the old man's son."

"I suppose the rest of the family's here now," grunted the guard.

"I've got a bad feeling about it," said Firaz. "What if he's here to bust the old man, and take over the business for himself?"

The guard snorted and tapped the side of his head. "Your imagination."

"If the old man knew he was coming, *he'd* have got me to collect him from the airport."

The guard shrugged, a sort of agreement. "You've got a point."

"I've got a bad feeling," Firaz said again. "If he's here to bust his old man, it's not going to be good for us."

The guard heaved himself to his feet, slung his rifle back over his shoulder and took a few steps, placing himself in front of the compound gates. He looked up into the surrounding trees, appearing to be listening to the clamour of bird call. But Firaz saw his fingers flex and curl, flex and curl. The guard was nervous.

After several moments of silence, the guard turned to face Firaz.

"What should we do?"

"I'm taking the son – if that's who he is – to Fethiye today," said Firaz. The guard held eye contact with him. Firaz had his confidence now. "You watch out for any signs of the wife and brother. They're bound to make an appearance soon. Find out what you can from them. Small talk."

The guard looked alarmed.

Maybe not, thought Firaz. "Just ask them about family – say it's nice to see Amin's family here, or something, and ask if they're expecting anyone else to join them."

The guard grunted.

"I'll try and work out what the son's motives really are," said Firaz.

He tossed the jeep key into the air and caught it again, moving towards the gate. The guard opened it and let him through.

"Be clever about it," said Firaz. And he clambered back into his ancient vehicle.

Chapter 56

Natesh was wide awake and listening to the call of the muezzin, amplified from a nearby minaret. The rising dawn sunshine poured in his window and warmed his skin.

To his relief, when he'd followed Firaz through the squeaky door the previous night, he'd found himself in a pleasant courtyard. In the centre was a small swimming pool surrounded by garden-style plastic tables and chairs. Making a wider circle around the courtyard was a block of rooms, all single storey. From every ledge and on every surface bloomed flowers of all colours, filling the small complex with an overpowering scent that irritated Natesh's nose and throat. However, it was a discreet, peaceful hotel carefully tucked away behind the humdrum of the main drag of the airport traffic.

Natesh had followed Firaz past the swimming pool, glancing only briefly at the few men who sat drinking and quietly chatting at the poolside tables, and nodding politely to a woman in a long voluminous skirt who was mopping the tiled floors. Firaz had shown him to a room, and he'd thrown himself onto the bed as soon as the door was locked behind him.

But sleep had evaded him. He was in Turkey, but what was he going to do now? More than once, he found himself beginning to ring Donna's number, but stopped, the threatening words in the note that he'd been given, along with the other items that had led him here, only too vivid in his mind's eye.

He yawned now and slowly sat up. The clattering of a plate smashing somewhere nearby made him start.

He made his way across the small bedroom and into the wet room. The shower made alarming noises, but produced a reasonable stream of warm water.

During the night he'd gotten back up and made his way to the hotel bar. He remembered coughing as the circling cigarette smoke enveloped him, and how he'd ached again for Donna. He'd ordered a bottle of water, and sat in a corner on his own, bleary eyed and dull-minded, and the patrons around him had let him be with hardly a glance. At one point he'd become aware of a set of eyes upon him. He turned, and saw a dark-skinned woman staring at him. The colourful scarf entwined through her hair caught his attention, but as soon as he'd looked at her, she seemed to evaporate into thin air and was gone. He'd finished his water, and returned to his room.

Now he followed the smell of cooking and the racket of laughter and loud chatter towards the hotel restaurant.

Miserable from exhaustion, and unable to form a plan to find out what had happened to Samira, he really wasn't in the mood for company. But he knew he had to eat. As he sat alone at his table, he forced himself to wonder what Donna would do in this situation. She would make sure she ate and drank, he knew.

He suddenly caught sight of a rainbow of colour at the other end of the restaurant. It was the dark-skinned woman from the night before. She was studying him closely, but when his eye focused on her, she quickly looked away. The hotelier arrived at his table, and set out an array of meats, cheeses, olives and breads, and when Natesh looked back across the restaurant, the woman was gone again. The hairs on the back of his neck prickled, and he was aware once again of Donna's words urging him to trust his instincts. Something wasn't right.

Firaz pushed the jeep's engine to its limit as he approached the junction before the airport, and pulled off the main highway for Dalaman town and Natesh's hotel. He sent a brief text to let his guest know he'd be there soon.

Surely the guard would be able to glean some information from Vidu Chaudrakar, he thought as he drove. He'd met Amin's brother on two occasions, and both times the free-rider had failed to impress. He clearly wasn't as clever as the old man, and Firaz was certain the reason he'd been summoned to the compound both times was because he'd been in over his head trying to run the operation from the UK side. Any time Amin had spoken of his brother, it was through teeth and lips poised to spit out something distasteful.

On the other hand, the way the old man cared for the photographs showed he still cared about his wife. But why leave it all this time to reconcile with her, Firaz wondered. And how did Natesh fit into all of this? It stank, the whole thing, and if he was going to remain out of the way of over-zealous law enforcers, he was going to have to work out which side Natesh was on, and take the appropriate course of action.

Natesh sat back in a chair by the pool, flicking through a newspaper and being dismayed that the best he could do was to look at the pictures. His heart was still beating rapidly, unnerved by the woman in the colourful scarf. He'd talked to Donna often enough about the difference between paranoia and real danger. It was a judgement call she had to make every day, so she was pretty good at it. Following her advice, he set out the facts of his situation.

He was alone in a country where he knew no-one. He didn't speak the language, had no idea of the geography. Those could all explain paranoia. But he'd been left a series of hints – the passport, the photograph, the bus ticket – that his mother was here. Had been *taken* here, in the same week during which one of her colleagues had been found murdered.

That wasn't paranoia. Neither was the threat against Donna. Somebody who knew him had written that note. Somebody who was linked to this place.

He stood up, deciding to track down the woman. He would confront her. Hell, he had nothing else to go on. Then he felt his mobile buzz, and a curse formed on his lips. Firaz would be here in a matter of minutes. He scanned the hotel complex from where he stood, but could see no sign of the woman.

Chapter 57

Fran was in casual gear, Donna noted, and found herself wondering if the DC had come to work straight from the hospital.

"Morning, Ma'am. Donna," said Fran.

"You should be taking it easy," said Donna. "How's the head?"

What had been a bloody gash on her head the day before was, today, a long bruise.

"It's fine," said Fran. Her desk was littered with print-outs, crime scene photographs and open folders. She was studiously avoiding eye contact with Donna.

Donna took off her heavy coat. The wind was whipping up outside, and there was a severe weather warning in place for gales the next morning. Just around the time she and Alice would be taking off on their flight to Turkey. She shut the thought down, and fetched a brush out of her bag. Her cheeks were still pink from the cold air outside, and she gave her hair a quick tidy before flicking on the kettle.

It was a Sunday morning, still early, and the rest of the team weren't expected in for another half an hour.

"Why did you do it?" she said softly, her back to Fran as she stood watching the kettle.

Fran sighed and put down the pen she'd been fidgeting with. "I just wanted to help," she said.

Donna sat facing her and set down two mugs of coffee.

"I might be crazy, but I'm not stupid," she said to Fran. "You did something I might have done myself at one point. But there's no need to try and prove yourself. We work as a team here."

"Ma'am."

"Donna."

Fran pushed herself back in her chair and sighed again, a loud exhalation. "I suppose I really wanted to impress you."

"You don't have to," said Donna. "I'm already impressed."

Fran tutted, annoyed with herself. "I know you think I got distracted...with Takeshi..."

"You *did* get distracted," said Donna. "And you lost a potentially valuable lead the other day. But that's no reason to go maverick and put yourself in danger."

She ignored Fran's mutterings of protest, and continued talking. "You should have told Alice where you were thinking of going yesterday, and you should have waited for approval and back-up. I can't have you going off doing your own thing. I need to be able to trust you." *My God*, she suddenly thought, *I sound like Ross talking to me!* She took a deep breath. She could see Fran fighting back the tears.

"Look," she said. "We're all allowed a balls-up now and then. God knows, I've had my fair share."

Fran met her eye now. "There won't be any more from me," she said. "What do you need me to do while you're away?"

"A few things," said Donna. Fran sat poised to take notes. "I need you to dig into the missing husband, Vidu Chalvez, find out what you can. Keep an eye out for Emma's DNA report. Also, see what else you can find on Marcus Edridge's ownership of Craigie Drive. Is there any link with Kozel's gang? Any link with this Vidu Chalvez character?"

She paused, taking a gulp of coffee while Fran wrote her notes. She looked up at the approaching sound of clanking boots, and smiled when Aiden Moore came into the room. He unwrapped a scarf from around his face, before making a bee-line for the kettle.

"I've asked Aiden to work with you while I'm away," Donna explained, seeing the question in Fran's eyes.

"Lucky you," Aiden smiled his shy smile. He joined them at the table, and Donna re-capped on her instructions to Fran.

"Lean on Peter Cowan some more," she went on. "I think he'll have seen Kozel's men hanging around Dundee. Maybe even Craigie Drive, though I doubt he'll have any idea what they were actually up to. But if we can place them there, for any reason, it's going to help." If Adam's sources had seen Kozel's men around, then she reckoned Peter Cowan must have, too. And at least his information could be used formally in the investigation.

"What about Christine Avery?" asked Aiden. "Do you think there's more she can tell us?"

Donna thought back to the interview in Christine's Arbroath kitchen. "I don't think so," she said. "But we do need to find the woman she mentioned..."

"Juanita," Aiden read from his notes taken on the day.

"That's right," said Donna. "I sent a couple of uniforms up to Aberdeen to ask around, but so far nothing."

Fran and Aiden exchanged a glance. Donna could sense Aiden's unease.

"You'll have Morrison and Akwasi for support," she said. "Fran, I want you to phone me daily and with any updates in between. You'll report to DCI Ross, both of you, until I get back."

She let her last words hang in the air. She had no idea when that might be, only that she wasn't coming home without Natesh.

"Are the two of you good to get on with this?" she asked, draining the last of her coffee and standing up. Fran and Aiden chorused that they were.

"Good," she went on. "Then I'm going to go and pack my suitcase."

Chapter 58

Amin Chaudrakar placed the old photograph back on the shelf. The bride's smiling face was smudged by his thumb mark. He couldn't believe she was finally here, after all these years.

He found himself checking his hair, his collar in the mirror. Looking back at him was the shadow of the young medic Samira had first arrived here with. Saw in that moment the hopes, the dreams and the ideals – *the principles* – he'd once had. How often, over the years, he'd scoffed at the idea of those principles, written them off as naive.

Samira had never understood the pressure he'd been under back then to keep them safe and provide a secure home for them, at a time when she was pregnant with Natesh and they had no-one to turn to, their options for returning home to Iran closed down in the face of their status as infidels, enemies of the state.

For what? he thought. Carrying a name that belonged to the wrong ethnic group? It was all part of a longer history that had seen him catapulted from his family home in Karachi as a boy. He recalled the fear on his grandfather's face back then, the man who, according to family lore, had stood firm during the Partition of India at the end of the War and refused to let them become part of the largest mass migration in human history, during which some 14 million people were displaced on the grounds of their religious affiliations. But by the early 1970s, when Amin was old enough to pick up on what the adults around him were saying, things had changed. Word was reaching them about the ethnic cleansing of East Pakistan by the Pakistani Army, three million of their fellow Hindus murdered in the genocide. Yes, the fear on his grandfather's face was etched deep on his mind. They'd made the short journey from Karachi across the border into Iran, at that time a safe place even for Hindus. Until, of course, the Revolution. Amin was not going to let it continue, the constant uprooting. The 1970s became the '80s. When he and his young bride fled to Turkey, he decided to use his medical skills in ways that might seem unethical to his peers, but which met a demand that at least didn't involve hunting large swathes of humanity from their settled homes. And, he reasoned with the ghost of his younger self reflected in the mirror, hadn't he made up for any wrongdoing that he had become involved in? He'd lost count of the trips he'd made to the refugee camp at Suruç, lost count of the girls he'd rescued. If there had been any other option for them once they left his care, he'd have insisted on it. But the life of prostitution they went on to was relatively brief, and it allowed them to buy their freedom, didn't it? Surely there were worse things in life, he reasoned. It was all relative.

But Samira didn't see it that way, he knew. Perhaps now she'd be able to understand his side of things. Principles were all very well, but life had its realities. Surely she'd be able to see now that he'd taken a route that led to a better destination than might sometimes have been obvious during some of the unsavoury twists and turns along the way? He could forgive her for thinking badly of him during those times. But surely she'd be able to see the bigger picture now?

He took a deep breath and made his way to the room where she was locked in.

He knocked on the door, and hesitated before unlocking it.

Samira sat defiantly in the middle of the room. She looked at him with contempt.

"What do you want?" she spat.

"Samira," he began.

"Just get to the point."

"We can work together again…"

"We never worked together," said Samira. "You lied to me. You hid your crimes from me until you could threaten me with harming our baby, because you knew I would never agree to be part of them otherwise. So, have you come to try and change my mind? You're wasting your time."

She refused to let the sting in her eye become a teardrop.

Amin sighed and pulled a chair opposite her, and sat down. She turned away from him.

"It's been a long time, Samira," he said. His voice was weary. "I thought perhaps, by now, you might come to see things differently. That perhaps we could trust each other."

He met her eye. She matched his determination blink for blink.

"The operation here is finished," he went on. "Finished, and now it'll all become exposed, with international police involved. But I'm not giving myself in to the authorities. Do you realise what that means? I will be hunted like an animal for the rest of my life. No, I'll go down fighting. And you'll be with me."

Samira said nothing in return. Amin waited, allowing a heavy silence to settle in the room.

"You know you can't go back to Dundee," he said eventually, unable to bear it. "Not with police now investigating two murders that they'll figure out you knew about."

"Yes," said Samira, looking up suddenly towards the doorway. Amin followed her line of sight, and saw his brother loitering there. Samira gestured towards him, and continued. "Thanks to his ineptitude. Two women died because of him. They were my friends! I can't forgive either of you for that, let alone what you've done to all of those other women. *Girls.*" A tear slid down her cheek. "And all this time," she went on, "I kept my side of the bargain. I kept quiet, and I never hinted to Natesh anything about what a monster his father was."

Amin flinched at the venom in her voice.

"Yes, I kept quiet," said Samira, "despite your brother's obsession with reuniting you and Natesh. Even when we left Dundee this week, he tried to insist on telling Natesh the truth. Did you know that?"

Amin spun to look at Vidu, to confirm Samira's words, but his brother was gone.

"It was me who protected your honour in your son's eyes," she said. "Me who convinced him his father was a hero – but for his sake, not for yours. So, I don't know what you're going to do, Amin. Vidu will go behind your back and bungle anything he has to do. And I'm not going to help you."

Amin regarded her, and felt a curtain close over the feelings he'd harboured for her all these years. She was, in fact, little more than another task he would have to take care of. A problem that he would have to erase, in the same way that he'd erased the problem with the American.

Samira's eyes grew wide, and she pulled her shawl tightly around her shoulders, as she watched him stand up and, without another word, leave the room.

Chapter 59

Heavy raindrops whipped Natesh's face as he sat in the exposed jeep. The drive to Fethiye that morning had taken just under an hour. With the sky now a rainbow of violets and blood-drenched clouds, and the sun pulling down the temperature with its own rapid descent behind the tree-tops, Natesh was relieved to estimate they must be close now to his hotel. Just as his back began to ache, he saw a familiar road, and Firaz brought the jeep to a stop outside the hotel's creaking doorway.

It had been a strange day, Natesh mused, as he clambered out of the jeep. He called out a thanks to Firaz, and made his way to his room.

Despite the cool air outside, the room was stuffy and uncomfortably warm.

Natesh sat on the bed, lowered his head into his hands, and tried to think of what he should do next.

Firaz had, at his request, shown him around Fethiye. Shown him the bus station there. The mosque that graced the town's centre. The remnants of a castle and the rock tombs that watched over the harbour town's activities with the eerie stare of never-closing eyes. Had walked him around the streets lined with shops and cafes. Natesh had been surprised at how un-touristy Fethiye was. He'd been captivated by the marina, tour boats moored up until the next season, but a regular ferry chugging back and forth across its slice of the Turquoise Coast to nearby Çaliş. Natesh had tried to feel some kind of vibe that might indicate a connection to this place, anything that might trigger a distant memory. But there had been nothing.

Sitting on the bed in his Dalaman hotel room, he felt as bereft of hope as he had done when he'd stood bewildered in line at passport control the previous night.

Donna took her passport and the printed e-ticket back out of her bag, and placed them in another pouch, then dug her warrant card from her pocket and placed it beside them. Took them all back out, and put them back where they'd been before.

This whole thing was crazy, she thought. Natesh could be anywhere. Turkey was a huge country, and even though they knew he'd flown into Dalaman, by the time she and Alice arrived there, he'd have two days' travelling time on them.

She shuddered, thinking of Natesh walking into who knew what kind of situation. Whatever it was that had led him there, he was up against people who had murdered two women, mutilated the body of a baby, and had spirited Samira away. His only hope, she thought, was to go along with their plan until she could find him. As long as he didn't do anything stupid, anything rash, she had to hope he would be safe until then.

Natesh stared at his own reflection in the hotel window. It occurred to him that he didn't know anything at all about Firaz. Adam had vouched for him, of course, but if he had caught wind of what Natesh was trying to find, there was a chance he could blab to the wrong person. He decided to make his own way to Fethiye the next day. He'd make casual enquiries at the mosque and around the traders, find out if anyone knew of Chaudrakars in the area. For once in his life, he was going to take the bull by the horns and take some control.

Monday

Chapter 60

Firaz sat at a low table in one of Kaya Valley's traditional pancake houses. Behind him rose the Ghost Village, the hillside sprung with the remains of the old Greek town. He'd not long returned from the top of the hill, from where he'd photographed the coves around Gemiler Beach, framing his shots through the deep-set window frames of the old houses. Now, being November, there were few tourists picking their way along the stony hillside paths, the remnants of once-bustling streets.

Firaz had the table to himself, and in between picking at his Nutella-laden pancake and sipping sweet Turkish coffee, he worked his way through the reams of images he'd captured on camera, selecting those most likely to earn him a convincingly legitimate income. Lost in his craft, he was content to listen to donkeys braying in a nearby field and to birds cackling on an overhead wire. Amin's compound may have been only minutes away by car, but it and its concerns were far from Firaz's thoughts this particular morning.

Adam scanned the press association email for the day's must-report news. Details of the murder hunt in Dundee were beginning to make the national headlines now, and Adam couldn't help feeling a glow that he'd been the one with the scoops so far. Thanks to Donna. He felt bad, though. She'd just rung to tell him she was flying out to Turkey to find Natesh. He could have told her about Firaz and offered to find out which hotel Natesh was staying at. But he had to think that one through. Firaz was in a difficult situation.

His thoughts turned to Natesh. What was his friend really up to in Turkey? What was it that had made him decide to go there? He hoped that Firaz had been of some help to him, but he felt a growing unease at the prospect of getting Firaz mixed up in trouble. Firaz was of Kurdish descent, a trait guaranteed to bring a person under the close scrutiny of the Turkish authorities. Adam, and indeed Firaz, understood why, of course. With the neighbours that Turkey had, law enforcement and peace-keeping often meant taking actions that elicited criticism from its European allies, who didn't have to share their borders with the neighbours from hell. Nevertheless, it meant Firaz had to tread a careful line, particularly given his trade. He was a photo-journalist, chiefly a photographer, but in the eyes of the authorities a journalist – as if being a Kurd wasn't bad enough.

Adam was acutely aware that if Firaz was found to be associated with the police activity around Natesh, it could spell trouble for him. So he'd kept quiet about that when Donna had phoned.

He closed down his emails, not having processed much of their information. He decided he'd better tell Firaz about Donna's plans. Give him fair warning and a chance to stay out of trouble. Donna, he was sure, would be able to figure things out without his help.

Donna's phone rang twice then stopped.

"That's the taxi here," she said. She and Libby held on to one another for a moment longer, then she stood up. The sound of the taxi horn pierced the air.

"Phone me as soon as you arrive," said Libby. Her jaw was set tense. They'd gone over the details that Donna could give, but none of them brought any comfort. They didn't alter the fact that Donna was heading into the unknown. And with Alice Moone – the bullet and blade magnet, as Libby had pointed out previously.

"It's important that you don't discuss this trip with anyone," Donna reminded her. Libby nodded her understanding.

Firaz sprang up from his comfortable spot at the pancake house. The phone call he'd just received from Adam changed everything. He replayed it in his mind as he hurried towards his jeep.

"She's a friend of his," Adam had said in response to Firaz's shock that police from the UK were coming to find Natesh.

So, Firaz concluded, Natesh was working with the UK police and was about to bust open Amin's lucrative operation.

"What's her name?" Firaz had had the wherewithal to keep his head while Adam was on the phone. "Maybe I can help with taxi rides, or whatever?"

Now, cranking through the gears as his jeep careered along the forest track to Amin's complex, Firaz worked out what he was going to do. Time to let Amin know his son was in Turkey, and to warn the old man about a possible international police ambush.

Donna Davenport, he tried the name several times. *We'll be waiting for you.*

"As long as nobody knows we're going," Donna told Libby as she stepped into the airport taxi, "we'll be fine. Nobody's going to be looking for us, so we'll be able to keep out of trouble."

Chapter 61

Natesh woke early again. His sleep had been fitful, punctuated by panicked realisations that his mother was somewhere nearby – somewhere reachable – and needing his help. He'd been left the package containing clues that its sender presumably believed gave enough information for him to figure it out.

As he showered, he felt the first spark of assurance that he was finally about to do something useful. A growing courage that, by going off on his own to Fethiye, he would find some of the answers that he so desperately needed.

He made his way to the hotel restaurant for breakfast, and fired a quick text to Erin that he was okay but missing her. He felt bad about lying to her that he'd had to leave in such a hurry for an unexpected family funeral. She hadn't questioned his story, and had even arranged for a delivery of flowers to the bogus undertakers he'd invented. He'd have some explaining to do when he got home, he knew, but he didn't have head space to worry about that just now.

The hotelier made cheerful small talk as he set out Natesh's breakfast platter, and Natesh took the opportunity to casually ask him about the easiest way to get to Fethiye. In mid request, he was startled to hear an old voice cackle from the corner, "Taxi here! I drive Fethiye, very cheap."

Natesh turned and saw that the words belonged to a wizened creature who looked to be a little under two hundred years old. The old man grinned, a dark toothless grin, at Natesh's surprise.

"No, really…" began Natesh, fearing that the man could very well have lost his eyesight during the Great War.

"Cheap taxi," insisted the ancient one, grunting as he rose from his seat. "Cheaper than Asda, yes, cheaper than shoplifting!"

To Natesh's horror, the hotelier nodded in agreement. "Taxi is best to go to Fethiye," he said.

Natesh resigned himself. What choice did he have?

The guard almost ran to the compound's gates to let Firaz in when the battered jeep pulled up.

"Did you find out what the son's up to?" he asked, making ash fall like sleet onto his grubby t-shirt from the cigarette he'd left dangling from the corner of his mouth.

"It's not good," said Firaz. He saw the guard subconsciously touch his fingertips to the assault rifle that was slung over his shoulder. Firaz went on, "I got a tip-off. The old man's son has brought the UK police with him."

The guard grunted.

"If we don't move fast, we're fucked," said Firaz.

The guard muttered a sound like irritation, and nodded Firaz towards the villa. "There's been no sign of activity, no extra security," he said. "Amin doesn't know about this. Go and tell him, and tell him we need back-up here at the gates."

Firaz didn't need telling twice. He sprinted towards the villa, while the guard paced back and forth across the gates, now holding his rifle at the ready.

Firaz pushed open the villa's door, and startled two teenage girls who were in the first room, washing tomatoes. When they saw it was Firaz, they offered a polite greeting and continued with their chore.

Amin Chaudrakar was pacing around one of the wet rooms, running an electric razor over his chin. The buzzing stopped, and Amin stared in surprise to see Firaz standing at the door.

"What are you doing here?"

"We need to talk," said Firaz. "It's urgent. Did you know your son is here?"

Amin seemed to stop breathing.

"Natesh, isn't it?"

Amin put down the razor. His mouth opened and closed a number of times, before he managed, "Natesh is here? Natesh?"

Firaz saw the shock in the old man's eyes. This was news to him.

They went into a room with comfortable seating, and at Amin's request, Firaz told him all he knew about Natesh's arrival and about the police involvement.

"Do you trust your source?" asked Amin.

"Adam is an old friend, a journalist," said Firaz. "He'd have no reason to lie to me. He was warning me to keep out of their way. He doesn't know anything about *this*." He indicated *this* with a sweep of his hand around the direction of the compound.

"And the UK police are arriving tonight, you're sure?" Amin checked.

Firaz nodded, *yes*.

The two men sat in silence for several long moments. Finally Amin stood up. "I have business to take care of," he said. "I want you to bring Natesh here to me."

Samira sighed as she watched through the window at chickens scratching around in the dust. She'd walked around the inside of the villa, now that Amin had stopped locking the door to the room he'd confined her to during the last few days. But whenever she got near any opening to the outside, some guard or other would appear, blocking her way out.

She caught glimpses of the Taurus mountains above treetops in the distance each time a brief gap appeared in the cloud, and she longed to feel the Mediterranean breeze on her skin again. She wondered how long Amin was going to keep her here. Or even how long he himself would remain now that things had changed.

She put her hand into her pocket, feeling for the tiny wrestling figurine. She clasped her fingers around it, her heart suddenly searing with pain for Natesh.

The roar of an old jeep engine from outside the other end of the compound sent the chickens flapping in alarm, and Samira jumped when the door to her room slammed shut. Amin was walking across the room towards her, and he had his medical bag with him. It briefly took her to a moment long ago, a snapshot of their younger selves meeting in the lecture hall, discussing the new rules for women that would prevent her from graduating in post-revolution Iran, of hastily packing their rucksacks, of dashing across the border into Turkey. She snapped out of her reverie, sensing a new darkness to Amin's mood.

"So much for holding up your end of the bargain," he said. His voice lacked emotion. He sat down, still holding the medical bag. "Why did you tell him?"

Samira froze. What had happened now, to make Amin think she'd told Natesh? Her heart skipped a beat. Was it possible that Natesh had found out, and had come here? "I think it's Vidu you need to talk to if you think Natesh has been told anything." She managed to keep her voice under control.

"I already have," said Amin. "He wouldn't betray my wishes by telling Natesh about me."

"You think he's never gone behind your back before? Never lied to you?"

Amin tapped the side of his medical bag. Samira was uneasy at the gesture.

"This is going to go one of two ways," he said quietly. "It's going to be better for you if you tell me what Natesh and his police friends know."

Samira eyed the medical bag, and shuddered. *Police friends?* Perhaps there was reason to hope, after all. Of course, she thought, Donna must have worked out what was going on. She had very quickly cottoned on to the Craigie Drive link. And no matter how much of this sordid story she might have pieced together by now, she would be on her and Natesh's side. No matter how bad the evidence looked. She thought suddenly about the baby clothes hidden beneath her floor at home. About that night when Eleanor Wallace had asked her to take them, confused about why Vidu had given them to her to dispose of. Samira had known, all right, that Vidu would have been trying to clear up after some blunder at the Craigie Drive flat. She remembered taking the clothes and reassuring Eleanor that there was nothing to make a fuss about. Hiding them as soon as the midwife was gone. Choosing to keep silent in order to protect Natesh from Amin's threat.

Yes, thought Samira, no matter how bad the evidence looked... But if Donna was to be of any help now, she realised, time was not on her side.

"He doesn't know anything," she insisted. "And I don't know what you mean about police friends."

Amin sighed, exasperated. His forehead was damp. Samira could tell his anxiety was rising. They'd been apart for a long time, and it was clear that he no longer knew how to read her.

"There's a lot at stake here, for a lot of people," said Amin. "I can't afford to take chances. And I don't have the time."

Without any more words, Amin went to the desk on the far side of the room and began to unpack the medical bag.

"What are you doing?" This time fear found its way into Samira's voice.

Amin placed steel items, a bottle of local anaesthetic, disinfectant and bandaging onto the desk.

"I'm giving you one last chance," he said, lining up the items as a surgeon might do. "Tell me the truth. Or you will pay the consequences."

Samira stared at the medical bag and at the items now arranged on the desk. She shook her head. "I have not told Natesh anything. You have to believe me."

Amin's narrowed eyes sent a chill through her. She felt herself begin to tremble, but remained silent. She listened as Amin phoned and ordered two of his men to come and assist him.

Chapter 62

Fran looked out of the Dundee Registrar's office window, and watched for a moment as a wedding party hurriedly arranged into formation on the picturesque stairway. A harsh frost had settled in overnight, and the air still bit into the skin. Fran checked her phone. Ten o'clock on a Monday morning. She'd been in here for almost two hours, and was beginning to wonder if she was wasting her time. She felt the pressure growing, now that the press had somehow got hold of details about the baby they'd found at the Craigie Drive address, and even knew about Samira being missing, although they hadn't named her, thank God. Still, it was creating a hysteria in the city, and their investigation was coming under ever closer scrutiny from above.

Her mobile rang. Emma, she noted.

"The DNA results for Natesh and the missing Chalvez man," said Emma, "are you ready for this?"

Fran felt a fresh buzz of excitement. "Go on," she said, trying to sound business-like.

"They're related," said Emma.

"Related how?"

"No way to tell," said Emma, "but we know now that Natesh is related to Vidu Chalvez."

"That explains the physical similarity," said Fran.

"I'm checking Vidu Chalvez's DNA against the unidentified samples from the Moira Cowan and Eleanor Wallace crime scenes," said Emma. "I'll call you as soon as I know anything."

"Thanks," said Fran. "I'll tell Donna when she calls in." It could be a while, she thought. Donna and Alice had not long set off on their journey.

Fran decided she was in the right place, after all. She just had to figure out a plausible story that would link all the pieces of information that were emerging.

She'd spent the night scanning the Web for any mention of Marcus Edridge. The name was fairly unusual, and she knew he was a medic, so she'd reckoned it wouldn't be too difficult to confirm that any hits she found were the correct person. He'd been in practice as a GP in Dundee for most of his career – and, depending on which online forums he appeared in, was variably a wonderful man or an incompetent arse – and there was also reference to him having some surgical experience around Europe prior to that.

Then a site had come up that made her heart beat faster. It was an old academic paper, the subject of which made no sense to Fran. Something to do with sedation and anaesthetic, as far as she could tell. But the paper, authored by a string of names, had been published by Ankara University. There was the Turkish connection again, she'd noted. Marcus Edridge had been one of the acknowledged research team in the paper, which looked to have been part of an international collaboration. Among the other 20 or so names listed, one stood out immediately to Fran: Amin Chaudrakar.

Fran had decided she'd make this visit to the Registrar's to see if anything else could be found on the Chaudrakar name. But, up until now, she hadn't found anything she didn't already know, and as she sat watching the wedding conveyor belt churning in and out of the building, an idea began to form.

Natesh had gone, inexplicably, to Turkey, and now Fran had confirmed a link between a Turkish university and Marcus Edridge – who had once owned the flat where Eleanor Wallace was murdered and where they'd found the baby. Fran shuddered. What was more, they now had a three-way link with Marcus, Turkey, and somebody else by the name Chaudrakar.

They were hunting for a 40-something Latino, the man known to have been with both Eleanor Wallace and Moira Cowan just prior to their deaths. The midwives had been unable to confirm whether the man captured on CCTV with Samira – the man Ross thought was Natesh – could have been the guy they'd seen Moira with at the nightclub. The picture was too unclear. So, thought Fran, what if the mystery guy wasn't Latino at all? What if he was actually South East Asian, like Natesh?

And now the phone call from Emma, confirming the missing husband, Vidu Chalvez, was related to Natesh.

What if…what if, thought Fran…was Chalvez a false name? Could Vidu Chalvez, she began to wonder, have changed his name from, say, Chaudrakar?

So she began to look for records of the Chalvez's marriage and the births of their two children.

Finally, when it was pushing noon and her stomach had begun to rumble loudly, she found that the younger of the two Chalvez children had two middle names. One of them was Chaudrakar.

Fran wrote up a set of notes on what she'd found, and took photos of all the paperwork. Next stop, she was going to take Vidu's photograph – the one his distraught wife had handed in – to the midwives. She had a growing hunch that they'd recognise him this time.

It was still going to be a while before she could get her information to Donna. She decided to grab a spot of lunch, then find out how Morrison and Akwasi were getting on with enquiries in Aberdeen, trying to trace the mysterious Juanita – a possible witness to what had gone on at Craigie Drive. She would update Ross after that.

Chapter 63

Natesh sat in a restaurant overlooking Fethiye marina, and sipped at a strong Turkish coffee in an attempt to settle his nerves following his hair-raising "taxi" ride here. Finally, he stood up and began to make his way back from the marina and into the town's shopping streets.

Looking into a shop that, oddly, displayed motorbikes and washing machines, Natesh drew a deep breath and went inside. There, he found a man dressed in a business suit and two younger men in mechanics' overalls, all in the middle of a heated discussion that involved lots of pointing at one of the motorbikes. The three men looked round, surprised, to see Natesh approach them. One of the younger men said something that Natesh didn't understand.

"Sorry," said Natesh. "Do you speak English?"

"Speak English, yes," beamed the man. "How can I help you?"

Natesh held out a scrap of paper onto which he'd written *Chaudrakar*.

"Do you know anybody with this name?" he asked.

The young guy squinted at the name, and shook his head, *no*. He then held out his hand and took the note from Natesh to show the other two. It elicited the same response from each of them.

"Thank you, anyway," said Natesh.

Having built up the courage to make this start, he now felt deflated, even though these were the first people he'd asked.

For the next hour or so, he worked his way along the street, going in and out of all the shops. He lost count of the number of people who looked at the name scrawled onto his piece of paper, but none of them showed the least hint of recognition.

Natesh felt sure he'd been given the clue to come specifically to this town. It was where the old photograph had been taken, and it was where the bus ticket had been from.

Making for a cafe, he sat for a while to regain his thoughts and his energy. He dug the photograph from his pocket and studied it closely again. Samira, the man who was probably his father, and the baby that was most likely himself. *Who had taken the photo?* he wondered.

He stared at it, trying to pick out any clues as to which part of Fethiye it could have been. There were no signs of water or boats, so not by the marina. But beyond that, there was simply not enough detail in the background.

Dejected, he decided there was no option but to continue scouring the streets. He decided to make his way end to end first from the outer edges of the town, working his way gradually back in towards the central mosque, which was his landmark for finding transport back to Dalaman. Although the air was still warm, and his task was tiring and made his feet ache, Fethiye was a small place.

At some point during the afternoon, he came to a shop that was stuffed full of small electrical items. The shopkeeper there glanced with scepticism at Natesh's note, then did a double-take. Natesh felt his lungs constrict. The man recognised the name, Natesh could tell. But to his frustration, the shopkeeper suddenly shook his head, *no*. Natesh wanted to shake him by the shoulders. He'd seen recognition on the man's face, no doubt about it, but the shopkeeper dismissed him, and turned away to concentrate on some task.

Natesh walked slowly back out of the shop, wondering whether it would do any good to confront the man. When he glanced back over his shoulder, he saw the shopkeeper speaking on a mobile, and their eyes met momentarily. Natesh knew the look – the look of someone discussing a person behind their back.

Suddenly he felt lightheaded at the thought of the danger he could be in. He left the shop and walked quickly along the street, trying to find his way back to the marina.

Glancing over his shoulder, he felt sick to see the shopkeeper following him at a distance. The shopkeeper turned abruptly, not subtle enough, when Natesh caught his eye.

Natesh found his legs carrying him in a sprint, and when he looked back, the shopkeeper was running after him.

The street was empty of people. There was nowhere Natesh could see to hide. No crowds to merge into. His adrenaline kept him sprinting, and his eyes frantically sought a way to escape the pursuit of the shopkeeper. At last, he ran around a corner where people were waiting for the dolmuş. He pushed his way into the middle of the crowd, and crouched down as if to tie his shoe laces.

From his position, he could tell that the shopkeeper had run past the crowd, but there was no way of telling if he'd stopped nearby or had kept going. The chug of the dolmuş drew the crowd of people apart, some surging towards it, others keeping back. Natesh scrambled along with those who'd pulled away from the approaching vehicle. If the shopkeeper was using any brain cells, he'd be alerted to the sound of the engine and would be checking for Natesh boarding the bus.

The retreated group reformed next to a monument, and Natesh took refuge behind it. From here, he forced himself to look along the street to see where the shopkeeper had gone. There was no sign of him. Natesh spun his head in all directions, but the shopkeeper was nowhere to be seen. Tears of exertion formed in Natesh's eyes, and the breath he'd been holding for an eternity came rushing out in sobs. His heart beat wildly, and for a moment he thought he was going to faint.

He needed Donna, now more than ever before. As his breathing began to slow to normal, and as he felt sure the shopkeeper really wasn't going to spring out on him, he looked around for anywhere that may have a pay phone. There was a news kiosk on the corner, with an A-board outside that advertised international phone cards. That was promising.

Walking quickly and taking care to avoid a cluster of road traffic, Natesh went into the kiosk.

"Phone card?" he asked.

The woman behind the till barely looked up at him as she exchanged a card for his proffered note. She handed over his change, and when he asked about a phone, she grunted and nodded towards a discreet booth in the corner of the shop.

The woman went back to her business, and Natesh felt he might cry for joy as he dug Donna's number from his wallet. Then he hesitated, remembering the threatening note, promising harm to her if he got her involved. He gritted his teeth. Donna would know what to do. He keyed in the first numbers, then stopped. But they knew where to find her. They'd photographed him with her, without their knowing.

Things were getting out of hand now. He had to talk to her. He keyed in the first numbers again. Stopped again.

He glanced over his shoulder. The kiosk was empty. He took a deep breath, and pressed the keys again.

But before he could complete the number, there was a commotion behind him, and he suddenly felt a sack being pushed down over his head, and rough hands grabbing him by the arms, as he was dragged, shocked, away from the booth.

Chapter 64

As the plane circled down towards Dalaman airport, Donna closed her eyes to stop her head from spinning. The four hour flight had passed by in an uneventful blur, punctuated by the rattling of the catering trolleys, the occasional, *Would you like to buy a scratch card, madam?* and the competition going on between the hum of the engines and Alice's snoring. Still with her eyes closed, Donna elbowed Alice.

"Wakey, wakey," she said. She could feel Alice attempt to stir against the extra dose of diazepam she'd taken. Who would ever have guessed that the indomitable Alice Moone, storm trooper extraordinaire and veteran of several tours of duty in the planet's most inhospitable hell-holes, was afraid of flying?

Bing! Alice jumped. "Whawassat?"

"Ladies and gentlemen, the Captain has switched on the fasten seatbelts sign as we begin our descent into Dalaman." The message was then repeated in Turkish.

"Wake up," Donna said again. This time she opened her own eyes and gave Alice's arm a shake.

"Mhnhmf," said Alice, as she struggled to open her inexpressibly heavy eyelids. "Awake. Ready for duty."

"That's us landing, General," said Donna. "The relaxing bit's finished."

"We've still got to land?" Alice's eyes sprang open in alarm. "This is the bit I hate the most." She gripped Donna's hand.

Alice survived touchdown, with only the slightest whimper escaping as the plane's wheels bounced on and off the tarmac, and now they sat waiting for the steps to be attached to the exit doors.

Holding their passports and visas, she and Donna filed from the plane and made their way to security, where they took up their places in the line of people shuffling their way through the airport procedures. The diazepam had all but worn off, and Alice was returning to her usual self.

"You know," she said solemnly to Donna, "as an officer of the law, it's my duty to do my very best to mix business with as much pleasure as possible on this trip."

"I'm impressed by your dedication to duty, Sergeant Moone," said Donna. "Which security booth has the cutest guard, then?"

"Middle one."

They joined the middle line.

When it came to their turn, Alice stood forward, offered her passport and visa to the security guard, and beamed at him. He glanced up at her, and catching the unexpected scar-shrouded grin, flinched in alarm.

"I have that effect on men," Alice whispered loudly over her shoulder. Donna sniggered. The security guard looked momentarily baffled for a response, before squaring his shoulders and sending back his fiercest scowl. Donna stepped in front of Alice.

"We're here on police business," she said. "Lieutenant Efe Demır is expecting us."

The young security guard blinked quickly at Donna then fleetingly at Alice as he took her passport. He tapped on some keys, glanced at the resulting information on his screen, and nodded.

"Wait here," he indicated to the side of his booth. "Lieutenant Demır has sent someone to meet you."

"I'm not having you steal my thunder with the local talent," said Alice to Donna, as she winked at the guard. The guard shuddered, and ushered forward the next person in line. Alice guffawed.

Late at night, the temperature in Dalaman was still more than ten degrees higher than it had been when they'd left Dundee in the middle of the afternoon. Donna was contemplating this, and wondering if Natesh had also arrived here in a heavy jacket and scarf, when a dark-skinned woman wearing a colourful scarf on her head approached them.

"Officers Davenport and Moone?" she asked.

"Yes, Detective Inspector Donna Davenport."

"Sergeant Alice Moone."

They all shook hands.

"Welcome to Turkey," said the woman. She held Donna's gaze for a moment longer than was necessary. "I'm Gönül Macar. I work with Lieutenant Demır. Please, come with me."

"You work with Lieutenant Demır?" Donna asked, noting the lack of a police uniform.

"In a private capacity," said Gönül, and she turned and led them away from airport security without further explanation.

Chapter 65

Firaz pulled up outside the hotel and waited. There was no reply from Natesh to his text. He waited five more minutes, then went inside. A knock on the room door got no response. He dialled Natesh's mobile. It went onto answer phone. Firaz cursed loudly, and made his way to the hotel bar.

"Your UK guest," he inquired, "do you know where he is?"

"Took a taxi to Fethiye," said the hotelier, glancing at the clock on the wall behind him. "This morning, around eight."

Firaz cursed again, and hurried back to his jeep. He quickly found Amin's number, and made the call.

"We have a problem," he told Amin. "Natesh has gone to Fethiye on his own. He must be setting up a stake-out for his police friends arriving. What are you going to do?"

"Come back here," said Amin. "I have a job for you. It should be enough to warn him off. I need you to deliver a message to his hotel. A pointer in the right direction, let's say."

Firaz heard Amin chuckle, a grim sound he'd heard before when the doctor was *working*.

Samira strained to pick up any sounds she could of the caller's voice on Amin's phone. She watched her husband's face grow red, saw his eyes narrow and his jaw set in determination, but although she didn't manage to make out any of the words that were being spoken to him, she knew the call was about Natesh. *His hotel…Warn him off.* It could only have been about Natesh. Amin had, after all, been waiting here for Natesh to be brought to him.

She had spent the morning begging Amin not to harm their son, and she had seen his conflict. She had seen how close Amin was to preferring a reconciliation with his son over a confrontation. And now, it looked to her as though neither one of these was about to happen. Whatever the phone call had been about, it looked to Samira as though Natesh couldn't be found. The disappointment and the fear were plain to see on Amin's face. And the decision he'd reached, it was equally plain, was not a good one for Natesh.

Samira twisted at the amber ring on her finger. Where could Natesh be? But a movement from the side of the room stopped her thoughts in their tracks. Amin had indicated to his two henchmen. One of them now came and stood behind Samira. She felt her heart constrict in fear, and panic began to rise up from her gut. She knew it would be no good trying to run or to fight as she saw the other man approach her with a syringe.

"Just something to relax you," Amin muttered. "You see, I'm not the monster that you think I am." He was removing more items from his medical bag. A small drill now. Steel wires. Samira heard herself begin to sob, then the syringe was in her arm.

"I'll reconstruct the hand, of course," Amin was going on, "to the best of my ability with the time we have at our disposal. It's not complicated. I have done it before."

"Reconstruct the hand?" Samira asked. Her head was becoming flossy now, and her words emerged thick and slow. "What are you doing?"

"Is the nerve block ready?" Amin asked one of the men. Either he'd ignored her question, or his answer had become swallowed up in her swirling brain fog.

From somewhere in space the echoey voice of the man replied that it was, and then Samira's consciousness fell into blackness.

Chapter 66

The air conditioned bus dropped Donna and Alice outside a pink building that was once pretty but was now held together by scaffolding.

"Last time I'm travelling on a Police Scotland budget," muttered Alice.

"Yes, whoever booked this is done for when I find them," said Donna.

A burly man in a damp white shirt stomped out of the building's main door and bellowed at them, "My guests! Welcome to my hotel!"

"Done for," whispered Alice in Donna's direction.

They followed him into their hotel, and their hearts sank as they made their way towards their room.

"This was the only room available at short notice," he said, with no hint of shame. "In two more nights I can move you to a room with two beds."

Donna and Alice were too tired to react. The sight of the bed made them both sigh with relief, even if they did have to share it. They threw their cases onto the floor, and bid the hotel manager goodnight.

Donna spotted it first, when she turned round to survey the room. An open plan bathroom.

"You have got to be kidding," she said.

Alice snorted in laughter. "Just keep your eyes closed when I'm in, and I'll do the same for you," she said.

"Did I piss someone off in a previous life?" said Donna.

"Well, I'm too tired to shower," said Alice. "I'm off to bed."

"Which side?"

They threw off their outer wear and collapsed into the bed, one at each side, back to back. A welcome cool breeze blew in through the room's open window, and with it the din of cars, trucks, buses and vans of all sorts, as well as a melee of music and cheery voices from surrounding bars.

"Typical," said Alice as she yawned. "A place brimming with gorgeous men, and here I am stuck in bed with a fecking lesbian."

"Alice," murmured Donna.

"Yes?"

"Shut up and get to sleep."

Tuesday

Chapter 67

"I've got lots to tell you."

Fran sounded almost breathless.

"Well, I've only left you for one day," said Donna. "I'd expect nothing less. What have you got?"

She had her mobile on speaker phone, and Alice was flossing her teeth at the wobbly sink as she listened, too

"Well," Fran hurried on, "first of all, the missing husband – Vidu Chalvez – is related to Natesh. DNA confirmed."

Donna and Alice raised an eyebrow at one another, registering surprise.

Fran barely stopped for breath. "And I'm pretty sure Chalvez isn't even his real name. I checked his kids' birth records, and one of them has a middle name – wait for it – Chaudrakar!"

Donna made a sound to begin saying something, but Fran kept going. "Now, Chaudrakar, you'll probably know, being Natesh's friend…"

"Breathe," said Donna. "Slow down."

There was a brief pause over the phone, then Fran continued as if operated by clockwork. "Chaudrakar is a Hindi name, but obviously Chalvez isn't. It's Latino, right?"

"I see where this is going," said Alice, examining the floss.

"This Vidu character," said Donna. "You think he changed his name?"

"His whole identity," said Fran, her voice rising an octave and several decibels. "Now, think about this: what if Vidu Chaudrakar-Chalvez is the man on the CCTV image with Samira? What if he's the Latino we've been trying to identify?"

"If he's related to Natesh and Samira, it explains why she might have gone with him," said Donna. "Sounds plausible. Ask Emma to…"

"I did."

"Of course you did."

"Morrison and Akwasi are taking Vidu's photograph to the midwives, to see if we can get a positive on the guy Moira Cowan met at the nightclub. So, by the end of play today, we'll be able to

225

confirm whether he's the Latino."

"Good work," said Donna. "If we get the positive ID, I want the information to go to the press as soon as possible. We need all eyes on the lookout for this guy and his associates."

"That's not all," said Fran.

"Oh, I forgot," said Donna. "You had all night, too, didn't you?" She heard Alice chuckle from across the hotel room.

"There's someone called Amin Chaudrakar," said Fran, undeterred. "He was part of a medical research team at Ankara University in the early 80s. He co-authored a report with Marcus Edridge."

"Bloody hell!" Donna gasped.

"I can't find any more reference to Amin Chaudrakar," said Fran, "but I don't think it can be Vidu Chalvez – he's a bit too young."

"Any joy with finding Juanita?" Donna asked.

"Morrison and Akwasi went up to Aberdeen yesterday," said Fran, "but we still can't find anyone who knows of her."

"Tell Aiden to keep pressing for enquiries from the Aberdeen officers," said Donna. "We need to find her."

"Understood," said Fran. "Oh, and just to give you the heads up – I don't know how, but the papers have found out about the baby, and about Samira, though they haven't named her. They're speculating like mad that Craigie Drive was being used to sell prostitutes' babies. I still don't know how they got the intel about the prostitute link, though."

Donna shifted her gaze to the far wall, to avoid giving anything of her discussion with Adam away to Alice.

After the call ended, Donna and Alice perched side by side on the bed.

"Marcus Edridge meets Amin Chaudrakar here in Turkey," said Alice.

"He comes home, buys the flat on Craigie Drive…"

"And we're talking the same time frame as Samira arriving in Dundee with baby Natesh?"

"Yes," said Donna.

They both paused, staring blankly ahead at the room door, as though the pieces of the jigsaw might appear there.

"Some sort of operation is being conducted, involving Craigie Drive, midwives, Vidu Chalvez-Chaudrakar, and Kozel's gang," said Alice.

"And a street girl called Juanita," whispered Donna. "We're close." She tugged at her bottom lip. "We're so close."

"Well, then, are you ready for the next bit?" Alice asked.

Donna stood up. "Ready as I'll ever be."

Natesh sat with his back against the wall of the tiny room. High above his head, and with no way to reach it, there was a small window with a metal grille across it. There was no furniture in the room. Simply an empty plate lying on the stone floor, a half empty bottle of water, a bucket that stank, and what looked like an old dish towel tossed next to it.

His head ached on one side, and he felt nauseous. He had no idea where he was, whether it might be a prison cell or not, nor how long he had been in here.

He remembered being in the phone booth in Fethiye, then waking up here. Since he'd woken, the only human contact he'd had was the arrival, twice, of a surly, lanky youth, who brought food, changed the bucket over for an empty one, and threw Natesh looks that could curdle milk.

Shocked by the whole turn of events, Natesh had simply sat and stared into space, only occasionally standing up when his muscles demanded it.

Whenever a thought entered his head, he chased it away, but he knew he was silently praying for Donna to find out where he was and come crashing through the door.

"This is the place," said Donna, re-checking Adam's text.

She and Alice got out of the taxi in front of the squeaking door. Going through it, they were surprised to see the hotel laid out in a complex of apartment blocks, all tastefully screened by greenery. The pool. The flowers.

"Better than ours," muttered Alice as a porter arrived to offer assistance.

The porter nodded his recognition of Natesh in the photo that Donna showed him, and appeared happy to take them to his room when she handed him a 50 New Turkish Lira note. The porter led them along the pathway to an outer block, and began to jingle the large set of keys he was carrying. As they rounded the corner to the door, they stopped abruptly at the sight of the apartment. The door was ajar, splintered at the lock. The porter's eyes grew wide in astonishment. Donna instinctively took the lead, and dismissed the porter with words that he didn't need translated.

Slowly, Donna inched her way into the room, Alice close in at her back.

Inside, the room was a mess. The bed was upended, glass shards littered the floor, the sheets were slashed, and Natesh's jacket was impaled to the wall by a hunting knife. The message was clear. Somebody wasn't happy at Natesh having been here.

There was only a bedroom and an adjoining bathroom, and they checked within seconds that nobody else was in here.

Donna touched the jacket on the wall, shocked to see this familiar item so brutalised.

"This is Natesh's," she confirmed to Alice. "He's walked right into a viper's nest."

"But they haven't killed him," Alice said quickly, seeing the expression on Donna's face. "There are no traces of blood here. Looks like someone's broken in while he's been out, and either he hasn't come back yet, or he came back, got a fright, and ran off."

"Well, let's have a look," said Donna after a deep breath. "We'll see if he left in a hurry. If there's one thing we know, Natesh doesn't think to cover his tracks."

In the bathroom, Natesh's toiletries were there, albeit in disarray. At the other side of the upturned bed, his suitcase lay with clothes spilling out of it.

"Wherever he is," said Donna, "he was certainly planning to come back here."

Alice was carefully lifting the heaped linen sheets from the bed, when she stopped suddenly.

"Boss, you're going to want to see this," she said.

Donna hurried to her side, and they stared at a box that had been hidden there beneath the sheets.

Donna's stomach lurched. She had an odd flashback to the moment she'd opened the freezer drawer in Craigie Drive. The same feeling swept up her gullet now as she tentatively raised the lid from the box.

"Oh, God!" Alice almost retched.

Inside the box sat a finger. Adorning the finger was an amber ring.

Chapter 68

Donna and Alice looked out of the taxi window, agog, as they arrived at the police station in Ölüdeniz. They'd called in the update about the finger to Ross, and had sent him all of the photos they'd taken in Natesh's room, leaving him to make arrangements with his Turkish counterparts. Then they'd sat in relative silence for the hour's drive from Dalaman to this picturesque town. It was time to meet Lieutenant Efe Demır, their liaison officer for this hush-hush operation.

"I'm putting in for a transfer," Alice muttered, staring at the sparkling turquoise waters of the world famous Blue Lagoon.

A large man with grey peppered hair greeted them as they got out of the taxi, and introduced himself as Lieutenant Efe Demır. He wore the dark green trousers and light green shirt of a Gendarme.

They exchanged pleasantries while he led them into a meeting room, where Gönül Macar was waiting for them.

"Thank you for meeting us," Donna said, once they were all seated.

Demır broke into a wide smile. "Welcome to my country," he said. "I am here to help, and you have already met Gönül, haven't you? She is a private investigator, often works with me. And now, I can show you the photos."

"You have the photos already?"

"Yes, yes," Demır seemed overjoyed at his own efficiency. He excused himself and let himself through a door on the other side of the room, leaving Donna and Alice there with Gönül. Donna became aware of Gönül's lingering eye, and turned away to avoid it.

Demır returned promptly, and placed a folio of passport photographs on the table.

"Impressive," Alice nodded in awe. Demır looked pleased.

Gönül leaned across Donna, and separated the folio into two separate piles.

"These," she said, "are the passengers from the UK from Tuesday last week. And these, from Saturday."

The Saturday pile was enormous. Alice picked it up and began to flick through. Donna did the same with the Tuesday pile, doing her best to ignore the fact that Gönül was still leaning across her, and to stop wanting a draw of Demir's cigarette. Then, almost immediately, she spotted the photo she was looking for.

"Here they are," she said, pointing to Samira and Vidu. "Can you get me their details?"

Gönül, surprised, took the photos from Donna. "Of course." She stood up straight, and looked at Demir. They exchanged some rapid words in Turkish, and he nodded her towards the door.

"My cousin is chief of airport security," she said as she left. "I can get the details quickly."

"Having a private investigator is an advantage," Demir smiled. "Not so tied by police procedure."

Gönül went out just as the Turkish equivalent of the tea trolley arrived with four cups of coffee.

"You are a mind reader," said Alice.

"Turkish coffee, you like?" said Demir.

"I think I'm liking every Turkish thing," said Alice, fluttering her eyelashes at him with melodrama.

Efe Demir laughed, a deep rumbling laugh straight from his gut.

"Didn't flinch, good sign," Alice whispered to Donna.

"One more to find," said Donna, her mood remaining serious, and taking half the Saturday pile from Alice.

"Right you are, boss," said Alice, as they began to scan for Natesh's mugshot.

"At least it'll be an up to date photo," said Donna.

"Yeah," said Alice. "I'll need to get a new one. My current passport photo hasn't got all my Belfast scars on it."

"Well, how on earth did you get through security?" said Donna.

"You saw how that guard had the hots for me," said Alice. "And by the way, don't think I haven't noticed."

"Noticed what?"

"The pretty Turkish delight has the hots for *you*."

"Oh, don't," said Donna, waving her palm in front of Alice.

"What happens in Turkey, stays in Turkey," Alice winked. "Just sayin'."

Donna ignored the comment and kept scanning the photos.

Demır sat watching them. His coffee and his cigarette were finished by the time Donna announced, "There he is!"

Sure enough, Natesh stared out at them from a page full of faces. She held it up to Demır. He stood up, took the photo, and without saying anything, left the room. In his place, Gönül came back, brandishing a sheet of paper with handwritten notes on it.

She sat next to Donna, and ran her finger down the writing.

"These are the woman's details," she said.

Donna read them, then sighed in exasperation. "False name," she said. "They've come in on false passports." She found herself glancing involuntarily at Gönül, as if to accuse her personally for the security breach. Gönül simply smiled back an apology.

Alice took the paper and read the details. "Independent travel," she announced. "No onward or accommodation details."

"Shit!" Donna sprang to her feet and began to pace around the room.

When Demır returned, Donna noted the look that passed between him and Gönül.

Demır set Natesh's photo in front of Donna and Alice.

A rattle of angry sounding words emitted from Gönül when she saw it, and the expression on Demır's face grew dark.

Donna and Alice both shifted uncomfortably, noting the sudden change in the atmosphere.

"Chaudrakar?" Demır said in a tone approaching anger. "Why do you look for this man, Chaudrakar?"

Chapter 69

The atmosphere in the police room in Ölüdeniz was tense. Donna and Alice sat around the small table with Efe Demır and Gönül Macar. Between them sat the passport photographs of Samira, Vidu and Natesh.

"This," began Donna, "is Natesh. We're worried about him, and we think he's in danger."

Demır and Gönül looked at one another and exchanged hurried words that didn't sound positive.

"This one here," Donna went on, tapping Samira's photo, "is Natesh's mother. The details here are false. Her real name is Samira Chaudrakar. We don't know who this man is." She indicated Vidu's photo.

Demır rubbed at his chin. He made brief eye contact with Donna, and she saw that he was in a dilemma. It was clear that he wanted to help her investigation, yet something told her that he felt compromised.

He knows something, she realised. Her stomach lurched. If Demır knew something, then it didn't seem to be something that Donna was going to like.

"I think perhaps we can help each other," Demır said eventually. He ignored the barrage of angry words from Gönül. "We have lots to discuss. Are you hungry?"

"Starving," said Alice, before Donna had the chance to be polite.

"Then we go eat and we talk," said Demır.

As they got up to go, he picked up each of the passenger information sheets and studied them.

Donna and Alice followed Demır through the main street of Ölüdeniz, past shuttered gift shops and along an empty beach front, until arriving at a small restaurant – one of the few that were still open in this late season. At a small hotel opposite, two men were sitting on the roof, working with hammers at some repair, and another was painting the exterior wall. Some of the gift shops were still open, but it looked to Donna as though their main activity now was to be cleaned and repaired in time for re-stocking for the following summer.

The town had a still air about it of having lost a large part of its population, which it had, since most of its summer inhabitants had already returned to their rural homes, relying on their tourist revenue to sustain them over the coming winter months.

A dog sat outside the restaurant, and wagged its tail at the approach of Donna, Alice, Demır and Gönül.

The restaurant owner shouted a welcome to Demır and Gönül as they entered, then disappeared into the kitchen following a cursory glance at Donna and Alice.

"We can talk here," said Demır. "Is safe."

Donna caught Alice's surprised glance. *Safe?*

"You're safe," said Amin.

Samira opened her eyes, and immediately felt queasy. Amin placed a bowl at her chin and she leaned over to retch. It was then that she noticed the bandaging around her hand.

"What have you done?"

"Rest," Amin said, placing the bowl back onto the floor. He sat down at her side, making her roll towards the edge of the bed. Her arm slid helplessly across her body.

"You've had a nerve block," Amin said. "Once it wears off, I can give you suitable painkillers."

"What did you do to me?" There was anger in her voice now.

"I had to send a warning," said Amin. "I couldn't risk having Natesh bring the police here. But it seems to have worked. He's gone."

Samira stared at him, her eyes heavy and bleary. "Gone where?"

Amin shrugged, a casual gesture. "He obviously found our little token in his hotel room, and decided to do the right thing. I don't know where he's gone. Back home, probably. But he's no longer here, so we're safe. For now."

Samira's heart sank. When she'd thought she couldn't feel any more despair, she found that she was wrong.

A young waiter slid a large tray of various dishes onto the table in front of Donna, Alice, Demır and Gönül, a mixture of cold platter and steaming rice, beans and meats. Then he slunk off in silence.

233

Demır indicated to Donna and Alice to watch, while he took a notebook from his pocket and began to sketch in pencil in it.

Donna looked at the notebook. "What are you doing?"

"Making a map," said Demır. "I will explain."

He placed his makeshift map on the table. "Turkey is a very big country." He marked an x on a particular spot. "Here is Dalaman airport." Then he drew a short line going south from Dalaman. "Here is...er...here." He pointed to the ground at his feet. "It's about an hour to drive, you already know."

He drew a longer line going south-east from there, and his expression grew more serious. "Here is a refugee camp next to the Syrian border. The town is called Suruç."

He put the pencil back in his pocket. Donna and Alice were leaning closer and closer towards him, wondering what could be coming next.

"Turkey houses many refugees," Demır went on, "for many, many years. They flee from Iran, Syria, run from bombs, from hunger, from bad soldiers." He looked up to confirm they were following. "Many women come to Turkey to be free. To go to university."

Donna and Alice stared at him in silence.

"When I was a young police officer," Demır said, "there was a revolution in Iran. Many people left there. We know one man came to Turkey from Iran. His name was Amin Chaudrakar."

Donna and Alice looked surprised.

"He was a doctor," said Demır, "but not working in the hospital. He traded the...the..." He patted his chest and his lower abdomen, not knowing the words he needed.

"Human organs?" ventured Donna. "Heart, liver, kidneys? He traded in human organs?"

"Yes," said Demır. "We believe he was doing this. Rich people paid him large amounts of money."

"Who were the organ donors?" asked Donna.

Demır tapped the last x he had marked on his map. "Here, we think. He took human organs in the refugee camps. We spoke to many people in the camps, over many years. They told us a doctor came. Once, maybe twice each month. He gave medical treatments, the people were so grateful, and they trusted him."

"How did he get the organs?" asked Donna.

"When the people trusted him," Demır said, "then he was able to offer them money. Not much, compared with the big money he made from the rich organ recipients, but enough that these people in the camps – destitute people – they agreed. Maybe sometimes they killed to find organs for him."

The horror of what Demır was telling them brought the small group into a heavy silence. Demır leaned in towards them, and his voice dropped almost to a whisper. "We think he stopped doing this after a while. The authorities grew suspicious of the hospital, and it was harder for him to hide what was going on there. Bad for international reputation." He gave a dry chuckle that gave away his disgust. "But he kept going to the camp. People still trusted him, thought he was a good man, and he began to tell them, *I will find a safe journey for your daughters.*"

"He's been smuggling girls out of the camps," said Alice. "Sending them abroad as prostitutes."

"Or as baby-making machines," said Donna.

"The baby in the flat!" said Alice.

"You have information about this man?" asked Demır.

"It looks like there is a link to our investigation," said Donna. "May I use your pencil?"

On another napkin, she drew two stick figures. Under one, she wrote *Eleanor*, and under the other, *Moira*.

"These two women," she said, "were midwives. Both were murdered. Eleanor almost two years ago. Moira last week. We believe the same man killed them both."

"I see," said Demır.

Donna drew another stick figure next to a question mark. Then another figure, writing *Samira* beneath it, placing Samira's passport photo next to it.

"She went missing," she said. "We were afraid she would become the third victim. She was seen leaving her home with this man." She pointed to the figure with the question mark beside it.

Demır looked sceptical, but nodded his head in understanding.

"And Natesh," said Donna, indicating to his passport photo, "has been falsely identified as the man she left with. He is her son."

"He has been set-up?" asked Demır.

"No," said Donna. "Mistaken identity. Look closely." She pushed the passport photos of Natesh and Vidu around for

Demır to study. Gönül moved round the table to look, too.

"What do you see?" asked Donna.

"They are both very alike," said Demır. "Maybe father and son?"

"Maybe," said Donna. "We don't know yet who he is, but we do know there is a family link between them. We have a possible name – Vidu Chalvez – but I don't believe it's his real name. Do you recognise it?"

Demır and Gönül both shook their heads, *no*.

"Our working theory is that Vidu killed Eleanor and Moira, and now he's here in Turkey with Samira," Alice told them.

Demır sat back in his chair, took a packet of cigarettes from his pocket, and lit one. He stared at the photos and at Donna's stick people while the smoke swirled lazily around his head. When he glanced up, he saw Donna staring hungrily at the smoke, and he held the packet out to her. Without a word, she took one and lit it with his lighter. She inhaled so deeply, Alice prodded her in the ribs to make her breathe back out.

"He is not Amin Chaudrakar," Demır said eventually, tapping his finger on Vidu's photo.

Donna took the pencil again and drew a house on the napkin. "Here," she said, "we found a dead baby." Demır's face registered disgust. Gönül took in a sharp breath. "It gets worse. The baby's organs were missing."

She watched Demır's eyes focus on each of the drawings and the photos, seeking a connection.

"This house," said Donna, "is where Eleanor was murdered."

"Here is my idea," said Demır, taking the pencil from Donna. He placed his hand-drawn map alongside her sketches. "Amin Chaudrakar, he takes the women from here," he circled the refugee camp at Suruç. "He moves them to here." He circled the flat on Donna's napkin. "He forces them to work as prostitutes, maybe have babies, which he sells. If they die, he sells the body parts."

"It works," said Donna.

"But how would Samira be involved?" asked Alice. "Remember, we found the baby clothes in her flat. She must have something to do with this."

Donna thought back to her discussion with Ross. Witness protection? "Could she have known Amin Chaudrakar? Run away from him? Or tried to run away?"

Again, Demır studied the photographs. "She may be his wife," he concurred. "Same age. But then, maybe she is helping him?"

"You need to consider that possibility, Donna," said Alice. "Samira has been in the perfect position, if you think about it, and this guy Amin will have needed someone in the UK with midwifery expertise. And the timeline fits. Samira must have come to Dundee around the time Demır says the people smuggling started."

Donna closed her eyes, bringing to mind the look on Samira's face the night she'd gone to watch the football with Natesh. Samira had known something about the murders, Donna had been sure of it at the time.

"But she never left Dundee," she said, knowing she was trying to find any way out for Samira. "Not even for a holiday. Would she really help her husband all that time, yet never meet him?"

"Perhaps she did," said Demır. "Perhaps he visited her?"

"No," said Donna. "Natesh would have asked questions. He never knew his father."

Demır looked puzzled. "How do you know this?"

"Natesh is my friend," said Donna. "I've known him almost my whole life. That's why I know he's innocent. I know him. His mother has been brought here, and God alone knows how, but Natesh figured it out, and he's come here to find her. They're both in danger." She watched Demır's expression intently while she told him about the discovery in Natesh's hotel room.

"You are a very senior detective," said Demır, leaning across the table to hold Donna in an eye-lock. "For a woman to become senior, you must be very good."

"She's the best," said Alice.

"Then, I believe you," said Demır. "I believe your friend is innocent. Perhaps Amin Chaudrakar has threatened his mother. I am sure she would do anything to protect her child, even though he is an adult."

"But then, who is helping Amin Chaudrakar?" asked Gönül.

"The house where we found the baby was owned by a doctor named Marcus Edridge," said Donna. "He bought it in the 1980s. We know that he worked for a while with Amin Chaudrakar, at Ankara University. Perhaps they concocted their plan, then

Marcus returned to Dundee to be the contact there. Do you know the name?"

"No," said Demır. "But you know him? You can interrogate?"

"Not so easy," said Donna. "He's very ill." She tapped her head. "He can't remember anything."

"Is it a tail-end for you?" Demır asked.

"*Dead* end," said Alice. "But actually, no. He might not remember what he did yesterday, but you can bet he remembers what he did 30 years ago."

Donna was already on her mobile. "I'll find out where we are with bringing him in for questioning. At least to find out if he'll admit to knowing Amin Chaudrakar in the 1980s." She rang Fran's number, and left a message for her to return the call as soon as possible.

"But this man, Marcus, won't know where to find Chaudrakar now," said Demır dolefully.

"Why would Samira return here?" said Alice, trance-like. "And why did Natesh report her missing, then come here? Someone must have told him where she was."

"Let's ask him," said Gönül with a sly smile. "I know where he is. Let me take you to him."

Donna stared in surprise as she ended her call.

"I think we will have the break-in soon," said Demır.

"Break-*through*," said Alice.

Chapter 70

Donna and Alice clambered into Demır's car behind him and Gönül. Donna noted the lack of seatbelts as Demır hit the accelerator and took off uphill and out of Ölüdeniz. Gönül refused to answer Donna's questions about Natesh's whereabouts. "You will see, soon," she kept responding, in between rapid phrases that shot back and forth between her and Demır. Although Donna couldn't understand the words, she could tell by the body language that the two Turks were distinctly uncomfortable about something.

Demır sped around hairpin bends on a narrow road that wound its way up a pine-clad hillside, his expression grim. From time to time, in amongst the forest, Donna caught glimpses of villas or hotel frontages, and when they reached the summit of the road, she looked out onto the trailing outskirts of neighbouring Hisarönü. Then, to her relief, they were on a straight road with very little traffic on it. She tried again, but could not get Gönül to tell her anything about Natesh. The private investigator and the police lieutenant appeared to have disagreed about something, and were now avoiding eye contact with one another.

Donna's phone pierced the icy silence.

"Returning your call, Ma'am…Donna," said Fran.

"Thanks, Fran, has there been any movement on getting Marcus Edridge in?" Donna asked.

"A little," said Fran. "We've finally got an Appropriate Adult, but Ross still doesn't think we can use anything he says."

"I'd agree with him there," said Donna, recalling the inability of the retired doctor to remember what he'd just said. "But do one thing – talk to him about his time in Ankara and anything he can tell us about Amin Chaudrakar. Anything we could use to track him down today, and anything to hint at their involvement with Craigie Drive."

"Consider it done," said Fran. "Oh, and the midwives positively identified Vidu Chalvez-Chaudrakar as the man that went home with Moira Cowan after the night club. We're still pressing Peter Cowan to admit who he thinks is on the CCTV image."

"Good work," said Donna. "We know Vidu is in Turkey now, so let the press know we have a definite lead – just don't mention where it's taken us." And she ended the call.

Demır kept driving at a steady – but fast – pace, and there was no more conversation in the car until they came to the crest of a hill, and stretched before them was the stunning view of Fethiye harbour and its surrounding hilltop villas. The car seemed to stream downhill now into the town. Demır began to point out various places of interest, as though this was a tourist trip.

Slowing the car, Demır brought them through the basin of Fethiye town and into a downtrodden suburb, where he suddenly came to a stop, and Gönül got out. Donna had no clue what the words meant that she and Demır exchanged, but they were terse.

"We are going a little bit further," Demır said, turning his head to address Donna and Alice. "Gönül will join us soon."

"What about Natesh?" asked Donna. "Where is he?"

"It will become clear," said Demır. Donna didn't appreciate the mystery, wondering why such an atmosphere had developed between him and Gönül, and she shot Alice a look of exasperation.

Natesh was grunting with exertion, doing press-ups in the tiny room that he had now convinced himself must be a prison cell, when he heard the door being cranked open. He scarpered back against the wall, and wiped sweat out of his eyes. When the door opened, he was surprised to see the woman from the hotel – the one who'd worn the colourful scarf in her hair. Natesh stared at her, and was about to yell at her, when she smiled at him.

"I must offer you my most sincere apologies," she said.

Natesh opened his mouth, but his voice failed him.

Gönül went on. "There has been a misunderstanding. Please, come with me."

She held the door open. Natesh took a hesitant step forward, half expecting the woman to start laughing and slam the door in his face. But Gönül gestured for him to hurry.

"Follow me," she said, leading Natesh from the room and into what looked like a sports locker room. "You must take a shower, and I have borrowed some clothes that you can wear today."

Natesh came to an abrupt halt. "I'm not doing a thing until you tell me what's going on." He folded his arms across his chest, hoping to look defiant and courageous.

"I am taking you to see Donna," said Gönül.

Natesh's eyes sprang open wide. "Donna? She's here?"

Gönül tried to hide a smile. "Shower first. You stink."

She pointed to a rack of towels and to a row of shower cubicles behind the lockers. Natesh almost tripped over himself in his haste.

In a secluded function room that was accessed through a bar, Demır set a tray of beers down on a table in front of Donna and Alice.

"I like this guy," said Alice.

Donna remained tense.

"Gönül and Natesh will be with us in half an hour," he said. "Please, relax. We will have dinner together, and we can exchange all of the information that you need."

"You could help by just telling me right now what's going on," said Donna.

Demır sighed and nodded in agreement. "I understand," he said. He began to pace the room. "I was hoping to avoid an altercation with you, but it is only fair to tell you the truth now. We have made a mistake, Gönül and I. We thought Natesh was working for Amin. When we learned that a passenger by the name of Chaudrakar was on a flight into Dalaman a few days ago, we followed him to see if he would lead us to Amin's whereabouts. But when he failed to make contact, we thought he must have known we were watching him, and so we...we captured him."

"You *what*?"

"Yesterday, we brought him into custody...of sorts," said Demır. He was visibly flustered now.

"Of sorts?" demanded Donna. "You're going to have to do better than that."

Demır continued to pace around the room, staring at the ceiling as though rehearsing his lines. Donna realised now that the reason for the silence was because the pair couldn't agree who was to blame for this epic blunder.

"Please understand," he said. "My investigations into Amin Chaudrakar have gone on for many years. I'm afraid my police colleagues no longer support this work. And I am sure some of them are taking money from Amin to ensure he remains hidden. I rely on Gönül for her expertise."

"Do you have *any* police resources looking into Amin's activities?" Donna asked, her heart sinking into that feeling of dread.

"Not at the moment," said Demır.

"Great," said Donna. She took a long gulp of beer. "That's great. So, we're on our own with this?"

Demır shrugged, apologetic. "This may change," he said, "now that we seem to be having the break-in."

"Break-*through*," said Alice.

Donna took in her surroundings, and wondered if it really would be possible for fiction to be stranger than fact right now. She raised her glass to Alice. *Clink*. "To the break-in," she said.

True to Demır's word, half an hour later there came the sounds of a commotion from the bar outside, and suddenly Natesh was walking into the function room, dressed in ill-fitting jeans and a t-shirt that had seen better days.

He spotted Donna, and took off at a sprint towards her, as she leaped from her chair, and the pair met in an embrace in the middle of the room. Then Natesh began to sob, his shoulders convulsing. Donna held him close, making soothing sounds, and Alice held her arms around both of them.

When they'd exhausted their emotions, they sat down and allowed Demır to pour them more beer. It was a much needed oil to help smooth out the tangled strands of the whole messy situation.

After three large glasses of beer sat empty in front of her, and a tray of cocktails appeared, Donna felt herself begin to relax. Now that Natesh was safe and with her, and dressed in clothing that clearly didn't belong to him...

Donna, "Ha ha, where did you get those? Steal them off a clothes line with your eyes shut?"

Gönül, "They're my brother's clothes."

Donna, "Oh."

...a warm glow settled in her stomach. She stopped caring whether she could walk in a straight line were she to stand up, and let Gönül re-fill her glass until she lost count.

The five talked long into the night. Natesh told of his panic when his mother disappeared, fearing it had something to do with the murdered midwives. He described the package he'd been left, and was particular to emphasise the note that threatened Donna's life. Demır was interested in the photograph, and told them everything he knew about Amin Chaudrakar. There were more tears. Natesh refused to believe Amin could be his father. Then he was angry. Then terrified for his mother when Alice spoke about finding her finger in the hotel room.

"But she must be okay," Alice tried to reassure him.

"Give or take the odd finger," the alcohol-infused Donna burst in with a snort of laughter. Gönül laughed along with her, and she and Donna clinked glasses.

Wednesday

Chapter 71

Donna felt the dry ash in her mouth then felt the ache at the side of her head. Then the piercing hunger that only a cocktail-induced hangover could produce. But she jumped in fright at the sight of a hand lying on her abdomen. It wasn't her own hand.

Her bleary eye followed the hand along a bare arm, and to the naked Gönül Macar who was fast asleep in bed with her. With a rising panic, Donna checked. She, too, was naked. Clothes were strewn around the room.

Oh God, oh God, what have you done? her mind raced.

She tried desperately to recall the events of the previous night, but after the table full of cocktail glasses became a patchy vision of what must have been dancing, there was nothing. Not a thing. She reckoned they must all have stayed over at the bar, though she had no idea how she'd ended up like this with Gönül. How could she have done this again? She thought back to the time before, when she'd cheated on Libby and ended up in that grotty bedsit on her own. Re-building the trust had been a long and painful process, and Donna was convinced she wouldn't have done it again. Would she?

No point asking the private eye: she was comatose.

Donna slid from under the arm, and clawed her way to the bathroom. When she'd showered and dressed again in yesterday's clothes, Gönül was still asleep.

Oh God, Donna groaned again to herself.

There was no sign of Alice. Donna wasn't sure if that was something to be relieved about or not.

As she tried to work out the situation, she jumped as a loud knocking came to the door.

"Alice," she said when she opened it. Alice was looking relaxed, but stopped abruptly when she saw Gönül.

"I know nothing," said Alice, tapping the side of her nose.

"Problem is, neither do I," said Donna.

Alice shrugged. "Nobody has to know."

"But I need to," said Donna. "And I made a promise to Libby that this would never happen again. How could I have done this?"

A loud snort and a yawn heralded the new dawn for Gönül. She looked up, almost surprised to see Donna and Alice. Not in the least abashed at her nudity, she rose from the bed and yawned again.

"Have fun last night?" she smiled at Donna. "You certainly slept well!"

With an enigmatic smile, she walked to the shower.

Donna glanced at Alice. "Ask her for me, will you?"

"You'll have to live with not knowing for now," said Alice. "We've got business to attend to. Efe got a call."

"*Efe*?"

"*I'm* single, remember," said Alice, with an enigmatic smile of her own. "Anyway, he says Amin has made contact and wants to negotiate. Are you ready to go?"

A baby

Pete Jenkins hurried down the street towards the bus stop, while pulling on his jacket and stuffing a cold slice of toast into his mouth, the sleep-deprived routine of a man with a full time job and a toddler. So tired, he didn't even drive to work any more. Couldn't be sure his eyes would stay open if he were to stop at a red light. It still shocked him, two years into parenthood, how little was openly admitted about how exhausting it all was. That perhaps, if the truth got out, people would just refuse to have children and the human race would come to an end.

A drizzle of rain began, and Pete wiped the last of his toast crumbs from his face, just as the bus stop came into view. Then his heart sank, as he saw his bus rounding the corner towards it. He broke into a sprint, wanting to throw himself on the ground and wail at the top of his lungs, just like Ruby would do. But an adult couldn't do that. He kept running, thinking he had more than a 50 – 50 chance of getting to the bus stop in time.

Then he saw it, from the corner of his eye at first. The words on the headline took a second or so to register.

Pete stopped running. He turned around on the spot, and stared at the news stand.

BABIES FOR SALE SCANDAL IN SCOTTISH SERIAL MURDER HUNT screamed the front page. Pete walked towards it, a knot forming in his stomach. He bought a copy of the paper, and forced his feet to continue carrying him to the bus stop. By the time he got there, he'd read the whole story, and his world was turned upside down.

In the office that day, there were comments from colleagues about how quiet he was being. That he didn't look so well. Was everything okay? He had barely mustered the energy to reply, and around 2pm his boss followed him down the corridor to the photocopy room.

Go home, he remembered his boss saying, but he didn't remember much about how he actually got home. Only that, when he pushed open the door, Ruby saw him first and ran to him, squealing "Daddy!" with open joy. Then Amanda appeared from the kitchen, looking exhausted but pleasantly surprised to see him home early.

He picked Ruby up, then felt vomit rush up through his gullet. He quickly put her back down and ran to the front door, leaned out, and threw up all over the doorstep.

Ruby wailed and Amanda said something about a tummy bug that was going around, but when he came back inside and showed her the newspaper, Amanda knew this was no tummy bug.

They'd taken an interest in the news story that had been running during the last couple of weeks. The hunt for a serial killer up north, in Dundee. Midwives had been killed. Something to do with prostitutes having babies. They'd been intrigued by the story, as they'd been to Dundee twice. The first time was to meet the mum and sign the adoption agreement. She'd been relaxed about the whole thing, they recalled. Very young, must still have been a teenager. Found herself pregnant during her travels and was more than willing to exchange the baby in return for substantial expenses. Legitimate expenses, though, Pete and Amanda had been assured, all through properly witnessed and signed paperwork following a thorough vetting by the adoption agency. Most of the paperwork and the vetting had been done by correspondence, before the first visit to Dundee. Pete and Amanda often remarked on how surprised they'd been at how relaxed Juanita, the young mum, had been.

Their second visit to Dundee had been to collect the baby. *Ruby*, they'd decided as soon as they saw her. They'd met at the agency's offices, a plush and cheerful place, and they'd been told that Juanita had, after all, been too upset to attend the exchange meeting, but they could arrange to visit her in the next month or so, for closure. The man at the agency had talked about the importance of that, and had been so reassuring. All their doubts about the morality of the adoption had been addressed. Pete and Amanda wouldn't have to go through the heartache of more failed IVF. Juanita could continue to travel the world on a healthy bank balance. Ruby would have a caring home and want for nothing. None of it had been underhand. Had it? There was paperwork. They'd been checked.

But the visit with Juanita never transpired. She'd taken off to her next country, apparently, and they had their final communication with the agency not long after they'd come home with Ruby.

Then parenthood had happened, with all its joys, of course, but mainly with its mind bogglingly fast passage of one week to the next, one month to the next, with no sleep, an endless conveyor belt of demands and tasks. And now Ruby was two. And the Dundee murders were being linked to the illegal sale of babies.

Pete and Amanda talked late into the night that night. Ironically, Ruby had fallen asleep in her own bed for the first time in their blurred memories, and it was their own need to work out what to do that had kept them up.

Finally, in the morning, Pete stood at Amanda's side while she keyed in DC Fran Woods' phone number. Tears trickled from her eyes as she read from the online details. Then she hurriedly ended the call as a voice began to answer.

"I can't," she told Pete. "I just can't. What are we going to do?"

Chapter 72

Firaz sat at the low table in the pancake house next to the Ghost Village. He didn't have his camera with him this time. He watched Lieutenant Efe Demır walk towards him, a tall woman at his side. Firaz was sure this must be Donna Davenport.

Demır's car sat some way back from the pancake house, but Firaz could make out a number of figures sitting inside it, and one of them was definitely Natesh. That was good, he thought. Amin's plan to use Samira as leverage was more likely to succeed if Natesh was here.

Firaz stood up to greet them. There was no warmth in either of their handshakes.

"I believe we have something you want," said Firaz.

"If you're talking about Samira Chaudrakar," said Donna, "she's not a bargaining chip. Leave her in a safe place where we can find her."

Firaz laughed. "Not a bargaining chip, no, but she *is* a form of insurance." He nodded to Demır. "I'm sure we can come to an agreement that ensures the best interests of both Samira and Amin."

"You cut off her fucking finger, you animals," spat Donna.

Demır placed a warning hand on her arm, and spoke to Firaz. "What has he told you to offer?"

Firaz spat out a piece of chewing gum. "Amin wants to reach an agreement. First, I need to see you remove your batteries from your phones. And I'll need your car passengers to do the same. I can't risk you calling for back-up."

There was a short stand-off, then Demır sighed. He drew his mobile from his pocket, and ejected the battery from it. Donna did the same, then Firaz walked with them to Demır's car. Ignoring the daggers that Natesh was shooting him, Firaz watched the three occupants remove their phone batteries in response to Demır's instructions.

"Okay," said Firaz. "Now here's the deal. Amin will release Samira to you if you supply him with your bank account details. He will place a large sum into the account…"

"Ha! So I can no longer investigate?" Demır's voice was angry this time. "Very clever."

Firaz shrugged. "It's the deal. If you want Samira, you have to give the account details."

"And where is the exchange to happen?" asked Demır, sounding disgusted.

"St Nicolas Island," said Firaz.

Donna looked at Demır.

"It's near here," he told her. "A short drive from here to Gemiler beach, then a boat across to the island. It's all clearly visible from the beach."

"Would we be vulnerable?" Donna asked him, whispered into his ear so that Firaz couldn't hear.

Demır took several steps away from Firaz before answering her. "They could see us arrive. We could also see them. It would be hard for either of us to surprise the other, so the island's a good choice."

"One condition," Firaz called to them.

"Here we go," said Donna.

"Amin will meet only with Natesh. No police."

Chapter 73

Firaz's jeep bounced along the rocky track that led past the Ghost Village to Gemiler beach. He'd been surprised when Amin had agreed to allow Donna and Alice to accompany Natesh, but he hadn't questioned the old man. Things were happening quickly now. The sooner he took his final payment and got out of this business, the better.

They rounded the curve that weaved between green hillsides, ending up on a sand dune, and Firaz killed the engine. The azure water stretched before them like frosted glass, and a short distance out from the beach, a craggy island popped up from the water.

Several small speedboats bobbed gently in the shallow sea, and Firaz waded knee-deep to one of them. He unzipped a key from his pocket, and started the boat.

Donna, Alice and Natesh followed Firaz onto the beach.

"Age before beauty," said Alice, shoving Donna into the water in front of her.

It took only minutes to reach the island, and the boat moored beside a rickety wooden jetty next to what looked like a sentry post. It turned out to be the locked-up ticket office that operated during the tourist season.

Firaz jumped onto the jetty and assisted the others out of the boat.

He pointed to a ruin at the top of the island. "Amin will arrive from the south. You can watch for his boat from up there – you'll have a view over the whole coastline." He busied himself with tying up the boat, while Donna, Alice and Natesh began to make their way along the rocky track that led into the remains of the ruin at the top of the small island. The pathway itself was embedded with uneven rocks, and the walking was slow and in some parts strenuous. The air was fresh, the sea clear blue around them, trimmed with pine clad hillsides.

"It's like a postcard," said Donna. "Pity about the circumstances." Then she heard the rev of Firaz's motor boat.

"He's leaving us here!" shouted Natesh, who almost fell

headlong as he scrambled around on the pathway.

Sure enough, they watched in dismay as Firaz steered his boat away from them and back towards the mainland.

"Now, what do you think he's...." began Alice, before they heard a crack in the air, and the stonework next to her head exploded into a dusty cloud of fine rubble. "Get down!" she yelled, and the three fell to the ground immediately. Alice retrieved the bullet from the ancient wall.

"We've been set up," she said.

"Like fucking sitting ducks," said Donna. She knelt up behind a tall stone and peered out towards the hillside, instantly drawing another bullet. It hit the stone she was keeling behind. Alice grabbed her back down onto the ground.

"Did you see the shooter?" Donna asked.

"No," said Alice, "but from that kind of distance and with that sort of accuracy, he's got a good eye and a pretty decent gun."

"We need to get out of here," said Natesh. "Can we swim it?"

"How far do you reckon that stretch of water is?" asked Alice.

Donna considered it for a moment. "I'd say around ten or fifteen lengths. We'd all manage that, no problem."

"Yeah, except for pop-a-shot over there," said Alice. "Look at that, mirror-still water, no obstacles, if we're in there swimming for ten minutes, he gets a whole lot of shots at us. I wouldn't risk it."

"Even *you* wouldn't?" exclaimed Donna.

"There must be a boat around here," said Natesh.

"Let's go and have a look," said Donna, "but keep within the walls of the ruin."

"There's always the option of waiting it out, and hoping he needs to go home before we do," said Alice, before they all heard the sound of another motor boat, this time approaching the island from around the southern hillside.

"I'm thinking waiting isn't an option," said Donna. "Looks like we've got company."

"It might be Demır or Gönül," said Natesh, squinting to see the boat better.

"The shooter isn't bothering with them," said Donna. "It's not a friendly boat. We need to get off this island pronto."

Chapter 74

Fran was surprised to find herself on a broad avenue, nicely lined by trees on both sides, houses with large front gardens. Not the sort of place she was used to interviewing street women. She'd driven up the A90 to Aberdeen as fast as the limits would allow, and a little more, as soon as Aiden got word to her that they'd finally found the elusive Juanita. She was positively buzzing. Emma had now confirmed that Vidu Chalvez was the Latin lover they'd been looking for, and the midwives had recognised his photo as the man they'd spent the evening in Spice with the night Moira was last seen alive. She was frustrated that she couldn't get Donna on her mobile to tell her they'd found Juanita. Ross had been pleased with the news, but she wanted to be the one to tell Donna.

She strode up the path to the front door, after re-checking the address that Aiden had given her, and was welcomed by a young woman who looked perhaps to be Middle Eastern. The woman introduced herself politely as Juanita. It was only once inside, faced with a row of locked doors along a hallway, that Fran realised this was a house with multiple occupants. Juanita led Fran to the third door along, unlocked it, and ushered the detective into a small but light and airy sitting room, where cups and a filled teapot were already waiting. The heat of the room after the biting cold outside made Fran's cheeks flush red.

Fran could tell that Juanita had been crying, although there seemed to be something odd, something she couldn't place, about the tears.

They exchanged pleasantries while Juanita poured tea, then the young woman sat facing Fran.

"You want to know about Eleanor Wallace?" she said, her English clear.

Fran nodded, drawing out her notebook. "Please," she replied. "Anything you can tell us that will help us find out who killed her…"

"I was there when she was shot," said Juanita. "I saw everything that happened."

Fran looked up, astonished. Was this really going to be it? The breakthrough? While she fumbled to get her notebook and pencil ready, Juanita continued talking, as if now that the floodgates were opened, she couldn't stop.

"One of the girls, I can't remember her name, had been having a difficult pregnancy. They called me and a couple of the older women to be with her when she went into labour. To comfort her, I suppose. They often did that."

"They?" Fran prompted.

"Vidu and Suleyman, they were the two in charge of the whole operation. And the doctor, Marcus, although he was getting old by then and he'd already retired. He'd been reluctant to attend that time, as there looked to be complications with the birth. But they had guns that time. They'd been talking to some other gang here in Aberdeen, one that did guns and drugs."

"Does the name Kozel sound familiar to you?" asked Fran.

Juanita paused in thought for a moment. "No," she said eventually. "We didn't know their names, the Aberdeen men. But they wanted to team up, use the girls to bring more drugs in, use the guns to bring more girls in. Something like that. Anyway, that day, two of the Aberdeen men were there in the flat."

"The Dundee flat? Craigie Drive?"

"Yes. That poor woman was screaming in agony, and Marcus just didn't know what to do. I remember hearing him begging for a midwife, as they wouldn't allow her to go to hospital. They finally agreed. Vidu had been seeing this woman, a midwife..."

"Eleanor Wallace?"

"Yes. She'd been at the flat a couple of times already, and she seemed to have realised there was something strange going on. But Vidu always seemed to talk her round, and I guess he thought the same thing would happen this time. Except it all got out of hand very quickly. When Eleanor arrived, she saw straight away that the woman and her baby were at risk and needed to go to hospital. I think Vidu and Suleyman would have let her go. They couldn't risk losing the baby, as the couple who would be taking it were already at the rented office, waiting for the exchange."

"The rented office?"

"Whenever an exchange was due to take place, they'd rent some plush office for a few days, to make it look like a legitimate adoption set-up. So the couple had arrived, and the baby would be taken straight to them." Juanita's voice quavered, and the strange tears formed again at her eyes. "The men started arguing. Vidu said they could trust Eleanor and that they should get the woman to hospital. The Aberdeen men said no, and they had the guns. Then the woman screamed, there was a lot of blood, and they were shouting that she was dead. I remember watching Eleanor check for the baby's heartbeat, but there wasn't one. She was arguing with Vidu, and wanted to phone for help, when one of the Aberdeen men pointed the gun at her and shot her. Just like that. No warning. Even before she fell to the floor, he was ordering Vidu and Suleyman to call the surgeon."

"The surgeon?" Fran asked. This was all beginning to feel too big.

"They had a list. Rich people who needed organ transplants. When they'd finished prostituting us girls and selling our babies, they took what they could from us." Juanita touched her eye.

Then Fran saw it. Juanita's left eye was a prosthetic one. Fran shuddered.

"Sometimes a baby would be stillborn," said Juanita. "It meant the exchange wouldn't go ahead, so they'd make money from them the other way, and the surgeon would come."

"Do you have a name?" asked Fran, fighting hard to stop a rising bile from engulfing her mouth. She was aware of her hand shaking now as she took notes.

"No, sorry. But it was a woman, and she must have worked locally, because the times I saw them call her, she was there very quickly. I think I'd recognise her again if I saw her."

Fran placed the notebook and pencil on her lap. "And why have you come forward after all this time, Juanita?"

"Because they're gone now. They can't stop me from finding my baby. I want my baby back."

"Aren't you afraid they might come after you?"

Juanita shook her head slowly, and took her time before answering. "They won't come back."

"How do you know that, Juanita?" Fran asked her.

Juanita seemed to think the question over. Finally she said, "After they killed the midwife, things went quiet for a while. I went into hiding, but Vidu found me not long afterwards. He persuaded me to go back to Dundee. He said there was a police officer helping them – to corrupt the evidence, or something, and quite soon afterwards, nobody seemed to be interested any more in finding out who killed her."

Fran wondered briefly if Donna already suspected this.

"Then more girls arrived, and for the next two years or so, Vidu and Suleyman continued as though nothing had happened," Juanita went on. "But I heard them arguing once with the Aberdeen men. They were adamant that another incident like that would mean they'd have to flee the country. Said the police wouldn't be able to cover up any more mistakes."

"And something else did happen, didn't it?" said Fran.

Juanita looked down at her feet as she began to speak again. "Yes." Her voice became a whisper. "A few weeks ago, Vidu was away on business, and there were complications in Dundee. We had to call in a midwife. When Vidu got back, I…I told him…I told him that we'd had to get the midwife in, and I made up a story that I'd overheard her telling somebody about us…" She began to quietly weep.

Fran leaned forward in her seat and touched Juanita's arm. "Just take your time," she said. "Tell me everything that happened. Was the midwife Moira Cowan, the woman who's been in the news?"

Juanita nodded her head, *yes*. "I thought that if the men believed she was telling other people what was going on in the flat, they would leave, just like they said they would. I didn't think…" She faltered again, bringing her breathing under control. "I didn't think Vidu would kill her. He wasn't like that."

Fran allowed a moment's silence, then said, "Are you prepared to come to the police station with me to tell us all of these details formally?"

"Yes."

Fran hurried back to her car while Juanita gathered her belongings. Her thin suit jacket was no match for the biting wind, but she felt the glow of pride in her belly. She'd found Juanita, and Juanita had unexpectedly given her the whole story about the deaths of both Eleanor Wallace and Moira Cowan. Eleanor murdered in cold blood while trying to save a woman and her baby; Moira the victim of a story made up by another desperate woman.

It all fitted with the other information she'd found, and she was sure it wouldn't be too difficult to find the surgeon that Juanita had referred to.

She punched the air when she took out her mobile and saw a text from Aiden, letting her know that Peter Cowan had finally told them he thought the man in the CCTV picture was involved with his dealer. He wasn't sure how, but he'd seen them arguing once in Craigie Drive when he'd gone to pick up his stash. He knew his dealer was scared of the guy, making Cowan doubly scared. But at least he was talking now.

Pratt's asked for immunity in return for the intel, haha, Aiden's text ended.

Fran swore out loud when Donna's mobile rang again as unobtainable. This was all too much. She left a brief message on Ross's phone to update him, and settled into the car to wait for Juanita.

Chapter 75

Donna led the way back down the stone track towards the jetty. She, Alice and Natesh ran almost on all fours; whenever screaming muscles made them stand up to stretch, there was a crack in the air and splintering stonework nearby. All the time, the sound of the motor boat arriving from the southern edge of the island grew louder.

"We don't have much time," gasped Donna as they reached the ticket office beside the jetty. "That boat's going to be here any minute."

"What are we going to do?" Natesh's voice was hysterical.

Crack!

"Keep down!" Alice ordered them.

"Get your clothes off," Donna said, already peeling off.

"What? I'm not undressing in front of you," said Natesh.

"For fuck's sake, Natesh, we're being shot at, and we've got to swim for our lives," Donna shouted at him.

Natesh kicked off his shoes and pulled off his t-shirt, while Alice did the same.

"What about this kiosk?" panted Natesh, standing in a pair of Superman y-fronts. "Could we push it into the water and float it like a boat? Use it as a shield?"

"That's not a bad idea," said Donna.

"It gives the shooter a bigger target," Alice shook her head in disagreement. "Increases his chances of hitting one of us."

"How about a decoy?" Donna suggested. "If we heave it into the water around that side of the jetty and give it a shove, while we swim around the other side?"

The three paused to consider the option.

Crack!

"Keep down!"

Natesh scrambled behind the kiosk and gave it a shove. "It's flimsy," he said. "Easy to push into the water."

"Do it, then," said Donna. "And let's get going. That boat's nearly on top of us."

Natesh angled himself behind the kiosk and pushed. It took

only two goes, and the sentry box-like cubicle toppled over and fell into the water. Alice peered around the rock towards the direction from which the shooting was coming.

"Quick," she said, "push it out in this direction."

They waded into the water behind the kiosk and pushed it as far out as they dared, then picked their way back onto the wooden jetty.

Crack! Crack!

Alice turned around and saw the kiosk splinter under fire, and it began to sink. "Crap! There goes our decoy."

"Get swimming," said Donna. "We've wasted enough time. Head for the beach."

"Keep low in the water, and keep well apart – give him as small a target as possible," said Alice.

See you on the other side, Donna thought, her heart beating wildly, as she launched herself into the sea. Barely aware of the sudden shock of cold, she quickly took the lead, thanks to her athletic abilities, and when she glanced back, spitting out a mouthful of salt water, she saw Alice some way behind and to her right, closest to the shooter. Natesh wasn't far behind her to her left. She caught a glimpse of a boat arriving at the jetty back on the island. She felt almost faint at their narrow escape, and hoped beyond hope that they'd remain out of view long enough to make it to the beach.

Crack! Crack!

Don't count your chickens, she reminded herself.

The swim turned out to be longer than Donna's estimate, and by the time she clawed her way on to the sandy beach at Gemiler, she was out of breath. She looked into the sea behind her, and saw a ripple moving towards her. Moments later, Alice came into sight and crawled, gasping, onto the sand next to Donna.

"Where's Natesh?" Donna's wavering voice gave away her growing concern. The sea looked mirror-still. No signs of anyone swimming towards the beach. She scoured the expanse of water that lay between Gemiler and St Nicolas Island.

Alice crawled next to her, shivering, and followed Donna's line of sight.

The water remained still.

"Where is he?" Donna demanded. Her voice rose in volume, and she began to stand up, ready to go back into the sea.

"Stop," said Alice. "They'll see us."

Donna ignored her, and had stepped back into the water when a sudden plume of white spray exploded in front of her; splashing towards the shore came Natesh. "Oh, thank God." She grabbed him around the waist and helped to haul him onto the sand. He lay coughing for several moments before he seemed to realise he was on dry land.

"We made it," he whispered.

"What do we do now, chief?" asked Alice.

The rifle shots had ceased, and Amin's motorboat bobbed gently by the jetty on the island. Donna, Alice and Natesh sat stock-still, cold and half naked on Gemiler beach.

"Move slowly and into the olive trees over there," said Donna, pointing to a tiny grove of parched shrubbery. "At least if we're hiding we won't get arrested for being scantily-clad on a Turkish beach."

Hidden in the scrub by the roadside, they sat shivering.

"What are we going to do now?" asked Alice again, but her words were drowned out by the roar of a jeep engine that sped towards them from the direction of the Ghost Village.

"Oh no," whispered Natesh. "Firaz has come to finish the job."

They watched, helpless, as the jeep appeared around the corner, and screeched to a halt before the sand, and directly in front of the shrubs they were hiding in. There was no mistaking it. The driver knew exactly where they were.

Chapter 76

The crunch of boots landing in the scree at the side of the jeep made Donna suddenly feel sick.

Then, to her astonishment, Gönül's face appeared in front of them as she parted the shrubs they were hiding in. For a moment Gönül looked as though she might burst out laughing, but instead, she shouted, "Quick, get into the jeep, we need to get out of here."

Donna and Alice didn't need to be told twice. They leaped to their feet and scrambled into the jeep. Natesh followed at their backs, shivering and holding his hands across the y-fronts.

"Hurry up!" Gönül yelled at him, and he bounded into the back of the vehicle.

Gönül tossed a set of blankets at them, and got back behind the wheel.

"How did you find us?" asked Alice.

Gönül met her eye in the rear view mirror, a look that said it all, without having to indicate the wet trail that so clearly marked the trio's scamper from the beach to the bushes.

"We heard Firaz coming back, then the gunshots," she said. "We knew then it was a set-up. Demir tried to track down Firaz, but he's vanished. We need to get to Ölüdeniz, to a safe house, before he comes back here to find you."

Donna huddled into her blanket, wondering what would happen now. She put her arm around Natesh's shoulder. He wasn't cut out for this sort of stuff. Hell, *she* wasn't cut out for it, and she was a cop with some pretty brutal experience behind her. Perhaps it was time to cut their losses and get back home. She'd found Natesh. She didn't rate their chances now of finding Samira, too.

Amin paced back and forth across the patch that had contained the ticket kiosk. He threw down the walkie talkie, having heard the news that the sniper had failed to hit either of the targets, who were now no longer trapped on the island, and furious at having found out too late to go after them.

The two armed men who'd arrived with Amin lurked on the

jetty, casting wary glances at one another. They'd never known the doctor to panic like this. It had been bad enough when they'd learned that his son had led the UK police here, after having to close down their activities. But at least there had been hope at this new plan, of cornering them here on the island. But now? Amin had lost his grip.

Gönül brought the jeep to a stop part way down a near-vertical slope, and parked close in to the verge. She yanked open the rear hatch, and held out a hand to assist her passengers out. Natesh almost tumbled head first down the slope, but Gönül whisked him off the road and onto a barely discernible path that led into the lush greenery of the hillside.

"Go in there," Gönül told Donna and Alice. "It's my home."

Donna was surprised to see the shrubbery open up to reveal a small stone single storey house sitting in a simple courtyard. Hens scarpered into the olive grove to the rear of the house, and a goat munched lazily on grass stalks while keeping an eye on the visitors.

The temperature inside the house was pleasant. It looked comfortable, its stone floor layered by colourful mats, and a built-in divan running around the walls. It struck Donna as her idea of a typical rural Turkish home. The air was delicately scented. Almonds, perhaps, thought Donna, from the surrounding trees.

The others trooped in behind her, and they stood, a sorry lot before Gönül, wrapped in their blankets.

"Efe will be here soon," she told them. "He has collected your clothes from your hotels. It won't be safe for you to return to them."

Sure enough, while Gönül was preparing a pot of strong Turkish coffee, there was a rap on the front door, and Demır appeared, carrying two large cases. He put the cases down, and immediately went to Alice.

"You are safe!" he beamed, embracing her.

Donna and Natesh exchanged a glance.

"Tonight we sleep," Demır said to all of them. "Tomorrow we make the next plan."

Donna had a feeling tomorrow was going to be a long day. But for now, she was happy to be alive. Even if it was half naked in Gönül's secluded house.

Thursday

Chapter 77

"Did you find the flight details?" asked Amin. He was pacing the room in his villa, banging his fist on every surface that he passed.

Firaz handed over a print-out of that day's flights out of Dalaman to the UK.

Amin sat down at the laptop which sat open on his desk, and began to type an email to Lieutenant Efe Demır at the police station in Ölüdeniz.

Donna replaced the receiver on Demır's office phone, and whistled softly. Alice, Natesh and Gönül were drinking coffee, in mid discussion about what they could do now without jeopardising Samira's safety. They were still none the wiser as to where Amin was hiding her.

"Fran interviewed Juanita," Donna announced. "She got the whole story about Craigie Drive, about what happened to Eleanor and Moira."

"Really?" Alice was suddenly alert. "So, what happened?"

"Well, apparently Eleanor Wallace attended a stillbirth," said Donna. She saw sorrow cloud Alice's eyes, and went on to explain the rest of the story leading to Eleanor's murder. "Then they needed another midwife, and that's when Moira got involved," she said.

"Did she threaten to report them?" asked Alice.

"No," said Donna, "but they thought she had. One of the women at the flat reckoned the thugs would just pack up and go if they thought word was getting out, so she made up a story that Moira had talked."

There was a moment of silence, then Demır suddenly exclaimed, having just opened an email, "Amin has given us an ultimatum. He is sending Firaz to escort Donna, Natesh and Alice to the airport." He checked the details in the email again. "They must board the Turkish Airlines flight to London via Istanbul that departs at 11.25 am." Demır glanced at his watch and frowned. They were going to have to leave Ölüdeniz within the hour. "Firaz will witness this, and when the plane has taken off, he will return to confirm with Amin. If Firaz does not arrive by 4pm with the confirmation, Amin says he will kill Samira."

"Then we have to find him," said Natesh. "We can't leave her here."

"He has police helping him to stay hidden," said Demır. "It won't end well if we try to approach, even if we knew where to begin."

"I'd hazard a guess he's somewhere around Kaya," said Donna, "since that's where he sent Firaz to meet us yesterday. Couldn't you search the area?"

"I don't have those kinds of resources," said Demır. "I'm sorry."

"But we can't leave my mother here!" Natesh said. "I'm not going without her. We have to look for them."

Gönül tapped Donna's arm, and beckoned her to the far end of the office.

"We have to talk," she told Donna.

She's really going to do this now? thought Donna, incredulous. At their backs as they stood looking out of the office window, the argument went on between Natesh and Demır. Gönül leaned close, and her lips brushed against Donna's ear as she whispered.

"I have a plan," she whispered. Donna berated herself. Gönül continued, "But it will only work if you keep it secret from Natesh. He mustn't know."

Donna nodded her head, the slightest of movements. "Go on."

It was with heavy hearts, and much protesting from Natesh, that they arrived at Dalaman airport. The deep rumble of approaching thunder shook the air.

"I can't believe you're going along with this," Natesh hissed at Donna.

"Trust me," said Donna, while Alice and Demır said their farewells. "Ross has been liaising with local law enforcement, ones that aren't connected with Demır." She thought back to her discussion two days previously with Ross after they'd found the finger in Natesh's hotel room. "He knows what he's doing, Natesh, he'll get the co-operation he needs to find your mother."

Natesh continued with the protests while Donna and Alice flanked him, ushering him towards the airport check-in area.

Firaz was waiting there for them, the way he'd been standing waiting for Natesh five days previously. Natesh felt the sting of fear mixed with failure. He'd come here to find his mother. He'd been led here. What was going to happen to her, now that he was leaving? Surely Donna wasn't going to walk away?

Firaz accompanied them to the departure gate, using his fake documents, and saw them walk onto the plane. First Donna, tall and distinctive from a distance. Then Natesh. Firaz almost felt sorry for him, and realised with a deep sadness in his heart that he'd lost Adam's friendship. Then Alice. They were all on board. Part of him wanted to run after them onto the plane and beg them to take him with them to the UK. But he sat on in the departure lounge, watching the plane through the viewing area, and when it began to taxi towards the runway, he stood up to make his way back to Amin's compound. He wondered, as he went, what Amin would do with Samira now. Perhaps he would kill her, anyway.

On board the plane, the pre-flight instructions were complete. Natesh was seated by the window, and Alice and Donna were seated two rows behind him. The plane was full.

He watched out the window miserably as rain drops began to fall onto the tarmac.

Hiding at the back of the plane was Gönül. From her place, she nodded her signal to the cabin assistant, who, according to her instructions, made her way to Natesh's seat and began to fuss over his seatbelt and hand luggage, chatting enough to keep him distracted for a few minutes. Meanwhile, Donna saw Gönül's signal, and she and Alice slipped out of their seats and sneaked to the back of the plane. Another cabin assistant held the rear exit open just enough for the three of them to slide out, on the side farthest from the departure lounge's viewing area. They dropped onto the soft top of an army truck, which then drove them out of the airport, just another vehicle on routine airport duties.

By the time the cabin assistant finished distracting Natesh, the plane was beginning to taxi towards the runway, ready for take-off.

"Don't you feel just a little bit bad, leaving him like that?" said Alice, while they snaked their way through the traffic out of Dalaman, keeping a discreet distance from Firaz's jeep. They were in Demır's car, having left Gönül at the airport thanking her cousin, the chief of airport security.

"A bit," concurred Donna. "But this sort of thing isn't for Natesh. I definitely feel better for knowing he's on his way home, and at least we have a chance now of finding Samira."

Demır remained silent as he concentrated at the wheel, letting Firaz unwittingly lead them to Amin's compound.

"That little shit had better stick to his end of the deal, and actually report back to Amin," muttered Donna.

Firaz didn't disappoint. He drove straight back to the Kaya valley. An hour's drive along the D-400, uninspiring except for the Göcek Tunnel, and they came to the turn-off that led into the Kaya Valley. Through the forest, past holiday villas with their swimming pools and carefully tended orange groves, a smattering of cottages and a small, white mosque up ahead. Now they were the only two vehicles on the road.

"Pull back," said Donna. "He'll see us."

To her horror, Demır stepped on the accelerator and brought his car close to Firaz's bumper.

"What the hell are you doing?" she shouted at him. Demır ignored her, and collided with Firaz's jeep, sending his ancient vehicle skidding across the road and into a wall that surrounded the small white mosque. The Imam rushed from the mosque, flapping his arms and shouting, but he ran back inside at the sight of Demır's police badge and revolver.

Demır jumped from the car, and raced towards Firaz, grabbing the journalist and pinning him face-down in the dust.

"It's too dangerous for us to go into the compound alone," said Demır, struggling to keep on top of Firaz.

"I don't fucking believe this," Donna shouted. "If he doesn't go and report to Amin, Samira will be killed."

"We will wait for back-up," said Demır. "After all this time, I am not going to risk letting Amin escape."

"You don't have any back-up," said Donna. She turned to Alice. "I'm going on ahead to see if I can find anything."

"Well, you're not going without me," said Alice.

Donna leaned down low, so that her face was almost pressed against Firaz's.

"Where is Amin?" she asked. She stared hard into his eyes, and saw the slight flicker of a movement that betrayed what he was trying not to tell her.

"This way," she said to Alice. "It can't be far from this spot."

"It's too dangerous," Demır yelled after them. But Donna and Alice had already taken off at a sprint past the white mosque.

A normal life

It was days like this he sometimes wished he had a normal life. When the sun was shining, when he had time alone to sit by his own poolside, when the mansion was still and quiet. Peaceful. No manager going on about contracts and tour dates. No band members arguing over who wrote what bit and how to play that piece. Hell, half the time his home was full of complete strangers, all there – seemingly – to take care of his complicated business affairs. He was sure normal people would know how much they had in the bank. He could even remember a time when he paid his own bills. Now he had people to take care of all that.

He carefully rubbed more sunscreen onto the scar, the part that he could see, and briefly thought about the kidney transplant that had saved his life. All of that had been arranged, too, by his people, without much input from himself. Someone as famous as he was couldn't exactly turn up at the local A&E. And besides, paying privately would mean he was one less person on an overloaded waiting list. It was right for him to have paid for the operation instead of using public resources, when he had the means to do so. Still, in the early days after the operation, it had bothered him to think he hadn't had to wait at all. He knew that people died while waiting for a suitable kidney donor.

You have a rare blood type, the doctor had told him at the time. We've *found a match, one that just wouldn't be suitable for the other patients on my list.* And why would anyone question that?

It had all happened so quickly, and his manager had done an ace job of keeping it all out of the papers. As far as they knew, the band was working on a new album, and tour dates for the following year would be announced. And they were. He'd had a team of private nurses, physios, nutritionists, fitness instructors, the works, to make sure he returned to peak physical health by the time the new tour got underway.

The sun poured straight onto this spot where he now sat. On the rare occasions he got to spend here alone, it was always pleasantly warm. Even now, in November.

He scrolled down the news headlines, vaguely interested in what might be going on outside the secure walls of the Surrey mansion. One of the headlines jumped out at him. Ordinarily he might have taken an interest, anyway, in a story about illegal organ harvesting. But this headline was different. This one was linked to a murder investigation in Dundee. That was where he'd been taken for his operation. The surgeon who specialised in his particular condition, with his particular complications, was based there, and so he'd never questioned it. Not then, when he'd been too ill, anyway. And not since, when he'd been too busy. He read on, and saw the appeal for information.

He set his tablet on the ground and studied his surrounds. There probably wouldn't be another time when he would be as alone as this, able to make his own decisions and to take responsibility for himself. It was probably nothing, anyway. He copied the number from the news report into his phone, and was surprised when the detective herself answered.

"Detective Fran Woods," he heard her say.

Chapter 78

Beyond the white mosque, a single track tarmac road led Donna and Alice past two villas with swimming pools. They discounted these as possibilities, being too exposed.

They continued on, panting as they ran, past a small patch of forestry, to where it seemed as though no more dwellings might be found.

Then, a single storey stone building with a rooftop terrace sat quiet and unimposing amongst the trees. A dusty moat of dry ground surrounded the building, giving it a 200-meter perimeter. An empty rocking chair sat on a paved porch outside the main door. Surrounding the moat-like perimeter was a wall with locked gates that faced the roadside. Away from the road, and particularly along the tree-line, the wall fell into varying states of disrepair. Standing one each side of the main door were two men, one skinny youth, one overweight and middle aged. Both had cigarettes dangling from their mouths.

"I'm willing to place a bet that not every villager here has their own private security guards," Donna whispered. "This has to be the place."

She and Alice crept to the edge of the perimeter by the tree-line, carefully keeping away from the forest track and hiding under cover of the ample foliage.

Instinctively they both hunkered down where the wall was nothing more than decorative. They could hear the men muttering and laughing.

"Doesn't look like they'd be able to give us much chase," whispered Donna. "I'd be surprised if the big one could run the length of himself, and I reckon the young one would piss himself if we jumped out at him."

"They're armed," Alice said.

"Oh, crap."

"AK47s," said Alice, keeping her eye on the guns that lay on the ground near the two men.

How had it come to this? Donna wondered. How had investigating a body washed up on Arbroath beach led to her hiding in the bushes in rural Turkey from two men with assault rifles? Libby's words, *Alice the bullet magnet*, came into her head. She shook the thought away.

"...not as bad as it looks," Alice was saying. "They're not trained shooters."

"How the hell can you tell they're not trained?"

"Their guns are lying on the ground," said Alice. "No military or police trained shooter would leave their gun on the ground. Especially AK47s, they're too prone to going wrong. Bit of grit gets into the gas tube, the dust cover's going to blow the whole thing in his face."

Donna turned and stared at Alice. "You sound like a Jack Reacher novel."

Alice touched one of the scars on her right cheek. A purple trace like the tail of a comet. "I know guns."

Donna stared hard at the men. The younger one took a long draw of his cigarette and threw down the butt.

"Does it help us any if one of them's left-handed?" she asked.

"It's all to the good," said Alice. "Rifles aren't a left-hander's friend."

"So, what are our chances here?" asked Donna.

The two men sat themselves down on the stone step of the doorway, taking up their weapons. Nobody was going for a snooze any time soon.

Alice wriggled and drew something out of her pocket. A handgun.

"What the hell?" asked Donna.

"Gönül gave me her gun," said Alice.

"Why did she give you her gun? Why didn't she give one to me?"

"Have you ever fired a gun before?"

"No."

"Then, there's your answer," said Alice.

"Are you going to shoot them?"

Alice shook her head. "Not from this distance. The bullet could end up anywhere, the chances of hitting a target aren't good. Then the bang would just tell them exactly where we're sitting and they'll let go a volley."

"Would we get hit from here?"

"They've got about 20 or 30 bullets apiece, they just need to let them spray in our general direction and we're down," said Alice. "That is unless their guns don't blow up in their faces."

"Is that likely?"

"AKs are known for it," said Alice, "especially in the hands of amateurs, like ones who leave them lying in the dirt."

They sat watching the two men. There were no other sounds from around the building.

"I'm going in," said Alice.

"No, you are not," said Donna. "We don't know who's inside."

"We need to know if Samira's inside," said Alice. "And time's running out for her. You've never fired a gun in your life. I'm trained, Donna. You need to trust me."

Donna thought for a moment, then nodded. "How do we do this?"

"Right," said Alice, "we use the oldest trick in the book. If we can lob a rock onto the road, they'll think someone's approaching from over there. If they're jumpy enough, they'll fire in that direction, use up all their bullets and have to stop to re-load. They're not going to think to check out this position, so you'll be safe as long as you sit tight here and Do. Not. Move."

"Okay, I don't move," said Donna. "What about you?"

"As soon as it's safe, I'll move in and get through the door," said Alice. "Once I'm inside, I'll need you to listen carefully. If you hear a double gun shot from inside the house, it's me who's fired it. *Pop, pop*, double gunshot like that. I'll need you to stay here, so I know where to get you if I come back out."

"You'd better come back out."

"If you hear a single gunshot, or more than two, it's not me. Anything except a double shot won't be me, okay? If that happens, you'll have to go and get Gönül and Demir. But go that way," she pointed in towards the forest and away from the road, "so they don't think to follow you."

Donna's heart beat so loudly she had to check that the two armed guards couldn't hear it. Her head was swimming. Alice's hand was on her shoulder, and her battle-scarred colleague looked directly into her eyes.

"If I don't make it back out, I love you," said Alice. "If I do get out, you never heard me say that." And before Donna could respond, Alice hurled a rock onto the road on the far side of the house.

As Alice had predicted, the two men jumped up and ran in the direction of the compound's gates, opening fire. Instinctively, Donna put her fingers in her ears, surprised at how loud the gunfire was, as Alice leaped from her position and sprinted for the villa's open door. Donna was vaguely aware of the young guard dropping his gun as a cloud of dark smoke erupted from it near his face, and within half a minute, a sudden silence engulfed the area. Then the sound of the older man shouting at the youth, before they backed in towards the doorway again, the older man pointing his rifle out towards the road and clipping a new magazine into the weapon. The younger man's gun lay in pieces on the ground.

Donna stared, open mouthed at the scene, before remembering Alice's instructions. She strained for any sounds that might be coming from inside the house. All of a sudden, she heard a single shot ring out. One single shot.

Chapter 79

Alice slipped in through the open door and stood with her back against the wall, pistol held close and ready, and glanced in every direction where there may be an assailant ready to hit her. She was alone.

She heard the yelp of the youth outside as his rifle misfired, as she'd suspected it might, and crept into the corner of the room she was in, so as to give herself the best vantage point.

She was in what looked like a boot room, or perhaps a tack room. The stone walls were in their original state, no paint, and a plank of wood that had been erected on one side contained a row of hooks upon which fleeces, jackets and backpacks hung. And two rifles. Alice inched her way towards the rifles, all the time alert to any sounds. More AK47s. She examined them. The lip of the dust cover was misaligned on one of them, so badly there was no way it would hold during fire. The other was missing its magazine.

Not worth the bother, she thought. They were no use to her, and no use to anyone who might want to have a go at her with them.

There was a large wooden table sitting in the middle of the room, and it was littered with beer cans and empty cigarette packs.

She continued around the room until she came to the door through to the main house. She pressed her ear firm against it and listened. She could hear a man's voice talking, but it sounded deeper into the house than the next room. She pictured the outside of the house, and measured it inside her mind to the dimensions of this room, working out what the shape of the next room through this door might be. Then she had an idea.

She crept back to the hooks and took down the rifle with the misfitted dust cover. She placed it on the table at the side nearest to the external door. If the guard whose gun had fallen apart came in now, he'd be looking for a replacement, and this one was sure to go the same way. She almost felt sorry for him.

She returned to the next door, listened again, then silently pushed it open a crack. Nothing. Then she threw her whole weight through to the next room, and had it scanned in a second. This room, too, was empty. The wall to her left was shorter than she'd expected from what she'd seen of the building's exterior, and so she guessed another room must wrap around the one she was in. That meant there were two possible rooms next to her that might contain danger.

She was pondering which way to go next, when her eye caught the faint light as the door directly ahead of her opened a fraction. Too late for her to react, a deafening shot exploded into the room, and Alice staggered, but kept her balance. A man who bore a striking resemblance to Natesh walked through the door, aiming a revolver at her, then she fell to the floor.

Chapter 80

Donna willed with all her might for a second shot, but none came. The two guards at the door panicked and ran inside, then the younger one was roughly bundled back outside to keep watch. A new rifle was in his hands, but Donna could see that he was shaking.

She made an attempt to turn to her left to begin her escape through the forest, when a searing cramp in her calf made her stumble. Twigs cracked and pebbles clacked under her weight, and the branches of the bush behind which she was hiding shook as she hung onto them for balance.

The young guard had heard something, and Donna could see him frantically scanning the area around her. But he saw nothing, and he seemed afraid of the rifle he was holding; he remained rooted to the spot.

Donna sat down carefully and stretched out her legs, circling her ankles and warming the cramped muscles. Then, keeping close watch on the guard, she manoeuvred herself into a sprinting start position, and waited for his attention to move away.

As soon as it did, Donna took off into the trees at full speed. Her old athletics training, and her regular running served her well, and she knew there was no way the youngster would be able to catch up with her. She was also pretty sure he wasn't going to risk firing his rifle, after almost blowing his own eye out with the last one.

She ran through the forest for about two kilometers, when all of a sudden the trees cleared and she found herself on a tarmac single track road. To her right were the two villas, with swimming pools facing onto the road, the two villas they'd passed on the way to Amin's compound. That meant the white mosque outside which Demır was parked with Firaz must be just up ahead. With laboured breathing, she set off at a jog in the direction she hoped was the right one. By now, she reckoned, Demır must have received the back-up he'd requested. If it was going to come at all.

When the small white mosque came into sight, Donna's heart sank. The jeep was still there, embedded in the wall where it had crashed. Only one other car, Demır's, was there.

He watched her approach, and rolled down his window.

"Where is Alice?" he called, worry etched across his brow.

"She's inside the compound," Donna puffed. "I think she's been shot, we need help. Where is your back-up?"

"I'm getting no help," said Demır, his voice dull. "Nobody is coming."

Samira listened intently, wondering what was happening on the other side of the padlocked door. She could hear Vidu struggling with something, huffing and puffing, but couldn't figure out what he might be up to out there. She had heard the sound of what could have been a gun shot at the other end of the villa, and was beginning to fear the worst. Now she heard what sounded like something heavy – a body? – being dragged towards the door.

Suddenly the padlock was being loosened, the door opened, Vidu stood there, and then he rolled the body of a woman into the room.

Samira gasped, and shuffled back from the body until she was pressed against the room's far-side wall. Vidu looked at her but said nothing, then went back out, locking the door behind him.

For several long moments, the only sound in the room was Samira's panting. She continued to stare at the body, and saw blood on the woman's leg, forming a growing dark stain over her thigh, but there was no movement.

Vidu, sweating heavily now, quickly scanned the room next to Samira's padlocked one. Amin wasn't there. He left the door open, and ran to another one. He pushed open the door so hard that the hinges cracked and Amin, who was at his laptop, spun round in alarm. He stood up, an expression of annoyance clear on his face, when he saw his inept younger brother there.

"What's wrong with you now?" he snapped.

Vidu wiped his brow with his shirt sleeve. "There's trouble," he said.

"There always seems to be trouble where you're concerned," said Amin.

"They got off the plane," said Vidu.

"What?"

"I've just caught one of them in here," said Vidu. "I shot her and put her in the locked room with Samira."

"My God," said Amin. Now his expression had turned to one of shock. "But Firaz saw them get on and confirmed the departure."

"Well, I don't know what he saw," said Vidu, "but one of the police officers is here."

"Get everyone to the tack room," said Amin, moving towards the door. "We need to prepare for the attack."

Vidu felt himself getting ready to vomit.

Cradling her own bandaged hand, Samira began to wonder about checking for signs of a pulse and whether she should use her shawl to try and stem the blood coming from the woman's thigh, when she was alerted to more footsteps approaching from outside.

She heard the padlock being snapped open, and the door flew open. Amin strode into the room, stepped over the body with barely a glance at it, and grabbed Samira by the arm.

"You need to come with me," he told her, pulling her towards the door.

She said nothing, concentrating only on keeping up with him without tripping over. Then she noticed that he was bringing a pistol to her head.

"We need to get Alice out of there," Donna insisted. Her head was inside the car window now, and she was nose to nose with Demır. "Right now. I know where Amin is. Forget *him*," she motioned to Firaz. "Bring your gun."

She saw the hesitation in Demır's expression, and she wanted to grab him by the hair and pull him out of the car. Then the roar of a jeep rose from the end of the road, and a cloud of dust and the screech of brakes brought Gönül to the scene.

"What's happening?" called Gönül as she jumped from the jeep. "Where is Alice?"

Donna told her what had happened. Demır and Gönül exchanged what sounded to Donna like angry words, and Demır finally got out of the car. Firaz took his chance and, bloodied and covered in dust, made a sprint away from them, just as a convoy of five police cars and a dark van came racing towards them, and surrounded them. Donna readied herself to run again, but she saw from the expression on Demır's face that police help had finally arrived. Green-clad Gendarmes swarmed from the cars, and six Agile Force officers in their navy blue uniforms jumped from the van, along with two excitable police dogs.

During a confusing moment of shouting and discussion, two of the Gendarmes caught up with Firaz and placed him in one of their cars, cuffing his hands behind his back. Then Donna found herself the centre of attention, surrounded by Demır, Gönül and more than a dozen armed officers.

"You lead," said Demır. "Take us to Amin Chaudrakar, we are going to find Alice. And Samira."

Donna didn't need telling twice. But she was puzzled. "What's changed their mind?" she asked Demır. "Why have they finally sent you help?"

As the troop made their way towards the compound, Demır spoke in hushed tones into Donna's ear. "They have found a dead body close to Dalaman Airport. They recognised him as the man I told them was helping to smuggle girls out of the country on fake passports. But he's an American citizen – they have to avoid an international incident."

Not for the first time, Donna found herself wondering how the hell she had ended up in a situation like this.

Chapter 81

Demır kept in front of Donna, holding his pistol low as they ran. Gönül was at her side. The gates of the compound came into view, and although the crunch of stones beneath all the boots was loud and probably carried far on the growing breeze, she saw one of the Agile Force officers use hand signals to divert his men into position around the grounds. Amin would hear them coming all right, but he'd have no way of knowing how many of them were aiming guns at him.

Demır slowed to a stop at the end of the wall and peered around the gate. Donna glanced over his shoulder. In the split second before diving back behind the wall, she saw a number of men – perhaps four or five – heavily armed and waiting in front of the villa. Across to her left, near the gap in the wall where she'd been hiding earlier with Alice, she caught sight of one man standing alone. She didn't see Alice or Samira. She felt Gönül take her arm as she hunched by the wall, as if to stop her from getting back up. She saw the Turkish private eye hold her gun out, shielding them both.

Three of the Agile Force officers took up position on the roadside behind her and to the right of the compound gates. One of the dogs was with them, and it crouched low and silent beside them, waiting for its command.

The other three took up similar positions, with the other dog, to the left of the gates. Donna and Demır were in the centre, and behind them stood the Gendarmes in a row, using the tree-line at the edge of the road as best they could for cover.

Demır again walked in front of the gates, and this time he stayed there, with his pistol held out in front. Immediately, the men standing in front of the villa trained their guns on him, and one of them yelled at the others, words that Donna didn't understand, but she saw the effect – the men formed themselves so that one had his gun aimed towards her and Demır, and the others had the remaining police officers within their sights. Donna's heart began to drum loudly as she listened to the agitated voices and shuffling of the officers behind her getting ready with their weapons.

Trying to slow her breathing, she edged herself from Gönül's side and came to stand in front of the gates beside Demır, knowing she was exposed to the firing squad at the villa and right in the middle of the crossfire that could erupt at any moment. She looked into every nook and cranny around the compound, as quickly as she could, scanning for any signs of Alice or Samira. There were none. She heard her own voice call their names. But as it rang out, her words were swallowed up in a sudden crack of thunder. She flinched, sure her time was up.

One of the guards at the villa flicked his eye and the nozzle of his assault rifle towards her. A knot tightened and gripped Donna's gut, then the guard resumed marking his officers.

Deep thunder rumbled on high in the darkening clouds. A breeze made the shrubbery sway. Just then, a movement at the corner of the villa caught Donna's attention. The man standing next to the gap in the wall saw it, too, and the armed man who was closest to it briefly followed his gaze. The other guards held firm at his words.

Amin came into view, with his arm around Samira and his gun pressed against her temple. Holding her like this, he walked into the centre of the compound.

Demır shouted something to him, and they exchanged words that were alien to Donna. She could feel the tension among the Gendarmes behind her. The dogs remained low to the ground on either side of the compound, though becoming restless. Two of the Agile Force officers on each side crept a few steps closer to the gates, fingers on their triggers.

Demır took a loud breath in, and it contained what sounded to Donna like a sob.

"Alice is inside with a serious gun wound," he told her. "But Amin won't let us get to her without a price."

Amin held a smirk on his lips as he stood defiant with the gun to Samira's head. Samira was looking frantically from side to side, as much as her situation would allow, and finally she saw Donna. She cried out Donna's name on instinct.

"We're going to get you out of here," Donna called to her. "Have you seen my colleague Alice?"

"The woman who was shot?" Samira's voice wavered. "I saw her, yes. I tried to help her, but…but I think she's dead."

"No!" yelled Donna. She felt herself advance on the gate, slam her fists against it, then heard a man's voice shout, before she was pushed to the ground as a ball of fire whizzed past where her shoulder had been.

Chapter 82

A plume of thick smoke filled the compound. From her position lying in the dirt and gravel beside the gates, Donna heard the movements of the Agile Force officers closing in on either side.

One of them fired several shots at the lock, opened the gates, and she felt the air around her move as the two dogs sped past her and into the compound.

Men's voices shouting.

Random gunshot.

Another crack of thunder, lightning streaking through the black cloud overhead.

Then suddenly, the smoke began to thin, and Donna heard a set of footsteps running towards the gate where she remained lying. A stumble, a grunt, green Gendarme uniforms, and then Vidu was lying on the ground next to her, being handcuffed following his failed attempt to escape.

Donna gasped when she saw his face. The image of Natesh, but older. The man on the CCTV footage, Moira Cowan's killer. Vidu grimaced and swore as the Gendarmes manhandled him to his feet and led him away.

The smoke dissipated to nothing almost as soon as it had engulfed the compound, but by the time it had gone, the scene inside had changed. Amin remained where he'd been, holding the gun to Samira's head. Two men lay dead beside the villa. Donna recognised one of them as the young guard who'd misfired his own rifle earlier. Donna looked towards the gap in the wall where she'd seen the other man, and not far from the spot she saw him with his hands on his head, an Agile Force officer, two Gendarmes and one of the dogs behind him.

Donna was sure there had been another armed man in the compound before the smoke grenade, but there was no sign of him now.

Amin was scanning the area around the compound. His head was moving rapidly from side to side as he assessed his situation. Two Agile Force officers crept forward slowly, until Amin looked at them and shouted words that made them stop.

Demır helped Donna to her feet. "He wants to do a deal," he told her. "He won't let Samira go, and he won't let us go to Alice until we meet his terms."

The rumbling thunder groaned across the valley, and a breeze whispered through the shrubbery. Then another movement caught Donna's eye. Beyond Amin and Samira, from behind the far corner of the villa, a chicken ran onto the porch. It scuttled for cover as quickly as it could. Something behind the villa must have startled it, Donna realised a fraction before she saw Alice emerge, holding a gun that was aimed at Amin's back.

Donna's breath caught in her chest, and she saw Demır and the Agile Force officers look in surprise at Alice's sprint across the yard. By the time Amin was alerted to the activity going on behind him, Alice was at his back and with her gun pressed to his head.

"I'll shoot her," Amin cried out. "Put down your gun."

Alice stood firm. "You won't shoot her," she said calmly. Donna could see that she had a scarf tied around her thigh, and that it was stained with blood.

"Ten seconds," Amin yelled. "If your gun is not on the ground in ten seconds, she'll be dead."

Alice kept the gun to Amin's head.

From within Amin's armlock around her neck, Samira turned towards him as fully as she could. Donna heard her say to him, "Look at me."

Her words disappeared into a thunderclap that shook the ground. Heavy raindrops began to fall, quickly turning the dusty ground dark and muddy.

"Look at me," Samira said again.

"I'll shoot her!" Amin's voice grew to a shriek as he called out. Then he slowly turned his head towards Samira. His grip tightened on his gun, and Samira winced in pain as he pressed it harder against her temple.

"It's over," Samira said. Her voice was calm. Strong. Amin stared at her. His mouth contorted and he gasped, bracing himself to pull the trigger, but still he held the gun to her head.

He seemed unaware now of Alice, who moved a fraction so that she stood midway between them.

"Do you understand?" Samira said to Amin, locking eye contact with him. "It's over. All of this. All of the horror that our families have endured for generations, it's over. You have a son. He's a fine man. He's happy and he lives in safety. He will settle where he's always known. He will always be able to call one place his home. No more running from wars, from persecution. You can stop now, Amin."

The rain lashed at their faces, but couldn't hide the tears that streamed from Amin's eyes. He let the gun fall from his hand, and he sank to his knees in the mud. His loud sobs filled the air. The Agile Force officers sprinted forward and shackled Amin's hands behind his back, then led him in silence from the compound while he wept.

Donna ran into the compound and met Alice and Samira in an embrace.

"Don't you ever get killed again," she muttered to Alice. But before Alice could answer, Demır enveloped her in his long arms.

Samira smiled at Donna, but there was worry in the older woman's eyes. "Natesh?" she whispered.

"He's fine," said Donna. "He helped us find you." *Actually, he was worse than useless, but you're his mum.* From the corner of her eye, she could see that Gönül had had the same thought, and they clapped hands in a high-five.

Then a cry from Demır alerted them. Alice lay collapsed on the ground, fresh blood oozing from the scarf tied around her thigh.

Demir was yelling an order at two of the Gendarmes, just as a team of paramedics rushed in through the gates.

The following week

Chapter 83

Donna and Alice walked the corridor in Bell Street, and stopped when they reached the door to the team room. The door was closed, but they could hear chit chat going on inside.

They paused before going in. Looked at one another, and smiled.

"Ready?" asked Donna.

"Ready," said Alice.

Cheers and clapping welcomed them as soon as they opened the door. The room was full. Party poppers flew into the air, and a large banner coloured the far end, displaying their names.

"Welcome back, chief!"

"Well done, General!"

The shouts were joyous and heartfelt. Donna and Alice were home safe. Akwasi and Morrison hurried towards them, in buoyant mood.

Donna strained to see across the swathe of officers in the room, but couldn't see Fran anywhere. Then she was scooped into Alice's arm link, to begin answering the barrage of questions that were being fired at them.

Donna allowed herself to bask in the warmth of the welcome, flicking off the unwanted thoughts about whether anything had happened between herself and Gönül, and she grinned widely as she listened to Alice re-tell the most gory parts of their adventures. She allowed her friend and colleague to embellish the superficial gunshot wound to her thigh, and to miss out the real explanation for her collapse following Amin's arrest – a drop in her blood sugar because she hadn't had enough to eat that day.

So, that was that, Donna thought, satisfied. Natesh was safely back home. Erin was treating him like a superhero, and he wasn't complaining. Perhaps she really was The One for him, she thought. She'd make an effort with Erin for his sake.

Samira was continuing to assist the police with their enquiries – Donna was keeping a distance from those interviews – until they could put enough details together to decide whether or with what to charge her. Was she responsible for covering up Amin's crimes, or was she a victim, under the threat of his blackmail?

Donna wasn't willing to place a bet on the outcome.

She carried some frustration at having to leave Amin and his gang behind, but she was sure Efe Demır would make sure they faced justice. And at least there would be no more women in Dundee forced to have babies that were then sold, or who had their organs harvested once they were no longer fit to prostitute themselves. That was a result, she thought, as she pondered the number of women now known to have been affected, revealed thanks to ongoing interviews with Juanita. And they'd found out what had happened to Moira Cowan and Eleanor Wallace. While it couldn't bring them back, and didn't bring any comfort to those who missed them, it was good to know that they were able to reassure the midwives that they were now safe. She did wonder, though, why she'd had such a strong feeling that Evanton had been involved in all of this. She knew, rationally, it didn't make sense, as Ross kept telling her. Perhaps she just had to accept that her healing process was not fully over.

The fall-out from this case, she knew, was going to be huge, and she was going to need her sharp wit to cope with it. Fran had a record of all the calls they'd received from worried parents, fearful of the legality of their adoption agreements, and there would be some difficult cases to deal with. And, of course, they still had to track down the surgeon who'd been helping the gangs. But where was Fran, she wondered again?

Just then the door opened.

Into the room walked Fran, carrying a large box. Steam was coming from the box, and Fran was grinning.

"A selection of sushi burgers," she announced. "And this time, DI Davenport, you're going to try one!"

Everyone in the room laughed, and there was a general swarm towards the box of burgers.

"Go on, then" said Donna. "I'm sure it can't do any harm to have just one!"

Libby sat sipping a coffee, letting her eyes drift over the paper she was about to submit. It was so good to have Donna home, she thought, not sure if she could cope with that sort of worry again.

A mobile rang, surprising her. She traced the melody to the bookcase in the hall. Donna's. She must have left it behind when she'd dashed out of the door for work. She was getting forgetful again. It went onto voicemail, and Libby's interest piqued when she saw that it was an international number. It must be something to do with the operation in Turkey, she realised, though strange it was on her personal mobile and not her work one. She decided she'd better listen to the message in case Donna needed to know about it right away. She played the recording.

"Donna?" said a woman's voice, husky and warm. Libby's stomach tightened. "It's Gönül. Just to check everything went okay with your flight home." There was a pause. The knot in Libby's tummy grew and began to twist. "You know," the woman's voice continued, "you should come back to Turkey, we could have a lot of fun together." Libby felt the sting of a tear beginning to form in the corner of her eye. *Dear God, Donna,* she thought, *don't you do this to me again.* The woman's voice went on, "Anyway. Your woman at home is very lucky. I would love to have somebody faithful to me like you are to her. My loss. You can't blame me for trying! Till another time. Kiss." And the message ended.

This time, Libby felt tears of relief.

DCI Angus Ross walked into the team room and made a bee-line for Alice. A grin began to spread across his face.

"Well done, you two," he said to her and Donna. Then to Alice, he said, "That's your annual leave request approved."

"Annual leave?" Donna quizzed her. She was surprised to see Alice's cheeks flush a little.

"I'm going on a short break to Istanbul," said Alice. "With Efe." Morrison wolf-whistled.

"Then," Alice went on, "we're going for a few days to Cappadocia, then taking a week's break on the Mediterranean."

"Well, good for you!" Donna beamed. For all the General's bravado, Donna was acutely aware of the pain hidden in Alice's heart. Perhaps Efe Demır was the guy who could heal it.

"You're going to have to tell me more about this," she told Alice, guiding her out of the melee and towards the fire exit. "And I need a fag."

The din from the team room faded into muted, indistinct chatter and laughter, as Donna stood with Alice at the fire exit.

She allowed her eyes to roam around the police complex. All the familiar comings and goings. The posse of journalists at the front entrance, poor sods. They must be freezing, she thought. Then Fran's guy at the burger van. She chuckled at the problems *that* had caused during their investigation. And she caught his eye. Staring at her.

Jonas Evanton busied himself around the oven plates, preparing burger buns for the queue that was set to appear at the next break time. Then he wiped his hands on a clean towel and leaned on the counter of the burger van, taking a break while he could. He smirked. *Fran Woods*, he thought. *She really needs to learn to stop the blabbing.* But her big mouth had served him well.

Amazing what a bit of plastic surgery could do, he mused, looking out through tinted contact lenses. Takeshi, the Warrior. What bullshit. *They've no fucking idea what's going to hit them.*

As he did so, he noticed two figures emerge from the fire exit at the side of the building. Alice Moone and Donna Davenport. He fixed his eyes on Donna, and felt his rage boil in his veins. *She has no idea*, he thought grimly. Then suddenly she was looking at him, and he knew she could see it. In the same instant that Donna took off towards him from the fire exit, Evanton threw down his towel, and fled from the van.

END

About the Author

Jackie McLean

Jackie McLean is a former government economist and political lobbyist from Arbroath. She subsequently ran her own business in Glasgow.

Jackie's first novel, *Toxic*, was shortlisted for the Yeovil Literary Prize in 2011 and Jackie has also been longlisted for the Dundee International Book Prize.

She leads Braehead Waterstones writers group and regularly speaks at Crime Writer events.

Also from Jackie McLean

Toxic
Shortlisted for the Yeovil Book Prize 2011
ISBN: 978-0-9575689-8-3 (eBook)
ISBN: 978-0-9575689-9-0 (Paperback)

The recklessly brilliant DI Donna Davenport, struggling to hide a secret from police colleagues and get over the break-up with her partner, has been suspended from duty for a fiery and inappropriate outburst to the press.

DI Evanton, an old-fashioned, hard-living misogynistic copper has been newly demoted for thumping a suspect, and transferred to Dundee with a final warning ringing in his ears and a reputation that precedes him.

And in the peaceful, rolling Tayside farmland a deadly store of MIC, the toxin that devastated Bhopal, is being illegally stored by a criminal gang smuggling the valuable substance necessary for making cheap pesticides.

An anonymous tip-off starts a desperate search for the MIC that is complicated by the uneasy partnership between Davenport and Evanton and their growing mistrust of each others actions.

Compelling and authentic, Toxic is a tense and fast paced crime thriller.

'...a humdinger of a plot that is as realistic as it is frightening' – crimefictionlover.com

More Books From ThunderPoint Publishing Ltd.

The Oystercatcher Girl
Gabrielle Barnby
ISBN: 978-1-910946-17-6 (eBook)
ISBN: 978-1-910946-15-2 (Paperback)

In the medieval splendour of St Magnus Cathedral, three women gather to mourn the untimely passing of Robbie: Robbie's widow, Tessa; Tessa's old childhood friend, Christine, and Christine's unstable and unreliable sister, Lindsay.

But all is not as it seems: what is the relationship between the three women, and Robbie? What secrets do they hide? And who has really betrayed who?

Set amidst the spectacular scenery of the Orkney Islands, Gabrielle Barnby's skilfully plotted first novel is a beautifully understated story of deception and forgiveness, love and redemption.

With poetic and precise language Barnby draws you in to the lives, loves and losses of the characters till you feel a part of the story.

'The Oystercatcher Girl is a wonderfully evocative and deftly woven story' – Sara Bailey

Changed Times
Ethyl Smith
ISBN: 978-1-910946-09-1 (eBook)
ISBN: 978-1-910946-08-4 (Paperback)

1679 – The Killing Times: Charles II is on the throne, the Episcopacy has been restored, and southern Scotland is in ferment.

The King is demanding superiority over all things spiritual and temporal and rebellious Ministers are being ousted from their parishes for refusing to bend the knee.

When John Steel steps in to help one such Minister in his home village of Lesmahagow he finds himself caught up in events that reverberate not just through the parish, but throughout the whole of southern Scotland.

From the Battle of Drumclog to the Battle of Bothwell Bridge, John's platoon of farmers and villagers find themselves in the heart of the action over that fateful summer where the people fight the King for their religion, their freedom, and their lives.

Set amid the tumult and intrigue of Scotland's Killing Times, John Steele's story powerfully reflects the changes that took place across 17th century Scotland, and stunningly brings this period of history to life.

'Smith writes with a fine ear for Scots speech, and with a sensitive awareness to the different ways in which history intrudes upon the lives of men and women, soldiers and civilians, adults and children'
– James Robertson

Dark Times
Ethyl Smith
ISBN: 978-1-910946-26-8 (eBook)
ISBN: 978-1-910946-24-4 (Paperback)

The summer of 1679 is a dark one for the Covenanters, routed by government troops at the Battle of Bothwell Brig. John Steel is on the run, hunted for his part in the battle by the vindictive Earl of Airlie. And life is no easier for the hapless Sandy Gillon, curate of Lesmahagow Kirk, in the Earl's sights for aiding John Steel's escape.

Outlawed and hounded, the surviving rebels have no choice but to take to the hills and moors to evade capture and deportation. And as a hard winter approaches, Marion Steel discovers she's pregnant with her third child.

Dark Times is the second part of Ethyl Smith's sweeping *Times* series that follows the lives of ordinary people in extraordinary times.

The False Men
Mhairead MacLeod
ISBN: 978-1-910946-27-5 (eBook)
ISBN: 978-1-910946-25-1 (Paperback)

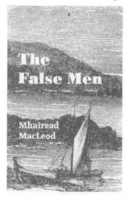

North Uist, Outer Hebrides, 1848

Jess MacKay has led a privileged life as the daughter of a local landowner, sheltered from the harsher aspects of life. Courted by the eligible Patrick Cooper, the Laird's new commissioner, Jess's future is mapped out, until Lachlan Macdonald arrives on North Uist, amid rumours of forced evictions on islands just to the south.

As the uncompromising brutality of the Clearances reaches the islands, and Jess sees her friends ripped from their homes, she must decide where her heart, and her loyalties, truly lie.

Set against the evocative backdrop of the Hebrides and inspired by a true story, *The False Men* is a compelling tale of love in a turbulent past that resonates with the upheavals of the modern world.

'...an engaging tale of powerlessness, love and disillusionment in the context of the type of injustice that, sadly, continues to this day' – Anne Goodwin

Dead Cat Bounce
Kevin Scott
ISBN: 978-1-910946-17-6 (eBook)
ISBN: 978-1-910946-15-2 (Paperback)

"Well, either way, you'll have to speak to your brother today because...unless I get my money by tomorrow morning there's not going to be a funeral."

When your 11 year old brother has been tragically killed in a car accident, you might think that organising his funeral would take priority. But when Nicky's coffin, complete with Nicky's body, goes missing, deadbeat loser Matt has only 26 hours in which to find the £20,000 he owes a Glasgow gangster or explain to his grieving mother why there's not going to be a funeral.

Enter middle brother, Pete, successful City trader with an expensive wife, expensive children, and an expensive villa in Tuscany. Pete's watches cost £20,000, but he has his own problems, and Matt doesn't want his help anyway.

Seething with old resentments, the betrayals of the past and the double-dealings of the present, the two brothers must find a way to work together to retrieve Nicky's body, discovering along the way that they are not so different after all.

'Underplaying the comic potential to highlight the troubled relationship between the equally flawed brothers. It's one of those books that keep the reader hooked right to the end' – The Herald

The Wrong Box
Andrew C Ferguson
ISBN: 978-1-910946-14-5 (Paperback)
ISBN: 978-1-910946-16-9 (eBook)

All I know is, I'm in exile in Scotland, and there's a dead Scouser businessman in my bath. With his toe up the tap.

Meet Simon English, corporate lawyer, heavy drinker and Scotophobe, banished from London after being caught misbehaving with one of the young associates on the corporate desk. As if that wasn't bad enough, English finds himself acting for a spiralling money laundering racket that could put not just his career, but his life, on the line.

Enter Karen Clamp, an 18 stone, well-read wann be couturier from the Auchendrossan sink estate, with an encyclopedic knowledge of Council misdeeds and 19th century Scottish fiction. With no one to trust but each other, this mismatched pair must work together to investigate a series of apparently unrelated frauds and discover how everything connects to the mysterious Wrong Box.

Manically funny, *The Wrong Box* is a chaotic story of lust, money, power and greed, and the importance of being able to sew a really good hem.

'...the makings of a new Caledonian Comic Noir genre: Rebus with jokes, Val McDiarmid with buddha belly laughs, or Trainspotting for the professional classes'

The House with the Lilac Shutters:
Gabrielle Barnby
ISBN: 978-1-910946-02-2 (eBook)
ISBN: 978-0-9929768-8-0 (Paperback)

Irma Lagrasse has taught piano to three generations of villagers, whilst slowly twisting the knife of vengeance; Nico knows a secret; and M. Lenoir has discovered a suppressed and dangerous passion.

Revolving around the Café Rose, opposite The House with the Lilac Shutters, this collection of contemporary short stories links a small town in France with a small town in England, traces the unexpected connections between the people of both places and explores the unpredictable influences that the past can have on the present.

Characters weave in and out of each other's stories, secrets are concealed and new connections are made.

With a keenly observant eye, Barnby illustrates the everyday tragedies, sorrows, hopes and joys of ordinary people in this vividly understated and unsentimental collection.

'The more I read, and the more descriptions I encountered, the more I was put in mind of one of my all time favourite texts – Dylan Thomas' Under Milk Wood' – lindasbookbag.com

The Bogeyman Chronicles
Craig Watson
ISBN: 978-1-910946-11-4 (eBook)
ISBN: 978-1-910946-10-7 (Paperback)

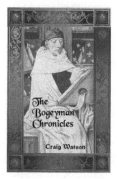

In 14th Century Scotland, amidst the wars of independence, hatred, murder and betrayal are commonplace. People are driven to extraordinary lengths to survive, whilst those with power exercise it with cruel pleasure.

Royal Prince Alexander Stewart, son of King Robert II and plagued by rumours of his illegitimacy, becomes infamous as the Wolf of Badenoch, while young Andrew Christie commits an unforgivable sin and lay Brother Brodie Affleck in the Restenneth Priory pieces together the mystery that links them all together.

From the horror of the times and the changing fortunes of the characters, the legend of the Bogeyman is born and Craig Watson cleverly weaves together the disparate lives of the characters into a compelling historical mystery that will keep you gripped throughout.

Over 80 years the lives of three men are inextricably entwined, and through their hatreds, murders and betrayals the legend of Christie Cleek, the bogeyman, is born.

'The Bogeyman Chronicles haunted our imagination long after we finished it' – iScot Magazine

Mule Train
Huw Francis
ISBN: 978-0-9575689-0-7 (eBook)
ISBN: 978-0-9575689-1-4 (Paperback)

Four lives come together in the remote and spectacular mountains bordering Afghanistan and explode in a deadly cocktail of treachery, betrayal and violence.

Written with a deep love of Pakistan and the Pakistani people, Mule Train will sweep you from Karachi in the south to the Shandur Pass in the north, through the dangerous borderland alongside Afghanistan, in an adventure that will keep you gripped throughout.

'Stunningly captures the feel of Pakistan, from Karachi to the hills' – tripfiction.com

QueerBashing
Tim Morriosn
ISBN: 978-1-910946-06-0 (eBook)
ISBN: 978-0-9929768-9-7 (Paperback)

The first queerbasher McGillivray ever met was in the mirror.

From the revivalist churches of Orkney in the 1970s, to the gay bars of London and Northern England in the 90s, via the divinity school at Aberdeen, this is the story of McGillivray, a self-centred, promiscuous hypocrite, failed Church of Scotland minister, and his own worst enemy.

Determined to live life on his own terms, McGillivray's grasp on reality slides into psychosis and a sense of his own invulnerability, resulting in a brutal attack ending life as he knows it.

Raw and uncompromising, this is a viciously funny but ultimately moving account of one man's desire to come to terms with himself and live his life as he sees fit.

'...an arresting novel of pain and self-discovery' – Alastair Mabbott (The Herald)

A Good Death
Helen Davis
ISBN: 978-0-9575689-7-6 (eBook)
ISBN: 978-0-9575689-6-9 (Paperback)

'A good death is better than a bad conscience,' said Sophie.

1983 – Georgie, Theo, Sophie and Helena, four disparate young Cambridge undergraduates, set out to scale Ausangate, one of the highest and most sacred peaks in the Andes.

Seduced into employing the handsome and enigmatic Wamani as a guide, the four women are initiated into the mystically dangerous side of Peru, Wamani and themselves as they travel from Cuzco to the mountain, a journey that will shape their lives forever.

2013 – though the women are still close, the secrets and betrayals of Ausangate chafe at the friendship.

A girls' weekend at a lonely Fenland farmhouse descends into conflict with the insensitive inclusion of an overbearing young academic toyboy brought along by Theo. Sparked by his unexpected presence, pent up petty jealousies, recriminations and bitterness finally explode the truth of Ausangate, setting the women on a new and dangerous path.

Sharply observant and darkly comic, Helen Davis's début novel is an elegant tale of murder, seduction, vengeance, and the value of a good friendship.

'The prose is crisp, adept, and emotionally evocative' – Lesbrary.com

The Birds That Never Flew
Margot McCuaig
Shortlisted for the Dundee International Book Prize 2012
Longlisted for the Polari First Book Prize 2014
ISBN: 978-0-9929768-5-9 (eBook)
ISBN: 978-0-9929768-4-2 (Paperback)

'Have you got a light hen? I'm totally gaspin.'

Battered and bruised, Elizabeth has taken her daughter and left her abusive husband Patrick. Again. In the bleak and impersonal Glasgow housing office Elizabeth meets the provocatively intriguing drug addict Sadie, who is desperate to get her own life back on track.

The two women forge a fierce and interdependent relationship as they try to rebuild their shattered lives, but despite their bold, and sometimes illegal attempts it seems impossible to escape from the abuse they have always known, and tragedy strikes.

More than a decade later Elizabeth has started to implement her perfect revenge – until a surreal Glaswegian Virgin Mary steps in with imperfect timing and a less than divine attitude to stick a spoke in the wheel of retribution.

Tragic, darkly funny and irreverent, *The Birds That Never Flew* ushers in a new and vibrant voice in Scottish literature.

'...dark, beautiful and moving, I wholeheartedly recommend' scanoir.co.uk

In The Shadow Of The Hill
Helen Forbes
ISBN: 978-0-9929768-1-1 (eBook)
ISBN: 978-0-9929768-0-4 (Paperback)

An elderly woman is found battered to death in the common stairwell of an Inverness block of flats.

Detective Sergeant Joe Galbraith starts what seems like one more depressing investigation of the untimely death of a poor unfortunate who was in the wrong place, at the wrong time.

As the investigation spreads across Scotland it reaches into a past that Joe has tried to forget, and takes him back to the Hebridean island of Harris, where he spent his childhood.

Among the mountains and the stunning landscape of religiously conservative Harris, in the shadow of Ceapabhal, long buried events and a tragic story are slowly uncovered, and the investigation takes on an altogether more sinister aspect.

In The Shadow Of The Hill skilfully captures the intricacies and malevolence of the underbelly of Highland and Island life, bringing tragedy and vengeance to the magical beauty of the Outer Hebrides.

'...our first real home-grown sample of modern Highland noir' – Roger Hutchison; West Highland Free Press

Over Here
Jane Taylor
ISBN: 978-0-9929768-3-5 (eBook)
ISBN: 978-0-9929768-2-8 (Paperback)

It's coming up to twenty-four hours since the boy stepped down from the big passenger liner – it must be, he reckons foggily – because morning has come around once more with the awful irrevocability of time destined to lead nowhere in this worrying new situation. His temporary minder on board – last spotted heading for the bar some while before the lumbering process of docking got underway – seems to have vanished for good. Where does that leave him now? All on his own in a new country: that's where it leaves him. He is just nine years old.

An eloquently written novel tracing the social transformations of a century where possibilities were opened up by two world wars that saw millions of men move around the world to fight, and mass migration to the new worlds of Canada and Australia by tens of thousands of people looking for a better life.

Through the eyes of three generations of women, the tragic story of the nine year old boy on Liverpool docks is brought to life in saddeningly evocative prose.

'...a sweeping haunting first novel that spans four generations and two continents...' – Cristina Odone/Catholic Herald

The Bonnie Road
Suzanne d'Corsey

ISBN: 978-1-910946-01-5 (eBook)
ISBN: 978-0-9929768-6-6 (Paperback)

Suzanne d'Corsey

The Bonnie Road

My grandmother passed me in transit. She was leaving, I was coming into this world, our spirits meeting at the door to my mother's womb, as she bent over the bed to close the thin crinkled lids of her own mother's eyes.

The women of Morag's family have been the keepers of tradition for generations, their skills and knowledge passed down from woman to woman, kept close and hidden from public view, official condemnation and religious suppression.

In late 1970s St. Andrews, demand for Morag's services are still there, but requested as stealthily as ever, for even in 20th century Scotland witchcraft is a dangerous Art to practise.

When newly widowed Rosalind arrives from California to tend her ailing uncle, she is drawn unsuspecting into a new world she never knew existed, one in which everyone seems to have a secret, but that offers greater opportunities than she dreamt of – if she only has the courage to open her heart to it.

Richly detailed, dark and compelling, d'Corsey magically transposes the old ways of Scotland into the 20th Century and brings to life the ancient traditions and beliefs that still dance just below the surface of the modern world.

'…successfully portrays rich characters in compelling plots, interwoven with atmospheric Scottish settings & history and coloured with witchcraft & romance' – poppypeacockpens.com

Talk of the Toun
Helen MacKinven
ISBN: 978-1-910946-00-8 (eBook)
ISBN: 978-0-9929768-7-3 (Paperback)

She was greetin' again. But there's no need for Lorraine to be feart, since the first day of primary school, Angela has always been there to mop up her tears and snotters.

An uplifting black comedy of love, family life and friendship, Talk of the Toun is a bittersweet coming-of-age tale set in the summer of 1985, in working class, central belt Scotland.

Lifelong friends Angela and Lorraine are two very different girls, with a growing divide in their aspirations and ambitions putting their friendship under increasing strain.

Artistically gifted Angela has her sights set on art school, but lassies like Angela, from a small town council scheme, are expected to settle for a nice wee secretarial job at the local factory. Her only ally is her gallus gran, Senga, the pet psychic, who firmly believes that her granddaughter can be whatever she wants.

Though Lorraine's ambitions are focused closer to home Angela has plans for her too, and a caravan holiday to Filey with Angela's family tests the dynamics of their relationship and has lifelong consequences for them both.

Effortlessly capturing the religious and social intricacies of 1980s Scotland, Talk of the Toun is the perfect mix of pathos and humour as the two girls wrestle with the complications of growing up and exploring who they really are.

'Fresh, fierce and funny…a sharp and poignant study of growing up in 1980s Scotland. You'll laugh, you'll cry…you'll cringe' – KAREN CAMPBELL

Lightning Source UK Ltd.
Milton Keynes UK
UKHW02f1504110218
317699UK00005B/191/P